**DISCLAIMER**
This book is a work of fiction. The characters, incidents, and dialogue are drawn from the author's imagination and are not to be construed as real. While references might be made to actual historical events or existing locations, the names, characters, places, and incidents are either products of the author's imagination or are used fictitiously, and any resemblance to actual persons living or dead, business establishments, events or locales is entirely coincidental.

# LIES, BETRAYAL, AND LOVE

MELISSA BENDER

*Bailey, Mason, Everly,*
*remember to look up at the stars, and not down at your feet.*

# FREE DOWNLOAD

Get these freebies and more when you sign up for the author's mailing list!

*http://melissa-bender.awesomeauthors.org/*

# PROLOGUE

OLIVER

The suspense was killing me.

My heart was in my throat as I nervously sat on the edge of the bed awaiting the results. I could feel my heart beating fast. I was almost sure it could be heard in the eerie silence.

Amy was beside me, showing no emotion at all, as I glanced up at her. Her blonde hair was pulled back into a tight plait that twisted down below her shoulders.

Shoving my hands into my jeans, I stood. I couldn't just sit and say nothing. I knew better than to ask, but I was a fool and asked anyway. "Do you think it worked?"

No reply. She just looked up straight at me. Her once bright blue eyes had turned dull. "No. I don't."

It was always her answer. It was the same for everything. It diminished my hopes more than I would admit. I didn't know what it would take for her to have a positive outlook on this and not make it feel like just another chore that had to be done.

Three long minutes and she glanced down at the white stick. "Told you so," she muttered clearly as she tossed it over to me.

It landed by my feet, on the carpet, before I could catch it. I frowned, bent down, and caught sight of the words *not pregnant* across the screen.

I wasn't sure how to react. I mean, sure, I was disappointed, but part of me was relieved in a way. I didn't dare tell her that though.

I had tried everything possible to be positive for her. Sometimes, it just wasn't enough. I didn't think it ever would be for her.

"Next time. We've only been on the shots for a month. I think next time, your body will be more adjusted. The doctor said it could take a few months." I'd do anything to give her a child of our own.

Amy looked at me as if I had said the wrong thing. "For fuck sake, can't you see! It's not working! None of this works, Oliver! How many times do I have to tell you this for you to finally believe it? You can't get me pregnant. Clearly, it's you and not me. You have one job, and you can't even do that right," she spat out harshly, shaking her head. "We're not going to get pregnant."

My fingers wound around the test in my palm firmly as I tried staying calm and not saying what I really wanted to say. "Maybe if you had a more positive outlook on this or even acted like you wanted to have a baby, then it would happen. You're so against us getting pregnant."

"Fine. I'm ovulating in a week. I will be ready then," she said, turning on her heel and walking out of our bedroom.

*Yeah, 'cause my dick is really throbbing to fuck you then.*

I sat back on the bed and placed the test on the bedside table, running my hands over my face and groaning as I fell back until my head hit the pillow. I missed having sex for the fun of it and not because I had to save all my sperm for one day a month, and then it was just me fucking till I blew minutes later.

She never came, nor did she want to. We didn't even kiss.

I felt like I was forcing her into it. It wasn't enjoyable. It was just something that needed to be done each month.

It was a struggle to stay hard, trying to think of something that would keep me hard as she lay there, silent and staring at the wall. I needed my damn dick sucked, or at least touched. Faking a damn interest would get me in the mood, rather than being told the time and day.

2

Each month was the same. Shower. Missionary. Job done minutes later.

I walked from the room to the hallway and found her sitting on the couch with a glass of red in her hand.

I sighed. I didn't want to start another fight, but I had to remind her. "You can't drink, Amy."

She wiggled the glass in her hand, and the liquid threatened to spill. "I'm not pregnant." Then, she proceeded to take a large mouthful and moaned with delight.

Of course, she'd moan for wine.

I walked over, taking the glass from her hand. "I don't care if you're not pregnant. We both have to make sacrifices. I gave up drinking and smokes. Can't you do the same? It'll be worth it in the end." I knew she had been smoking. The packet in the toilet was her giveaway.

She stood up, shaking her head, and then I felt the sting of a cold hard slap against my cheek. I dropped the glass from my long fingers.

"What the fuck?"

"Stop telling me what I can and can't do. I'm sick of all these rules, all the shots, and exams. I just want to give up, Oliver. You piss me off so much with you going on about it all the time!" She hissed, standing and pushing past me with a nudge.

She'd slapped me at least five times this year already. I slumped backward on the sofa, watching as she returned with a cloth and spray bottle to clean the liquid up. Her words hit me. I knew I was acting like a bastard.

"Amy, I don't mean to make you feel like shit," I said quietly.

"Yeah. Well, you do. I'm sorry if I don't find having sex with you arousing or exciting. God, it's just something that needs to be done. We dated then married, and now we need a baby. That's the way it goes!"

My ego was bruised. She could cut deep at the best of times.

3

"Do you even want to have sex when we do have it?" I asked her even though I already knew the answer. Tilting my head, I wasn't sure what she meant. "What do you mean, it needs to be done? A baby isn't something that you just automatically get just because you marry."

When she didn't answer immediately, I knew I had my answer.

I went to stand when Amy pushed me back down. Her hand stayed and squeezed my shoulder. "I'm sorry. It's me, not you. I know you're trying, but we've been trying for ages. I just don't see the point anymore."

"You want a baby. You said no to adopting or surrogacy. If you want a baby, then we keep trying. All right?" I said firmly. I wasn't giving up.

She talked this way each month, and it was beginning to grow old. The same fight. The same complaints. It was all the same.

Amy looked at me. Her blue eyes weren't what they used to be six years ago. They were dull and dead looking. She rarely smiled, but I still found her beautiful. I knew the girl I had fallen for was still in there somewhere. She had to be.

I cupped her cheek gently, stroking softly with my thumb as she leant into my chest and quietly began to sob. I let her cry and held her until she was ready to move. What else could I do? I felt nothing on the inside. My emotions were completely fucking gone over this.

"Maybe we're not meant to have kids. I can live with that," she whispered, finally pulling away.

I had to fight the instinct to agree. I didn't want her to know that was what I thought too. But part of me did want to be a father. I wanted children and had always thought I wanted them with her.

Christ, if I didn't want kids, I wouldn't be so damn willing for the once a month fuck. Surely, that was good for something.

Finally, I pulled back just enough to reach down and wipe away her tears. She broke eye contact with me instantly.

4

"It'll work out. Whatever will be, will be."

"I think I might go to bed, Oliver. I just need to sleep. You go out with Tony. He will want you there with him," she said softly.

Fuck. With all that was going on, my best mate's buck's night was the last thing on my mind. "I don't have to go."

"No. Please. Go and have fun. You need it. You can't let him down," she urged.

I found it strange that she was encouraging me to go out and get shit-faced, but I nodded. I picked her up against her wishes and carried her toward our bedroom.

It was a simple room with a dresser and a queen bed in the middle. I wasn't much of a designer, but the room felt cold at its best. I laid her in the bed and drew the covers back over her small frame.

I knew that glass of wine wasn't her first. She'd had a fair bit of drink while I was lying in the bedroom.

"Rest sweetheart." I bent down, pressing my lips to her forehead.

After a shower, I put some wax on my hair and sprayed on some Hugo Boss. I wasn't in the mood to go out, but I couldn't let Tony down. He was finally tying the knot, and with a great chick at that. I'd love to say I threw on a suit like the groom demanded and rocked a pair of leather boots, but I went with a cleaner casual look.

~

"A round on me!" Tony shouted. He was already half tanked by the time we finally made our way from dinner to the first bar. "Actually, throw it on the best man's tab!"

I walked up, slapping his back with a laugh. "How's that fair? You're the one racking the bill up." I winked.

He smirked, draping an arm over my shoulder as he hung off me. "You're my best man. You need to be drinking as much as I am."

Grinning, I nodded for the go ahead with whatever Tony was ordering. "Just slow down, or you'll be unable to walk. How can you fuck the missus when you're bent over spewing?" I laughed.

He grinned back. His eyes were wide and humorous as he dropped his head back laughing as he held his last shot of whiskey. "Trust me, I'll manage." He winked and downed it with a grunt.

I couldn't help but laugh and eagerly reach for a new round when they were poured. "Yeah, true. You finally found someone who can tame your wild ways. Never thought I'd see the day."

He smirked. "Find a girl who'll do anything in bed. That's the one you marry."

"I must have done it wrong then." I winked, smiling.

There was nothing wild about my wife.

Shots were down, and I took a swig of beer.

"Did Amy mind that you were coming out? How'd it go today?" he asked.

He knew all about our troubles with trying to get pregnant.

We were like brothers. When we were still kids, we lived next to each other. We had grown up together and became inseparable. This was why after twenty years, he was still my best mate.

I shrugged, shaking my head. "Another negative. She's giving up, and I think I'm about to also. I can't keep trying to put on a fake smile when she yells and doesn't seem interested in it."

"Fuck. I'm sorry, man. She needs to just let loose and have a good time once in a while. I don't think I've seen her smile in years." He pointed out with a grimace.

He was right, and I hated it.

"Yeah, I know. I keep asking, and she's always busy."

"Cass invited her out the other day. She never called her back though." He looked at me.

I knew he wasn't into girl drama and all that, but he was my best mate, and it made sense for Cassie and Amy to be friends as well. Well, we had hoped for them to be.

6

"She never mentioned it. I'll talk to her. You guys should come around for lunch tomorrow. We'll need it after tonight." I grinned.

Tonight was definitely going to be big by the looks of it.

He raised his hand when the bartender walked over with the round of shots. She slid it down and walked away after giving him a wink. Tony slung his arm over my shoulder, wearing a shit-eating grin.

"Brother, tonight we're going to get drunk until neither of us can walk or piss straight."

That, after the day I had, sounded like a fucking good idea.

I couldn't remember the last time I drank so many shots and jaeger bombs. I think it was in college before exams.

I felt like a prick for drinking while Amy was home in bed, but I needed to clear my head. I needed this. I fucking needed a night out. My brain was overloaded with schedules and routines. Tonight, I needed to just put it aside on the back burner and have a good time. I knew once tomorrow came, we'd be back to marking out the dates on the calendar and working our routine out for the month.

We had gone from bar to bar. Eight of us were stumbling our way through pubs and clubs. Tony was trying to make the most of his night and hiding the fact that he was slightly disappointed we hadn't ordered the stripper he wanted.

Sorry, friend. Katarina the Russian was already busy this evening. Not to mention, about five grand too much.

He settled in trying to out-drink some eighteen-year-olds in the bar. Watching him do it was more than amusing. That was until he couldn't handle his liquor and puked a good mouthful over some chick. Then, he got slapped across the face, and we were thrown out of that bar.

We soon moved onto another.

It was hours past midnight, and according to my friend, the night was still young. Knowing that he was already wasted, one of us rung Cassie.

She was on her way after she was told that her soon to be husband was a wasted mess and embarrassing himself.

I had decided to catch a lift back home with them if I didn't pass out before she arrived.

I left Tony with the rest of the guys, telling them that I needed some air.

Right now, I was out having a smoke. Fuck Doctor Lucas and his rules. I needed the air more than anything. The sight of couples making out and grinding just pissed me off. Usually, I didn't care. It never bothered me. Tonight though, I was a miserable bastard on the inside. Probably because I found out that my wife hated fucking me and only wanted a kid because she needed one.

I couldn't even give her that. No wonder she was fucking miserable.

Sitting here in my own misery, I wasn't paying attention to anyone until a soft voice pulled me out of my own thoughts.

"Can I sit here for a moment?"

I looked up and noticed a woman standing beside me, pointing to the stool right next to me. I should have said no, but I didn't. "Sure. No one else is using it." I gave her a drunken grin.

"Sorry. I'm waiting for someone, and it is too crowded in there. I didn't really want to stand and look like a loser." She tilted her head, motioning into the club. "You're alone, and the other tables are full."

I laughed, wanting to scoff. "Doubt you'd have any trouble looking like a loser in there."

What the fuck was I doing? I should get up and just walk away. I needed to leave.

"I'm Sage, just so this isn't weird. I promise I don't normally go up to random men and ask to sit with them." She let out a laugh, smiling down at the table, and then she looked up.

Her eyes were what hit me in the chest, and I struggled to look away.

8

They were big and blue, not like Amy's blue, but a grey-blue.

*Amy, my wife. Remember, you have a wife, idiot. It's not that hard. You've been married to her for two years. Together for eight.*

"Oliver," I said. I glanced around, trying to distract myself. I tried figuring out where my phone was and what to do next. However, the following words that came out of my mouth were the wrong ones. "You want a drink?"

What did I ask that for? I was going straight to hell.

"Alright, just one, then I need to go. Finish your smoke first." She then reached over and took the glass tumbler from in front of me. "I think you need some help with this though." She bit her plump red lip as she brought my drink of Beam to her mouth, then downed the last of it.

Licking her lips afterward, she set the drink down. I couldn't take my eyes off her mouth. It looked so soft with full lips. It was hard not to wonder what they'd feel like wrapped around my cock.

Shifting on the stool to try hiding the tightening of my jeans, I cleared my throat and took a long drag. I had to think of something else. I tried thinking of anything to distract myself, but I couldn't. My mind was shot to hell, and my arousal was getting the best of me.

I stood up, putting the smoke out in the ashtray. I needed to fix this.

"What are you drinking?"

"Vodka will do." She stood, and I got a better look at her body.

She was short, coming up to my shoulders, even though she was wearing fuck me heels. Her body was covered in what I guess chicks called a dress, but this thing left very little to a guy's imagination. It was just a piece of black material covering her tits, pussy, and ass. Her back, arms, and legs were fully exposed.

I swallowed hard.

I was too fucking drunk for this.

9

Taking her hand, I stumbled through the club, over to where the bar was. The music was too loud for either of us to hear each other. I grabbed a bottle of water, and she a vodka. Clarity was something I needed. I needed to sober up and fucking fast.

I tried to find Tony, but I couldn't find him anywhere. Luckily, I saw Rhys standing by the male's restroom. Sage waited for me outside while I talked to Rhys. I told him I was ready to go, and he pointed at Tony who was currently bent over on a sink and emptying the contents of his stomach. He told me to wait for them on the second level where there was a lounge section. He would bring Tony up the stairs once he was done, and we'd wait for Cassie.

I went back to Sage and gestured toward the stairs. She walked in front as we made our way up. I couldn't stop staring at her ass, wondering what type of underwear she had on.

Probably nothing.

"Now, I can hear myself think." She giggled, slightly tipsy while sitting on the lounge chair.

I sat beside her and nodded. I tried not to get distracted. However, she made me curious. She looked young.

"You don't look old enough to be in a club." I pointed out.

"Trust me, I'm old enough. Twenty-one and you?" She ran a hand through her dark hair, tossing it over her shoulder and revealing her creamy white collarbone.

My eyes shifted back up to hers. "Too old to be in a club."

I was only twenty-six, but sometimes I felt much older. Years of fucking stress would do that to you.

She laughed loudly and leant closer, giving me a flirty smile. I inhaled her sweet perfume as she raised her hand and pointed down to the stairway. "Well then, I think the old men hang around the exit doors to prowl on the young women, trying to pick them up while they're too drunk to know any better."

I laughed. "Fuck. I'm only twenty-six. I guess I've got a few good years left in me before I have to resort to that." I winked, grinning.

10

Damn, it felt good to laugh.

We locked eyes again, and I was done for.

I didn't know how it happened. Well, I did know. I just didn't know why I wasn't stopping myself.

I snaked my hand around her neck as my other one went to the curve of her hip, and I pulled her onto my lap. My mouth closed over hers, and I soon thrust my tongue down her throat. Tasting the mix of alcohol and smelling her perfume, I was intoxicated. God, I was lost in her right now.

When I gripped her ass to grind her against my aching dick, she moaned against my mouth, and I could have almost blown. It'd been so long since I heard a woman moan like that. My fingers slid down and slipped up underneath her dress, and I felt the soft lace fabric of the thong she wore.

Christ, I was a dead man.

Her hands were all over my chest, sliding up and scratching me. I growled over her mouth and broke the kiss, only to continue kissing down her neck and sucking lightly against what I had wanted to taste since I first caught sight of it. I ran my tongue over her collarbone.

I hissed through my teeth as she slid her hand in my jeans. She fisted my cock and pushed her palm hard up and down, rubbing against me.

"Sage…" I groaned, trying to focus, but everything was clouding my judgment. Her hand was on my dick, and I couldn't fucking think straight.

"We should stop. I can't do this…" She moaned. "I'm not like this, Ollie."

"We should." We needed to stop. Otherwise, I wouldn't be able to.

My thoughts vaguely went to Amy but soon disappeared as she withdrew her hand and slowly ground against my dick.

"God I'm so drunk…and you're so fucking hot…"

"You're definitely drunk if you think that," I smirked, sliding my fingers inside the fabric of her panties and tracing her slit, my fingers teasing as I pushed one inside of her.

I looked around as she slid between my parted thighs. I was relieved that the door was shut and no one else was in here. Sure, there was a huge window so we could see everyone down below us, but luckily, no one could see us from down there.

She pulled my jeans down, and I jerked my hips forward when I felt her warm tongue over my shaft, her mouth soon sucking me as her hands played with my balls.

Fuck.

"Fuck, I'll blow if you keep that up," I said, holding her head while tilting mine back as she sucked me.

I couldn't say I'd blown down a chick's throat before because I hadn't. Tonight, I did.

Sage came back up, wiping her mouth with her palm after sucking me dry and swallowing. "You taste so good." She bit her lip. "I think you're so sexy."

Ignoring her comment, I pulled her back down to my lap. My cock was hard and needing its release again. I wanted to taste her.

"Turn around and lean forward on the table," I said huskily against her ear.

She looked nervous but did it. I bit my teeth into the soft flesh of her ass, pulling her thong aside and then running my tongue down her wet slit from behind. I slipped a finger in her, and fuck, she was so tight. I groaned, loving the warmth of her and tasting her.

I couldn't stop. I could have eaten her pussy for hours. I kept licking, sucking, and rubbing her clit until she cried out and came, gripping the table while grinding against my mouth.

Another first.

Not wasting a second, I spun her around and pulled her down on my hard cock. She was so damn tight. I groaned as she lowered all the way down, moaning and letting her eyes roll. It was a fucking sight; that was for sure. My jeans were around my ankles, and her dress was hiked up around her waist as she leant back, rocking her body up and down my cock. Her eyes opened and looked directly on mine.

"I'm going to cum again, Ollie...Oh my god...You feel so damn good." She leant forward, mouth almost on mine as her fingers ran through my hair, tugging while she slowed to a deep grind.

"You're so fucking beautiful." I squeezed her ass, pushing her down as I flexed my hips upright.

"I want you to fuck me. I want to feel your body on me," she moaned, moving faster yet again. "Fuck me."

I shouldn't have done it. I knew I'd regret it afterward when I sobered up, but at this moment, right now, it felt too fucking good to stop. To have a gorgeous woman ride my cock like she was on a wild horse, kissing me back just as hard, and moaning out my name as I held her body close against mine—made me remember what a woman felt like.

I picked her up, still inside her as I knelt down, laying her on the floor behind the chairs, so we weren't seen as I gave her what she begged me for.

My thoughts about everything else vanished. I wasn't thinking about Tony coming into the room, or anyone seeing us. I forgot about my wife, and I selfishly thought with my dick.

Her legs wrapped around my waist, feet digging into my ass as I started moving. My hand cupped her face. I kissed her hungrily as I slid in and out, over and over, my dick only growing harder with each moan and beg she made. She told me how she wanted it and didn't hesitate in taking what she wanted from me. Her fingers were dragging up and down my back, teeth biting into my shoulder as she shuddered beneath me. I kissed her, enjoyed her. Our bodies were moving together in sync, fucking in primal bliss.

She made me remember what it was like, what it felt like when someone made me feel wanted.

13

# CHAPTER 1

SAGE

I groaned as I tried to cover my eyes, shielding the burning sunlight that came into the bedroom. I didn't want to get up. I felt like utter hell. My pounding head didn't make me feel any better either. I yawned as I grabbed a pillow and rolled over, covering my head with it, trying to pass back out.

The sleep I was trying to get back into was short-lived when I heard a loud knock on the door.

"Sage, it's almost two in the afternoon. Please tell me you're up."

I yawned, groaning with annoyance. "I'm up, Mum," I said back to her. "Just wait."

My feet hit the wooden flooring, and I rubbed my eyes, looking around for my underwear. I grabbed what I could and slid on some sweats and a shirt. Walking past a mirror, I glanced at myself. My hair was nothing short of a hairy scarecrow. I didn't look that hung over though, but I knew Mum would be able to tell I had a late one. Hell, it was more than late.

"Sage!" she called out again, her voice hurting my head more than I liked. She was enjoying this. I could tell.

I opened the door of the guesthouse, which was now my living space while I was home from school. "I'm up." I yawned, covering my mouth yet again.

Mum gave me a disapproving look as she made her way in. "Late night? What time did you get in?" she asked, sitting on the large sofa.

Obviously, she wasn't going to be making me breakfast or coffee anytime soon.

"Around four, I think it was." I sat across from her, lying sideways and resting my head on the fluffy cushions.

She shook her head. "Your father won't be happy if he finds out. I told him you got home around eleven. Stick to that story please."

Mum was more laid back than Dad. To him, I was his innocent little girl. I was innocent most of the time, but there were days where I liked to go and have some fun.

I sighed. "Cassie was meant to pick me up, but I didn't see her, and my phone died. I'm sorry."

"How did you get home?" she asked, eyeing me cautiously.

"A taxi," I said.

It was the truth.

She nodded, straightening the stack of books on my coffee table. "Your sister will be married in a couple of months. Please tell me you're going to make it."

"I'm the maid of honor. Of course, I'm going to make it." I laughed. "She needs to chill out and stop stressing."

"You know what your sister is like. Everything needs to be perfect for her day." She laughed, sitting back and smiling. Her wrinkles were showing more—laughter lines as she called them. "How's school been? Any boys you like?"

I blushed, fighting the smile. "Good and nope. No boys."

She hated when I gave her short replies like that. Mum liked to know what was going on and how I was doing, especially when it came to my love life.

"Sage," she said again, this time, a playfulness in her voice. "Why are you smiling?"

If only she knew why I was smiling. I wasn't dating anyone, nor did I want to. I was smiling about last night or this morning. Heck, I couldn't remember. All I remembered was shagging in a club and getting carpet burn on my ass and knees.

15

The guy was definitely a hottie. At least, I thought he was. My mind was still a little blurry. I went to bed deliciously sore and woke up the same. My lower half was aching. I just couldn't believe we had done that in a club when anyone could have walked in. I had no idea who he was, and it didn't bother me. I never had one-night stands or went to clubs, but I was glad I did.

It was definitely a great end to a bad day.

I realized Mum was still waiting for my answer. "There was a guy, but we didn't work out, so we're just friends." It didn't work out because he was gay.

"Oh, well. I'm sorry to hear that," she said softly.

"It's fine. He is actually coming to the wedding. He's my date." I smiled.

She looked very confused. "I'm sorry. What? You dated, and now he's your date?"

"He's gay. We're more brothers and sisters than anything."

"Gay? You dated a gay man?" she asked, obviously amused by this.

I shook my head. "No. He didn't tell me he was at the time. Then he did, and now we're just close friends."

"Okay. Well, I need to head back to your father. Please stay out of trouble. If you need anything, just let us know, okay?" she asked, standing and walking over to me, placing a kiss against my cheek.

"Thanks, Mum." I got up behind her and locked the door when she left.

I desperately needed a shower. I went into the bathroom and stripped off. As I went to step into the shower, I noticed it: the bruises and marks over my body. I turned around and gasped. There were teeth marks on my ass. God, he did bite hard. I had small bruises on my hips from his fingers and even love bites over my breasts. Damn, this guy went to town with marking my body all over.

As I washed, I wondered if I left any marks on him or if he was thinking about what happened as much as I was. Probably not. It was just a one-night stand. I was sure he had plenty.

He did offer to pay for my ride home after we had finished, and I realized my sister had already left. It was a little weird when we fixed ourselves up. He was very quiet once we both finished, and I felt completely embarrassed that I had done all that to him.

I mean sucking him off and swallowing was something I would only do in a serious relationship and not for a guy in a club. Then when he asked me to bend over so he could eat me from behind, God, I had almost died of embarrassment.

Until his tongue hit me, then I lost it.

When I stepped out of the shower, I went to my room and slid into some silk summer pajamas, climbing back into bed and wanting to sleep the day away.

My thoughts slowly drifted back to the man who touched me last night.

~

OLIVER

I stood in the shower, arms out in front of me as I kept my head down, spitting out saliva as guilt consumed my whole body. I couldn't think straight. My head was filled with flashbacks of what happened at the club. The way she felt and her mouth on mine. Remembering how she sounded when she came started to stir my insides enough for my cock to grow.

Then just like that, my hard cock was gone with a single thought. I cheated on my wife.

I cheated on her with some random girl, and I never stopped it. I let it go on even though I knew it was wrong at the time. I felt sick. I wanted to throw up at the thought of what I had done. I went out and let a gorgeous woman suck me off and then I fucked her.

My heart was pounding. My tears were too hard to stop as they ran down from my eyes, mixing in with the water. It was salty, and I sniffled hard, running my hands over my face, wiping them. I had no idea what the fuck I was going to do. Guilt was eating away at me.

"Oliver." I heard Amy call out.

Fuck. She couldn't come in here. She'd know instantly. Just one look at my guilt-ridden face and she'd know I cheated on her. I hated myself more than anything right now.

"Just a minute," I yelled out to her. I ran my hands through my wet hair and took in a deep breath, trying to calm my nerves down.

"Hurry. We need to talk," she called back.

I could tell by her tone that she was annoyed.

I sighed and turned the water off. I dried off quickly, noticing in the mirror that my back had red fingernail marks scratched down it. Even my ass had two bruises from her heels digging in. There was no explaining those without some ridiculous lie about falling into a rose bush naked.

I couldn't get her eyes out of my mind, her smile…I shook my head. I needed to stop thinking about her.

What I needed to do was to tell Amy, but I didn't even know how to do that.

How would I begin to tell my wife that I sunk my dick inside another woman? More than once.

Once was a mistake. Three times wasn't. Three fucking times I blew in her, not counting the blow job she gave me. God, those lips. Fucking hell.

I splashed some cold water over my face to cool myself, pulled on a shirt, and then I opened the door. I walked out. My eyes glassed over, which hopefully, she would assume was mostly from being so hung over.

Amy gave me a smile, and I felt sick.

"What's up?"

"You were out late last night? Where did you go?" she asked, her eyes on mine.

I hadn't spoken to her all day. I slept in the spare room to avoid her. Yeah, I was a fucking coward.

"Just around, few different bars and clubs." I shrugged, trying to keep my voice normal.

She just looked at me. "You didn't come to bed either. Why?"

Fuck. "I, uh, didn't want to wake you up. You say I snore when I drink, and I'd had a few."

"Okay. Well, Cassie called. Something about a lunch today that I knew nothing about?" She crossed her arms. "You know I don't like to be put on the spot, Oliver. You should have asked if I minded before you go making promises to people. I don't know her, and you're lucky you were asleep. I used that as an excuse to say no."

I frowned. Even though I was completely in the wrong, I was pissed. "You what? No. I asked Tony over for lunch, which will now be dinner."

I walked away, but I heard the low hiss of a "Fuck you, asshole" being spat at me.

I spun around and shook my head. It was moments like this when I didn't regret fucking someone else. It was easy for me to think, well, she deserved it. I felt like utter shit over it, but now I didn't know if I did entirely regret it.

"What did you just say?" I asked her, standing closer to her now. "You need to show me a little more respect, Amy. The things I do for you around here."

"Oh, here we go. Blah, Blah. I put a roof over your head. I provide the food and all the nice things you have." She was mocking me; talking like me in a sarcastic, childish voice; and throwing everything I did for her in my face. "I don't give a fuck if you're the only one working, Oliver. I do a lot around here. Who cooks the food you eat? Washes all your clothing? Me. I do it all, so don't start your rant about me being ungrateful. I was working until—"

19

I cut her off sharply. "No. You were working until you quit your job without talking to me about it first. Your excuse was that work and all the baby talk had you too stressed to focus on your job. We meant to focus on children, but it's not happening. Don't think I don't know about you spending your days shopping with friends. You don't do it all. I cook and clean as well, so don't you dare throw that at me."

"Fuck you, Oliver. Get out!" She snapped angrily.

"You're acting like a spoilt child," I growled, feeling my blood rising at the anger I felt, mostly for myself, but she was making it so much easier to be mad at her right now.

Amy scoffed. "Whatever."

A smile grew over my lips. I was mad but somehow amused by her tantrum. "Well, I guess you're right. I won't have kids when you speak to me like shit. You call Cassie and Tony back and ask them over for dinner."

"No. I don't want them here! Why can't you understand it! You're not the one who doesn't get pregnant each month. You have no idea what it feels like!" She gave my chest a hard push, and I didn't budge.

I was really getting sick of her pushing, shoving, and slapping me.

"I'll be sleeping in the spare room. Good thing I'm used to the no sex around here because I'd be fucked if I'm going to make an effort for it. Not that I turn you on or anything because you told me it doesn't do anything for you." I shook my head angrily at her. "I mean it, Amy. The baby is off the table, and for your information, I do know what it feels like because I'm the one who can't get my wife pregnant. That goes through my head each fucking month."

She had really pissed me off. I walked out and slammed the bedroom door shut.

I called up Tony and invited them over, knowing she wouldn't do it. He sounded as bad as I felt on the phone. His fiancé was at her parent's place, something about her younger sister visiting and she needed to talk wedding stuff. I laid down on the bed in the spare room and stared at the door. I should go and work things out. Hell, calling me a fucking asshole was the least she would call me when she knew what really happened last night.

Amy never came out when Tony came over for dinner. He and I sat on the back deck with a couple of beers and steaks. I wanted to tell him what I had done last night, just to get it off my chest.

But I couldn't. Instead, I just sat there and thought about her.

# CHAPTER 2

"What's going on with you?" Cassie asked me as I stood on the round platform stand in front of the three large floor-to-ceiling-length mirrors, giving a perfect view of the dress.

I shook my head, ignoring her burning gaze. "Nothing, just tired." It wasn't a complete lie. "Plus, I may be over trying on dress after dress." I smiled.

We'd been at it for more than four hours. All the other bridesmaids couldn't agree on the same dress. One even turned up hungover and had to leave for a quick spew. My sister wasn't the slightest bit impressed and threatened to throw her out of the wedding.

She laughed, brushing it off with a wave of her hand. "Oh, don't lie. You love it, and secretly, I think you enjoy all this dressing up, don't you?"

"Yes. I think you're right. My main goal in life is to play dress-ups." I giggled back as I slid the straps down and tucked them under my arms. "I prefer strapless. It looks younger on me this way, not too old."

Cassie nodded, agreeing and came closer. "I like the colour on you as well. The navy goes with your tanned skin." I then noticed her eyes going wide as she let out a screech. "Oh my god. What is that!"

"What?" I asked, backing away from her as she came closer.

"Sage, are those hickeys?" She grabbed my arm, pulling me closer and pulled the top of the dress down a little more.

22

I groaned. They were still there, and still a deep purple colour. He sucked on me hard.

I tried to deny it, but my blush was giving it away. "No. They're just bruises from books that fell on me at the library."

She raised a brow at me, scoffing with a snort. "Uh huh. Don't try to lie to me. I can't believe you, you little tart. Who was he and when? Oh, don't you dare say it was when you went out? Sage, you hooked up with a random guy?"

I lifted the navy dress straps back up and rolled my eyes. "I'm twenty-one, not nine. I can have fun if I want."

"Since when do you have fun like that? Please tell me you were safe," she asked, whispering the last part so the other bridesmaids didn't hear as they came out from the changing room in different styles of the same colour.

I nodded, patting down the fabric again. "Course we were. I'm not stupid."

My stomach churned. I wasn't on the pill, and he didn't use anything. God, I felt sick. I kept a fake smile on, but all I wanted to do was burst into tears. What if I was pregnant? I couldn't be. I doubted it. He probably did use something, and I just couldn't remember. My mind was still a little fuzzy. All I could remember was these damn sex bruises that he gave me.

I did remember his smile and his dark blue, bedroom, fuck me eyes. They were hard to forget.

I'd been dreaming of them for the past five days.

For five days, all I had thought about was the man who remained a mystery to me. It played on my mind what would happen if we saw each other again, and I would eagerly want a repeat. I'd want to spend a night with him completely sober so I couldn't forget anything.

Sighing, I looked at my sister.

She was smiling. "You've got it bad for him, haven't you?"

"You can't fall for someone who you don't really remember." But I did remember him.

The other girls bitched and moaned about looking too fat or not looking good enough. I couldn't care. My head was now elsewhere, and it would be until I got my period in a couple weeks. I couldn't believe I had been so careless to not think of something as important as that.

Fuck my life right now.

The dress fittings went well after Cassie told them all to suck it up and wear what they were told. We all ended up with floor-length Grecian style gowns. The three other girls had their straps on differently as I kept mine with a strapless, but we all had the same colour.

"Where's Tony?" I asked her. "Aren't you two like inseparable now that you're living together?"

My sister poked her tongue out and made a face. "He's at work, and then he had a suit fitting afterward. Your partner for the wedding is his best friend. You'll like him. He's nice and easygoing."

"Single?" I asked, smirking.

"Ah, no. Married and taken, I'm afraid." She winked back.

"You couldn't have let me be partners with someone single and hot?" I grumbled playfully, turning in my seat. "So this guy, his wife won't give me daggers all night, will she?"

Cassie's smile etched from side to side. "No. She's really quiet and nice. I don't see much of her though. Tony said she's just busy and shy around new people."

Well, that was a relief. "I'll have Greyson there anyway. He's flying out tomorrow to stay."

"What? You've got another guy on the go? You are my sister after all." She winked.

I cringed, shuddering at the thought. "Eww, you're gross, and no, I don't. He's gay and pretty much my only friend at college."

"I doubt he's your only friend. Do Mum and Dad know he's coming over?" she asked, going all big sister on me. "I could tell Daddy for you."

I nodded, proud of myself that I had actually asked them. "They know. They also know he is gay, so Dad's mind was put at ease knowing there was going to be no tumble in the sheets. He's really nice and very cute."

Cassie smiled, asking more about Greyson as she drove us back to our parent's house. I went on and told her how my classes were going. I didn't think my sister and I had ever bonded this way before. It was nice to get along with her like this. Usually, we would be arguing and fighting over something petty. I was surprised she wanted me as her maid of honor. I expected only a bridesmaid.

She was telling me more about Tony and where they were going for their honeymoon. They chose London. When I thought of a honeymoon, I thought of exotic beaches and private villas on the beach. Maybe I'd get that one day. Not that I was looking to settle down. I wasn't ready for that.

I walked into the kitchen behind Cassie. Dad was over by the cupboard, making coffee. "Hey, girls. Have a good day?"

"Yep," I answered, sitting up on the counter bench beside where he stood. "I think I may be prettier than the bride." I winked teasingly.

Dad threw his head back and laughed loudly. "Oh, I have no doubt about that. You look more like me than your mother anyway."

That was true. I looked a lot like my father with my tanned skin, grey-blue eyes, and dark brown hair.

Cassie pinched my arm. I let out a hiss, and she smirked. "Another one to add to the collection."

I could have killed her. Dad looked and frowned. "Another what?"

"Bruise. I fell over and hurt myself. You know me." I shot my sister a look, warning her not to bring it up. "Clumsy."

"Yes. Sage tripped in her dress and bruised her ass," she fibbed, winking as she jabbed me in the side. "Let's hope she doesn't fall at the wedding."

25

I rolled my eyes, jumping off the bench with a squirm. "Just make sure you don't slip and fall down. Nothing like a bride tumbling down the aisle to make a good YouTube hit." I teased her back. That was her biggest fear.

"You're so going to get it." She laughed, trying to chase me around the island counter.

I laughed, squealing loudly when Dad picked me up. "Hmm, Cass. What do you think the pool is like today? I think Sage should test the water for us."

My eyes grew wide with fear. "Don't you dare! I will so pull you in with me!"

Dad just chuckled. "Just teaching you a lesson for stirring your sister up." He laughed loudly, tossing me over his shoulder and heading outdoors for the pool.

I was kicking and screaming the entire time Dad dropped me into the freezing cold water.

~

OLIVER

"I look like a grade-A wanker."

Tony laughed, raising a brow. "Then we both look like wankers. We're in the same thing."

"Yeah, but a bowtie? She isn't serious, is she?" I asked, walking and picking out a different tie from the rack to switch with the one around my neck.

He just shrugged, checking himself out in the mirror. "No idea. I just go along with whatever she says to me, and it's normally the saying 'Happy wife, happy life.'"

I raised a brow at him. "Oh?"

"Isn't that how it goes?" He laughed, looking clueless.

A happy wife meant fuck all in my house.

I kept quiet and just nodded. "Yeah, something like that."

I'd been unable to bring myself to confess to Amy or anyone about my one night of epic fuck ups. Things weren't too good at home. They usually weren't, but this time, they were worse.

26

I just didn't know how to bring it up. Let alone even tell my best mate when he was about to get married after years of fucking around with different women.

"How're things with you anyway? Amy okay that you're in the wedding?" he asked.

I scoffed. Yeah, she was eager as fuck to go. I wouldn't tell him what her actual reaction had been. She threatened not to go to the wedding if I went with another woman. Meaning, she didn't want me as his best man and being paired with the maid of honor. She flipped out and told me if I didn't decline, then I was going alone.

"I don't know. I mentioned it, and she didn't say much. Just that it was good, and that's all really. So I assume she's fine with it. Anyway, it's not like this chick is my actual date. It's just one walk, one dance, and sitting together at dinner, yes?" I asked, making sure that was all.

He smirked. "Yeah, that's all. Maybe more than once dance and all those photos. Oh, and a car ride but that's all."

"Fuck, this wedding is sounding like a road trip and circus." I chuckled, looking at myself in the mirror as I buttoned the black jacket.

"Well, you were married at a courthouse. This is how the other half do it." He winked, looking at the silk tie I had swapped over. "Yeah, the tie looks much better."

I handed him a tie also. "Ha, don't knock it. It was alright. I need to figure out my best man speech. That's going to be fun. I think I have a few college stories I could whip out. Go on about your hit it and quit it ways."

He snorted out a laugh. "Fuck, don't bother. Cass doesn't even know just how bad I was. Plus, you could do it with Cass's sister. She's in town," he suggested. "Could be nice to make a toast together."

I frowned for a moment. My brows knotted together as I tried to think. "I don't think I've met her."

27

"Nah, you haven't. She normally keeps to herself anyway when she's back here. Think she's around twenty-one and in college," Tony said with a shrug. "She's hot. Amy may get pissed, but I couldn't have my best man paired with someone who's not as pretty as he is."

I looked at him and broke out into a grin. "You're checking out your sister-in-law? Classy." I rolled my eyes.

He burst out laughing as the man in the store looked at us confused. "Well, I can look but not touch." He winked. "Trust me. You'll be looking too when you meet her."

"Doubt it," I mumbled to myself. I doubted I'd ever look at another fucking woman again.

We spent the next hour going over different ties until we settled on black ones. Typical men we were. If we looked at colours, we'd pick the wrong ones and then be screwed with Cassie. We chose the safe option. Black went with almost everything.

After choosing the ties, I went home.

I started to undress as soon as I had walked into the spare room. I'd been sleeping in here ever since that night. Even if I hadn't cheated, I would be in here regardless. The tension was thick. It was like living with a roommate.

Amy always had her door shut if she was in the bedroom. Today was no different. I knew she was ovulating, and I was waiting for her to bring it up to me. I was always the one who mentioned it. Maybe it was just the excitement of finally getting laid for the month. After screwing that woman last weekend, sex with my wife was the last thing I could do.

There was no way I could bring myself to even attempt it.

I stripped and headed for the shower.

Work killed me today. I was never one for sitting on my ass behind a desk. I liked to be out and moving around. I normally got to do that, but today, it was all paperwork and going over site plans.

I'd been working in construction since I finished college. My dad had a company and asked if I'd join him, as my brother wouldn't. He liked sitting behind his big wooden desk too much to go and get his hands dirty. I, on the other hand, fucking loved it.

There was a knock on the door mid-shower. I froze at her voice.

"Oliver, we need to talk," Amy said, trying to open the bathroom door, but I had locked it. She kept trying to push it open.

I groaned quietly, turning the water off and grabbing a towel. I didn't answer her. I had nothing to say. Once dressed again, I opened the door and looked at her.

"What?"

She just stared at me with a sullen, sour look that didn't impress me. It sure as hell wouldn't make me cave in and give her what she wanted.

"Never mind," she said quietly.

I frowned, blocking her from walking away. Clearly, something was important. "No, tell me what you want. You almost caved the door in trying to ask me something, so ask."

She sighed, giving me a shrug. Her eyes locked to mine for a brief second before looking away. "Are we going to fuck? You know what today is."

*Are we going to fuck?* Words every man wanted to hear.

Usually, I'd always be up for a chance to get my dick wet. But now? I couldn't believe it that was all she wanted. She had an ulterior motive, and after the week we've had, I wasn't keen.

I shook my head. "Real nice, Amy. That's really going to get me in the mood to just fuck you."

"Well, god. What do you want? I show you some interest, and you push me away!" Her voice raised, but I was too exhausted to fight with her tonight.

"Amy, when we tried making a baby, I never just fucked you. I made love to you, but that's all it was to you, just a quick screw. I'm not in the mood for this tonight or tomorrow. I said it once already. I'm done trying for now. I'm going to bed." I went to walk past her, but her hand, wrapping around my forearm, stopped me.

29

"Oliver, I'm sorry," she whispered, stepping closer. Her grip loosened, and she moved both hands to slide around my waist, resting her head against my chest—a gesture I would appreciate any other time.

I raised both arms and hugged her back. Standing frozen to the spot, I couldn't move. I almost kissed her forehead but stopped myself.

"Amy," I started. I had to tell her. I couldn't do this. "I need to talk to you about something."

"No. I'm sick of talking. I just need you to give it to me. It's time, and I don't have long." Amy began to slide a hand down towards the waistband of my sweats.

I grabbed her wrist, stopping her before she got any further. I looked at her, and it killed me.

"No. I can't. I'm sorry."

"Why not?" she demanded. Trying to free her hand and with no luck, she tried using her other one. "Yes!"

I groaned, shaking my head. This wasn't her. She never wanted my cock.

"Amy, do you honestly think I can get into bed with you after what you said to me? You think I enjoy sex? I don't. I feel like I'm forcing you most of the time. I had a shit day at work, and now I just want to go to sleep." I was fucking tired.

She scoffed, her eyes dancing with humor as she let out a barely audible snort. "I'm sorry if you don't know how to touch a woman. That's not my fault."

Her words didn't hurt me. I knew that was far from true. I'd managed to make the girl scream with an orgasm before my dick had even touched her. The first of plenty.

"Amy, I'm not going to fight with you tonight. Now you can see what it's like to be turned down for once." I ran a hand through my hair, leaning against the wall.

We both stood in silence, facing each other from across the hallway. I had nothing to say. What I wanted to say wouldn't end well, and it wasn't the time. Although, I didn't know when the right

30

time would be to tell her. That was a fight I knew wouldn't end well.

Finally, she tucked her hair behind her ear and asked, "So, what? You don't want a baby with me anymore?"

My gaze softened, and I shrugged. I couldn't exactly say no, so I softened the blow. "I do want a baby, but I don't think it's the right time for us."

Her blue eyes welled with tears, and she nodded. "I'm sorry. I didn't mean to say those things." She stepped forward and was soon crying against my chest.

"Amy, you're stressed as much as I am. Fighting won't solve anything. We just need to try and get back to where we were," I suggested. "A baby won't fix anything, and clearly, we have issues."

She didn't answer me, just giving me a nod instead.

I carried her down to our room. She didn't speak, and I ended up lying beside her on the bed. I stayed there until she fell asleep, and then I quietly made my way down to the other bedroom. I closed the door and locked it. If she woke, that lock would save another fight that I really wasn't up for.

Sitting on the double bed, I sighed. Running a hand through my hair, I tilted my head to the side and rubbed the base of my neck. My life was a fucking mess right now.

The glass caught my sight, and I reached over to the wooden bedside table, picking up the unopened bottle of Jack Daniel that had my name written all over it. It was taunting, begging me to drink. I unscrewed the cap and took a large swig, ignoring the burn as I took another.

That was how the rest of my night went, staring at the cream plastered wall and drinking alone in the bedroom with every thought under the sun running through my mind.

I had no idea what I was going to do.

I had a woman I loved, a woman who needed to know the truth deserved to know.

I just wondered if it was all worth it in the end.

31

# CHAPTER 3

Summer was one of my favourite seasons. I could lie around by the pool and enjoy the warmth as I sipped on cocktails and ate watermelon. It was one of the good things about being home for the summer break, and as summer was nearing an end, I vowed to make the most of this heat while I could.

Stretching out on the sun lounge, I smiled, catching sight of Greyson making his way towards me with another drink and a fresh plate of food to nibble on. I'd already eaten the last one before he could enjoy some.

"Remember, sharing is caring." He winked, joining me.

"This heat just makes me feel so hungry and thirsty," I confessed. "I haven't felt this lazy in months."

"It's called holidays, and I see you're definitely in holiday mode." He laughed.

I laughed, tilting my sunglasses and making sure he could see my eye roll. "I don't see you doing any work either." I pointed out, lying back down. "Was anyone inside?"

"No. Your mum went to the store. Apparently, she has a daughter who's eating all their food," he said seriously. Then his charming smile was back on the show. "Now that she's gone, do you want to take a naked dip? Fool around a little?"

"Okay." I laughed, reaching for a handful of chips. "Remember, you have to actually touch me and not imagine it."

"Fuck. It looks like I'm out of ideas then. Why don't we go watch a movie, or are you still too worried to do anything?" he asked on a more serious note.

I looked at him and nodded, hating that he brought it up. I didn't want to think about it. I hadn't told my family the whole story. I was freaking out over a pregnancy that might or might not be happening.

If I were, I would tell Mum first. She'd know what to do.

"I feel sick thinking about it, Grey. What if I am?"

"You're not. Stop stressing over nothing. Have you made an appointment yet?"

I shook my head, finishing my mouthful of food before I spoke, "No. I couldn't. Mum would know, and then Dad would freak out. I don't want to think about it, but when I do, I convince myself that I have all the symptoms."

I heard him groan, and I looked up to see him leaning in closer. "Sage, you're eating all the time, but that's probably because you're worried. Stress eating will do that to you. Just take the test, and then I'll make you an actual drink with alcohol in it rather than your mocktails."

"Yeah, thanks for keeping me in check." I laughed dryly. I would love something stronger right now.

I smiled, thankful that I had him here to keep me sane right now. I was due for my period any day, and I was praying it would come soon. Otherwise, I was damn right screwed.

I lay on my back, closing my eyes and relishing in the feeling of warmth over my bare skin. "Do you parents mind that you're here?"

"No, they're working anyway. How's your sister's wedding plan going?"

My smile grew. He would love this. "She's turned a little obsessed. Everything needs to be perfect."

Cassie had gone a little crazy with everything that involved her wedding. She was now on a detox to clear up her skin, body, and mind. I thought. I didn't pay much attention to her at all when she was rambling on about that. All I knew was that she had to look her absolute best. I couldn't blame her. I'd want to look the same too.

Tony joined us for dinner last night, telling her that whatever she wanted she could have. I swore he did it just to keep her happy and not pouting. She had a knack of getting her own way when she wanted it. He had let slip that he picked out the ties, and she wasn't happy that her bowtie dream had ended. I had to giggle until Dad shot me a glare.

Greyson nudged me, pulling me from my daydream and inner thoughts, and I opened my eyes. "Yes?"

"Let's go in your room and watch a movie. I'm burning up. Unlike you, I don't tan." He stood, shielding his body with a towel and acting like he was going to burn to a crisp.

There was nothing wrong with his body. He loved working out and prided himself over the fact he could eat an entire pizza and still sport a six-pack. Sometimes it was hard to believe he was gay. If he were straight, we would still be dating. With his dimpled smile, we would still be dating.

I followed him, not leaving the bowl of chips behind. "What would you like to watch?" I called out as he disappeared into the guest house.

Not missing his humorous tone, I found him on my bed, holding the TV remote as he skimmed through shows on my hard drive. "Anything but *Scandal*. I can't handle Fitz and that chick getting it on anymore. I want him to leave his damn wife."

"Olivia?" I asked and sighed dreamily. "I love Fitz. He's so sexy."

Greyson rolled his eyes, scoffing. "I could totally see you hooking up with a married man like her."

He had a way with words.

"Don't be gross. Anyway, it's just a show, so shut up and watch it. I have the new episodes that we haven't seen yet."

He smirked, slipping underneath the covers in just his boxers. "Well then, come cuddle and watch."

"That's all you're going to be getting from me, too." I winked, grabbing my clean clothes from the chair beside the door.

I didn't change in front of him. Yes, I could be very shy at times and modest.

I lay on the bed, beneath the covers beside him. His arm was draped around my waist as we started watching *Scandal*. He was tired, and it didn't take long for him to fall asleep. I kicked his leg every time he began to snore.

I used to love this show, but now, whenever Oliver and Fitz would kiss or when there were sex scenes, it just made me want that night over again. I wanted his hands back on my body, his lips against mine, and his cock deep inside me. I couldn't even remember his name, but I was sure that if we ever met again, I would know those eyes and that smile.

One could only hope, and I hoped that day would come.

When it was clear Greyson wasn't going to wake up, I decided to take a soak in the tub.

The bubbles filled to the edge of the spa. I lay back and closed my eyes. It had been a good couple of weeks of being back home. I missed the family dinners and the days spent with my parents, even just going and getting groceries with Mum. I thought about staying here and not going back. I liked school, but I wasn't in love with it.

As I stood naked, I stared at my reflection in the mirror. All signs of that night had vanished. My marks were gone, and I had nothing to be reminded of him. I peered in closer at my breasts, wondering if they were bigger. I couldn't tell. Turning to the side, I still looked the same. I was paranoid.

After I dressed, I went to leave the bathroom, but something stopped me.

"Screw it," I whispered to myself, biting my lip as I opened the vanity drawer and pulled out a store brought pregnancy test.

I was nervous. I was beyond anxious, but I knew I needed to take it. I was never a patient person when it came to waiting around.

"Sage?" I heard Greyson call out.

He scared me so much I almost dropped the test in the toilet.

"Just a minute," I called back out, trying to keep my nerves under control. "I'm just changing."

It wasn't a complete lie. I knew if he knew that I was taking a test, he'd want to be in here with me. I needed to do this on my own. I had to see if it was just my thoughts eating me up or if it was something else, something much bigger.

"Okay, well, I'll go over these takeout menus for dinner," he replied. "I'm thinking Mexican or Chinese? Even sushi?"

I rolled my eyes. He was distracting me with food, and I wanted them all. "Sounds good!"

Nerves filled me. Was this what it was like? To sit in complete and utter panic for three minutes? To overthink and worry about every single decision that you had made leading up to this? I was terrified. I wanted to throw up.

My heart was in my throat.

I didn't know what to do. I just kept praying for the results to come fast. My eyes were glued to the stick as it flashed, waiting. Waiting, which seemed to go on for a lifetime.

Until it stopped.

There was a tiny ounce of relief when it stopped flashing, but that lasted as soon as it came. Then, complete panic set in.

~

OLIVER

"Alright, what's going on?" Tony said, turning around and facing me. "I know when something's up with you. I can read you like an open book. Is it the pregnancy problems?" He studied my face, staring at me with seriousness.

We were in the middle of another suit fitting, and I wasn't feeling it. I just couldn't be fucking bothered with it today. Cassie had demanded bow ties yet again, and we ignored her.

I shook my head, brushing him off. "No. We've put that on hold for the time being," I said, loosening my tie. I felt like I was about to choke.

Babies were the last thing on my mind.

"Then what is it? You've barely said anything, and you haven't even laughed at my hilarious jokes." He pointed out.

With his smile, it only made me feel worse. I couldn't pretend anymore. I had to tell him.

"I fucked up." I didn't even know how I got the words out. They were like bile in my throat.

He waved the tailor away, giving us some privacy. I took a seat, and he walked over sitting opposite on the stool.

"When you say fucked up, how big are you talking? Like forgetting to pick your socks up or not bringing milk home." He paused. "Or do you mean you really fucked up?"

I looked at him, running both hands through my hair and then over my face again with a groan. "Really fucked up."

Tony stood again, glancing around to make sure we were completely alone then came back to the seat he previously sat on and leant forward. "What did you do?"

Pinching the bridge of my nose, I took a couple of deep breaths and wiped my eyes. "I…" I couldn't get the words out.

"Oliver, shit. What the fuck happened?" Tony asked. I felt his hand on my shoulder, nudging me to continue. "Talk to me."

"I fucked another woman." The words were out before I knew it.

He was silent for a moment, then blew out a hard breath. "Fuck."

I nodded. "I know. I have to tell her. I feel so guilty."

His eyes went wider, and the panic I had been feeling was evident in him. "No. You don't say anything to her. She will kill you. No doubt about it, man. She will fucking kill you."

"You think I don't know that? I can't even look at her without wanting to throw up. I really screwed up. I can't believe I let it happen," I muttered. I was so pissed with myself.

"Listen, I know you think coming clean would be the right thing to do, but I don't know. It only happened once, right?" he asked, nodding for me to agree.

I hesitated, looking at him. "Once would be one night?" I asked.

God, I knew that wasn't the case with me.

He shook his head with caution. "No, I mean one load, and then you left."

I shut my eyes hard, shaking my head. "She sucked me off, and I fucked her three times after that."

"Fuck." He pulled back. His mouth opened and closed again. "Are you kidding me? What were you thinking? When? How? Where?" He rolled out a ton of questions.

"I wasn't thinking. I was off my head at the bar for your bucks. She was there, and we were alone upstairs. Next thing I knew, I had her on me, and I couldn't stop. Amy never fucking touches me. She hates having sex, and in that second, I wanted a woman who couldn't keep her hands off me. She was on her knees, and I just let it happen." It didn't feel any better to talk about this or relive the night's events. "I never even mentioned I was married." I snapped, punching my fist down against the arm of the chair.

Tony sighed, rubbing his temple with one hand. "Look, it's not obvious to a lot of people that things aren't going well for you and her, but to me, I can see it. She's angry and pushing you away. I know she is, so don't deny it. I know what it's like when a woman has her mouth around your dick. All rational thoughts leave your mind, and you only have one thought on your mind, and that's to fucking blow down her throat…" Well, he was right there. I had been thinking about nothing but her mouth around me. His next question threw me off. "Where do you sleep at home?"

There was no point lying about this. "Spare room. We got into a huge fight the other week after your buck's night, and she wanted me out. I told her I was done trying to have kids, and we've now barely spoken to each other. I don't know what to do." I admitted. "She just wants to screw to have a baby, and I can't even imagine having sex with her, let alone having a kid."

I needed to go home and come clean to her.

"I'm sorry. I shouldn't have put this on you," I said, standing again.

Tony stood, putting both hands on my forearms and frowning. "No. You should have told me after it happened. We're brothers. I won't mention it to anyone, not even Cassie. I don't think you should tell Amy, not yet anyway."

I nodded, still not sure of this. "Thanks. I tried convincing myself not to tell her, but then I feel like a bastard, and I hate lying to her."

"You did wear a rubber though, right?" he asked when we both walked to the door.

I stopped dead in my tracks. Fuck. I was racking my mind and came up empty. I looked at him and shook my head. "No. I think I blew in her each time as well."

"Well, if you can't get Amy pregnant, then I'd doubt you got this chick knocked up. She'd most likely be on something anyway. They all are these days." He grinned, slapping me on the back. "Fucking good boy Oliver finally played up a bit."

I groaned. That wasn't funny. I chose to ignore his praise and think about a possible pregnancy. "Yeah, I highly doubt I could knock anyone up." I felt slightly relieved but only for a moment though.

A kid to another woman was something I didn't need. It would send me into an early grave.

I headed home, stopping by the florist and did the pathetic husband sucking up thing. I picked up a bunch of flowers for Amy. I needed to try to work things out with her. I didn't want this coldness that was around us or the dreaded feeling of coming home to either a fight or silence. I wanted the kisses and desperate "I missed you" sex on the floor.

"Amy?" I called out, entering the kitchen. She walked in the kitchen wearing her pyjamas. I was confused. "Are you feeling sick?" I asked, gesturing at her flannel sleepwear.

She shook her head. "No. I just had nothing to do today. Why?"

"You're not dressed. That's all." I walked around the island and over to her, handing over the colourful assortment of flowers. "I missed you today."

"That's a first," she muttered under her breath and took the flowers, looking at them for a second and tossing them on the counter with a sigh. There was no appreciation for them. She turned around and began picking up some fallen petals. "Do you want to order yourself dinner?"

I frowned, hurt that she didn't care what I had done to try and make her happy. "You've already eaten?"

"Look, I'm tired. I'm not in the mood for whatever this is, Oliver." She shrugged, brushing me off.

Was she serious? I wasn't sure what was going on. Sure, I hadn't been the best company, but I was trying here.

"You spent the day in bed while I busted my ass off at work, and you couldn't even wait to eat dinner with me? Why not text and tell me to grab something on the way home?"

"Because it didn't cross my mind. I was hungry, so I ate. Big deal." The worst part was she was actually pleased with her answer as she glanced again at the flowers. "Thanks, but they don't match the house."

They were flowers. How the fuck were they meant to match?

Shaking my head, I didn't have anything to say back. I couldn't respond, and I was done with the conversation. I went to the bathroom, clearly needing a shower and a way to relieve the vented up stress my body was aching from.

My hand reached my cock, and I threw my head back with a quiet moan. My dick was hard, dripping with pre-cum. My balls were heavy, aching for their release as I closed my eyes and stroked. I knew this wasn't going to last long.

Probably a good thing because I needed it fast.

The worst part was during the blissful start of my orgasm, I fucked my fist faster, thinking of the girl at the club and how good her mouth felt around my cock.

# CHAPTER 4

Sage

"Have you heard from Daniel at all?" Cassie's question threw me off during dinner.

I gave her a look before my slow reply came. "No, I haven't. Why?" I asked curiously, ignoring the look Greyson was giving me.

She shrugged, going back to slicing her chicken breast. "Just wondering. He's in town, or so I've heard."

"He is? How do you know?" I raised a questioning brow, knowing full well that she was baiting me for a reaction.

Daniel, oh charming Daniel. He was my ex-boyfriend. Or, as I liked to remember, the man who took my virginity and used me until something blonder and with bigger tits came along. I knew I should have expected it. I mean he was older. But unlike all men, he had made me feel special.

I was way too young and definitely naive.

Also, very stupid. I was stupid and blind when I went out with him.

She bit her lip and ran a hand through her hair, glancing from Tony to me with hesitation. "Tony told me he's in town. He is here for the wedding. He's a groomsman."

I shot Tony a look, and his cheeks blushed slightly. "Sorry, Sage. It slipped my mind."

"Thanks for the notice," I mumbled, eye-rolling to no one in particular as I sighed. I didn't want to see him after he left me heartbroken and devastated for weeks. Another thought crossed my mind, and I shot him a wide-eyed look full of panic. "Is he my partner for the wedding?"

"Christ, no. I wouldn't do that to you," he retorted.

My shoulders sagged in relief as I began to eat again. "Good. I wouldn't be in the wedding otherwise."

Cassie gave me an apologetic smile as she reached over and squeezed my arm. "I'm sorry. I didn't know until a couple days ago. You're still coming out on Saturday though, right?"

"What's on Saturday?" I asked, my mind coming up blank when I tried to think.

She rolled her eyes, nudging me. "We're having dinner and drinks with Tony's and my friends. I want you there. It's kind of like a joint bachelor and bachelorette party."

"Your bachelorette party was a few weeks ago though. How many do you need, bridezilla?" I teased, grabbing my fork and stabbing the fettuccine with it. I brought it up to my lips and took a bite.

"It's not really a bachelor, bachelorette thing. It's more like a friendly outing with the bridal party before the big day." Tony winked, correcting me. "No one will be drunk."

I rolled my eyes at him. He was such a sucker for pleasing her. He wasn't the type of guy I thought she'd end up marrying. Tall and athletic was what I pictured. Tony was tall but slim and kind of playerish. Well, that was what I picked up when I first met him. He was like a brother now, and we teased the utter hell out of each other a lot.

"Well, I may be drunk for it." I laughed, but the humor wasn't in it.

Mum looked up from her bowl and sighed, clearly tired of this conversation. "Sage, when you get married, you can make your own rules up. Your sister wants to do this her way. Stop teasing, and just help out a bit more."

"I don't think I want to get married. Playing the field is far more fun." I winked. Tony held in his laugh as I looked up, waiting for Dad to stop reading his paperwork and join the dinner conversation.

As if on cue, his head snapped up and eyes narrowed in on me. "Want to go for another swim, dear?"

"You'd have to catch me, old man. Don't worry. I was kidding. My wedding is going to send you broke, so keep working and saving." I smiled brightly up at him. "I can't wait for my hand-stitched dress that'll need to be insured."

Greyson laughed with a scoff from beside me. "Sage, your wedding is most likely never going to happen. You need to find a guy first."

"True. She's too fussy with boys," Cassie chimed in again.

Tony threw his head back with a wide grin. "I don't think any man would match up to her list of wants and needs."

"Bullshit. I am not that fussy, and I don't have a list." I rolled my eyes laughing as my cheeks tinged pink slightly.

Did they really think I was that choosy?

Dad laughed, his smile meeting his eyes. He looked tired and overworked. "Oh, darling. I know you've set your standards up to your old man. I can't help if there's no other man like myself."

Cass and I both let out a groan. I shook my head from side to side. "Eww, you've got tickets on yourself."

Mum sighed, obviously agreeing with Dad. "He's wonderful and exactly right. There's no other man around like him."

"Whatever." I groaned. The conversation was over for me.

I wasn't picky. I just knew what I wanted, and that wasn't easy to find. Yes, I could easily go out and have plenty of one-night stands, but I didn't want to do that. I wanted someone who wanted to know me and not just my body. I wanted the man who touched me in ways I had never felt before. I wanted him so badly that it hurt.

Plus, a boyfriend was the least of my worries and definitely the last thing on my mind right now.

I had bigger issues to think about. Way bigger issues.

45

Like the pregnancy test I took.

Taking my bowl out to the kitchen, I put it in the dishwasher and headed for my area. I liked relaxing in front of the fire, sipping hot tea, and wrestling with my inner thoughts while Greyson sat opposite, scrolling through Facebook and Instagram. He fitted in perfectly at home here. It was as if he were the son they never had.

I didn't know what got into me, but I picked up my phone and started to write out a text to Daniel. I hadn't seen him in almost four years. Last time I saw him, he had his tongue down another woman's throat and hand up her skirt. Opting against it, I erased the message. I wasn't going to bother with him. He never made me feel like he regretted it.

"Let's get to bed. You look tired." Greyson's voice startled me as he walked behind me. He poked my side, which had me jumping before I let out a shriek.

I managed to push the door open and tried to block him out. "I think you can sleep outside tonight, pretty boy." I bit down on my lip and giggled, sounding like a schoolgirl, as he fought to open the door from the other side.

"I'm not sleeping on a deck chair. Open up, or I'll huff, and I'll puff, and I'll blow your house down," he said, his voice deeper, as he puffed out his chest and stood tall. He then proceeded to blow a breath of warm air on my face.

Scrunching my face, I gave in and let him enter. "Big bad wolf, please go and shower so we can lie out here and watch a movie."

"Shower with me? Oh, no. That's right. You can't handle this." He teased, slapping my ass as he took off to the bathroom.

I rubbed my backside. "You're going to sleep on the couch, Greyson!"

I could hear him laughing while I slipped into my pyjamas and went in to wash my face while Grey was showering. I laughed as he hissed when I turned the tap on, and the hot water hit his skin. I left before he could splash me with a handful of water.

46

Just as I made myself comfortable, my sister's unannounced visit took me by surprise. "Hey," she said quietly, joining me. "I'm sorry. I didn't mean to upset you."

Looking at her confused, I wasn't sure what she meant. "Umm, I'm not upset. Probably more surprised, but I'm not upset." I looked at her, playing with my sleeve. "Will he be at dinner?"

"Yeah, that's why I told you tonight. I told Tony to warn him to stay away from you, or else."

I had to laugh. "Well, let's hope for his sake, he listens to Tony." I grinned, sitting up, and turned to face her, glancing at the door to make sure Greyson wasn't nearby. "I need to talk to you. Do you remember that night I told you about."

She nodded, looking cautiously. "You mean, about Mr. Bedroom Eyes who fucked you on the floor?"

I blushed, regretting telling her that. "Do you have to call him that? It's embarrassing."

She threw her head back, laughing. "I love teasing you. Yes, I know who you mean. Now continue."

There was no easy way to say this. I wanted to stop, but there was no going back now.

"Let's just say, what would people think if I ended up pregnant? I mean with the guy that I don't know and will probably never see again." I couldn't look at her. The floor was my only source of comfort right now.

Cassie squished my cheeks together and forced me to look at her. "Oh my god, Sage! Are you kidding me? You said you were careful."

"I didn't say I was dumbass. I was asking a hypothetical what if?" I pushed her hands away, gaining control of my own face back.

She sighed, laughing and finding my annoyed state funny. "I don't know. I mean you're young and single. Then you'd be pregnant to a man you don't know? How do you think Mum and Dad would react? Mum may be okay. She is more chill than Dad, who, by the way, would search this entire city to find the guy who

47

knocked his little girl up without putting a ring on it first. Then he is going to beat his hot ass up, which, by the way, I know he's got to be hot because you are so damn fussy and wouldn't shag just anyone."

"Cassie, be serious." I hated it when I asked her something that was so serious and then she just joked around.

She was right though. He was the most gorgeous man I had ever laid eyes on.

"Babe, I am serious. Dad would flip out. Mum would probably cry, and I, well, I'd be the coolest aunt ever. Now, spill. Are you preggers? It's been around five weeks since that night, hasn't it? So, you'd know by now if you're late," she asked, pulling her phone out and skimming through the calendar.

She had literally freaked me out big time. I knew what would happen. I didn't even know why I bothered to ask her.

Dad would flip out. He would roar the house down, demanding to know who, when, and where. He would disown me and possibly throw me out of his house.

Mum would cry, saying that I had ruined my life and all the hard work I was going to school for.

I laughed, shaking my head as I brushed her off with a smile. Putting on my "I'm fine voice" to pretend nothing was wrong. Saying the words broke my heart. "God, of course. I'm not pregnant."

I was.

~

OLIVER

*I felt a pair of hands sliding down my chest. A mouth kissed and licked at my stomach. She pulled my boxers down as she took my hard dick in her mouth, moaning. She licked and sucked while grazing her nails down and up my chest. Closing my eyes, I leant my head back slowly into the pillow.*

*I was in bliss right now.*

*"God, you feel so good. Keep going, baby."* I groaned, still half asleep as I raised my hips, pushing up to slide further down her throat. She took me in and used her hand to stroke at the same time.

*I reached out and felt her long hair, taking a handful as she bobbed her head faster and faster. I wanted to see her face. I propped myself up on my elbows, looking down at the woman sucking me off with her skilful, soft mouth.*

*Then she looked up at me. Those grey-blue eyes were smiling at me as I spilled my thick white seed down her throat, watching as she took every last drop hungrily.*

That was when I jerked awake.

Covered in sweat, I sat up, my breathing hard and ragged. I flicked on the lamp beside me and sighed in relief.

What a fucking dream.

I groaned. Yep, I'd woken up hard and on the verge of blowing in my boxers. I looked over at a sleeping Amy beside me and sighed regrettably. After my talk with Tony, I went back sleeping in our bedroom.

How could I even dream about something like that with my wife beside me?

I looked at her sleeping body and went to touch her. I hesitated and decided against it. She hated being woken up.

I lay back down and wiped the sweat from my forehead with my shirt and turned the lamp off.

What the fuck was I dreaming about her for? I needed her out of my damn mind.

I couldn't lie here next to my wife and pretend all was forgiven between us, but we were both trying. She hadn't yelled at me this week, although the weird tension was still there between us.

Reaching over, I grabbed my phone and checked the time. It was almost 5:00 AM. I rolled over and faced away from Amy. Yawning, I tried to fall back into sleep again, trying to block out dreams I began to have.

~

49

Groaning, and not in a good way, I opened my eyes. Amy was standing in front of me. The sunlight was almost burning my sight.

"Fuck, close the curtains." I yawned, blocking the light with my hand.

"Get up. It's almost 8:00 AM, and your parents are coming for lunch today," she said, crossing her arms over her chest and waiting for me to budge.

I shook my head and rolled over, facing the other way. "I'm tired. I've hardly slept and had a busy week with new plans at work. It's a Saturday, Amy."

Yes, I was up dreaming about another woman.

"I don't care. Get up and help me get ready. The house is a mess, and I need to go to the store."

I yawned again, mumbling my reply, "Mum's bringing something over, and you don't need to make anything."

I heard her scoff as she pulled the blinds further open and opened a window, letting the breeze blow in.

I got her message, and it was well truly received.

She walked to the foot of the bed, and I could see her with her hand on both hips, glaring at me. "What? So my food isn't good enough for them to eat?"

"What?" That was when I sat up, frowning and looking at her as my back hit the bed head. "Do you want me to call her and tell her not to bring over anything? She's just trying to help and be nice."

"Don't worry about it. Now, I feel like she thinks I don't do anything around here. I can't even cook dinner for my in-laws." She sighed, waving a hand through the air. "It's fine."

I wanted to roll my eyes. Fine. I hated that fucking word. Everything with her was just fine.

There was no way I'd fall back asleep.

I tossed the blankets off. "I'm going to shower, then I'll do the lawns. There's no point going back to sleep now."

"Good, and the house needs a vacuum once you're done." She smiled with victory and left the room.

Dad and Mum had arrived just as I finished the front lawn. I went over and kissed Mum on the cheek as I took the bags from her. She was always trying to help, and I wished Amy could just see that. It wasn't anything intentional or her trying to be rude.

"Parents are here," I called out. I was going to put the lasagna in the oven, but I froze. "Amy, what did you do?" I asked, staring at the lasagne already baking in the oven.

She walked out and smiled. Her eyes told me not to fuck with her today. "I cooked lunch. Put your mum's in the freezer. We're eating mine today."

"Amy, are you kidding me right now? She'll be offended if I do that." I just stood there with Mum's lasagne in my hands as my wife's was in the oven, bubbling up.

I heard my parents making their way inside, and I sighed, closing the oven door. I set the one Mum made on the bench top and tried to figure out a way to clear the air.

Mum walked over with a salad and a couple of bottles of apple cider. "Oliver, that only needs around twenty minutes to reheat." Mum smiled, then looked at Amy. "Nice to see you again, dear. How are you?"

Amy walked over and kissed her cheek. She had done her makeup today, and some bronze thing on her cheekbones stood out the most. "I'm good. Thank you, Jean, and I see you brought lunch." She put on a fake laugh. "I feel horrible. I already made lasagne, which is almost done. I'm sure yours will be great another night when we're too tired to cook. Oliver, can you put that in the freezer for me please?"

Well, fuck. The tension in the room was now thicker than ever.

"That's okay. I look forward to trying yours, Amy," Mum said, forcing out a smile.

I could tell she was offended, and I felt sick. My mother meant a damn lot to me, and Amy was pushing it.

51

Luckily, Dad spoke up, and I was grateful. "Your mother and I are going to go on a holiday soon. She wants to visit the vineyards and museums while I sit at a beer garden."

"Yeah? A seniors' trip?" I smirked, finding a spot for Mum's lasagne on the middle shelf.

Mum laughed, helping pull out the plates. "Ever so cheeky, I see. It's one of those group trips. We will see all different places and tour in a group."

"A seniors' trip." Dad chuckled. "Yes, it's probably going to end up like that. Unless you two want to tag along?"

I grinned, grabbing a beer out for him and sliding it over the bench. "Love to, but there's too much at work. I've got the contract for the new shopping complex to get sorted. Around fifty new stores are going in there. It's going to keep me busy for a good year or so."

Amy piped up, adding in, "Yes, but you need to take some time for yourself. A holiday would be great. Don't you think, honey?"

I knew where she was going with this: a holiday that my parents would end up paying for. As much as I'd love to go away, now wasn't the time.

"Another time. Anyway, Mum and Dad should go explore on their own. I don't find any of that tourist crap fun. Looking at paintings and statues isn't really my thing." I flashed Mum a charming smile.

"You were never one to sit still. Always on the go. Your father and I want some alone time, anyway." She laughed at my sudden change of expression, which had turned sour.

Amy went to speak up again when the timer went off. "Lunch is ready. Go sit, and I'll dish up."

It was still nice outside, so we set up out there for lunch and waited for Amy to join us. I was trying to avoid my mum's stare, but she snapped her fingers, which got me looking her way. Damn, I fell for that every single time.

"Yes?" I asked.

She looked behind her and Amy was still inside. "Are you still not having any luck?"

"It's just on hold for now. Until we figure some things out," I said, keeping my voice down. My eyes flickered up at Amy. She was watching me through the window. "Don't bring it up again, Mum. She's not in a good mood."

When was she ever?

"Oh, I can see that. I feel like we're intruding on you both," she whispered back accusingly.

She and I were close. I knew she'd be able to sense something was up. I had talked to her about our problems and struggles. She'd always been there to listen. I had no doubt in my mind she knew something was off. I also knew the moment she found out about my cheating, she'd never forgive me.

I sighed, rubbing my chin. "Just drop it, please. I don't want to piss her off and make anyone feel weird. Amy just wanted to cook for you. I'm sorry that I forgot to mention it to you yesterday when you called. Don't be upset with her. It's my doing."

I had to take the blame for this one.

"Ah, good luck with that. Women are complicated creatures. Happy one minute and then..." Dad paused as Mum raised a brow at him. "Like I was saying. Happy one minute and still happy the next. Unless you do something to land yourself in the doghouse."

I'd definitely be in the dog house.

Amy walked out, setting the lasagne down. Through lunch, it was all quiet talk. They asked about Tony's wedding, and I told them about that and our suit fittings, plus the dinner next weekend. Amy didn't say anything, so I guessed we were still going.

I didn't have the heart to tell Amy her lasagne almost snapped a tooth of mine from the uncooked sheets of pastry. She seemed pleased with it, so everyone agreed that it was good.

Unfortunately, Mum keeping her mouth shut about us having the baby plans on hold didn't last long. "Amy, Oliver tells me you're taking time out from trying to get pregnant again."

Amy's eyes snapped to mine. I could almost hear her teeth grinding together. "Did he? Well, seems as if Oliver can't keep his mouth shut."

"Oh, dear. I didn't mean to upset you. I pried it out of him. I think it's actually a wise decision," Mum said, trying to control the situation and simmer it down.

Dad nodded. "Yes. Go out and see the world, then have kids. They're hard work, and with Oliver working so much at the moment, it's good to just save while you can. Maybe in a year or so, it'll happen for you both. If not, no big deal."

"Well, I wasn't given much of a choice to stop. Your son decided that all on his own," Amy mumbled, keeping her eyes dead on mine.

"You're not ready," Mum said softly. "You're both still young and growing up."

I winced at her words, wishing she wouldn't meddle or get involved in this. She didn't know.

Amy, who was clearly hurt and angered by her words, dropped her cutlery on the plate loudly. "Well, when Oliver and I decide to have a baby, that'll be between us, and not on you to dictate when we should start a family." She didn't hold back staring my mother down.

I sighed, rubbing my neck. Lunch was a disaster.

After waving goodbye to my parents, who left soon after finishing their food, I headed back inside to catch sight of Amy, slamming the fridge door close. She glared at me and stormed off down the hallway.

I followed. "Amy."

"Leave me alone, Oliver. I don't want to talk to you!" She snapped. "How could you!"

I pushed my hand on the door before she slammed it in my face. "What did I do now? You can't be serious?"

"Oh, I am serious. I saw the way she looked at me, all disapprovingly and like I was rude to her. God, she can't come around here if she's going to be rude to me, Oliver. I mean it! What was with her saying we're not ready for a baby? She made it seem like we were teenagers. I don't want her back here." She looked at me dead serious as she laid down the rules.

This wasn't going to go well.

"I love you, but I won't ban my mother from visiting. My brother and his family live away, and she doesn't see them often. You have no right to tell me who can and can't come here. I wouldn't have a good job and income if it weren't for my parents." I gritted out with one hand still on the door holding it open. "Oh, I didn't notice you looking too pissed off when they were offering us to come on their trip with them. That was fucking rude, Amy. I won't use my parents like that, and you shouldn't either. I'm all they've got now. She didn't mean to be rude to you."

"You didn't notice because you were too busy sulking to notice the scrunched up posh face she wore when eating lunch!" She scoffed, walking away and tying her blonde hair up in a band.

Her calling my mother that really struck a nerve, but I held it in. I was trying to calm myself before I lost it completely.

"Amy, it nearly broke all our fucking teeth. You never made lunch for any other reason than out of spite. I don't know what you want from me anymore. I can't keep up with your crazy mood swings."

She spun around, grabbing the photo of us and throwing it at me. I dodged out of the way to keep it from cracking my skull open. It shattered to the floor, leaving a dent in the wall.

"Don't you dare call me crazy, Oliver."

I walked out of the room, letting her slam the door close as I walked away from her. I was expected to have something thrown at my back as I went into the spare room and closed that door with a loud bang, just to prove some ridiculous point.

So much for a good fucking week.

# CHAPTER 5

"What am I meant to wear to this thing tonight? Is it casual, formal, or lazy?" I asked, flicking through the racks of my clothing that hung in the large closet.

Greyson walked up behind me, checking out the options too. "I don't know."

"But isn't clothes your thing?" I asked, trying to bat my lashes at him.

He cocked his head to the side, raising a brow. "Just because I'm gay, doesn't mean I'm a fashion designer. I'd wear a shirt and jeans, but that's just me. Where are you going?"

"My sister's thing," I said with a duh tone. "It's mandatory."

He flicked the side of my arm. "I know that. I meant, where is it at? A restaurant? Bar or someone's house?"

Now I felt stupid. I laughed awkwardly. "Oh, umm, it's at a steak and grill place in the city, which is good. I want steak for dinner." I smiled big. I was so hungry for steak all day.

"You're weird." He laughed. "Okay, sit on the bed and let me help you out with something to wear. Go and do your hair. It needs to be straightened, and do that cat eyeliner you do. It makes your eyes pop, not to mention you look like the girl who'll do anything." He wiggled his brows.

I burst into a loud fit of giggles. Once calmed down enough to talk, I sat up and shook my head. "Nope, not a fashion designer. Maybe a beautician with the way you gave me that description."

He smiled. "I know. I have never felt gayer than right now. Laugh it up. Now go and get pretty."

Doing as he said, I managed to give myself the thick cat-eyed liner with a pink-tinged gloss. My hair was left out and straightened. I did pin the side up a little to keep it from getting on my face all night. Greyson walked in holding up a navy blue patterned playsuit with lace trimming around the bottom of the shorts.

"No way." I shook my head. "It's a steak bar. I will look so overdressed."

"I knew you'd say that. I have some black skinny leg jeans and a white t-shirt for you to wear. Tuck the bottom of the top into the band of the jeans, but not all the way. Just a bit. It's casual but shows off your body." He walked back out of the bathroom.

I groaned. He could deny being into all this fashion stuff, but I knew he liked playing dress-up as well.

"Can't you come with me?" I pouted, dragging my feet behind him.

He shook his head. "Sorry. My parents are in town and want me to come to visit them for dinner."

~

Luckily, when I arrived, everyone who was already there wasn't dressed up. They were in casual but nice outfits. Thank god I argued Greyson on wearing heels, sticking to a pair of flats instead.

Looking around, I couldn't see my sister as yet. When I spotted the giggling girls who were in the bridal party, sipping on their cocktails, they gave me a wave. I didn't really know them that well to want to go sit with them.

I did see one familiar face, and I fought back the groan. I didn't want to see Daniel. I was planning to avoid him as much as possible. Plan failed as he walked over and placed his hand on my shoulder, leaning in and kissing my cheek softly.

If Greyson were here, he'd have punched him.

"Sage, wow, it's been what? Three years?" he asked, pulling back. His baby blue were eyes smiling right into mine.

*Do not fall for his charm.* "Four." I corrected, standing tall. "How have you been?"

"Good. Come sit at the bar with the others. What are you drinking?" He flashed his teeth, giving me another smile.

My heart rate quickened. I hadn't thought about the whole not drinking thing. Shit, I completely blocked out the being knocked up to a stranger thing.

"Just a Coke with raspberry. I'm driving tonight."

"Ah, good girl. So, what have you been up to? I had no idea you were back for the wedding," he said sitting at the bar, gesturing for me to join him.

"Just finishing my degree and that's about it, not too much going on. What about you?" I asked. He would have to be married or dating someone by now.

A smiled twitched on Daniel's lips. "Nope, no one at all. Just busy with work mostly."

"That's good then," I replied. Yeah, work and screwing everyone who spread them for him.

"And you? Seeing anyone interesting?" he asked, a smile pulling on the corner of his lips.

I shook my head at him. I should have lied and said dating, but that would lead to more questions, and I wasn't a good liar. "No. Single and I like it that way."

There was a pause between us. I sat there quietly sipping on my drink when I heard him sigh. "Sage, I want to tell you again that I'm really sorry for what I did to you. There's not a day when I don't regret it."

"You never apologized for it." I corrected.

"Sage, please—"

"Dan." I slipped up, calling him what I used to. "Please don't. I finally got over it. I don't want to bring up the past. What's done is done. Nothing more we can do about it."

He held his drink to his lips, not taking his eyes from mine. "I miss you," he whispered.

I couldn't look up at him. If I did, I'd most likely cave. "You shouldn't," I whispered back.

I fought the urge to push away any feeling I still kept for him. I just couldn't do this again. Not tonight, not ever.

Even if I did miss him, things were never going to be the same. I was pregnant with another man. No guy would want to date a girl like me now, and Daniel sure as hell wouldn't want too. Not that I'd take him back. He might be cute and dreamy, but he still cheated on me. I couldn't trust him after that happened.

Not with my head, and definitely not with my heart.

How could my heart trust him when I was pining after someone I would never see again? It was like being in love with a ghost. It almost brought tears to my eyes, realizing that I would never see that man again. It hurt. How could I be so affected by something so brief?

Except it wasn't brief. It was going to last a lifetime for me.

I heard my sister's loud voice coming up behind me. I spun around to witness her giving Daniel a questioning look.

"Sorry, we're late."

"It's okay. Is everyone here?" I asked, looking around for others.

"No. Tony's just getting his friend and his wife. They're on their way. They should be here in around five minutes. Did you get a drink?" she asked, not slowing down as she went over to her friends.

"I have a feeling their wedding is going to be like this." I pulled my hair to the side and looked at Daniel.

He nodded. "Definitely. Let's go get a seat at the table. I want to hear more about what you've been up to and how's school been going. Did you end up doing the courses you told me about?"

I nudged him playfully in the shoulder. "Dork, it's been years. I can't remember that far back."

When I slung his arm around my neck, I realized he had been drinking more than I thought. The smell was strong and not agreeing with my stomach.

My eyes landed on Tony's when he walked in, and I smiled at him. He grinned back.

"Hey, I didn't think you'd be out of bed in time to make it." Tony winked, then eyed Daniel's arm. "I'm watching you."

I faked hurt, ignoring that he warned Daniel, who didn't seem too fazed as he waved the waiter over for another drink. "I have my ring on so the sun doesn't burn my body. We vamps do have to eat sometimes, you know."

Tony broke out into a loud laugh, clapping his hands and shaking his head. "I see you brought your lovely wit with you. Come on. I'm starved since your sister has me on this crazy detox as well."

"Ooh, I pity you, brother. Not fun at all. I'm going to eat a big delicious steak and watch while you sit and eat your rabbit food." I poked his stomach.

He chuckled. "Bitch."

"You know it. Come on, Daniel. I'm hungry." I looked back at him. It felt so good to be back around my old friends again. "Oh, wait. Isn't your friend coming here, too?" I asked, noticing him alone.

Tony shook his head. "Wife's sick, a migraine or something, so he stayed in with her."

"More like was forced to stay," Daniel muttered with a cough.

I was going to ask what he meant, but my stomach churned again. I just hoped I could keep my food down and not throw it all up like the previous nights.

~

OLIVER

I sat on the couch with a cold beer and flicked the TV on. I was pissed off and annoyed. Amy had been lying on the couch, feeling sick, or so she told me. I had a feeling it was just to get me to stay in and not go out with the guys.

Eventually, she stood up and left the couch. After a while, Amy walked over with a bowl of popcorn and sat down.

My eyes glued to her. "Feeling better, I see."

"The shower helped. Plus, it can be a night in for us." She smiled. Her smile seemed too happy for me.

I laughed, tilting my head back. "Date night?"

"Yeah, why not. It's been ages since we did this." She put her feet up on the table and sighed. "Look, if you don't want to spend time with your wife, then you can go out with your friends, Oliver."

Well now, I felt guilty. "Amy, it's not that. It's just..." I paused. "Tony's my best mate. We grew up together, and he's getting married. It means a lot to him if I go to these wedding party things with him. I'm the best man. You were invited too."

"Why wasn't I asked to be in the wedding? I mean doesn't that bother you?" She looked at me.

I just stared. Honestly, no. It never bothered me at all. "I, uh, never thought about that at all. I mean Cassie had her sister and friends. You and her, you don't really hang out. Are you really that pissed off about it?"

Amy rolled her eyes back at me. "No, I'm just glad we didn't have to go through that with our wedding."

I couldn't hold in the laugh. "Yeah, but we missed a lot. Don't you think? I mean it was like a ten-minute engagement. Not even that long. I didn't even propose to you."

"Are you saying you didn't want to get married? Oliver, we'd been together for six years. I wasn't going to wait much longer." She shrugged, taking a handful of popcorn.

"I'm not saying that at all. I just thought, you know, girls have this whole engagement, and then the wedding, the dress, flowers, and cake." Fuck, I was rambling on and on. "Sorry if I was too slow at proposing to you."

"No, I forgave you for that anyway. You can make it up to me on our anniversary. Maybe a nice new ring? Something a bit more sparkly?" She winked. "And I have you. Why would I need the other crap that goes with a wedding? I think Cassie and Tony are going overboard. I mean, it's just a day."

Yeah, a day to share with your friends and family.

I bit my tongue, kicking my boots off, and cocked a brow. "Is that a hint that you don't like the ring I gave you?"

"It's fine," she said, giving me another smile and returning to watching the TV.

Fine. There was that word again.

My mind was going over everything she had said to me, wondering if she was as happy as I were, or wished I was. I unscrewed another beer and took a large mouthful.

It shouldn't be like this. We were so close but so far apart. I had every intention of proposing to her, but a week before Valentine's Day, she beat me to it, dropping the hint that since we were in the city, we should go make it official. Within an hour, we were married. We brought rings and looked at a house to buy.

I didn't think much of it. I thought it was kind of spur of the moment and romantic. When we told our parents, I regretted it. A few months later, Amy let it slip that she didn't want my mother to have a say in how the wedding would have been, so us doing it quickly and on a whim was the only way she'd get her way.

The TV was on low. I lay back and kept drinking. I was horny and hard. I could have gone in the room and just fucked her, but I knew once I did, I'd regret it. I'd regret screwing my wife because it wasn't what I wanted anymore. I wanted more.

I wanted to feel something other than empty on the inside. I wanted to get that rush of excitement coming home after work to see the woman inside, instead of dread and guilt, wondering if I had to get myself dinner or if we were going to end up in a screaming fight again. Our neighbours must really love us.

"Oliver, can you bring me a glass of water?" Amy called out.

She decided that sitting out here watching the football game was too boring and went to the bedroom.

Lying there a moment, I hoped she would forget she asked me. I couldn't be fucked moving.

"Oliver." Her voice rang through my ears louder this time.

I sighed, getting up and doing what her majesty asked of me. I walked in the room, and she was texting on her phone. Well, her plan worked. She got me to stay in and miss a great night out with my mates. It was probably a smart idea. After the last time I went out, I wasn't too keen on risking anything again. I ended up getting wasted on my own while she watched movies in the bedroom.

~

I woke to a knock on our front door. I closed my eyes again, not wanting to get up and deal with whoever was there.

"Amy, get the door." I yawned as the knocking went on more.

I tossed the blanket off myself and almost tripped over the bottles on the floor. I hadn't realized just how much I had drunk. My head was pounding with a headache. I opened it and came face to face with Cassie and Tony.

Shit. I had forgotten about today.

"You look like hell." He winked, not mincing his words. "Rough night?"

"Long night." I covered my mouth and yawned, looking back down the hall at our bedroom door still shut. "Amy will be out in a minute."

"Is she feeling better?" Cassie asked, walking past and into the house as I closed the door behind them.

I nodded, following them to the living room. "Yeah, she is. How was last night?"

I felt like shit that I never came out. I should have. I should have put my damn foot down and went out with them all.

Tony picked up a warm beer and took a swig, pulling a face. "Shit. No wonder you look like hell. Last night was alright. Daniel's trying to get his ex-girlfriend back. You know the one he cheated on. His attempts were shot down each time. Fucking hilarious."

"My sister." Cassie gritted. "She's too smart to fall for him again anyway."

I grinned, unscrewing one for myself. Best way to cure a hangover was to keep drinking. "You hope anyway." I winked. "We all know what a charmer Danny boy can be."

Amy walked out, her hair down for once, and noticed Tony and Cassie sitting opposite me. "Oh. Hi." She smiled. "I didn't know you were coming over."

Running a hand through my messed-up hair, I leant back on the couch and just looked at Amy. She didn't get my heart racing like she used to. Sure, I loved her with everything I had, but that spark was just gone. I wasn't sure if it was just the stress of what had been happening between us and the constant digs at each other. It was all doing my head in.

What surprised me was Amy came over and sat on my lap, wrapping her arms around my neck and kissing my cheek. "I'm heading out soon."

I frowned, wrapping my arm around her small frame. I didn't like her so thin. I felt like I was going to snap her if I held her too tightly. "You are? Where you going?"

Why the fuck was I just hearing about it now?

"I need to get something to wear for the wedding. I don't have anything, and Mum offered to take me shopping. Is that okay?" she asked.

I could feel Tony's stare at me.

How could I say no to her when she looked this happy? It was a rare occasion, but there was a nagging feeling in the back of my mind. I thought she had already brought her dress last month.

"Yeah, I could take you if you wanted to."

"No." Amy shook her head. "I mean, I don't need you to come. You'll be bored anyway."

"How about I tag along? I'd love to help." Cass suggested. "I need a couple of things, and it'll give us a chance to get to know each other more. We could even grab lunch?"

Amy looked up at Cassie. I could feel her tense up, and I put it down to being nervous around her. "Uh, you don't have to. I don't want to spoil your plans for the day. Plus, Mum might be annoyed if I cancel on her."

"Don't be silly. I'd love to come with you. Plus, the guys are just going to sit around and drink all afternoon. We can have a girl's day with your mum, too. Come on. I won't take no for an answer." Cassie kissed Tony on the cheek and grabbed the keys from him. "Pick you up later. Behave."

He laughed, nodding towards me. "Oh, I don't know. I'm kind of digging this guy's caveman look."

"Yeah, keep looking, buddy. You couldn't handle what I gave you." I joked back.

Amy was the only one who didn't find it funny. She rolled her eyes and walked away with Cassie.

Tony smirked, lowering his voice to make sure no one else heard. "Nope. Doubt I could handle you, but someone else sure could."

I almost choked on the mouthful of liquid I had been swallowing.

"I bet she gagged on it, too." He added, laughing.

"You're going to get me killed," I muttered dryly, then smirked. "But you're right. She handled it pretty damn well."

# CHAPTER 6

"Oh my god. You're getting married tomorrow!" I grinned, jumping up and down on the large king-sized bed with my sister, who was as equally excited as I was.

Cassie laughed, nodding furiously. "I know. I can't wait for this night to hurry up and be over with."

"You've had too much to drink. I need to stop, or I'm going to fall off the bed." I held her forearms to try steady myself again.

I was either going to fall off the bed or throw up. My pregnancy was still a secret. Telling my mother was easier said than done. I couldn't muster up the courage to break her heart and tell her that her youngest daughter had gone screwed a random guy and ended up pregnant to him.

Cassie jumped off the bed and picked her flute of champagne up. "You're not drinking. Why?" she asked, taking a large sip.

Another day. Another lie. "I'm remaining sober so I can enjoy your wedding. As your maid of honour, I have lots to do tomorrow, and making sure your drunken ass is sober enough to walk down the aisle is my main priority."

"Good call. Oh god, I should sleep. Tony is probably freaking out. I'm waiting for him to call and say he's gotten cold feet." She admitted, probably not meaning to.

I laughed, taking the glass from her hand. It was time she went to sleep.

"Nope. I got him some socks to wear in case he does gets cold feet. He's fine and going to show up."

"What time are the girls getting here tomorrow morning? What time do we have to leave to go to the church?"

I wanted to slap her across the face. This was her wedding that she had planned very carefully. How was I meant to know when we had to leave?

"Mum will be here at 6:00 AM. Then the girls will arrive at 7:00 AM. Hair and makeup is at half eight, and then we get dressed. If you're getting married at twelve, then we leave fifteen or so before that. It's not far away."

"I love you. I don't know what I'd do without you." She smiled, finishing off her champagne.

"Love you, too. Now, go. Get into bed and sleep. You want to wake up looking pretty and refreshed, not like you normally do." I grinned cheekily, heading to my room before she could torture me in her own evil way.

Lying in bed, I just stared at the ceiling. My hands slowly slid from the side of my thighs upwards to my stomach, resting gently. I hadn't seen a doctor. I was too scared, too, knowing that once he confirmed it, it would be real. I was kind of hoping for my period to arrive, but it didn't. Each day went by, and I only became more and more nauseous.

Daniel had been texting me on a regular basis, asking to catch up sometime soon again. I wasn't sure if I wanted to do that. I was still getting used to him being around. Thinking of the baby and my ex, I began to drift off and fall asleep.

Waking up to a banging on the door, loud squeals, and girls giggling and laughing, I sat up way too fast and held my forehead, glancing at the clock. I had slept in. It was almost 8:00 AM. Oh no. This wasn't good.

"Shit." I hissed, getting out of bed and walking out to where my sister and the others were.

"Oh, hello, sleepy head." Mum smiled, placing a kiss on my cheek. "Are you feeling okay? You look pale."

"I'm okay. Just got up too fast, that's all." I yawned, hugging her and resting my head on her shoulder as she ran her fingertips through my hair softly. I closed my eyes, relishing in comfort.

Cassie looked over from where she sat by the table, eating strawberries and drinking champagne. "Morning. Looks like you were the one who woke up looking like hell and not me."

I poked my tongue out at her and closed my eyes, trying to overcome the round of nausea I felt.

"Sage, why don't you sit and I'll make you something to eat?" Mum offered.

Food. That was the last thing I wanted right now. "Just a glass of apple juice will be good, Mum. I'm not that hungry."

"You need to eat, dear. It's going to be a long day with everything happening." She sighed but poured me a glass anyway. "Oh, before I forget, Greyson told me to tell you that he will see you at the church. He's not able to make it this morning."

"Yeah, I got his text last night when we were stuffing our faces with pizza and Chinese because someone couldn't stand the detox she was on." I eyed Cassie, then my mouth watered for another reason. "Ohh, is there cold pizza in the fridge?" I asked, growing hungry at the thought of it.

I got up and opened the fridge. Sure enough, there was still some left. I moaned as I took a bite. It was so damn good. There was nothing better than cold pizza especially right now. I grabbed another slice, and as I took another bite, I noticed everyone looking at me.

Monica, another bridesmaid and Cassie's best friend from work, laughed. "Oh, god. Come on. You need to get ready for hair and makeup. They're arriving."

Two hours later, my hair was straightened, curled, and twisted back into a loose low bun, which was all pinned in. Soft beach curls were framing my face. It looked sexy glam, or so the stylist said. I loved it.

My makeup was much more than I'd normally wear. I never wore lipstick, but the makeup artist put on a red lipstick after doing my eyes. My eyes shimmered with the liner and were framed by thick black lashes. Waking up tomorrow and looking like a panda was definitely, most likely going to happen.

My sister looked gorgeous. Her hair was pulled back and with the same curls but more tightly tucked in. Tony was going to die when she walked down that aisle. I just knew it. I, for one, would be a blubbering mess.

"Where's my dress?" I called out to anyone who was listening.

"In the bathroom, hanging up. I steamed them dry," Mum called back out.

I walked in and sighed. It was gorgeous. I stripped down to my panties. Slipping on the dress, I froze when I went to do it up. The side zipper stuck just a good few centimetres under my arm. Oh, no. God, no. This couldn't be happening. Not today of all days.

My boobs had grown. Shit.

"Uh, I need someone to come and help me," I called out, trying not to cry.

Debbie, one of our friends, walked in, noticing my problem and closing the door. "How far along are you?" she asked quietly.

"What?" I choked out.

How the hell did she know?

She smiled, holding my dress as she worked the zipper. "I've had three kids. Trust me, I can tell a pregnant woman from a mile away. Your boobs grow first, then soon, the stomach follows."

I remained silent. If she could tell, then I wondered how many others could also. A sigh of relief escaped my lips as the zipper was closed.

"Please don't tell anyone. I haven't seen a doctor yet."

"Don't worry. I can keep a secret. The zip was just caught on the material. You'll be fine, but you're going to need to tell someone soon, Sage, before you start showing," she said softly. She

69

squeezed my hand and smiled, looking at me through the mirror. "Does the father know? Wait, it's not Daniel's, is it?"

"No, definitely not his. I haven't told the father yet. I'm still getting used to the idea." I used a piece of tissue and dabbed my eyes, carefully trying not to take any makeup off. I looked at the dress on me. It fitted perfectly, but she was right. My boobs looked much bigger.

Debbie smiled warmly. "You'll be a great mother. Now, your sister is ready, and I think we need to go out there and get some photos taken. She's freaking out. Tony changed his bowtie to a tie without telling her again." She laughed.

I groaned. "Oh, god. She'll murder him."

Debbie agreed and unlocked the bathroom door. "Oh, and the pizza was a giveaway for me. I craved the weirdest food during my second pregnancy."

I blushed, biting my lip. Cravings. Was that what this was?

"I'm probably going to eat the rest of it before we leave the house."

"Do it. They'll just assume you're hungover." She winked and left me alone in the bathroom.

With a groan, I stared at myself in the mirror and couldn't stop the soft laugh that escaped. "This is insane, little baby. Today is going to be insane."

~

OLIVER

"Nervous?" I grinned.

Tony sat on the chair and grabbed a pair of socks. "No. Yes. Actually, I'm freaking out. She found out about the tie."

I laughed, sitting opposite him and taking a sock from him. I read the bottom, which was printed with white ink. "Just in case you get cold feet."

"Yeah. Sage got them for me. She's a funny one." He grinned, slipping the other one on.

"Sage?" I asked, slightly confused. I swear I had heard that name before.

He nodded, pulling his foot up to pull the other sock on. "Cassie's sister. She thinks I'm going to bail and decided to give me a warning."

Shaking my head, I laughed. "Her and me both. I still can't believe you're getting married. The man who stood up on a pool table and said commitment was for the…What was it? Oh, yes. Weak and pathetic."

"I was blind drunk. I can't help it if Cassie came along and fucked those plans up. I see a future with her. She puts up with me and takes all my bad ways as good." He grinned, looking up and leaning back in his chair.

He was definitely a man in love. I hadn't seen him look so happy. "I'm glad, man. You deserve it. She's a lucky girl to end up with you."

"Thanks, brother." He checked his watch. "Shit. We need to leave. I have to be there half an hour before she turns up. Why can't the guy turn up after the bride?"

"Unless you're wearing a big white dress, then I wouldn't even attempt to try that. Come on. Let's get going before Dan gets too drunk and passes out." I got up and downed the rest of my Johnnie Walker can.

The nerves were setting in a little for me, too.

Once we arrived at the church, I saw Amy sitting and waiting at the church with my parents and brother. She did look pretty in her dress and all done up. I dipped my brows. She was in something entirely different than what she planned on wearing. It was a little more revealing than I would have liked her to wear, but telling her that was like getting water through a brick. She wouldn't see the problem.

"Now, don't you look so handsome," Mum gushed, "and you too Tony…Are you okay? You look pale."

"He's good." I slapped his back. "Nerves are getting the better of him."

"You told me my life was over on the way here." Tony bumped his elbow into my side.

I just laughed as did my father and my brother until I realized my wife was already standing next to me and had overheard too. "Uh, I was kidding, of course."

"Liar." Haddon, my brother, laughed. "Don't worry, Tony. You'll just need to do everything she says for the rest of your life regardless if you want to or not. Oh, and you'll never get laid again except on scheduled nights."

The look on Tony's face was priceless. "Stop scaring him. He might actually take off."

"Yeah, some support system you guys are. Amy, what the hell did you see in this guy?" Tony asked her.

She shrugged, lightly poking me in the side. "I'm beginning to wonder about that now."

I faked hurt, placing a hand over my heart but still grinning. "Oh, I'm not that bad."

"You can be." She winked and walked back to her seat.

To everyone else, she was kidding. To me, I knew I was in a lot of trouble with her, especially after last night when I told her she didn't need to come today if she didn't want to. Yeah, I think I needed to stop talking when I was drinking around her.

The wall also now had a huge hole in it from her flinging the spare room door open so hard. The handle went right through it. She wasn't even fazed, and it wasn't her money that had to fix it. She just told me if I gave a shit about her, then I'd make it up big time.

"Amy." I walked over and sat beside her, taking hold of her hand. I sighed when she pulled it from mine. "You know I do want you here, right? I don't want to fight with you right now. It's a good day. No need to stress. Just relax and enjoy yourself, please."

Her eyes just stared ahead. Finally, she leant in closer and spoke. She wasn't happy at all. "Oliver, just watch your drinking tonight. Please, don't make a fool out of yourself when your speech comes around. The last thing I want to do is watch you slur your words and then go dance like an idiot."

My jaw hardened. Her tone was not something I appreciate being spoken to. "Thanks, Amy. I appreciate the fucking moral support you offer. If you were going to be a sulky bitch, you could have fucking stayed home." I snapped.

The chair scraped on the hardwood floor as I stood up abruptly then made my way back to Haddon and Tony, who was with his parents.

Just my luck, I had to stand up there with my best mate and friends while my wife sat in her chair throwing daggers with her eyes at me.

"What did you do this time?" Tony whispered, trying to keep a straight face.

I kept my eyes ahead, ignoring Amy's burning gaze. "What don't I do wrong is more like it." I looked down at my watch and sighed. "Cassie's cutting the time short. It's almost half past. Maybe she realized she could do better."

"Some best man you are." He laughed.

"I've been warned not to dance like an idiot tonight. What do you say we pull out the old moves?" I chuckled, giving him a nudge.

"Fuck, yeah. Just don't let me do too many shots. Cassie said if I threw up on her, then she's annulling the marriage first thing tomorrow. Then she's taking her sister on the honeymoon." He tilted his head back and laughed. Then, he stopped and looked at me. "Seriously, man. Don't let me do shots."

I nodded, patting his shoulder. "Don't worry. I won't let you get too wasted. I also think we should stop saying fuck in a church."

"Shit. Agreed." He fixed his tie and looked back ahead.

I could feel his nerves picking up just by standing beside him as the music came on. I wasn't that nervous though. I was just curious to see what Cassie looked like and this girl who was my partner for the evening.

73

Debbie came up first. I wasn't paying too much attention because they all looked the same—until the woman behind Monica, one of the bridesmaids, began walking, and I thought my heart just about stopped.

My throat went dry.

Her eyes, the body, and my god, she was just as beautiful as I remembered. Instantly, flashbacks of her body against mine played over and over in my mind. I found it very hard to think straight or to concentrate on anyone else. I wasn't even looking at Cassie behind her. My eyes were just on the woman walking towards us.

No wonder her name seemed familiar. I heard Tony whispering, "That's Sage, Cass's sister."

Well, fuck. I just nodded. My eyes glued to her.

My first thought was *Don't get hard.*

The second: *The girl I screwed was my partner for the entire day.*

My third: *My wife is going to blow a fucking fuse if I'm caught looking at her for any longer.*

The fourth, well, I didn't get that far because Sage's walk began to slow down and her eyes widened. Those soft full lips parted, and she just stared at me, looking as if she remembered the exact same thing I had been.

She smiled at Tony as she passed him and then stood on the other side. Her eyes drifted back to mine, and she looked completely panicked.

What shocked, or more so amused me was when she lifted the flowers in her hand. One of her fingers slid up, and she slightly raised a brow, smirking as she slyly gave me the finger. The flowers prevented anyone from seeing what she had done.

A grin spread across my face. I was playing with fire right now, and I didn't really care if I got burned.

# CHAPTER 7

*He was married. Was? He is married.*

How on earth could he have done such a thing? Oh, god. If he was here, then that meant his wife was also in this room.

I groaned. I couldn't believe I had given him the finger in the church, of all places. What the hell was I thinking? That was right. I wasn't thinking. Neither was he apparently since he had gone out and screwed me while he was married.

Married. Married. Fucking married.

"Sage?" I heard my name being called out.

I looked around. Cassie stood there looking absolutely stunning in her gown. "Oh, right. Where do I stand?"

"Next to Oliver. Then, you and he would sign after us." She smiled, looking ever so radiant.

My sister was now a married woman.

I walked over, not wanting to stand beside the tall, gorgeous man who had bedroom eyes. Oh, god. He was going to be a father, and he had no idea.

Realization hit me hard. I was pregnant with this guy.

I felt physically sick at what this meant. I had slept with someone else's husband, a taken man. It was against everything I believed in, and I was now disgusted with myself. Tears threatened to spill, and I fought ever so hard to keep them at bay. It was the worst feeling ever.

What a fucked-up situation. The guy who knocked me up was married to another woman, who obviously had no idea about us or the fact that her husband was fathering a child with another woman. That was if I told him. I wasn't so sure I wanted to.

"Don't talk to me," I muttered quietly, keeping my smile on my face.

"Sage," he whispered. Damn the way he said my name. "We're sharing a car. You'll talk to me then."

I shook my head, watching my sister and new brother-in-law sign their names on the marriage certificate. "I don't have to talk to you, Oliver. Your wife may be watching."

He was silent. I knew that probably struck a nerve. Just my luck that silence didn't last much longer. "I'm sorry. I should have told you."

"When? After you came the first time? Or before you offered to buy me a drink?" I couldn't help my sarcastic reply.

"I know what you're thinking—"

I felt so sick, mostly with nerves. "No, you don't. You men are all the same, cheating assholes."

How could I have been cheated on and then went and slept with a married man? If I had known he was married, I wouldn't have done it. I wasn't that girl. I wasn't a home-wrecker or anything like that. I was stupid. Yes, I was the stupid girl who fell for a gorgeous smile far too easily.

I signed my name and just wanted to get the hell out of here. The smell of Oliver was bothering me. He smelt so damn good. All I could think about was the night we were together and the things we had done.

Startled when he slid his hand in mine, I was about to slap him away when I noticed the others doing the same. This was getting too much.

"I want to break your hand." I gritted through my teeth, squeezing harder.

He laughed. "You can try, but the way you're squeezing isn't hurting much."

"Stop it. I'm not talking to you." I didn't want to talk to him, let alone share a car.

He sighed, stopping behind Cassie and Tony to wait for them to stop hugging. I looked to my left and noticed a blonde woman looking very mad. My insides churned.

"Is that her? In the red dress? Your wife?" I asked, looking back ahead again.

"Yep" was his only reply. He didn't sound very happy about it either.

Clearly, he was as rattled as I was to discover we'd be spending the day and evening being partnered together.

Oliver went over to who I assumed were his family and wife just as the photographers started taking photos. My cheeks hurt so hard from constantly smiling as photo after photo was taken.

Needing to sit down, I walked over to Greyson.

He told me about some dressed up woman who slipped on her ass while she walked on the grass, spilling a tray of drinks all over herself. I couldn't help but laugh with him even though I felt awful for her.

He smiled. "I must say, you're looking damn fine today."

"Thank you. I try." I smiled back, laughing softly.

My eyes drifted slowly back over to Oliver. There was no denying he got lucky with the gene pool. He was tall with broad shoulders and a smile that could melt anyone. His wife was definitely a lucky woman to have landed a guy like him.

The suit, damn that looked good on him. His dark hair was neatly done and slightly combed over to the side. I remembered running my fingertips through it and the growl he made against my mouth when I tugged against it.

I felt my cheeks heat up when he caught my gaze, giving me a wink. I narrowed my eyes and looked away to find my sister. I found her with our parents, getting more photos taken. How many did someone need for a wedding day? Cassie smiled, waving me over to come and join in.

"Oh, hang on. There's Oliver." Cass stepped away. "Oliver, you need to get some more photos with Sage and you. We don't have any with just you two yet."

"Do you need them? Isn't this meant to be just you and Tony?" I asked, and she shot me a look that said, 'Do as you're told.'

The photographer looked at us and laughed. "Okay, you two need to move closer, and Oliver, wrap your arm around her. This isn't a mug shot."

As I felt his arm sliding around my waist, I instantly found myself moving in closer against him. His body was hard against my side. I tried to ignore the feeling I felt from him. My heartbeat was racing like crazy. My hand went to the front of his stomach as we stood smiling like a loved-up happy couple.

After more photos and different poses, we were able to leave and do our own thing. I walked back to where my purse was and picked it up when I heard footsteps behind me.

"Sage, we've got to head off in a few. We've got the second car," Oliver said, standing opposite me.

I nodded, refusing to look at him. "Alright then. You can sit in the front so I don't have to talk to you anymore."

"They're rally cars. We're in the back seat together. I really want to talk to you and explain and ask you something as well," he said. It was more of a statement than a question.

"Is it important? I mean, if you're worried about me telling her, then you don't need to worry. I won't mention it to anyone, Ollie. I don't want to get involved in some mad drama," I said.

We needed to get this conversation over and done with quickly.

He laughed, and I hated that I loved that sound. "You think I came over here to warn you? I couldn't give a fuck about that at the moment."

"Please, just don't." I glanced up. "She's coming over here, Ollie. Talk about something else."

He cleared his throat, looking to his side when his wife stopped by his side. "Amy, this is Sage," he said, his voice strained. She just stared at me. "Cassie's sister."

"Oh, hi." She smiled, but I could tell she wasn't really smiling at me. It was just for show.

"Nice to meet you," I replied. "Excuse me. I need to go figure out how I'm going to fit inside this car without ripping this dress."

I walked away quickly. My god, there was nothing more awkward or embarrassing as that. She was just like Daniel had mentioned. She was quiet, but you could tell she wasn't someone who held back. I was very intimidated by her. She was gorgeous, and my god, she was slim like really tiny.

The bright green car was tiny, and the roll cage on the inside had me worried. How on earth was I going to get in? I threw my purse in and hoisted my dress up in a bunch above my knees, sitting in and lifting my bum to put the dress back down.

Oliver opened the door and frowned. "I think I'm too tall for this."

I laughed, agreeing with him completely. "Your legs will probably touch your chin. Looks like you need to sit elsewhere."

He rolled his eyes. "You wish."

He, somehow just as I did, managed to sit in beside me. His tall, broad frame was close to my body. I felt like a giant in a matchbox car.

The driver followed the canary yellow car slowly. I put my purse on the floor and looked out the window. While I was focusing on the road, Oliver's arm was stretched out on my back, and his fingers rested on my bare forearm.

I tried to ignore the pounding of my heart. I knew he didn't mean anything by it, and I felt sorry for him. He was so big and tall that stretching his arm was the only way that he could sit back comfortably.

When he went to scratch his chin, I found my head being jerked into his side.

79

"Oh, god. Don't move." I hissed in panic, staring up at him. "Your cufflink is caught."

"Shit. Uh, hang on. Let me try to get it out." He reached with his other arm and gently began to untangle his link.

My eyes were still against his. I reached up and held my hair, so he didn't pull it out.

"There got it." His eyes lit up with a smile. "Sorry."

"It's okay." I patted down the back of my hair. "Nothing is out of place, so you're safe from that."

We resumed sitting back down until the driver began to drive the rally car like he was in a race. He was overtaking the cars in front of us as the other one behind us followed. It was thrilling and frightening at the same time.

My hands shot out, one grasping his thigh and the other clutching at his side. "Shit." This wasn't helping my nerves.

Oliver just laughed. His arm was back around my shoulder. "Don't like fast cars?"

"Not when they're taking off unannounced like this," I said, slightly panicked.

The driver looked at us through the mirror and winked. "Sorry, love. Hold on."

As soon as he said that, he floored it again. The red one behind us overtook us. Debbie and Daniel were waving and yelling out the window as they passed us.

Oliver and I both laughed and waved back as we followed, catching up to them.

Slowly, his fingers began to stroke my bare arm up and down. I was lost in hazy lust right now. Looking up at him, I chewed down my lower lip and tried to control my breathing. I could feel him hardening. My wrist was lying over his hip where his obvious length was lying across.

"I need to see you again. I don't know why. but I just do," he said, his eyes still ahead on the road and voice husky and low.

"Ollie," I whispered. "You're married."

80

His face was somehow much closer to mine. Why was it that I felt so drunk beside him when I was completely sober?

"Tell me you feel this too. I know it's wrong, and I thought it was just the alcohol, but I don't know anymore. I'm drawn to you. For weeks I haven't been able to not think about you. I need to stop, but I can't." He reached up with his other hand, and I expected him to touch me. He didn't. He locked me in as he twisted his body and placed his arm above my head, holding onto the handle above the door.

Closing my eyes, I shook my head. His cologne was wafting underneath my nose, and I was lost again. "You smell the same. God, I dreamt about you so many times, but this is wrong. I can't…We can't…"

He pulled back, only to move in closer as I gripped him tighter. "I know. I'm married, and this is fucking wrong, but why do I want it so much."

"Because you're stupid."

"I'm smart, Sage," he said softly. "I'm smart enough to know that you feel it too. This isn't just heat. It's a fucking burning fire between us right now."

I knew what he meant. I felt a pull from myself to him. I never thought I would react this way, especially once finding out that he was married. I flushed, breathing hard as I opened my mouth to speak, to tell him I felt the exact same thing he did. I needed to tell him.

He pulled back abruptly, and suddenly, the heat between us was gone. Shifting back, his gaze went cold and dark.

"We're here."

I hadn't noticed we arrived. I removed my hands that were unintentionally gripping him tightly and let him go. I was suddenly feeling far more nervous than I ever wanted to feel.

~

OLIVER

Fuck. How the hell did I lose control like that again? This woman had something on me. She was so innocent-looking and so damn beautiful.

I wanted to fuck her again. I felt the need to fuck her, to touch her and to explore her body more than I had done. I wanted to do it. I groaned. What the hell was wrong with me? I had a wife. Why the fuck was I giving into temptation that I didn't need? I didn't need it, but I sure as hell wanted it.

"Ollie."

God, the way my name sounded off her lips. I was fighting the urge to not get hard again, but I couldn't stop it. Being so close to her like this was torture, agonizing torture.

I swallowed hard. "Sage." I started but noticed Amy walking with my brother, and I stopped myself. Instead, I just opened the car door. "Wait there. I'll come around and help you out."

She didn't fight me, which I had been expecting her to.

I took her hand. My eyes were on hers as I pulled her up. Her footing stumbled, and she placed both hands against my chest to steady herself.

"Sorry. I didn't mean..." She stepped backward.

"Stop apologizing. Are you okay? You seem pale." I noticed her swaying a little, and I took her by the arm again. I guided her towards the bench to sit down.

She nodded. She glanced around then quietly said, "Oliver, I need to tell you something."

"What's up?" I asked, curious as her eyes weren't meeting mine and she looked nervous.

Sage opened her mouth, only to close it again when Amy's heels came to a stop in front of us. Shit. Just what I needed right now. I looked up and could tell she was pissed.

"You okay?" I asked, standing.

"No. I thought my husband could take me to our table, but obviously, you're busy." She gave Sage an intimidating stare.

82

**Haddon** could see Amy was going to lose it. I immediately stepped in and shook my head. "I'm sorry. I thought you knew. We've all got to wait out here until Cassie and Tony get back, then we go sit at the bridal table together for the evening."

"Where do I sit then? Alone?" Amy snapped bitterly.

"Ollie, it's okay. You don't have to sit with Tony." Sage sat up straighter. Her colour was coming back into her cheeks.

Amy smiled in triumph. "Good. Glad that's sorted then."

I bit my tongue, looking happy, but on the inside, I was starting to grow livid with her. She was pushing me too much today. I wasn't in the mood to be treated like a child. I had sat at my brother's bridal table, and I planned on doing the same with my best mate.

I put my hand on her back while Sage and my brother started introducing themselves and began to talk about the food for the night. I escorted Amy closer to the group but far enough not to be heard by others.

"I think you need to chill out. You're overreacting and causing a scene."

"Ollie?" Amy asked, ignoring me. "You hate being called that."

I shrugged. "I'm not going to tell the bride's sister to stop calling me that. God, Cass is already pissed at Tony for getting rally cars. You think I want to complain about that also?"

It was a good excuse. Truth be told, I did hate being called Ollie. I had always hated it, but when Sage called me that, I wanted nothing more than to taste the words coming from her sweet tongue, that or make her moan it over and over again.

"You're sitting with me, Oliver. I swear to god, I will make a huge fucking scene if you walk over there and touch her again. Did you need to sit in a car or hold her hand while getting photos?" She snapped, glancing around the outdoor area.

I just stared at her. It wasn't like I had kissed Sage or felt her up. Yes, I might have wanted to, but I could control my urges while I was in a room full of people.

83

"Christ, it's a wedding. Why can't you just enjoy yourself for once? I'm beginning to think you're not happy unless I'm home and doing as you tell me to. I'm actually having a good time, Amy. Why can't you just relax and do so also?" I asked with a heavy sigh.

Amy just shook her head. "I don't want you sitting at the bridal table. If you do, then I will leave, Oliver. I mean it. Choose wisely, or I'm heading home."

I stepped closer, my anger rising to a point where my voice was so much lower, and my eyes darkened. "Don't you ever threaten or give me an ultimatum again, Amy. I'm not a puppet. You don't pull my strings and have me instantly do what you say."

I might have just cost myself a week on the couch or at my parent's place by saying this, but I didn't care. I headed back to where Haddon was now sitting, not sure what Amy was going to do, but right now, I didn't give a fuck.

"You guys ready to head in?" Tony came up behind us all.

"Yeah. We're all starving and thirsty." Daniel grinned, walking over and sitting beside Sage.

I didn't know what was going on with them or if something was starting up, considering their past. I did know that I had fucked one of my good friend's exes.

The tension in the reception was undeniably thick. Amy had left, pissed and angry that I didn't fall for her demands. Yes, I was starting to see her true colours. If she was at her friend's wedding, no way would I demand she sit with me and not with the others in the wedding party.

Sage was beside me at the round table and sipping on water. I'd not seen her drink anything alcoholic today. It was odd. The first encounter we had, she was on vodka, and now, nothing.

"Can you do me a favour? If you don't mind and it's no bother," she asked, leaning in closer.

I looked down and grinned. "Depends. What is it that you're wanting?"

"Dangerous choice of words, Ollie," she said in a sultry and low voice. She licked her lips and said, "I'm hungry. Could you get me something to eat?

A wide grin came across my face. "I don't know. That's an awfully big thing you're asking of me. Why can't you get that for yourself?" I asked.

A blush formed across her cheeks, which made me smile even more. "Because you're bigger than I am, and I don't want to go up there alone."

I laughed, confused, but nodded anyway. "Okay. Come on, Sage. I'll get up with you then."

She smiled, but then it disappeared. "Oh, no. You shouldn't. She might get mad."

"Who? Amy?" It clicked in my head. "Oh, no. She left after I refused to sit with her."

"Oh. Bad boy, Oliver." She laughed, standing up.

I nodded. "I have been."

I was definitely bad around her. Not that I wanted to be, but I just couldn't control it.

I followed behind her, and like at the club, my eyes slowly drifted down to her ass. I looked back up before she caught on or anyone else did. She wasn't like any other girl I knew. I guessed I'd been so caught up with Amy and how she was that I paid no attention to anyone else.

Sage grabbed a large steak instead of the fish and looked up to give me a nervous smile.

"I'm hungry. I didn't eat all day yet," she said, looking embarrassed.

I winked, easing her nerves. "Well then, move over before I take the steak off your plate for my own."

"Ass." She laughed, walking over to the sides.

"Yeah, so I've been told." Numerous times actually.

By the time dessert came around, Sage and I somehow ended up sharing a bowl with both desserts, too full to eat one each. As her fork went in, I purposely took her piece and put it in my mouth, watching her face turn to shock as she flicked me with her finger.

"Seriously? That was so mean." She rolled her eyes, taking another piece and eating it.

"Yeah, but I'm an ass, remember?"

"What's going on with you and that guy? Boyfriend of yours?" I asked. Not sure why it bothered me, but he'd been coming over here nonstop.

"Who? Daniel? No. We're just kind of friends, and that's all it will ever be," she said, and I shook my head, not Daniel. "Oh, do you mean Greyson? Nope. We dated, but he's into something I don't have if you catch my drift."

When she winked, I threw my head back and laughed. "Oh, god. You're a crazy one."

"Can be." She sighed. Even though she looked happy, her eyes told me different.

Which reminded me. "You wanted to tell me something earlier? What was it?" I asked her.

Something in her posture changed. She looked stiff and nervous again. "I don't know...I mean, I can't remember."

I could see right through her. "You're a bad liar. You know that, right?"

She shrugged, giving me a wink, and then we continued going back to our dessert war. I let her have the last piece of cheesecake. She halved it and told me she couldn't eat it on her own. I didn't think I had ever grinned so much in my life right then.

If Amy were here, she'd blow a lid witnessing the on and off bantering between Sage and me throughout the night. If she stayed, it would have been a very different story. It wasn't as if I was putting on a show of purposely flirting around, but I was very attracted to her, and I hadn't smiled or felt this at ease in years. She was easy to talk to, and I enjoyed talking to her.

When the music came on, I groaned.

Regardless of what happened before, we had to get through the night. "Come on. I owe you a dance as my official duty as best man. Just don't step on my toes."

"Get off your high horse. You're the one who's going to break my toes." She laughed, standing up.

Following Tony, I led Sage over to dance. I wasn't really in the mood to dance after my mother had lectured me for letting Amy leave without going after her. I probably should have, but today wasn't about her. It was a day for two other people and their celebration.

Amy had given my mother a long-winded story, claiming I told her to fuck off and leave. I was pissed because I hadn't said that at all. Amy was just fucking taking things too far.

It was almost midnight, and I was far drunker than I should be. Tony had done shots regardless of our warnings and proceeded to down three. The dance moves that Amy told me not to do were in full swing. I was probably far too drunk to be dancing, and I should have cut myself off hours ago. Especially when the reason I cheated was right in front of me, laughing loudly and dancing just as dorky as the rest of us.

Cassie's father announced we would continue with the drinks back at his place when Tony and Cassie decided to call it a night or head off and start their all-night fucking. Waiting outside for a taxi to come, I saw Daniel throwing up in the garden while the chick he'd wrapped up for the night was storming off, realizing she wasn't getting laid.

"We need to talk." Sage's voice came up behind me, grabbing my arm roughly and leading me towards the car lot.

I stumbled behind her, slinging my arm around her when we were out of sight. "What do you need to discuss?" I asked, swaying on my feet for a moment.

"This." She gestured from her to me. "What's going on with us all night. It can't go on anymore," she said, trying to sound firm, but the way she looked at me when she stopped walking seemed like she was trying to convince herself.

I nodded slowly. "Because I'm married."

"Yes," she said, groaning. "You're married, and I won't be some side fuck for you. Daniel screwed me over pretty bad, Oliver. I am not that type of girl."

I agreed. "No."

"No?"

I shook my head, stepping closer. "No. You most definitely are not that kind of girl. Do I get to see your room?" I asked, giving her my best boyish grin.

"My god. How drunk are you?" Her laugh came out soft, and she pushed me away, but I didn't move.

I shrugged, unsure. I was hoping the cold air would sober me up quickly, but it was having an opposite effect. "Drunk enough to know I won't fuck you again...unless you want it."

"Oliver." She gasped, glancing around to make sure no one heard.

I laughed. "I'm kidding. Come on. I need to get in a taxi and head home."

"You're not going to drink with the others?" she asked, leaning against a car.

"Why aren't you drinking?" I asked, ignoring her question. "You've not drunk any alcohol all night."

I noticed her raising a brow as she crossed both arms over her chest. Her breasts pushed up higher, and my eyes went straight to them.

"You're very observant. I didn't think anyone noticed."

"Only when things interest me, then I am." I winked, looking back at her. I stood, looking around as I began to walk backward. I had to leave. "Are you going to answer my question?"

She paused, unlocking the car, and then I realized it was hers. "Get in. You've got friends waiting for you at mine, and you can crash in a room there. As for your other question"—she opened the door and turned back towards me—"get in, and I will tell you."

"Did you have someone drive your car here earlier?" I asked, curious as to why she had her car parked here.

"A friend drove it here. I wanted to have it here so I can go whenever I want without worrying about transportation." She went inside the car.

I slid in the passenger seat beside her and pulled the chair backward, giving myself more leg room as she went to the front seat. She looked at me, and I didn't look away. I couldn't take my eyes from her. Reaching up, I softly cupped her cheek, and she leant into my palm and closed her eyes.

"Are you going to tell me now?"

Just as she went to speak, the door opened, pulling us apart quickly, and that other guy she was with tonight jumped in, laughing. "Fuck. Daniel spewed all through the taxi. Give me a lift back to yours."

I laughed, cringing. "He could never hold his liqueur."

Sage just sighed. "We should have used something, Ollie."

I heard her soft voice as she started the car up, but by then, I was far drunker than I originally thought. My reaction? Well, I passed out in her car on the drive to her parents' house.

# CHAPTER 8

Oliver was snoring over Halsey and G-Easy playing in the car. I couldn't believe he passed out like that. Especially after I worked up the courage to tell him I was pregnant. Well, not in so many words, but I did try to tell him.

It was true what they say; men didn't take hints well. I had to tell him the words clearly. Otherwise, he'd never know.

Greyson was slumped against the door in the back seat. His mouth was open as he snored too, but not as loud. I pulled into a McDonald's drive-thru and ordered a McDouble, Coke, and large gravy fries. I was still hungry.

I pulled into my parents' garage shortly after and parked my Grand Cherokee in the garage. Reaching over, I nudged his thigh with a mouthful of burger.

"Oliver," I whispered.

He didn't do a thing and just kept snoring. I leant over, placed both my fingertips to his nose, and squeezed. His snoring stopped, and he woke with a jerk.

With eyes bloodshot and breath reeking of booze, he frowned. He looked around the car until his eyes landed back on mine. There was confusion until he realized where we were.

"I fell asleep?"

"Yes, and you snore horridly loud." I couldn't stop my grin.

"Sorry." He smiled, then noticed I was eating. "Did you buy me something too?"

I grinned, shaking my head. "Nope. You fell asleep, and I was hungry."

He groaned, which was something I couldn't understand. He closed his eyes and let out a yawn. I thought he was about to fall back asleep.

"Come on. The others are already inside. I'm going to bed, so I'll show you the way." I offered as I got out of the car.

He followed, but then his hand captured my wrist. "You're beautiful. You know that, right?"

I shook my head. "Oliver, you're drunk. Don't do this."

"Do what? Kiss you? Because that's all I want to do. I want to touch you so badly, Sage," he spoke, and I kept my eyes on his. His words—gah—they were doing something to me so badly right now.

Oh, god. Yes, I wanted him to touch me. All night had been torture for me. Being so close and the constant light flirting we were doing. What the hell was I thinking? Oh, that's right. Around him, I didn't think. I became this girl who was crushing hard on a married man.

My god, I was pathetic.

"You can kiss me again—" I leant in closer and waited until our lips were so close, then smiled "—when you're single," I said, backing away to create some space between us.

"Single." He was testing the word against his tongue as he repeated it again, his eyes narrowly looking into mine.

The subject of the kiss had changed. I knew once I brought that up to him, it would shift things. It was good. It was what I needed to happen.

I looked back towards the car. Greyson was starting to wake up, and he struggled to get the belt off. He noticed us standing there, and he pushed the door open.

"Oh, shit. I'm so drunk."

I laughed as he stated the obvious. "Yes, you are. If you're going to drink with the guys, then can you take Oliver with you and show him the way?"

91

"I have been here before," Oliver spoke up. "I know the way."

My brows raised in surprise. "When?" I asked.

How did he know where I live? Maybe he'd been here with Tony.

I shook my head. "Never mind. I'm going to call it a night. I am exhausted, and I need my sleep."

"See you in there later then," Greyson called out with a wave. I could see the smirk growing over Oliver's face before he turned and walked away.

Once I was inside my room, I immediately went for a shower. Standing in the shower, I moaned loudly as the water fell down my naked body. God, every part of my body was on fire. I had no idea how the way he looked at me and a single touch from him could drive me wild.

Then, the one thing that drained the colour from my face was the fact that he was married.

A married man.

What the fuck was I thinking?

Shutting down my lustful thoughts of him, I finished my shower and went back to my room. I put on some clothes and lay down, trying to sleep, but the loud music and my thoughts about my future kept sleep at bay.

I was relieved that it didn't click on when I mentioned the birth control. I didn't want him to know I was pregnant. It would just complicate things. I'd go back to college to finish my course and figure out what I was going to do.

The thumping music was driving me insane. If I weren't sober and trying to sleep, I would be out there joining the after party. Right now, I just couldn't think of anything worse to do.

Finally, exhaustion pulled me to slumber.

~

"Sage!" A drunken slur came out from someone banging on my door. "Unlock it, or we'll climb through a window."

I jolted up. We? When I glanced at the clock, I saw that it was 4:00 AM.

*What on earth were they still up for?*

The banging kept going. I swore I could hear singing and even a sound of beatboxing. I laughed, opening the door to see Daniel, Oliver, and Greyson swaying away as a carton of beer was tucked under Dan's arm, and three pizzas were in Oliver's.

"Can I help you three?" I asked, leaning against the frame in my boxers and a tank top. "I'm trying to sleep."

"We"—Greyson grinned, pointing from him to Daniel, to Oliver, then back to himself—"we came to the party."

"Oh, is that right?" I looked at them all, trying to fight the smirk off my face. Mostly, I was trying to avoid eye contact with Oliver.

Daniel stepped forward, clearing his throat. "Sage, you need to invite us in."

That was it. I couldn't stop the laugh from escaping my throat as he quoted *True Blood*. Finally putting them out of their misery, as I doubted I would be able to get rid of them now, I opened the door.

"Oliver, Daniel, and Greyson, would you like to come in?"

I moved aside as the three men walked in, even drunker than when I last saw them. I followed as they made their way into my small living room and they all took a seat. I wanted to sit on the couch, but the only spot was in the middle of Oliver and Daniel. I stayed standing instead.

"You look tired. Did we wake you?" Oliver grinned, sitting back.

I nodded, looking up at him. Big mistake, he was staring at me with those eyes—the dark eyes that haunted my dreams and fantasies for so long.

"I am, in case you are all too drunk to remember. I was asleep only to be woken up by a bunch of drunk men singing."

They all laughed. "Yeah, sorry about that. Sit and have a drink and some pizza."

The pizza smelled good. I wouldn't lie. "Alright, only because I'm up and it'll give me something to do while I watch TV."

"You're not staying out here?" Greyson asked.

"No. You guys can have your male bonding time. I'm going to lay back in bed," I said, reaching for the slice of pizza that Oliver was about to bite into as I walked back to my room. It wasn't intentional, but I didn't miss the heated gaze between us again as our fingers skimmed across each other.

"Oh, your mum said we can crash in here since there's a spare room," Daniel called out.

Typical of her, playing the good host by sending them out here, not wanting them to throw up on her good linen sheets inside.

"Have fun snuggling each other."

The TV stayed off. I just lay in bed, listening to them all laughing and talking away about the most random things ever.

My eyes began to slowly close, and I snuggled further down the sheets. Just as I was about to fall asleep, I heard my door open, and two men entered, laughing as they stumbled their way through my room. The bed dipped behind me. It then dipped again in front of me, and I opened my eyes.

"Who's in here?" I asked, trying to pull the blankets back up higher.

"Daniel's a mess. There is no way I'm going in that spare room." Grey busted out laughing while Oliver behind me shook with laughter. "He shat himself. I mean literally shat and then spewed."

I squirmed, wriggling around like a half-squished bug. "Oh my god. Shut the freaking hell up! I don't ever, and I mean ever want to hear things like that again."

Both men, if it was possible, laughed even harder. I rolled over onto my back and cringed as I heard Daniel spewing.

Oliver managed to stop laughing and spoke, "He's so drunk. I don't think I've ever seen him this wasted."

"Wait. Where did this happen? I am not cleaning anything up, and god, that is disgusting." I really felt ill just thinking about it even if it was funny.

Oliver rolled to his side. I knew he'd be too big for my bed. It wasn't large, just a queen, but with him, myself, and Greyson all squished in, it felt like a single. I couldn't ignore the thumping of my heart as I looked to my right and stared up at him. His shirt was half unbuttoned, and his chest was exposed enough for me to see his tanned skin as he sat with his back against the headboard, drinking a Corona.

He smiled, looking down at me. "Let's just say, keeping your door shut is a good idea. If you've got a weak stomach, then it's best to stay in here until he's sorted himself out."

"How are you even still drinking?" I was more shocked by that than the fact Daniel had done the unspeakable in my little lounge room.

He shrugged. "I hold my liquor well. What can I say?"

I raised a brow, snorting. "If you say so."

We all heard the shower, and I cringed. I was never going to step into that shower again. I heard the faint steady breathing of Greyson behind me, and I knew he was passed out. Closing my eyes, I put my head back against the pillow. Oliver's warm breath blew across my face when he lay down. I bit my lip, willing myself not to move or open my eyes. I didn't know what I would do if I opened them again.

"Goodnight, Sage." Oliver's voice was the last thing I heard as I began to fall into a deep sleep.

A twitch of a smile came across my lips as I sighed softly. "Night, Ollie."

~

OLIVER

I just lay there watching her sleep.

Yeah. I wanted to punch myself in the face. That just made me feel like a creep, but it was something I couldn't help. She was hard to look away from. I just wanted to reach out and hold her and never let go. I shouldn't do it.

Fuck it.

I reached over, stroking her cheek and pushing a strand of hair from her face. I just lay there watching her. Why couldn't it be this simple with Amy and me? Why didn't I want to go home to my wife and hold her instead of another woman? So many questions were going over and over my mind until the darkness came and overtook my inner thoughts.

It was well into the late morning when I woke. For a moment, I thought I was back home, and my wife had her arms wrapped around my waist. Instead, it was still another woman who was sleeping behind me. I lay there, almost laughing at the fact that she was trying to big spoon me.

I was going to move, but she started waking up, and the last thing I wanted to do was embarrass her. Feeling her hand moving from my waist and her leg coming off the back of mine, she sat up and climbed over my body. Slowly walking away, she grabbed some clothes and slid open a door near the closet. It must be her walk-in bathroom.

The shower began to run, and after a few more minutes, I slid out of bed. I had to get back home. I needed to face the reality of the hell I was going to walk into.

Greyson was the first thing I saw when I walked out of the bedroom. I hated to admit it, but the guy had grown on me last night. "Hey, man. You look like shit."

"Feel like it." I yawned, stretching. "When did you get up?"

"Not long ago. Daniel's wrecked." He laughed as he walked back into the kitchen.

"Where is he?"

"Still sleeping. Spare room." He grabbed a Coke and passed one over.

Cracking the lid open, I laughed. "Doubt he will remember any of it. I've never seen him so wasted before."

"You two morons want to keep it down. My head's a pounding mess." Daniel walked out, rubbing his eyes and yawning loudly. He looked over at us. "What the fuck did you give me last night? I feel like I was fucked in the ass."

Greyson's Coke sprayed out of his mouth, coughing loudly as his eye bulged. "Uh, trust me. I didn't give you anything. I wouldn't be able to after what you did to yourself."

I had to laugh again, shaking my head with a grin. "Dan, there's a woman in that bedroom who wants your blood. Tell me you've thrown your clothes out."

He looked at us, standing in his boxers and nothing else. "Uh, fuck. I didn't—Wait. What? I didn't shit myself. Fuck, did I?"

"Daniel Arthur Adams, I swear that spare room better be clean." We all stopped laughing upon hearing Sage's voice.

When she walked out, I was sitting on the couch, trying to get the headache to go away by saying over and over that I was never going to drink again. I looked at her. Her wet hair was tied up and no make-up on, whatsoever. My cock twitched. She had an uncontrollable effect on me.

"Feeling better?" I asked, moving over.

"No." She rested her head on my arm, and I didn't think she realized what she had done until she suddenly pulled away. "Oh, god. I am sorry. I wasn't thinking. It's just a habit."

"To half lay on any man you sit beside?" I asked, nudging her.

She rolled her eyes and scrunched up her nose. "No. I normally lay down on here. Do you need a lift home?"

"No. I'll catch a taxi back." I shook my head, realizing I needed to leave soon.

She yawned and lay down on the opposite end. I leant back and closed my eyes. I couldn't be fucked moving, getting up, or heading home. I rested a leg over hers, and hers were over mine. Both of us passed out again.

My phone woke me up, the vibration not stopping when another call came in. I slid my hand in my pocket. Sage's leg was lying over my thigh, her foot very close to my groin.

I went to answer, but when I realized it was Amy, I let it ring.

"Oliver."

I kept my eyes shut. "Yeah?"

"Let me give you a lift home. I'm awake now." Sage sat up, putting her feet back down.

I stayed there for a moment and then got up. "Drop me off just before mine. I'll tell you where."

"I need a lift also." Daniel yawned.

I looked over noticing him hanging his legs over the armchair.

We piled into her car and didn't bother with the radio. I think hearing music right now would blow our heads off. Sage dropped Dan off to his mother's and then she turned back around to mine.

I knew it was a thicker tension between us again. "Sage," I said, looking at her. She didn't answer but turned to me then looked ahead again. I kept talking. "I want to see you again. I can't not see you. Yesterday, last night...I need to see you again."

"Ollie, you're making this harder on me."

I laughed. "You think it's hard for you? You're not the one sitting here with a hard dick."

"Don't say that," she said.

I groaned. My cock stiffened even more at her soft voice, and I watched as her tongue swept across her lips. She was driving me so fucking wild for her.

"Sage, I want you so fucking bad right now. I wanted you last night in the bed and this morning on the couch."

Her breathing picked up. I noticed her shuffling in the seat. "Ollie, god, you need to stop. I'm fighting control right now. I can't do it. I want to, but I won't."

"Pull over," I said, unclipping my belt.

"What? No. I'm not getting it on with you in the car, especially in broad daylight!"

I chuckled, smiling over at her. "Baby, as tempting as that sounds, I need to get out. My house is up to the road."

She pulled over and looked at me, realizing that this was it. "It was nice to see you again, Oliver. I hope you get home safely."

A broader grin swept across my face. "I want to kiss you," I said, leaning in closer, my voice somewhat lower and deeper. Her eyes rolled a little. "But I won't, not just yet anyway." She looked taken aback. She was about to speak, but I pressed my finger to her lips to stop her from speaking any more. "I will see you again. I hope, and soon."

I made my way into my house with my mind on the woman in the car. I should have kissed her, but she was right. I wouldn't touch her again until I was single.

I sat down, thinking about everything that had been happening with Amy and me for a couple of months now. Was I just giving into temptation? I had never looked at another woman that way before, but with Sage, it was different.

I sighed. If Amy were the one, the temptation wouldn't bother me at all. I should be able to resist it easily. Now, it was getting harder to do that I knew who Sage was and that I'd most likely be running into her more often.

Could I give up my marriage for something I didn't know would work? Was this just going to be another hookup? Was it worth leaving the woman I had been with for the past eight years to find out if it was something more?

I realized that my marriage wasn't what I had thought it had been. I thought it was pretty damn good until it hit me that it wasn't at all. I was just too fucking blind to see anything clearly.

"Where'd you stay last night?" Amy's shrill voice snapped me out of my thoughts.

I was still annoyed about her dramatic antics at the wedding.

99

"Oliver!" She punched my shoulder blade. "Fucking answer me!"

I jumped up, not in the mood for this any longer.

My fists curled to my sides, turning white as I stepped towards her. "Hit me one more time, and I will show you just how it feels to be slapped, punched, and have things thrown at you. Enough is enough!"

Her eyes went wide, but she wasn't afraid. I knew she'd love for me to hit her back. I think she was egging me on most the time.

"Answer my question then. Where or who did you sleep with?"

"I spent the night at Cassie's parents. Her father threw a party after the wedding, so we went back there. I crashed on a bed with another guy after Daniel threw up everywhere." It wasn't a lie, but there was no way she'd get the complete truth out of me now. I was too fucking angry.

"Okay. I'll be checking to make sure." She shrugged.

I shrugged back. I didn't care.

I walked around to the fridge and grabbed a bottle of water. Sitting down at the table, I looked at her as she slid into the seat across me. "I don't appreciate you lying to my mother. I never told you to fuck off. You left the wedding on your own terms. I never forced you to leave."

"Yeah, but you didn't fight for me to stay. Damn, Oliver, is it that hard to pay me some attention? You didn't even get a photo with me." She crossed her arms and narrowed her eyes. "If you loved me, then you would have sat with me and not complained."

Amy stood up, starting to walk away when I laughed. If I loved her? It was right then and there that I realized something, which also led me to another realization; I had to tell her I cheated.

Exasperated, I slammed my hand down on the kitchen table. The vase in the centre rattled loudly as she looked at me, stunned as I raised my voice and spoke firmly. "Amy, dammit! Sit the fuck down. We really need to talk, and it's going to happen right fucking now."

# CHAPTER 9

"Hi, what can I get for you?" the young guy at Starbucks asked as I came to the front of the line.

I wanted coffee so bad. "Uh, just a caramel frappe, and a coffee frappe, too. Thanks." I smiled.

"Sure thing, pretty." He winked and off he went.

I fought the urge to roll my eyes at him.

Greyson was sitting at a small table when I walked over with our drinks. He was still so hung over. He was wearing thick black frames and a baseball cap as he leant back in his chair. One would say he was asleep.

"Hey, coffee's here." I smiled, sitting down opposite him.

He gave me a nod, but I think he was still snoozing on and off.

It had been an hour since I dropped Oliver off, and I missed him. Damn. Where did that come from? I shook my head, breaking those thoughts from my mind. As much as I wished he kissed me, I was glad he didn't.

Ugh, I needed to tell him. It was hard, and I didn't know how to say it.

I didn't even have his number to text him and let him know. I didn't even know if I was really going to see him again. Now that Cassie and Tony were off married and on their honeymoon, I doubt I'd see him at all. We didn't normally hang out. We were just random strangers who fucked in a club and seemed to have a strong, intense connection.

"You have a good time last night?" I asked, taking a long sip of my iced drink.

"Yeah, I did. What about you?" he asked, taking his glasses off and rubbing his eyes. "I am so fucking tired. I feel like hell."

I smiled. "I had great fun."

It was true. I had a really good time being out with my family, dancing and simply being surrounded by them, and the food was sumptuous. My highlight was definitely the night and having Oliver in my bed. Damn, I didn't want to wash those sheets ever.

"Why was Daniel blowing at both ends?" I asked him in almost a whisper, making sure no one heard me.

He burst out laughing. "You don't want to know. Trust me, that guy got his payback for cheating on you from me. He deserved it, Sage. I couldn't hit him, so I did the next best thing."

My curiosity piqued up. I didn't like where this was headed. "Greyson, what the hell did you do?"

He just kept a grin across his face. I nudged his foot with mine and glared.

He sighed and nodded. "Okay. We made him a milkshake and may have dosed it up with some laxatives, and I mean like a lot of them. I swear, we had no idea it'd work so fast that he'd not make it to the toilet."

I burst into a fit of giggles, holding the side of my palm in my mouth and biting down, so I wasn't too loud. "Greyson, that is horrible. God, he must have been so embarrassed."

"He doesn't remember doing it. He was that drunk." He smirked.

"Did Oliver know what was going on?" I asked, trying to keep my cheeks normal and not flushed at the mention of his name.

"Yeah, he did. He was all for it. I tell you. He's pretty fun. We're going to catch a game next week sometime when he's off work," he said, divulging in a deep conversation about his new bromance.

I sat there listening to it all. "Seems like you have made a new friend then."

"Don't be jealous. You're still my number one girl." Greyson winked.

I laughed. "I better be, or else."

While we sat there talking over our drinks, I couldn't help but think about him and Oliver being friends. I wasn't sure how I felt about it. What it was going to be like when I see him again, especially if he was still with his wife? I knew I should feel guilty and horrible, a homewrecker even, but I couldn't help but want to see him again. I wanted to know more about him. Maybe it was just my hormones, or maybe it was something more between us.

I knew what I wanted wasn't ever going to happen. I couldn't be with him, the father of my child.

I sighed. "I need to see the doctor next week," I said aloud.

Greyson stopped talking and dipped his brows. "Why? Are you okay?"

"Yeah, I just need to get a couple things checked out." I couldn't bring myself to tell him either.

What was wrong with me? Why did I feel so afraid? Why couldn't I just tell my best friend I was pregnant?

I was embarrassed.

"Do you want me to come with you?" he asked. "I can, you know. I don't need to go back Monday morning."

I shook my head. "No, it's okay. You go back. Your classes start up soon, and you can't miss them."

"True." He smiled. "Let me know how it goes though. You've got me all worried now."

"Don't worry. I'm not." I smiled.

I was more than worried. I was freaking out on the inside. This was all about to become real. Much more real than I ever wanted it to be.

We left Starbucks and made our way through the mall. Neither of us was in the mood to shop. We just went browsing through the windows. An hour of that and we headed back home, grabbing some takeout on the way to lie around the house and eat while watching movies.

On the way down the pathway to my little home away from home, I was stopped by my father's voice. "Sage, wait up. I'd like a moment please."

Oh, god.

I looked at Greyson. "Meet you inside. Choose what you want to watch."

"Sons." He wiggled his brows.

"Hmm. Jax Teller. Give me him any day, and I'll be happy." I licked my lips, failing at being seductive.

He winked. "You and me both."

"You can have Clay. He's more your type." I teased.

He groaned. "Bitch. Hurry up, or I'll start without you."

I laughed, making my way over to where Dad sat in the patio. I sat across from him. Then Mum walked out with some hot tea and biscuits on a tray. Something was up.

"Sage, feeling okay today?" Mum smiled, offering me a cup.

I couldn't refuse her tea. It was always good. "Thanks, and I feel okay. Except I am tired from the party Dad threw."

Dad chuckled, setting his teacup down. "Oh, sweetheart, your sister and Tony were heading off just as all the oldies left. That's when the real party started, and boy, did we drink back here."

"I know. I had three men wanting to crash in my space. Not cool, Mum." I shot her a playful glare.

She sighed. "I wasn't letting them throw up on the good bedding. From what I heard, Daniel was quite sick. Must be something he was allergic to."

If only she knew what really happened.

Dad cleared his throat as I opened my mouth. "I know you start school soon again, but we have an offer for you."

Now I was curious but also wary. "Yes?"

"More of a bribe. Stay here and don't leave," Mum blurted out.

I sighed. "Mum, I have my course to finish."

"Yes, but you can still finish it online. Why don't you look at opening up your own store here? Your father has told me about some great space that's going to be available soon. He's head of the council and in charge of the new shopping division. I think it would be a great opportunity for you." She beamed, looking happy.

I looked up at Dad. I wasn't sure how I felt about it. It was possible. I could finish the course from home, but running a business, I didn't know if that was something I could do.

"Let me think about it. Just don't push it on me and give me a week to think, please?" I asked, looking at them both.

"That's better than a no." Dad smiled. "Okay. Let us know your thoughts next weekend, and I can show you the space if you like. I know the building manager, and I'm sure he wouldn't mind helping out."

I stood up and kissed them both on the cheek. I waved goodbye and went back to find Greyson.

As I lay on the couch, I couldn't help but think of Oliver, lying here with him and sleeping. I enjoyed the way his body felt beside me and the comfort I received from him. I sighed. Why couldn't he be single? It was obvious why. He had a gorgeous male, and it was not a shock that he was taken.

His wife seemed so lovely, and that was where I began to feel guilty. I wouldn't like it if my husband was doing what Oliver and I had done behind my back. I hated it when Daniel cheated. I really needed to stop it. He was married, and it was just the alcohol talking.

He loved his wife. He still loved her.

My stomach started feeling a little weird. I really needed to see a doctor. The last thing I wanted was to wake up and have a balloon-sized stomach popping out. I was so in the dark about babies and pregnancy. I never really thought about having kids. Maybe in my late twenties, but not now. I was still so young. I'd make a horrible mother. I wouldn't know what to do.

I slowed down with my eating and pulled the cover up higher. I wrapped it around my body as I lay to my side and closed my eyes while listening to the TV, thinking about the one thing I shouldn't be.

I should have let him kiss me.

~

OLIVER

I sat there waiting for her to speak.

My heart pounded a million miles an hour. We had been silent for an awfully long time.

"Amy, did you hear me? I'm really sorry. I didn't mean to do it or hurt you. It just happened. I'm so sorry."

Her eyes flickered up, mouth in a grim line. "You're telling me you cheated? You went and slept with another woman?"

I nodded, wincing at her words. "Yes. I slept with another woman."

"When?" she asked, calmly.

"Tony's buck's night." I wasn't going to lie about when it was. No point.

She sighed, her fingernails tapping on the wooden round table. "I'm sorry. You're seriously telling me that you...you went out and got so drunk that you picked up another woman and fucked her?"

I nodded. "Yes."

A smile spread across her face like she was enjoying this. "How? How did you do it and what did she do to you? I want details and all of them."

"I don't remember. I was off my fucking head." I remembered it all. I wouldn't ever be fooled by that trick of admitting any details.

Amy sat there with her arms crossed as she clicked her tongue. "Not good enough. You're going to remember. Did you enjoy it?"

"Christ." I ran a hand through my hair. "Amy, I felt like shit afterward. I've felt shit ever since it happened."

Did I feel bad about it though? Sure. At first, I regretted it, but now, I didn't think I did. I thought it was the moral shock of going and doing something like that. I wasn't raised to treat a woman badly. Swearing or hitting one wasn't what my mother would be proud of. Cheating, she'd be disappointed.

Amy was silent for a moment. Then she spoke quietly, tying her blonde hair up in a twist thing. I'm a guy. I had no idea what the fuck it was called.

She sighed and looked me dead in the eye. "I'm sorry. I just don't believe you cheated."

"You're kidding me?" Well, fuck. I didn't expect that.

She shook her head, leaning forward to push herself off the chair. "Oliver, I know what you're doing, and it's not going to work."

"What do you mean?" I was completely stumped. I had no idea what she was on about.

She picked the vase up from the table and hurled it across the room, smashing it into the wall. Shards of glass splintered everywhere. Water soaked through the carpet, and the flowers now looked dead and plucked, as the leaves had mostly fallen off.

Shit. She was mad.

Her eyes went back to mine. "And in this indiscretion, did she suck you off?"

I swallowed hard. "Amy, don't."

"Don't? Don't want, Oliver?" She grabbed the table with both hands tightly and flung that so it hit the wall.

The table leg snapped off. Next thing I knew, she picked up a chair and slammed it down to the floor. Two legs on that snapped, and the chair fell down to the ground. She was pissed. I just kept telling myself that I caused this. I cheated, and she had every right to flip out, scream, and shout.

"I'm sorry, but I don't think you did cheat on me. If you did, then you'd be sucking up to me, buying me expensive gifts, taking me on holidays, and fucking me constantly. You haven't done any of that. Therefore, you didn't cheat. You're making it up!"

"Amy, I'm trying to come clean to you. I fucked another woman."

Maybe if I said it in a harsher way, she would believe me. It was as if everything I was telling her was just going in one ear and out the other. She was blocking it out, denying the truth to herself.

My cheek was burnt with a stinging slap. I had expected that. I deserved that for sure. I just blinked, sitting there, trying to remain calm as my eyes watered.

"You're lying to me. Stop it!" she screamed, her voice loud and raspy.

"Amy." I sighed, standing up. This was tougher than I thought. "I'm sorry. Things aren't working with us. I can't keep doing this anymore. I think we should take a break. I'm not happy. You're not happy. You're never happy anymore. It's just not working. I shouldn't have cheated on you."

I hissed in pain as she slapped me again, this time dragging her nails across my face. I knew there was blood. I just stood and took it. I deserved that too.

She let out a cackle, walking behind the kitchen bench, and grabbed a large butcher's knife, waving it around.

"Oliver. Oliver." She picked up a carrot from the vegetable bowl and cut the end off, loud and fast. Her eyes snapped up, voice firm. "Who was she?"

"I don't know." Like fuck, I was going to tell her that. I could only imagine what she'd go and do to Sage if she knew it was her.

"So, you slept with a random woman. She could have diseases." She seemed pleased. I didn't know what she was smiling for. "That would serve you right. Your own fault."

"I used something." That was a lie, but the way she was cutting that carrot was fucking making my cock want to shrivel up and hide.

She laughed, and a sickening feeling spread through my body. "Oh, how thoughtful. Well then, I think you're going to be checked out after this so-called affair. Oh, wait. Affair is too generous. We'll call it the night a woman takes pity on you. I mean, you've not slept with me and I know I'm clean because I have been faithful to you. Now, tell me. Is your cock itchy, Oliver? Does it hurt to piss? Or do you have any unusual bumps? Did the woman leave disappointed after you humped her like a man having a stroke? Did she turn the lights out so she didn't have to see your thinning hair?"

She was hitting a nerve. My eyes glared at her. "Amy, stop it."

I wasn't concerned about getting something off Sage. She didn't look like the type to fuck around and then spread diseases. I hoped not. Fucking hell.

"Oh, Oliver. I was just teasing you. I know you're smarter than that. Well, I thought you were. Was this woman beautiful? Did she make you cum hard? I know you can't get her off, so I'm wondering if you really enjoyed it?" she asked, chopping harder with each slice.

Fuck sake. I wanted to say yes, very damn hard. I didn't answer.

"You know, I don't appreciate being lied to. You cheated, but I don't believe you. If you did, you'd have owned up to it. I know you, Oliver, and you seem to forget that. You forget that I know when you're hiding something and you don't look like you are. You're looking like you just want an excuse to leave me."

"Amy, fuck. Why would I lie about this?" I asked, growing more and more frustrated.

"I've smoked bigger joints than your dick. That's the reason why." She walked around the bench and towards me.

Fuck, now she was back to the small cock digs. She thought she was messing around. She didn't know what that does to my confidence. Shattered it. I never worried about my size until lately.

"Don't. Amy, put the damn knife down." I warned, stepping back.

110

She laughed, tauntingly. "You've gained weight, and I wonder if I poke your belly, will it wobble back at me? Let's try it."

I frowned. I hadn't gained weight. I didn't think I had.

Next thing I knew, she was jerking the knife towards me. Playing around or not, I stepped back again but wasn't fast enough. The end had hit me in the side, and my eyes widened with shock. She couldn't be serious. She didn't just put a fucking knife into me.

I stood there in shocked, the pain stinging as I just stared at her with an open mouth.

"Oliver, I am so sorry. Oh god, baby, what have I done? I promise I didn't mean it." She pulled her hand back and dropped the knife, blood coating the end. She started to walk closer to me and reached out to touch me. I backed away, not wanting her anywhere near me.

"Stay away from me, Amy." *Fucking crazy bitch*, I screamed in my head at her.

I reached down and touched the wound over my shirt that was soaked with blood. It fucking hurt. I lifted my shirt up and stared at the gash. It was as long as the diameter of a fifty-cent coin but with a thick slit, open and bleeding.

"You're not going to a hospital, are you?" Amy called out, sounding panicked as I walked toward the door.

"Well, do you suggest? Go and tell them my wife flung a knife into my abdomen? I don't think so, Amy, but maybe I should. I don't want you anywhere near me." I tried to put pressure on my stomach where the cut was starting to sting more.

Amy sighed, tears running down her cheeks. I didn't give a shit if she was crying. She wiped her eyes and pulled out a chair that wasn't broken.

"Sit down. I'll stitch you up, Oliver. I still have my medical bag with supplies. God, baby, I didn't mean it. I swear. I was just so mad. You made me do it. You made me so mad."

Gee, wasn't I lucky that my wife used to be a nurse?

I sat down and kept my eyes to hers as she stitched my stomach up, hissing and wincing as the needle went in. She began to sow until eight stitches were pulled tight. Then she covered it with a bandage.

I said nothing to her. I was in shock and stunned at what she had done. This was a new side to her that I was only just seeing. I didn't like it or care for it in any way.

Amy stood up and gripped my chin tightly, bending down low and looking menacingly into my eyes, but somehow, she was smiling and talking ever so calmly. "Don't do it again. Got it! You're mine, Oliver, until death do us part. You're not getting a divorce, so don't you suggest it. You're not getting a separation either. That would be far too easy. You're going to go to the doctor's this coming week and get your sperm checked again. Something has to be wrong with you if you can't get me pregnant. Then you can continue with how things were. You will try to please me by giving me a child because if you broke a marriage vow, then you'd do anything to fix it? Isn't that right?"

I was frozen. She had just gone batshit crazy, stabbed me, and expected me to still want to be with her. Let alone even think of having a child with her. I was done. Fuck that for life. I didn't even nod. Her hand did it for me, moving my head while she smiled in a false assuming victory.

"Good boy. Now go shower. You smell horrible and look like hell."

"Amy." I warned. I was seconds from snapping and absolutely flipping the fuck out.

She said nothing as I got up and walked down to the spare bedroom. I was confused but exhausted.

Falling down to the bed, I groaned. Finding it hard to breathe this way, I rolled over and shoved a pillow under my side. I admitted to the cheating. She didn't believe me and then pushed a knife into my side. My wife was insane and one crazy ass bitch

So why the hell was I just realizing this now?

# CHAPTER 10

"I'm going to miss you." I smiled at Greyson as I leaned forward, engulfing him in a tight bear hug. I had been doing that all morning.

He hugged me back just as tight. "I'm going to miss you, too. You better hurry and join me so I'm not alone." He pulled back and kissed my cheek softly.

I nodded, giving a wave as I watched him enter his car and reverse out of the driveway and drive away.

I slumped against the doorway.

It had been three days, and I hadn't seen Oliver, not that I wanted to. It was better for everyone that he stayed away.

I checked my watch. I had another hour before I needed to make my way to the doctor. Nerves were consuming me so bad right now. I was far too nervous. This was what I had been trying to avoid: the confirmation of my pregnancy.

Today was the day to see the baby that was growing inside my stomach and to find out if all was good. I was about to place my hands on my stomach, but I heard footsteps behind me.

"Dear, would you like some lunch?"

I glanced over my shoulder to see Mum there.

"Sure. What are you cooking?" I asked, following her into the large kitchen, and I peered over into the large metal saucepans on the stovetop.

Food was my only comforting distraction, and I wasted no time in taking her up on her offer for a bowl of vegetable soup and Turkish bread.

113

~

Hurrying into the doctor's room at the hospital, I was flustered and nervous.

The room wasn't completely filled up, but there were heavily pregnant women and a couple of small children.

I walked over to the receptionist and handed over my health care card. I smiled at her as she told me to take a seat.

I was early, which was a good thing because I didn't want to be late. This way, I could calm my nerves and work my way up to go through the white door in front of me. In that room, I would hear what I needed to make myself believe and not think that it was all a false pregnancy.

"Sage Mathers. The doctor will see you now," a woman called out.

Shit. This was happening way faster than I wanted. I shakily picked up my bag beside me and began to walk ahead to the door the young woman was holding open.

"Please change into this and lie down. The doctor will be in shortly." She smiled.

I changed into the hospital gown that she gave me, and just as I lay down, the doctor came in.

"Hi. I'm Dr. Carlson. Are you ready?" He introduced himself and sat in front of a monitor.

"Hi," I said nervously.

"I'm going to lift this up and apply some lube so we can get started. Okay?" He smiled.

He then took an equipment and squeezed some of the lube on it. After that, he gently pressed it on my stomach. All in all, I thought I was coping quite well until I heard the loud *thump, thump, thump*. My heart rate picked up, and I blinked furiously, staring at the monitor as Dr. Carlson moved the stick over my stomach and pushed down. Damn, my bladder was about to burst.

He tilted his glasses down over his large nostrils and squinted his eyes, a smile finally appearing. He pointed at the screen, and I could see a tiny blob, which resembled the size of an olive. It was tiny.

"Yes. You're most certainly pregnant. The foetus is nine weeks, and the heartbeat is sounding nice and healthy."

Foetus? How technical.

In my mind, at that very moment, I thought, *It was a baby. Mine. Oliver's. Our baby.*

I wiped my stomach with some rough paper towel and sat up. I couldn't believe it. I wanted to throw up or go home and then throw up. I needed to tell someone. I couldn't keep this a secret any longer.

Dr. Carlson held the door open for me. "Come back and see me when you're fifteen weeks. We'll do another ultrasound then."

I nodded and still in a slight daze as I made my way to the reception desk and waited behind the couple in front of me. I was almost knocked off my feet when the woman spun around, and her eyes locked right on mine. She gave me a friendly smile, and my skin prickled.

"Oliver, look who it is."

*Oliver? Oh, no. You've got to be fucking kidding me.*

The man turned around, and I wanted to gasp. He looked so angry, so cold, and empty. His eyes just glared into mine. He looked away again while his wife smiled sweetly and placed her hand on his lower back as she turned around, resting her head on his shoulder the same way I had done the other morning.

I wanted to rip it off her. Some intense and crazy feeling was overwhelming me.

"Dear, you can come over here." An older lady slid open the connecting glass screen.

Just great. I didn't want to stand there while he was there. I made my way up, ignoring his sideways glance. I didn't know what his problem was, but giving me a glare wasn't the reaction I expected from him.

115

I guessed it was true. He was just a typical horny man who cheated and then crawled back to his wife.

The woman looking over my details slid a piece of paper towards me. "Please sign, dear. It's bulk billed today. Do you need to make another appointment?" she asked.

"Yes. Umm, I don't know when." I was trying to work the weeks out in my head. If I were nine weeks now, then he'd want to see me...I didn't get to tell her when.

She spoke up, loud and clear. "Oh, yes. Dr. Carlson has it written here. You'll be fifteen weeks in six weeks. I'll put you in for the morning at nine. Is that okay?"

"Perfect. Thank you." I smiled back, itching to make a run for it.

Oliver's hand that had been furiously writing on a piece of paper came to a sudden stop. I could see him gripping the pen from the corner of my eye. I really hoped he hadn't been listening.

"We will see you then." She slid over the card, and I reached for it and left hastily, not bothering to stick around.

~

My back hit the bed, and I broke out crying. I couldn't hold it in anymore. The entire drive home, all I thought about was him. He was there with her, and she was most likely pregnant if they were in an ob-gyn clinic, or trying to get pregnant.

Why on earth was I crying?

I didn't care what he was doing. He was married, for crying out loud.

So why did it hurt so much?

Between overthinking everything and crying, I began to grow tired. Curling onto my side, I shut my eyes and let sleep take over.

A light tap on my bedroom window woke me up.

What the?

I lay there, frozen. I wasn't one for horror movies, and this was beginning to freak me out.

116

"Sage, unlock your door or open the window," a soft voice spoke as a tap went again.

My heart rate was picking up. Everything in my mind was racing. It couldn't be, could it?

I pushed the covers off and got out of the bed, peeking through my curtains. I felt sick.

"What?" I asked, not meaning to sound rude as I hissed it out.

"Open it," he said again, stepping backward.

"Go to my door. You won't fit through the window. It only opens halfway," I whispered back.

Why the hell was I whispering? No one could hear me.

When he walked, I quickly ran to the door. My parents, as laid back as they were, would kill him and me if they knew what was happening right now. I opened the door, and Oliver walked in immediately. He turned and instantly locked the door then looked back at me.

His eyes were burning with desire as he looked me up and down.

Oh, god. Yes. No. I meant no.

My feet, moving on their own accord, stepped backward as he walked forward with his hand reaching out. My back hit the wall, and he stood in front of me, wearing nothing but a dark navy hoodie and black sweats. His hair was covered by a beanie.

He reached up and pulled it off. His hair was all flat, and my fingers were dying to tug on it.

"You've been crying," he murmured softly. "Are you okay?"

I melted against his palm as he caressed my cheek.

"What are you doing here?" I asked, my voice a hoarse whisper.

"I need to know something," he said, taking another step toward me.

Oh, shit.

"What?" I asked, trying to control my rapid breathing.

"We should have used something. Is this what you were trying to tell me the other night? That you're pregnant?" he asked, eyes softening as he looked me over. His voice sounded like a sweet melody.

I didn't want to, but I needed to tell him. Oh, hell. He already knew. I knew that he wasn't stupid. He knew all right, and with one simple, soft word, I responded.

"Yes."

He closed his eyes tightly. His breathing picked up as his hand felt harder against my cheek. He pulled away and ran both hands through his hair, gripping it as he groaned.

"Fuck. This isn't what I fucking need right now."

Ouch. That was not the reaction I had expected. My chest tightened, and a lump formed in my throat. I felt sick.

"I'm sorry," I whispered, feeling more sobs coming on. If there was a time I had ever felt stupid, it was now. "Can you leave, please?"

He turned, looked back at me, eyes widening, and his mouth parted. The grim line was still there. "Fuck. No. I'm not mad at you. It's just...Shit! Shit! Shit!" he yelled. "God, Sage. My life is so fucked up right now. I can't give you what you need."

"What I need?" I asked, shocked.

Oliver pushed his body to mine, and he walked me back toward my room. "Are you sure it's mine?" he asked.

"I don't sleep around. I won't tell anyone it's yours," I said quietly, looking away from him.

"I'm not worried about that. I'm just more worried about your safety right now. I can't have anything happen to you, or our child." He breathed out. "You had a scan. Yes? Is everything okay? How far are you?" he rambled on and on.

"Nine weeks. The baby is good and healthy." I assured him then frowned a little.

What did he mean? What was going to happen? I had so many questions I wanted to ask.

I frowned, noticing a scratch along his cheek. I reached up to run my fingers along it, but he snatched my hand and pulled his head back.

"Oliver, what happened?"

"Nothing," he said blankly. "I need to go. I just needed to hear it from you. I thought I misheard today. God, I'm the one who is sorry for putting you in a situation like this, Sage. It's not fair on you." He stepped closer to me.

"How did you get in here?" I asked. He would have needed to go through the garage, and he didn't know the hidden way.

Shrugging, he said. "Jumped the fence. Not that hard or high to do."

I was caught by surprise when I could felt his hard erection pressed against my body. I gasped, gripping his hoodie tighter. "God, Oliver. What are you doing? You're killing me right now."

"No, baby. You're killing me. All I want to do is hold you and not let you go," he murmured again, fingertips stroking through my hair.

I bit my lip, needing to ask him. "Is she pregnant? Your wife?" I asked, breaking eye contact.

~

OLIVER

I blinked. Why would she think that? Then it hit me. We were also at the doctor.

Fuck.

"God, no. Definitely not. Well not by me, anyway. We were trying for a long time, and well, nothing happened. Then you…seems as if I got you pregnant instantly," I muttered with a blank stare.

"Oh." She blushed, looking away from me. I wanted to hold her tighter. "I'm sorry. I just assumed."

I was fighting the urge to strip her naked and make passionate love to her right now. She was pregnant, and that answered my question when I walked out of the doctor's office five

119

minutes after Sage had taken off. I refused to jerk off into a cup and then have a tube stuck down my cock for another exam.

Amy was growing on my nerves. She was demanding things in a way that made it sound as if I had come up with the idea myself.

"It's mine, yes?" I asked again. I knew she already answered, but for some reason, I wanted to hear her say it to me again. My eyes locked on hers and all I could see was a sad beauty within her eyes.

She nodded slowly. "I'm sorry. I didn't. God, all of this is my fault. If I hadn't been to the club, then you wouldn't be in this situation."

"Situation?" I asked, frowning and slightly amused as I had just used that line on her. "You think I'm mad at you? I don't give a fuck if you were on the pill or not. You're carrying my child. That's amazing, but..." I couldn't tell her the truth. "It's just...things are really hard at the moment. I can't give you what you need, and I don't know when I will be able to."

I couldn't give her sweet fuck all. Not when my wife was at home on a rampage. I actually just took off, giving some excuse about needing a run. Apparently, I was still on the fat side, so she was happy I took the incentive to start wanting to look better.

"Ollie, this is so fucked up."

I smiled, resting my forehead to hers. "Yes, I know."

Kicking off my shoes, I pushed her gently back down to her bed and straddled over the top of her, not wanting to hurt her in any way. "I'm meant to be out running," I said, running a finger up from her yoga pants band and over the flatness of her stomach. I lifted her top up to reveal her bare skin. "Have you told anyone else you're pregnant?" I asked softly as my fingertips moved up and down her stomach.

"No. I don't know what to say to anyone," she said, sucking in a sharp breath. "I tried to tell you, but you fell asleep."

I chuckled, smirking. "I know. I heard you. I just thought it was the alcohol and I was tired."

"It's going to be hard," she whispered with a sigh.

I lay to her side and cupped her cheek again, not liking the tears that were sliding down the corner of her eyes. I brushed my thumb over and wiped them away. "I know. I wish I could make it easier on you."

"Oliver." She sighed. "You're married. I'm not going to come between you and her. I can keep it a secret."

"You shouldn't have to though. You should be able to tell the world you're pregnant. I've taken that from you," I said. I hurt her in more ways than I wanted to.

I rolled to my back and sighed. I couldn't believe it. My one-night stand was pregnant, and my wife wasn't. This was fucked up alright. I fucked up. My thoughts drifted to Amy. If she knew Sage was the girl I slept with, and she was now pregnant, well, I would hate to think what she'd do to her or do to the child.

My wife was someone else. She was a woman who turned into a possessed, crazed animal.

I had barely spoken to her. She knew she fucked up. The moment that knife hit my skin, it was over for me. My instincts told me to just walk. No matter how many times she apologized or cooked all my favourite meals, it wasn't ever going to be enough. Dead weight was inside me when I was with her.

I just did what I could to try keep her calm and happy, but in the back of my mind, the thoughts were still there. What else was she capable of if I did leave her? She already warned me about leaving, but little did she know, I was still fucking leaving her.

The insults, I could take, but slowly they were wearing me down. Maybe I was a lazy bastard who needed to do more for her. Did I really take her for granted and not show her any love or affection?

I couldn't remember. It seemed that these past days were now a blur. Between work, the fights, and everything else, I was exhausted. My stomach was numb most the time, and I blocked that pain out. A small price I paid for pissing her off with my casual

"Oh, honey. I needed to tell you that I fucked another woman" speech. It was not my best times.

I didn't regret sleeping with Sage anymore. This woman made me open my eyes to what I was really living with. I just didn't know if I could give myself to someone like that again.

I felt a hand sliding up my chest, and I stiffened, not used to the intimate touch. Looking down at Sage, I watched as her hand kept moving upwards and sliding over my shoulder, massaging gently.

"You're not leaving her, are you?" she asked, finally after a moment's silence. "You won't leave her."

I sighed. "It's complicated, much more than you know."

"It always is. God, I don't even know what I'm saying. I'm chasing after a married man." She pushed me down and sat herself up. "What the hell are we doing? You're married, Oliver. I can't be that girl. I don't want to be. I'm sick of being the second choice."

I sat up. "What do you mean the second choice?" I asked softly, stroking her hair behind her ear.

"Daniel cheated on me. You're cheating with me. I don't want that." She began to cry. "I can't have a baby with a man who's married. I can't do it. I'm not ready to be a mother. I don't know what the hell I'm going to do."

"Hey." I cooed, pulling her close to me in a hug. I didn't want to admit how good it felt to hold her this way. I ran my hand up and down her back, trying to calm her sobs, which turned into hiccups. "I want to see you tomorrow, same time."

"Where? Is that a good idea?" She sniffed, pulling back so I could look into her crying eyes.

"Here. I can say I'm running. I can visit you if you want me to. I don't want this to end like this. I can't walk away now when we've not resolved anything." I didn't want to walk away from her.

She looked at me, not saying anything. I leaned in closer and stroked her cheek again, keeping my eyes on hers for reassurance that she wanted me to do this. I was so close, yet we were so far apart.

My mouth lightly brushed against her lips, and at that moment, I felt something inside me come back alive. Her mouth began to move, and her hand slid around my neck as the heat of the kiss began to grow more intense. My tongue swept out, and I groaned, tasting her sweetness against me. I lowered her back down to the bed and slowly moved on top, supporting myself with my arms while I gave her all I could give her right now.

Just a kiss. I wouldn't take it any further. I wouldn't do that to her. I fucked her up enough as it was. I just needed her to know that I was here, and I cared even if I couldn't tell her that in words.

Pulling back, I rubbed my nose against hers, caressing her forehead with my hand. "You're so beautiful. Don't ever doubt yourself, Sage."

"I'm sorry," she whispered, her breathing slowing down.

I smiled weakly. "Don't apologize, not to me ever."

I hated that fucking word right now. Sorry. That was all Amy ever was. Sorry and fine. Two words I hated.

"You're so gorgeous. Your eyes and body..." she whispered, blushing as she went to pull my shirt up.

I backed away, shaking my head. I didn't want her to see the disgusting mess underneath this top. She would be disgusted, and I didn't want her to see me this way. I was a fucked up mess, nothing to be attracted to.

She opened her mouth, and I pushed my finger against her lips, talking for her. "I know you're afraid. I am too. I won't force you into keeping a child that you're not ready for, but I would like you to think about it. I know it's a lot to ask, and I understand if you don't want this. It's just, we made a baby, together or not." I looked at my watch. Fuck, I had to leave very soon. "I need to leave now. I will come around tomorrow if you want me too?" I asked her, stroking her cheek again.

Biting her lip, she blushed. "I...Yes. I want to see you tomorrow," she whispered, looking nervous.

A smile grew across my mouth again. "I was hoping you'd say that."

"Ollie, what's going to happen?" she asked sleepily.

I placed a kiss to her nose. "Let me think. I will come up with a plan. Just give me tonight to work something out."

Walking to the door, I watched as she unlocked it and pulled it open. "Goodbye, Ollie. And if you walk past my window a little more, you'll find a hidden gate next to the purple flowers."

I chuckled. "Good to know." I stepped closer, wrapping my arms around her waist, drawing her close again. Our faces were inches apart. "I can't give you all of me, not just yet. Just, please, baby. Know that one day, if you're willing to wait and willing to give me all of you, I can give you all of me."

~

I walked into the house, and it was awfully quiet. A dimly lit candle was flickering in the corner of the living room, and immediately, I spotted Amy. She was staring right at me with a dark look. I almost didn't recognize her. She had coloured her hair. It was not blonde anymore but stark black.

"Christ, you trying to give me a heart attack?" I growled, kicking my shoes back off. I wanted to tell her she looked like the chick in *The Grudge*, but I held my tongue.

"Where's your hat?" she asked, tapping her fingers against her arm that was crossed over her chest. She stood and walked toward me. "You left with one on."

*Shit. I must have left it at Sage's.* I shrugged. "I stuck it in my back pocket while running. It must have fallen out. It's dark, and I didn't see anything."

"I see. Well, I'm going to bed. Just wanted to make sure you got home safely." She stopped in front of me and stared. "I'm happy that you're trying to get fit again. I liked the way you looked in college, slimmer."

I clenched my jaw, holding back from snapping. "I'm going to bed. I have work early tomorrow."

Her posture changed, and she smiled. I knew what that smile was. It was the same one she gave me before she flipped out the other day. It only had me very wary of her.

"Goodnight, Oliver. Sleep tight."

I went to the room that was now my own. Stripping off and lying in bed, I stared at the ceiling and thought that out of all the shit I endured this past week, there was one thing that made me smile, and that gave me a little bit of hope that things would turn out okay.

I was hopefully going to be a father.

# CHAPTER 11

Anxious. I was so anxious today.

Oliver was coming back over. Oh, god. I couldn't believe we had kissed again. It was amazing. The way his lips felt was better than I had imagined. It was a perfect kiss, and definitely, more than I remembered.

But it was also wrong, so very wrong.

I should have told him not to come over not until his wife was out of the picture. Something felt off about him. He seemed to be hesitant when I touched him like he didn't want me to. Maybe it was just regret about what we were doing; sneaking around.

The baby. Of course, I couldn't get rid of it. It was a child, after all, a tiny human with a heartbeat.

My nerves suddenly shot up. I realized that I didn't remember what time he was coming over here. Last night, it was pretty late. Maybe he wouldn't come over. He would need to get away from her first. Ugh, the woman he was married to.

I threw on some leggings and an oversized shirt. Tying my hair up, I made my way into the kitchen of my home away from home. I opened the fridge up and smiled. Mum had re-stocked it for me.

I grabbed the things I needed to make a salad and began to slice up a lettuce.

My skills in the kitchen weren't that good. I could cook with a microwave, but to make something from scratch, that wasn't me. I sucked, and food usually ended up burnt.

The door opened just as I sat on the couch and my heart leaped from my chest. It was not even 9:00 PM, and he was here. Strolling over casually, dressed in running gear, he gave me a slight smile as he sat opposite me.

How was I meant to eat now? He was just so casual as he walked in and sat down without a care in the world.

"Eat up. How was your day?" he asked, sitting back. His eyes stared at mine.

I just stared at him. "It was good. Quiet but busy. Uh, have you eaten?" I asked a little nervously.

He shook his head. "I'm fine."

"Oliver." I laughed. I put my bowl aside and got back up, walking my way to the kitchen. "I'm not eating in front of you if you don't eat either. That's just embarrassing and rude."

He followed, and I could hear the exasperated sigh. "I didn't come here to eat."

"No?" I faked shock. "What is it that you came for, Oliver?"

He laughed, loudly. "Just in the neighbourhood. Thought I might call in and see what you're up to."

"I see." I smiled, using the wooden tongs to put some chicken salad in a bowl for him. "I don't cook," I mumbled, thinking that he might think what I was serving up was disgusting.

Oliver stepped around, and I felt the heat from his body as he stepped behind me and reached around to take the bowl. "I didn't come for food. I don't care if you can cook or not, but this looks good. Thank you."

Oh, damn.

I kept still until he had moved and walked over to the couch where I was sitting a moment ago. I followed, and we both sat in silence and ate. It wasn't uncomfortable, but there was an odd feeling between us. My subconscious scolded me for what I was doing with him, but I pushed the thoughts from my mind and stared at Oliver.

"Did you go to work today?" I asked. I had no idea what he did for a living.

He nodded. "I did. It's a very busy day, and it's going to be a busy year."

I set my bowl on the table once I finished. "What do you do? Am I allowed to ask that?"

Looking at me, he smirked. "Course, you can. I'm in construction. I took over my father's company, and now I work hard to make it my own."

Suddenly, I was picturing him all dirty and sweating. I blushed and sat up straighter. "That's interesting. Maybe you can tell me more about it one day?" I suggested.

He seemed surprised by my question but quickly masked his expression. Putting his bowl down on top of mine, he stood up. "Bed. You look tired."

"Excuse me?" I asked, almost choking on my own breath.

"Let's go to your room. I don't want your parents to walk in and find me here," he said and walked toward my room.

Quickly putting both bowls away, I followed and found him lying on my bed. I walked around and lay down on my back. The last time we were here, we kissed.

"What are you thinking?" I asked. Lying sideways facing Oliver had my heart racing.

He shrugged, turning to roll on his side also. "How wrong this is, but I don't care."

A smile crept over my lips. "It's more than wrong, but I understand."

"You do?" he asked, his pinkie finger brushing over mine.

I tried to ignore the growing feeling from his simple touch, and I nodded slowly. "No. I have no idea. I'm not married, but I just can't imagine it's easy for you."

His mouth set in a grim line. "It's not easy, but I don't want to bore you with details." He then cleared his throat, glancing at me nervously. "Have you, uh, decided what you want to do?"

My heartbeat quickened some more, and I nodded. "I'm going to keep it," I said softly. "I know it makes things difficult for you, but it's a baby. I can't go through with anything else."

A smile grew over his face. "Good. That's a good decision."

I laughed softly, rolling my eyes. "You know, I'm not holding you to stick around."

Oliver's arm slid over to my stomach and lifted my shirt up, hand resting and fingers splayed out across my stomach. "If Amy found out about this, I'm afraid what she would do to you."

"What do you mean?" I asked quietly.

"Just that she's been wanting a baby for over a year. I told her about us. The club," he whispered, and my insides churned. That took me by surprise.

"You did? Wait. She forgave you?"

Damn. If my husband had cheated on me, I would have kicked him out after breaking his nose.

He laughed, shaking his head. "Not exactly. She's a little on the mad side, but it's nothing I can't handle. I think she thinks if she can control me a bit more, then I won't stray."

"Have you strayed before?" I wondered, realizing I asked that out loud without meaning to.

He smiled, and a playful smirk came across his face. He moved closer toward me. "No, Sage. I haven't ever felt the urge to fuck someone else."

"Do you want to fuck me again?" I asked boldly.

He nodded. "Yes. I do badly, but I won't."

"You won't?" That surprised me. Also, my core tightened at the thought of him wanting me again.

"No. I won't. I don't want you to feel used, but I do want to kiss you again. I enjoy feeling your mouth against mine." With that, he pressed his mouth to mine only for a mere second, but it was enough to set me on fire. "Kissing only if you want."

I was sure he could hear my heart pounding. "Me too, and I'm glad about the sex thing. I want to as well but not like this. We don't know each other very well yet. I want to know more about you, Ollie."

He breathed out, smiling as he slid his hand back up my body, and pulled me closer, wrapping his arm around me and kissing my nose. "I can get away for around an hour each evening. It's all I can do right now."

I couldn't hide my slight disappointment. "Oh."

"I'm sorry," he said softly.

I hooked my leg over his thigh, hesitantly sliding my arm over his hip. He tensed up a little but eventually relaxed.

"It's okay. I get it."

A groan escaped his throat. I tried to fight the moan as his fingers tightened around my back, running down the curve of my ass and over my thigh.

"You shouldn't have to get it. That's my point. I want to strip you bare and have my way with you in a bed and not on the floor of a club, not that I didn't enjoy it thoroughly."

"I liked it too. I'd never done that before." I teased, fighting off my blush.

He looked at me curiously, amused. "Done what?"

"Had sex." I lied.

"You're kidding me?" His brows shot up, looking at me like I was insane.

I laughed, rubbing my nose to his gently. "Course, I am. I meant in a club with a strange man. I don't normally do it."

His eyes burned into mine, pulling me closer against him if that were possible. "I'm going to find my own place. Hopefully, in a week, I've got something."

"Yeah? Is that what you want? I mean, it must be hard. I hope you're not leaving because of what happened between us. I don't want to break your marriage up," I whispered, a little scared.

He nodded. I didn't press, but I wanted to find out more. "My marriage isn't a good one, Sage. I will help you with the baby. I can help you out financially if you need. Don't worry about that. If you need help, just ask."

"No. I mean, don't think that's what I want. I've got savings. I just need to decide where I'm going. I am meant to decide if I'm going back to school this week or not." I frowned. I didn't want his money at all. That wasn't what this was about.

He looked at me, taking in what I had said to him. "What do you mean? You're leaving?"

"My parents want me to stay and open up my own business, but I'm not sure. It's hard, but I don't think going back and being pregnant is a good idea also." I closed my eyes, feeling slightly tired. I didn't want him to leave, and I didn't want to leave him.

"I don't want you to leave. I want you to stay so I can watch your stomach grow and help out," he said quietly, almost sullen.

"Can you come back tomorrow?" I yawned, snuggling more against him. "Sorry. Even if we're just friends, I don't mind."

"Sleep, baby. I'll be back tomorrow night and the night after that. How could I not when I've found you again."

That was the last thing I heard him say before I fell asleep.

~

OLIVER

I slipped out of her hold once she was fast asleep and pulled the covers up over her.

Kissing her cheek, I sighed, whispering, "What are you doing to me, Sage?"

I headed home, running back all the way. My feet hit the pavement hard. Everything was a fucking storm in my eyes. I had a pregnant woman that I knew I was only going to hurt in the long run. I didn't want to hurt her, but I knew I would.

Pushing the front door open, I slammed it shut and headed for the shower. Running seemed to take the need to fuck out of my mind. Slipping under the hot water, I groaned. Why and how did everything get so messed up?

"Baby, you want me to join you?" Amy purred.

131

Shit. I forgot to lock the door.

"No." I didn't want her anywhere in here.

She began to take her clothes off, and I turned the water off. I grabbed a towel and wrapped it around my waist before she pulled the curtain open.

"I said no."

"Oliver, I was trying to be nice. I thought you'd want to?" she asked, letting the bra fall down from her chest.

My eyes didn't flicker down like they used to. My cock didn't get hard either. I was immune to her.

I shook my head. "I don't want you anywhere near me, Amy. Got it!"

"Don't fucking lie!" She snapped.

"Why would I lie to you?" I scoffed. "I'm telling you. I don't want to shower with you. I'm tired."

"You're always tired." She spat, walking over to the sink.

I heard a noise, but I didn't see what was turned on or off.

I laughed sarcastically. "Yes. Well, some people do need to work for a living. Should try it sometime instead of living off other people. Get a fucking job. I won't be giving you shit anymore."

As I reached the door handle, I pulled it open only to feel something extremely hot on my hip. Jerking my body violently away, I looked down at the red welt forming on the side of my hip and trailing around to my back.

"Fucking hell!" I yelled loudly. "What the fuck!"

Amy glared, still standing naked as she held her hair straightener in her hand, snapping the tongs together. "You're going to talk to me better. You wonder why I do this, Oliver! It's all you. You hurt me with your horrible words. I am your wife. Don't fucking yell at me!"

I stepped closer toward her, my eyes glowering at her. "Get out of here now before I take that thing and snap it around your neck! Now, get the fuck out!"

She just laughed and began to straighten her hair. "You don't scare me. I know you're just a big pussy with a little dick."

I pulled the cord from the power socket and snatched the straighter from her, tossing it across the bathroom. "Leave!"

As soon as she walked out of the bathroom, I slammed the door and locked it. Fuck. My side was stinging awfully. I raised my arm, looking in the mirror at the burn.

*She's crazy.* I bit my tongue hard and pinched the bridge of my nose, holding in tears and telling myself over and over the same thing. *Men don't cry. Men don't cry. Men don't cry.*

She was right. I was a pussy. I was a fucking useless pussy.

I went out of the bathroom and lay down in bed while keeping a cool washcloth against my side. I couldn't sleep. Not now, not when my lower hip was on fire. Honestly, I couldn't believe she had done such a thing. But this was the woman who stabbed me, so I shouldn't have been surprised.

Thoughts of hatred soon eased when I thought about Sage. She was so different from Amy. She was just different in every way from her smile to her frown. I knew there was something between us. I wouldn't deny it, but I didn't know just how far I would take it. I wanted more, but then I'd had more with Amy, and I wasn't sure if I could do it again. I knew there was going to be more with her. It was inevitable. After all, she was pregnant, and I would be there for her. Just not the way I wanted to.

I picked my phone up and was about to dial my brother, but I ended the call before it rang. This was my mess, my own fault.

~

Four hours sleep was all I got through the night.

Getting up earlier than I needed to, I showered and dressed. The burn was a fucking sore mess. It was all raised and slightly blistered. I put a bandage over it and headed to the front door when Amy's voice stopped me.

I was on high alert, turning around as she stared. I hated her black hair. She looked awful.

"Oliver, please stay home, baby." She yawned, walking towards me.

What the fuck!

"No." My voice meant to come out firmer, but it was a whisper instead.

"No?" she asked, raising her brows. "Oh, why not?"

"I need to go," I muttered. I wasn't turning my back on her though. Who knew what she'd jab at me again.

She burst into tears. "I'm sorry, baby. I didn't mean it. I promise. I swear I would never try to hurt you on purpose. I just...I'm so upset and stressed from not being able to get pregnant. I want it so much, and it's just not happening."

A couple of months ago, I would have believed her. Now, I was immune to her crying and seeing her like this. I felt absolutely nothing for her anymore.

I was going to leave, get a divorce, and fuck her off for good. Or so I hoped.

"You don't love me," I said, barely a whisper. "I don't think you ever did."

That seemed to get her tears to come to a halt. She looked up and raised a brow as if to say, 'Fuck you, asshole.'

Amy leaned on the armchair and sighed. "Oliver, no one will ever love you the way I love you."

"I'm going to work, Amy. I can't deal with this anymore." I sighed, running a hand through my hair.

I made the mistake of closing my eyes. Next thing I knew, I was pushed backward with a thump to the door. Amy's hands slapped and punched me.

I grabbed her hands and pushed her off, pinning her against the wall with my body. She was small but strong. I was breathing hard, and my stomach was killing me like a bitch. She spat saliva in my face, and I swiped my face with my arm, shaking my head.

"What the hell is your goddamn problem?"

"You! I hate you. You're right. I never fucking loved you. You were just what I wanted years ago. Fell right into my plan. I mean it, Oliver. What's to love about you? You're not a man. You never were. Just a fucking useless boy. You can't even fuck a woman. You can't do anything," she screamed, her face red and eyes dark with anger.

I just stared at her in shock. What the hell was wrong with her?

"You used me?" I asked, my voice barely a whisper.

She snickered. "Oh, once upon a time I may have wanted you, but not anymore. You're nothing. You are stupid, and god, your mother. Don't get me started on her. She's an overbearing troll who thinks she's better than anyone else."

She could lash out at me, but attacking my mother, that wasn't something I appreciate. I squeezed her wrists harder. "Stop it. Just stop."

"No!" she screamed, her legs flailing to try to kick me.

I pushed against her harder, growing angrier with her.

I shook my head, pushing her into the wall while I pushed myself off her. "I don't love you either, so we're good there."

That got her to shut up. She stood there huffing loudly.

"Oliver."

"No! Don't you dare Oliver me!"

"Do you remember Jonah? Your college roommate? I fucked him back then with every chance I got." She smirked.

I shook my head, amused but not showing it. "He was gay. Don't try lying to me, Amy. I'm not that stupid."

"I should have fucked him." She spat. "Remember when we first met? Well, you may have noticed me for the first time, but I knew you before. I knew you well."

I frowned. "What the hell does that mean? God, you're insane. You're an insane controlling bitch!"

Another slap across my face was well received.

"Shut up, asshole!"

I clenched my jaw and rubbed my cheek. "Don't like that? Not nice is it? Now, if you get out of my fucking way, I need to get to work, and I suggest you get packed and out of this house. I mean it. I'm done. We're done."

"I'm not leaving!" She spat.

I laughed, walking back toward the bedroom. "Okay then. I fucking will."

My wife stood and watched as I packed a bag. I ignored her while she hurled profanities at me and a few shoes. I was tired, in pain, and fucking exhausted. She was calling me every name under the sun, telling me how useless and pathetic I was and telling me she wished that I'd go drive off a cliff and die.

Being worn down this way, I pretty much wanted to jump off a cliff and make sure I hit the bottom.

"Are you really leaving me?" she asked, and her tears were back on.

For Christ's sake, I couldn't keep up anymore. "You brought this on yourself. You did this to us, Amy. I thought everything was going good, but you've just shown me how awful things have really been."

"Walk out that door, and I will make your life a living hell." She hissed, menacingly.

I nodded, heading toward the front door. "I intend on doing the exact same to you."

My second mistake this morning was turning and walking away from her.

# CHAPTER 12

"Are you excited?" Dad asked, smiling wide as he parked the car.

I shrugged, glancing around the large lot with trucks and machinery everywhere. "I don't know. I'm kind of nervous." I was extremely nervous to see what Dad had organized to show me.

"It's okay, princess. I hope you're going to like it and it may help you decide to stay?" he asked, giving me a hopeful look.

I knew what he meant. He wanted me to stay and be close. I thought now that Cassie was off and married, my parents were feeling lonely. If only they knew that pitter-patter of baby feet would be here in around seven months.

Glancing back over at my dad, I sighed. "I don't know. Just let me look, and please don't pressure me into anything. Please?"

"I won't, dear. I promise." He smiled and kept driving.

We went through large metal gates and into the new mall complex. I saw men everywhere, working outside, driving around in white utes, wearing hard hats. I gasped at the size of the building in front of me.

"Shit," I said loudly.

Dad chuckled beside me. "Do you like it?" he asked with a brow wiggle.

I laughed. "Let me look inside, then I will decide."

Apparently, due to regulations, I had to wear a hard hat too. It was not what I wanted to wear, and I had to let my hair down due to it not fitting right. Also, I was told to wear a fluro orange vest, and I could have cried. It was awful and didn't match with my outfit and was way oversized.

Dad laughed at my pouting.

"I'll lead you up, ma'am." An old man smiled, his grey hair peeking out from his own hard hat.

"Oh, I can stay here. I don't mind," I said nervously and embarrassed.

My dad, being in the council, put in a call to the project manager and told him we were coming over. It was very odd and strange. I could have waited until they were completed. I felt like one of those privileged kids who had everything given to them.

"It's okay, dear. Follow him up, and I'll meet you back out here when you're done. Remember, I will let you have your time to think, and I won't come to hassle you even if I want to." He smiled and kissed my cheek. Turning to the man, he patted the man's back. "Charles, show her up to the top left, then come back. I'd like to go over some ideas with you and Mr. Bailey when you've got a chance."

"Sure thing, sir." Charles nodded.

I ignored all the looks I got from the men as we walked past them. The escalator had stopped working, and we climbed the stairs, all forty-two steps of them.

Charles led me to where my father had suggested. He pushed the plastic covering back and walked me into a room, a large empty room.

"Here you go." He smiled.

I ducked. "Thanks."

Standing alone, I felt like an utter idiot. What on Earth was I meant to do now? I had no idea about businesses. I wanted to take off my hat, but I was a little worried about the ceiling caving in on me, so I opted to keep it as much as I hated it.

Hearing the plastic open again a few minutes later, I sighed. Yawning, I spun around on my heels, and I came face to face with a man who I had no idea worked here.

"Ollie?" I couldn't hide my surprise in my voice as I smiled.

He looked devilishly handsome in his work gear. I wanted to reach out and touch him, but I didn't, not when everyone here knew he was married. I was just someone he visited during evenings.

He gave me a grin, stepping closer. The smile he had wasn't a real one. Something was up. "You know, this is a very pleasant surprise."

"Is it?" I asked, cocking my head to the side. "You don't look happy."

He nodded, giving me a shrug. "It is. I've just been busy working hard. How are you? I hope you're not mad that I left last night when you fell asleep."

I felt my cheeks flame, remembering that when I woke this morning, he was gone. I couldn't believe I had fallen asleep like that.

"I'm not mad. I slept very well actually."

A broader smile swept across his face. His body was now only at arm's length away from me. "Good. Now tell me what are you up to in here looking around all nervous and confused?"

"Well, my dad wants me to stay here as you know. He thinks I should buy one of these spaces and start a business, but I don't know." I felt so embarrassed right now. All my dreams were usually kept hidden, but this was one I had always wanted.

He nodded, pursing his lips together. "Oh, yes. You leaving, right?" He sounded almost sullen.

"You're as bad as he is. I haven't decided." I sighed. "I don't know. It's hard."

"Something else is hard." His eyes were on mine, and I felt a shiver down my spine to my core.

Blinking, I had to swallow and regain myself. "Don't tease me."

He laughed. "What are you going to put in here if you do stay?" he asked, changing the subject. Taking a step closer, his hands slid around my waist slowly and pulled me closer.

A smile twitched over my mouth. I slid my hands up his chest and tilted my head back. "Well. I have been studying things about the body, health, and beauty. I want to, one day, open up a body shop that has a range of skincare products, from children to adults and men and women."

His brows raised up, looking surprised by my answer. "Makeup?" he asked.

I laughed, nodding. "Makeup, shower and bath scrubs, fragrances, and all that type of stuff that is good for the body and skin."

"Interesting. I think you should do it, but I do worry about something else. Will it be too much for you?" he said softer, eyes flickering down between us to my stomach.

"I feel okay. If I don't, then I take it easy and sit down," I said softly and not wanting him to worry. "I know it'll be hard, but I can do this." I was sure of it.

"Have you been unwell?" he asked, his fingertips playing with the end of my hair falling down my back.

Jesus, this was so wrong, but it felt so good.

I nodded, gripping his shirt tighter. "Yes. Apart from some morning sickness which happens randomly and mostly in the evenings, I am good."

"Don't cook tonight. I will come over earlier if you want me to?" he asked, lowering his head.

My breathing hitched up slightly. I swallowed hard, nerves filling me. "I want you to come over. Yes," I whispered back.

He went to kiss me, or so I thought. He hesitated and stopped, pulling back and stepping aside not before giving my helmet a tap. "This suits you. Now, do you want to have some shelves built in here? I can have one of the guys do it since I am the boss and all."

"You are?" I asked surprised.

He grinned. "I am. Now tell me what you want."

Oh, boy. If only he knew. "Well, apparently, since I am staying here, I would like a row of shelves, probably four from here to here," I suggested, pointing to the sidewall. I turned around. "Also, over there, too, and a long table island in the middle. Put in slats downwards and have a flat part along the top. Does that make sense?" I asked.

He scratched his chin, then I noticed his slight limp when walking. "I can work something out. I can build you a counter as well if you want. Just get some photos of ideas to show me."

"Are you okay?" I asked, staring at him.

He stopped walking and just looked at me, a slight frown appearing. "I'm fine," he grumbled, shooting me a look, and a slight chill ran down my spine. I could sense slight anger in his voice. "Let's get you back down to your dad. He's waiting for you."

"Wait." I stood there feeling like an idiot. "Are you upset with me?"

He shook his head. "No, Sage. I'm not," he whispered and walked over, cupping my cheek with one hand and kissing my forehead gently.

Maybe it was me being paranoid. I was so nervous being around him that I didn't want to come off being a weirdo. I went to slide my arms around his waist when he sucked in a sharp breath, wincing as he pulled away quickly.

"I'm sorry," I said, stepping closer again.

"Let's go. I need to go back to work." He was blunt as he walked away.

Something was off with him. He was acting so strange. I just followed, not saying another word to him. I kept my eyes to where I was going. The last thing I wanted was to fall down the stairs or through a floorboard that wasn't bolted down. Oliver stood at the top of the escalator and motioned for me to go first. I did so but didn't say another word and started walking down.

I never said goodbye. When I got out of the building, I just took my hat and vest off. Then I walked over to Dad's car and sat inside it. He was busy talking with Oliver. I noticed Oliver looked over, but he didn't smile or show any type of emotion. He was a blank canvas. I had a strange feeling that something was wrong.

Maybe he was changing his mind. He probably thought this was all too real now and he didn't want to deal with it.

What the hell was I doing? I was thinking about a life with a man I didn't know, a man who had a life with another woman. Jesus, what the hell were we doing? This wasn't going to work. I couldn't be that stupid to think he was going to leave her.

Dad came back, and I didn't say much as he drove back on the highway. Silent tears ran down my cheeks as I sat there staring out the window, mulling over the fucked up mess my life was becoming. I was attached to a man who wasn't into me.

Dad reached over and squeezed my thigh. "Sweetheart, are you okay? Sage, are you crying?" He sounded worried as he pulled over on the side of the road.

I shook my head and began to sob harder. Everything wasn't okay. Nothing was okay. My lip quivered as I faced him, shaking my head again. "I'm pregnant." I choked out a sob and buried my face in my hands as I cried loudly.

Oliver was right. I couldn't tell anyone who the father was.

Our baby probably wouldn't even know who his dad was.

Dad embraced me in his arms, holding me tightly as I cried into his chest on the side of the road.

~

OLIVER

"What's going on with you?" Smithy asked when I sat in the office. He was my right-hand man here and the only guy I trusted to help with the company when I wasn't around.

I looked up, confused. "What?"

"You're limping and extremely quiet, mate. What's going on?" he said, sitting in front of me.

I sighed, shaking my head. Why couldn't everyone just fucking drop it? I didn't want to talk about it, and I definitely didn't want to think about it.

I laughed it off. "Dropped a power drill on my foot at home last night. I think I broke a toe. It's nothing I can't manage."

He chuckled, shaking his head. "Ah, well, that explains it then."

"Yeah. Anyway, I'm taking a few days off. I've got some things to sort out. Will you be alright here?" I asked him, standing up and walking to my car. He followed me out.

I didn't get into personal life at work or with anyone apart from Tony, but he wasn't around, and I just needed some time off to sort my shit out.

Once I got in the car, he said. "Course, just let me know when you're coming back. Everything will be alright here, and I went over those drawings. I'll have a couple young guys do the shelving in room eighteen up top. It shouldn't take too long." He hit the roof of the work ute and nodded.

"Thanks, man," I said and wound my window up.

I headed for a drive but not home. I had my bag in the back seat while I headed to a hotel. Home wasn't an option for me anymore. I couldn't go back after what happened when I left. She had me too damn afraid to go there. I, a fully grown man, was afraid of a tiny woman. It was a joke. I was going to be a laughing stock.

No one would ever believe she could do something like that. She was too kind to other people, but behind closed doors, she was an insane monster. I had been waiting for her eyes to change to red and have horns growing from her head.

What she said this morning had made me question everything from the day I met her up until now.

Sitting on the couch in the small room, I flicked the TV on and cracked open a beer, needing to just drink everything away that I felt right now. The anger was rising up. I was so mad and so angry at myself for letting this happen. Why the fuck didn't I stop it or leave sooner? I just hated myself right now. I was a weak man.

Everything Amy said to me was right. I was pathetic and a coward. She definitely had a bigger cock than I did. I sighed and tossed the beer I downed into the bin across the room. Grabbing another, I didn't hesitate to down most of it.

What the fuck had my life become in these past couple weeks?

The hours flew by, and my phone rang constantly. It was Amy every single time. She was leaving voice mail messages, screaming down the phone, and demanding I come home. The final voice message was her apologizing and saying she wanted to talk when I was ready. I sighed and tossed it to the small bed.

Maybe she was right. Maybe I wasn't worth anything and needed to go back to her.

Checking my watch, I jumped up when I realized it was almost midnight. Fuck. I was meant to go around to Sage's tonight. Fuck sake.

Everything was screwed up. I knew she'd want to touch me. I wanted her to, but it was just harder now. I couldn't handle being touched after having a set of books thrown at me. Amy just lost it. The bookshelf was now empty from the dozens of books hurled into my back, chest, legs, and she even tried to get my groin, which I covered pretty well.

I hurriedly drove to her place. It was a good thing that there was no traffic this late at night and I was able to arrive there in a few minutes.

I parked my car and locked it. I went in, hoping that she was still awake.

Arriving at her door, I wondered if she locked it. I was relieved when it pushed open, and I closed it quietly. Sage was sitting up in the bed, watching TV, when I walked in her room. I just leaned against her doorframe and watched her. She was truly beautiful and so peaceful-looking. I felt somewhat better just being around her.

She looked over at me and smiled softly. "I didn't think you could come over."

"I couldn't not see you. I'm sorry it's so late," I said, still looking at her.

She lay down and patted the bed. "It's okay. Is everything okay?"

I owed her the truth, but I couldn't say it.

I felt like an ass.

"I'm sorry. I've been..." How could I get by this without seeming like an arrogant ass? I blew out a breath and scratched my neck. "I'm just sorry. You've eaten, I take it?"

"No," she said quietly, looking at me with her big eyes.

I frowned, sitting down on the bed beside her. "No? You've got to eat. Why haven't you?"

She sighed, shrugging. "I wasn't hungry. It was a long day, and by the time I realized I hadn't eaten, it was only like an hour ago, so I didn't see the point."

"Come on." I jumped off the bed and pulled the covers off her. "Tell me all about it while I cook you dinner. You need to eat."

"Ollie," she grumbled as I pulled her out of bed.

I smirked, ignoring her. "Come on. You two need food." Leading her out to her kitchen, I sat her on the stool and walked over to the fridge, peering in to see what I could find. "So, why was your day such a bad one?"

"I told my parents I was pregnant," she said out of the blue.

"Oh?" I stood up and looked at her. I wasn't expecting that to come out of her mouth, but I knew it couldn't be kept a secret for much longer.

She rested her chin on her palm and nodded, sighing. "Yeah. It was a long afternoon, sitting and talking. I'm just sick of worrying and crying over it."

"You're not happy about the baby?" I asked.

How could she be? I was basically trapping her.

145

She stood up and walked around the island towards me. I sensed her hesitation before touching me. She went to wrap her arm around my waist, but she stopped.

Was I that obvious about not liking to be touched?

Sage leaned against the counter and looked at me. "Don't get me wrong. It's just when I imagined myself pregnant, I was married and in love. Not the case here, is it?"

She was right. Absolutely right.

"Sorry. That's my fault."

"Don't be sorry. It takes two to make a baby. We can be friends and have a baby. No pressure, okay? I'm not forcing anything here. I don't have expectations." She smiled.

"That's so fucked up." I let the words out before I stopped myself.

How could she not see what she just said was crazy? Two people, who knew fuck all about each other, were now having a baby. It was insane. Fucking fucked up.

"Indeed." She giggled.

I nodded, returning to her hot plate and turning it on. The red glow somehow made my hip sting without realizing it. I sighed, grabbing a pot and filling it with water.

"Your parents. Tell me what happened. Shit. I should have been here for you sooner."

"My parents are happy. That's the whole shock of it. They're not pushing me with asking who the father is, but they said this isn't a bad thing." She laughed. "God, it's insane. I was expecting them to go and kick me out, but they're happy about it. And I agree. It's not bad."

When I put the pasta in the pot, I turned around and walked over to her again. Grabbing her waist, I picked her up and slid her on the counter, skimming my mouth over hers. "It's not. It's a good thing. A very good thing."

Her breathing picked up, and I dived in, kissing her before she spoke again. I needed her badly, but I didn't want to push it. I couldn't. Well, I could, but I knew that she didn't want it. For now, I needed to just fucking kiss her. I had to taste her on my lips.

My cock instantly hardened, proving that I had no control when it came to her and how she affected me.

"Today...Seeing you at work, God, I was so hard." I groaned, running a hand through her hair and tugging the braid backward, so her head tilted upright.

"I thought you were mad." She moaned, hissing as I bit her lower lip.

I smirked. "I can't get mad at you. You're too pretty."

She broke the kiss by laughing over my mouth, and I found myself loving that sound. Her hands wrapped around my back and I tried not to give anything away, but her hands were resting on my shoulder blades, and well, it hurt a lot.

"Cooking me dinner. I'm very impressed. Do you cook a lot?" she asked, her thighs wrapping around my waist tighter.

I smirked. "My mother taught me that the way to a woman's heart was to cook for her." I leaned in closer, placing a line of kisses against her mouth and up along to her ear, then whispered. "But no. I've never willingly cooked for a woman like this."

"Well, I'm honored you're doing so. Thank you," she whispered, running her hands through my hair and tugging it as our mouths connected again.

I kissed her more forcefully as images of Amy flashed through my head. I wanted to get rid of Amy. I didn't want to think about her when I was with Sage. Right now, Sage was what I wanted. She made me feel things again.

After we ate, we ended up lying back in her bed. My body moved against hers as I kissed down her collarbone and slid my hand up her top, feeling the smoothness of her skin. I groaned as she bucked her hips and I rolled my hips into her. I'd damn well near blow a load if she kept going.

My cock was itching to slide inside her, and her bucking hips told me she wanted it too. I wanted to taste her. She was a drug, and I was addicted.

"I want you." I groaned, cupping the curve of her breast with a squeeze.

She pushed into my palm, moaning. "I want you so badly."

"You're so fucking sexy..."

Somewhere in the middle of making my way down her chest with a trail of kisses, she pulled back and gasped loudly. "Ollie! Oh god, you're bleeding."

I sat up and stared at her. I hadn't realized she had her hands sliding up my back. I couldn't speak. I just frowned.

*What?*

"Oliver?" she said again.

I got off her and backed away. Fuck. I never wanted her to see me like this.

She went to get up as well, kneeling on her bed. I could see she was curious. Fuck, how could she not be?

"Let me look. I can help and clean you up."

"No." I finally found my voice. "I need to go. This isn't going to work out with us."

"What? You don't mean that. What's going on? Why won't you let me see your back?" she asked, looking confused and getting off the bed.

"It means what I just said. It means whatever this is"—I pointed between her and myself—"isn't going to work. God, I'm fucking married, Sage. You don't want that shit in your life."

"Ollie." She frowned, running her hands over her face, looking more confused. "I don't understand. We were good. I'm pretty sure we were about to end up naked and have sex. So what changed? Why won't you tell me? I just want to make sure you're okay. Jesus, I don't understand."

I shook my head at her and pulled on my boots. "No. I'm sorry. I thought I wanted it, and I thought I wanted the baby, but who are we kidding? I'm no good for you. The baby deserves a father who's strong enough to help take care of you both. I can't do that. I won't leave my wife for you."

It needed to be done. I felt like a fucking jerk, but I knew being with her would only hurt her. I wasn't good enough for her. She needed a man who could take care of her. With Amy hot on my ass, I couldn't do that. I couldn't have Sage and our child suffer anything that Amy would throw at them. They needed a man who was strong enough to leave a woman who beat him…and I wasn't that.

"Why come here then? Why give me some false hope that this was working?" she asked, biting her trembling lip.

There was only one way to end this and make her see that I wasn't the man for her. "I wanted to fuck you again. That's all. I love my wife, and I won't leave her."

"I don't believe you," she said firmly. "You're lying to yourself if you believe that."

Looking at the mother of my child one last time, I felt my heart ache as silent tears ran down her cheeks. "I'm so sorry, Sage. It's for the best. You deserve better than this."

"Please." She sobbed. "Don't leave. I can't do it without you, Oliver. You said that you would be there for us."

I shook my head sadly, trying to fight my own emotions as I walked toward her and cupped both her cheeks hard. "I know I did. I shouldn't have made a promise I couldn't keep. I don't want to leave you both, but baby, I need to."

Placing a kiss to her forehead, I brushed her tears with my thumbs and regretfully let her go.

# CHAPTER 13

SAGE

"Dear, you need to eat for the baby's sake if not your own," Mum said softly, stroking my cheek.

I shrugged. "I'm not hungry, Mum."

"I know. Please come eat the soup. It'll help." She leaned forward and kissed my forehead.

She was wrong. Nothing could help the pain I felt right now. The pain of feeling someone walk out of my life before it began. I didn't know what I did wrong, but every day I played that scene over and over in my mind.

We were fine until I began to lift his shirt off and felt something warm and wet. I didn't know why he was bleeding. It wasn't much but enough to worry me that I had scratched him too hard or something.

Mum was still looking at me, waiting for my answer. I sighed. "Okay. Just give me a minute."

"Good girl. I'll go get your bowl ready. Two slices of bread and butter with it?" she asked, looking more hopeful.

I just stared at her. "Don't push it. I said yes to the soup."

"Oh, nonsense. Who doesn't eat bread and butter with soup? Now, get up, and I'll meet you out there." She smiled and closed my bedroom door.

I groaned and pulled the blankets off my body. My legs ached, and my feet were sore. Grabbing a tank top, I slid it on and pulled it down over my very swollen stomach. I looked in the mirror as I re-tied my hair up.

Memories of the day I told my father I was pregnant flashed through my mind.

~

*"You're what?" Dad finally spoke, kissing the top of my head. All I could do was nod as I clung to him, sobbing harder. "Oh, sweetheart, it's okay. It's all going to be okay. Let's get you home."*

*The drive was silent, but Dad held my hand the whole time. Even when we arrived at the house to tell Mum, he never let me go. Mum knew something was up immediately.*

*I couldn't stop crying. I was so afraid to tell them.*

*"Mark, what happened to Sage?" Mum asked, rushing outside and welcoming me in open arms.*

*"Well, it looks as if we're going to be grandparents. I thought Cass would give us that news, but Sage beat her to it." Dad chuckled, hugging me into his side.*

*I sniffed when Mum began to cry. "I'm sorry." It was all I could say. I was sorry that I had gone and done this.*

*"Don't cry, baby girl. Let's get some hot tea boiling and sit down to talk," she said softly, pulling me into her arms.*

~

Nothing could get me to smile anymore except for her and the little kicks she gave me each day. I already loved her with everything I had in me. She was going to be here soon, and I was excited, but also dreading it. Dreading it because then I was really going to be alone, a single parent.

I walked out to find Mum sitting at the table waiting for me. She was my rock throughout this. I couldn't get up and do anything if she hadn't been here to help me.

I was still in the house out the back of my parents'. The second room or the room where Daniel had thrown up was re-painted and made into a little nursery. It was the other thing that made me smile. All the pink and purple was making this so much more real.

"You're going to pop soon." Mum smiled. "You're growing so quickly."

151

I laughed a little. "I feel like it. I'm really uncomfortable right now. Her foot is digging into my ribs. I'm barely sleeping because of her kicking."

"Wait until she's born. You won't be sleeping much then." And with a change of topic, she looked up. "Have you thought of any names?" she asked, taking a sip of her water.

"I can't really decide. It's so hard to pick just one."

That was a lie. I knew what I wanted to call my daughter, but I was afraid because if I called her that, then everyone might know who the father was.

I hadn't heard from Oliver since the day he walked out of here and broke my heart. I didn't realize how much I needed him at that moment when he said it was over. I needed him so much. I knew he was married, and I didn't want to pressure him, but I felt something more for him.

I wouldn't go as far as love, or maybe I did love him.

Whatever it was, there was a connection between us, and I wanted to see where it could lead us. I knew it was dangerous, and I had put him in an uncomfortable position, but what was I meant to do? He was the father of this baby. I wanted him to be around, but it couldn't happen without destroying a happy marriage, breaking apart a family, and hurting his wife, the woman who deserved none of this.

That was what I felt most guilty about. I had gone against all girl codes and allowed myself to do things with him. Even after I knew he was married, I still fucking wanted him.

It hurt too much to think about him. I'd spent weeks replaying our last conversations and wondered if I had kept my mouth shut, would it have ended differently. I just wanted to go back to that night and not mention the blood part.

I pushed him away and lost him forever.

I was eating lunch in silence until the door flung wide open with Cassie walking in. She smiled. "Hey, how's my little ladybug doing?" She sat beside us and rubbed my stomach.

Telling her was worse than telling my parents. I was so nervous, but it turned out she already knew. She guessed it from the size of my breasts at the wedding and the fact I practically inhaled that cold pizza without being hung over. She and Tony were nothing but supportive and excited. If only they knew it was their friend who got me pregnant then left because of the awkward position I had put him in, but I wouldn't cause drama for him. I didn't want to hurt anyone else more than what I have done.

"Ladybug wants to come out." I smiled down at my belly, rubbing it. I wanted her out and in my arms desperately.

"Yeah? Well, I was talking to Dad, and he said your shop is complete and ready. Do you want to go see it?" She wiggled her brows, looking excited. "Because I really do. Please, let us go and look at it."

I shrugged with a sigh. "I don't know." That place reminded me of Oliver when we went over the layouts, but the last time I had been there, there was someone else working, and Oliver was nowhere to be seen.

"Oh please, let me take you there. I'm dying to see what you filled it with, and we can go to the other shops and get some baby things that you need," she asked, and hope was in her eyes. "I know you can't pass up a cute baby store."

I felt awful for denying it and rolled my eyes. She did have a point. "Okay. Let's go and see the shop."

"Yes. I knew you'd cave eventually." She gave a victory punch and got back up. "Okay. I'm going to call Tony and tell him to meet us there. I think Oliver is with him."

My insides froze. What? No. I didn't want to see him.

The entire drive, I was panicking. I was so afraid and nervous and on the verge of breaking down. How could I see him after all this time, now that I was almost eight months pregnant?

There had been no contact since the last time, and seeing him after all this time would be hard.

"Got the keys?" Cass asked, and I looked confused. "For the store silly."

Oh, right. I hadn't even realized that we had already arrived and we were standing in front of the shop.

I pulled it from my bag and walked to the tinted glass door, which kept peering eyes from seeing my big reveal. I pushed it open, and Cassie followed. After flicking on the light to my left, the room lit up, and I looked around with a satisfied smile.

It was utterly perfect. I couldn't wipe the smile from my face.

"Sage, holy shit. This is amazing! My god, I need to buy a lot of things here. Sister discount?" she asked, walking to the large table in the middle and turning the button on. Everything lit up on the white stand with a bright light behind it.

The smell of perfumes filled my nostrils, and I loved it. It was definitely worth coming here for. I walked over to the bath lotions and picked the Forbidden Fruits Scrub. It was a favourite of mine.

"You're going to be working here while I'm home with the baby. You don't need sister rates."

The door opened again, and I froze. Shit.

"Hey. Oh gee, this place looks fantastic. Now Cass doesn't have an excuse not to smell this good." Tony winked and walked over, giving me a kiss on the cheek and my belly a pat.

"Where's Oliver? I thought he was coming with you?" Cassie asked.

I mentally thanked her. I didn't want to ask that since to them we barely knew each other.

He sighed. "Had to go home. I don't know. Something is up, and I'm really confused."

"Why?" The words slipped out before I could even stop them.

Tony sat on the stool behind the counter and scratched his chin, playing with his beard that he'd been trying to grow. It was taking him a while, but he was determined.

He looked at Cassie as she came over.

"Yeah. Why?"

"He's just different. Quiet and always does what Amy says. Haddon said he's barely spoken to any of his family and hasn't seen them for a couple months." He shrugged. "Maybe he's just busy with work."

"Or she's got him harder under the thumb. She is a little controlling, don't you think?" Cassie asked quietly, placing the body oil down and picking up a lip balm to smell.

Tony frowned, giving her a shrug. "She's just upset. I don't know. I haven't been around his place in ages."

"Did he tell you what happened to his arm?" she asked.

"Yeah. He fell off a ladder and broke it." He stood up and rubbed his stomach. "Come on. I'm starving and need food."

All three of us left and went down to the café in the mall. Tony and Cassie went to eat while I strolled the mall. I got a box of Krispy Kreme donuts because, well, how could you just buy only one? I was pregnant and craving anything sweet.

The thoughts of what Tony had said kept going on in my mind. Oliver broke his arm? I didn't know what to think. I felt bad that he wasn't seeing him as much, but I guess Oliver and Amy were trying to work things out and make a go of it.

I wondered if they knew Oliver cheated on her.

I headed into a baby store and looked at the rack of clothing. I didn't need anything else, but it never hurt to keep buying outfits. She was going to look gorgeous with little headbands on. I wondered if she would have his black or my dark brown hair.

It didn't matter as long as she was healthy. That was all I cared for.

Leaving with two bags of things I didn't need, I felt slightly uneasy. A shiver ran down my spine. I kept walking toward the restaurant that Tony and Cassie were eating at, but the feeling wasn't going away, and my baby was kicking like crazy. I was almost at the restaurant when I looked over my shoulder. I didn't see anyone I knew until I looked ahead again and almost crashed into Daniel.

155

"Oh, god. I'm so sorry," I said as he helped me steady myself.

He laughed. "It's okay. What are you up to?"

"Just shopping and waiting for those two to finish eating," I said, nodding towards Cassie and Tony.

"I see. So…You're having a baby? I didn't really see that one coming." He looked at me. I knew he was trying to think who could be the possible father, but I wasn't telling.

I just gave a shrug. "I know. It is very much a surprise." I laughed nervously. I hated talking about it with anyone other than my parents and sister.

It just felt weird. Even Greyson wasn't sure what to think. When I told him I wasn't coming back to school and that I was pregnant, he went into panic mode, hanging up and then calling me back to say he was going to keep an eye out for maternity clothing. Typical. He was due this weekend for my baby shower, and I couldn't wait to see him.

"I should get going, but we should see each other sometime." He flashed me a smile.

I nodded, wondering if there was more to his gesture but didn't dwell on it. "Yeah. That sounds good."

He leaned forward and gave me a hug, kissing my cheek. "It was good to see you, Sage."

Seeing that Tony and Cassie weren't done yet, I went to the bookstore instead. After a while, they came and found me stocking up on more books. Not pregnancy and birth but cooking ones. I wanted to learn how to cook. I was determined to try to do it on my own and take care of myself and my daughter.

~

OLIVER

"Can't you do anything right? For fuck sakes, Oliver, I am so done with your shit. All you do is sit on your ass, and that's it! You're so pathetic. God, I don't know how you look at yourself every day without hating what you are!" Amy screamed, punching the bedroom door.

I had it locked twice. This was the only place I could come and just lie down and not have to look at her. I could handle hearing her voice, but seeing her and not smacking her around the face was becoming more and more difficult.

I hated her, my wife. I absolutely hated her.

"Oliver, open the fucking door!" Her voice was raspy but still loud.

I just lay there and stared at the ceiling, thinking about anything else but her screaming. For some unknown reason, she was mad all the damn time.

My phone buzzed in my pocket, and I grabbed it. If Amy knew I'd been texting Tony, she'd flip a lid. I was apparently not to be trusted on my phone anymore. All my calls were monitored. If my parents called, I'd have to have them on speaker so she could listen in. She even put an app on my phone to let her know my movements each day.

Work then home. Work then home. That was all I ever went each day.

I should have left when I had the chance months ago, but I fucking came back home to give my marriage another shot after Amy begged me to come back. She'd even promised to go see someone to do with her anger, but that never happened. A few days after I came home, she swung my old cricket bat into my back and threatened to call my parents and tell them that I was beating her up.

My parents and I weren't talking anymore. I just couldn't do it anymore and ignored all their calls. Amy seemed happier when I did that. But my brother was still persistent, and I couldn't keep up the lies anymore.

I sighed, reading the message from Tony.

*Come around for dinner?*

157

Pushing everyone away was the easiest thing to do. I couldn't do anything else. I was weak, and Amy reminded me of that every single day. Typing back a quick message, I told him I wasn't up to it, and we could do it another time. Then I erased the messages.

I couldn't tell him the truth that my wife had banned me from having friends.

Why did I stay? I had no idea, but I knew she'd make my life a living hell if I left. I hated that I was stuck here. I wanted to leave and just get out of here and never see her again. Doing it wasn't that easy though. She'd find me and bring me back.

God, I hated this. I fucking hated the pitiful man I had become. My confidence had been shot through a wall. I was nothing. I was just nothing but worthless to her. She had burned it into my mind that I was as good as nothing.

I asked her why she didn't just leave if she hated me so much. She just laughed, slapped me across the face, and walked off.

My sex drive was shot. I didn't want it anymore. Even jerking off hadn't happened in months. There was no need for it. I felt nothing.

The only thing I felt was something for a woman I had pushed away. She'd never want someone like myself. I couldn't even take care of myself, let alone her and our child. A daughter, I'd been told. The night Tony let it slip that Sage found out she was having a girl, I cried.

I cried because I wanted to be there for both of them. I wanted to protect them and show them both the world and what it had to offer. But here I was, stuck in a prison with a woman who changed her mood within a few seconds. I couldn't keep up, and I was done trying to.

I gave up months ago. Now, I rarely spoke to her and just did what she said, hoping that it was enough to keep her happy.

Cooking dinner one night, I had burned the onions on the frying pan. Next minute, a wooden rolling pin came banging down on my arm, snapping my wrist instantly. It was the worst pain I'd ever felt. Actually, no, it wasn't. The worst pain was walking out and leaving Sage. It killed me every day.

Sleeping seemed an easy escape, and I finally dozed off.

~

I woke up to more screaming, but it wasn't Amy doing the yelling. It was Tony.

*Shit.*

I jumped out of bed and pulled on some clothes while they were going at it loudly.

"Get out of my house! You can't just show up here!" Amy hissed.

"Your house? What the hell is your problem? Where is Oliver? Why the fuck isn't he calling back or seeing anyone?"

"Oliver is fine. I suggest you get out now, or I will call the cops!" she screamed.

*Fuck. I need to get out there.*

Tony laughed as I was coming out. His eyes narrowed on her as he waved his arm in the air. "Go ahead and call. You're the crazy bitch they'd lock up, not us."

Shit. It wasn't going to end well for him or me soon.

He looked up when I walked out, and he froze. "Get your things, and we're leaving. Don't fucking argue with me, mate. I mean it. I will keep hold of her. Just grab a bag."

"Oliver is fine. Aren't you, dear?" I could sense the threatening anger in Amy's voice, and I just looked at her.

Could I keep doing this? Living in a lie? Being with a woman who controlled every aspect of my life and flipped out on a spur, making me regret things? She loved it when I was unhappy and had me absolutely loathing myself.

I had zoned out, not paying attention until I felt a hand on my shoulder, which I jerked away. I hated being touched. I hated that Amy had me afraid of people touching me because all I was used to was her hitting me.

"What do you need? Anything or are clothes just okay?" Tony asked softly, noticing my fear.

159

I had tried so hard to mask these feelings. I never wanted anyone to see what was really going on here. It was a humiliation, a complete embarrassment.

"Uh, I…" I said. I couldn't look at him.

"Oliver." Amy hissed. "You're not leaving."

"Oh, shut the fuck up. He's going, and you're not going to do a damn thing about it. If you do, I sure as hell will do something about you." Tony narrowed his eyes, walked closer to her, and pointed his finger into her chest. "I don't know what the hell you've done, but I promise if I find a single mark on him that came from you, you're going to regret it. You can't control him anymore, Amy. I heard how you spoke to him a couple hours ago when I stood at the front door. It ends today. He's coming with me, and he won't be back."

She looked shocked, and he was furious. She slapped his hand away and gritted her teeth.

"You just believe what you want to. You're the one filling his head with lies."

They were soon back into it, yelling and screaming at each other. I left them to it and walked down to the room I had been living in. It was a tiny room that gave me some peace. Sighing, I grabbed the duffle bag and tossed my things back in it. I also grabbed the phone charger and car keys.

I didn't need anything else in this house. It wasn't my home anymore. I felt like a child, afraid to do anything for fear of getting punished.

After grabbing what I needed from the bathroom, I looked at myself in the mirror. There was a faded bruise on my chin and a scratch along the side of my neck going down to my collarbone. I slammed the cupboard and made my way out to the two who were having at it as if they were on a battlefield. Tony was finally seeing her true colours.

"I'm ready." My voice came out much stronger than I thought it ever would. I was a fucking mess.

Tony looked over, and relief flashed through his eyes. "Good. Thank fuck. Now let's go."

"Wait," I said quietly.

I looked down at my hand, shakily stretching out my long fingers and bruised knuckles. I reached up and began to slide my gold wedding band off, or as I referred to it now, the collar she had on me. I looked up at Amy who was wide-eyed and stunned. After a split second, she was staring at me with fury. Her rage was coming back to boiling point.

"You're making a mistake." She stepped forward, but Tony pulled her back. She flung her body around and clocked him in the jaw with her fist.

He pushed her to the chair we used to sit on instead of the couch and rubbed his mouth. "Fuck, you're insane!" He snapped.

I slid the ring in my pocket, agreeing with him. I shook my head and picked up my bag. Walking to the front door, I looked at her as she sat on the chair, glaring at me. "It ends today. I'm done and want a divorce."

With that, I walked out of the place I now called my prison.

Tony never said anything while driving back to his place. I didn't know what to say as well. I hated that he had to see all of that.

It didn't take long, and I was soon in his spare room, sitting on their bed. Cassie never said anything when we walked inside. She just smiled and kept cooking.

My phone was going off constantly, and I ignored it, but I was going to keep all the messages. I kept everything she sent me. If only she knew I had taken photos of all the injuries she inflicted. The hurt and pain I constantly received from her was all saved in a security-hidden app that she couldn't get into.

There was a soft knock on the door, and Tony walked in. I had been so afraid of everything that even the softest sounds had my heart racing. It was humiliating to feel this way. Now that others knew, I wondered what they thought of me.

"Mind if I come in?" he asked with hesitation.

161

I shook my head, looking away. "Not at all. I'm sorry for all this."

"Don't, mate. Don't you dare apologize, especially for her. I don't want you to worry about anything while you're here. Sleep and just take it easy," he said quietly. "You don't need to do anything."

I nodded, resting my forearms on my thighs. "Okay."

"I have to ask—" he cocked his head to the side as his brows dipped "—where's the couch?"

I laughed quietly, rolling my eyes. "She was cold, and we had no firewood, so she cut it up and used it in the heater."

"What the fuck?" He looked bewildered as he grinned, running a hand through his hair. "Didn't she think it'd be just easy to order a load of wood from her old man? He does that for a living."

"You'd think. Oh well, least it was only a cheap couch." I tried to see the funnier side in it, but it wasn't funny when I came home from work to see her with a saw in the living room.

He stood up and sighed, looking back toward me. "Can you do one more thing for me?"

"What's that?" I asked, looking up at him.

"Just please, don't go back to her. You deserve better than that." His voice was shaking, and before I knew it, he was breaking down in front of me. "Fuck, I should have known sooner that something was up."

I shook my head, not stopping my own tears. I cried all the damn time and hated it. "Don't feel sorry for me. I'm a grown man and should have stopped it when it first happened. It's no one's fault but my own."

"No." He cleared his throat and spoke firmer. "It's not your fault. None of this is."

I wished he was right, but I knew it was my fault. I should have been man enough to stop it and piss her off when she first flipped out. I let it go on and let her continue with it all. She thought it was okay to hurt a man, and I only proved to her that I was weak.

I didn't have fight left in me.

"I think I might grab a shower and just sleep. I, uh…I will talk more when I'm able to speak about it. Right now, I'm too damn ashamed of myself. Do you mind giving Mum and Dad a call and letting them know not to go near her or the house? I don't want her doing anything to them," I asked, getting off the bed. "God knows what she would say to them."

He nodded. "Of course. Just tell me one thing. Was it bad? What she did?"

I sighed, giving him a sad look and nodding. "Fucking brutal."

# CHAPTER 14

SAGE

I walked out of the house and let the warm, soft breeze hit my skin. I made my way toward the main house. I was really excited and so happy right now.

I could hear everyone talking, and the smell of pastries and summer fruits flowed underneath my nostrils as I entered the large kitchen.

I was wearing a maxi dress. It was the only thing I could wear without feeling too uncomfortable other than my yoga pants, a maternity bra, or tank top, which I wore a lot when I was alone and let my stomach hang out. The restriction of clothing just made me feel tight and bloated.

"Aww, you look gorgeous!" Cassie smiled, snapping a photo of me.

I laughed, turning on my side as she motioned for me to do so she could take another photograph of my pregnant stomach. I looked at her dress and grinned. She was beautiful.

"As do you."

She giggled. "I know. You get your looks from me anyway. Okay, no more pics for now. I need to save the battery life."

"Always the one to take credit." I teased as she hugged me.

Dad walked over and wrapped his arm around me. He had a plate of food in his free hand. "Picked a name yet? I'd like to call my granddaughter something other than a ladybug."

Cassie laughed loudly. "Dad, that's the name Sage picked."

She gave me a wink to tease our father.

"Of course, it isn't. Dear god, you're going to give me a heart attack you two. Now I need to go before your mother catches me sneaking the food away." He kissed us both on the cheek and went to his office. It was a "girls only" morning.

Blindfolded, I was led into the living room. I could hear some hushed whispers and wondered what was going on. The cover was ripped off, and I was met with the rest of my family, all women, of course. Cousins, aunts, both grandmas, and to my surprise, Greyson. I smiled widely, feeling slightly overwhelmed at everything. I looked around. Everything was decorated with pink and very girly.

"Welcome to your baby shower, darling," Mum said, coming over and kissing me gently on the cheek.

Gifts. Oh god, did I receive some amazing gifts. The beautiful things people had brought, and gosh, the tiny clothing were all so adorable. I loved each gift so much. To my surprise, Mum and Cassie had brought me a pram, which was the one I wanted to get, and it made me cry with happiness.

I wanted to push it around the house, and I did just that with a small teddy bear inside. Plus, I carted everything back to my home in it, saying that it was much easier than carrying everything by hand as my excuse.

Playing so many games today had me worn out, mostly from laughing. My sister trying to fold a cloth diaper was pretty damn funny. "That's it. I will never have kids!" she announced and tossed it away from her.

I couldn't fold a cloth nappy if I tried, and I was sticking with the disposable ones.

"You look so well for someone who is almost nine months pregnant, Sage. Are you all ready for the big day?" my cousin Ellie asked. She was the cousin we all weren't too fond of, but we put up with her for the sake of it.

I rubbed my stomach when I got a big kick, smiling at her. "I can't wait." I couldn't. I was so excited to have her here and in my arms.

She put her hand over my belly and rubbed it. Funnily, the kicking stopped. She pouted a little and sighed. "We've all been warned not to mention the baby daddy. Do you know who he is or was it just a random hook up?"

My insides tensed up. "I know who he is."

I knew damn well who the father was, and I wouldn't be intimidated about it.

Ellie looked surprised for a moment. "Really? Did he bail?"

"Ellie, how about you take a hint and bail? Your car's waiting for you." Cass smiled, coming up behind us.

Ellie, not taking the hint, laughed her off. "How's married life, Cassie?"

"It's going great. How's single life?" Cass said, and I could tell she was trying to keep her cool.

"You know, fun playing around the field." She looked at me and raised her brows. "Although, this one here has very much changed my priorities. I would die if I got pregnant with a one-night stand and with no man who would stick around to help with that mess."

"Mess?" I asked, gritting my teeth. "My daughter isn't a mess, nor a mistake. Unplanned, yes, but far from a fucking mess."

"Sage, calm down." She sighed. "Overdramatic much."

"I think you need to leave. It's getting late, and you have to drive back." Mum scared us all with her sharp voice as she interrupted. She leant in closer to Ellie and grabbed her by the arm. "I suggest you leave now. Otherwise, I won't bat an eyelash to what either of my daughters will do to you."

She looked shocked, blinking and nodding fast. Her face turned a shade of pink under her mop of blonde hair. It was a funny sight to see her stumble away that fast.

"Now you two, we four need to talk," Mum announced.

"Four?" Cassie and I both said together.

Mum nodded. "Your father and us three. He's inside, waiting."

166

My nerves picked up a little. I had no idea what he'd want to talk about. I followed behind Cassie who looked as equally confused as I felt. It was odd. They rarely wanted to speak to us, since family meetings rarely happened around here. The last one was to do with Cassie's wedding, and she'd organized that herself.

"What's going on?" Cass asked, sitting on the sofa while I chose the large bean bag on the floor.

Lying back and relaxing, I could have easily dozed off. My feet ached. No, scrap that. Everything ached. My boobs were sore, and my pelvis felt shattered and then stuck together with tape.

Dad furrowed his brows, clearing his throat slightly with a cough. "Your mother and I are going away for a week."

"Oh," I said. *Oh, that meant I'd be here alone with no one around.*

Mum looked over at me as I kept my face free from any emotions. "Are you going to be okay?" she asked.

"Course. I won't be going too far." I tried to make light of the situation. I wasn't a baby after all. I was sure I would be perfectly capable here on my own.

"Are you sure? We know it is short notice since we leave tonight, but your pop isn't doing too well, and we wanted to go visit him and to help out a little," Dad said quietly.

My dad's father, our pop, had cancer. They'd given him a year at most. That was three months ago, and he was suffering quicker than expected. The cancer was spreading rapidly.

"It's okay. I promise." I assured them. I could have me time and not get out of bed at all unless it was urgent.

"Cassie, do you have a free room at the house? Maybe Sage could stay with you. I just worry she'll go into labour and be on her own." Mum looked worried.

I wasn't due for three more weeks. It was way too soon to be having little miss. I was sure she'd be content in her little warm home until my due date.

Cassie looked over, chewing on her lower lip. She was nervous about something. "Uh. We've got a friend of Tony staying over. He's a little messed up. I don't know if having Sage around would help or not. I don't want to put her in danger."

"Danger?" my father asked, looking extremely worried.

Cass rolled her eyes, laughing at him. "Not like that. I could ask Tony. I'm sure it'll be fine."

"No," I blurted out. She was either lying, or they were fighting. "Please, I want to stay here, and I promise I will be okay. I can visit her if I need something or have her come here. I don't need a babysitter. It's a week. I am good on my own."

It was a feeling I wasn't too sure I liked. I didn't like feeling as if people needed to watch over me. I could do things on my own, and I even proved that while I was away at school. It was time for me to be alone and to do things without help from others.

"Plus, if I go into labour, she's just a phone call and a five-minute drive away. I will be fine here."

Agreeing that it was a problem solved, I began to wonder who the friend was that was staying over her and Tony's. She didn't mention it to me before, and I was a curious girl at times. Maybe it was Daniel, and she didn't want to say. My mind did flicker over to Oliver for a slight second, but I doubted that. He had his wife at home with him.

A pang of jealousy flooded my insides. I hated his wife. I shouldn't, but I did. She got to have him, and I didn't. Our child didn't get to have that with him, but his other children would.

"Help me up, please," I asked, blushing and holding my hands up to Dad when he stood.

He came over, bending down and helping to lift me. "God, you almost broke my back." He teased with a wink.

I laughed, acting offended. "Thanks a lot, old man. Now I won't eat."

He chuckled. "I don't think that's possible. Plus, I ordered you some Chinese since we're leaving in an hour."

My stomach suddenly grew hungry. "Yum. Thank you." I turned to Mum and hugged her. "Thank you for today. It was lots of fun."

"Don't thank me, dear. I'm glad you enjoyed yourself." She smiled back, hugging me tighter.

They left, and Cassie soon headed out a little after them. I made my way to my room with the Chinese in tow. I was starving but still had lots to clean up, starting with all these gifts. Sitting in the nursery after I showered and changed into some boxers and a maternity bra, I sat on the floor and began to unpack everything and fill out the baby diary that I kept.

My phone buzzed, and I looked down at the text.

*Take it easy on him. Just hear him out before you kick him out. Please.*

I stared at it oddly. Who the heck was Tony talking about?

I thought he had the wrong number. I didn't reply. I just shoved the phone back on the floor and kept going over everything in the baby's room, sorting out the nappies and wipes to go on the changing table. There was so much to put away, and I had a feeling it would take a while.

~

OLIVER

I walked out of the bedroom. Today I was going to do something other than lay in bed and try not to doubt myself and the decision I had made. I headed to the shower. I was going to shave off this pathetic half beard I tried to grow.

The marks on my back had faded. I had a couple scars but nothing that was noticeable except the huge mark on my side from the straightener. I had snapped that thing and everything else she could burn me with. I even tossed the iron in the garbage. She never noticed anyway, as she was too lazy to do the laundry.

Tony was on the couch when I wandered out. It was evening, and he was playing the PS3. He paused the game and sat up. "Hey, you're up."

169

"Yeah. I figured I should get up before the bed grew into my ass." I sat down and rubbed my neck. The shower had done me good and made me feel more alive.

He smirked. "Well, I wouldn't like to be the one to cut it out of you then." He laughed.

I knew what he was doing. He was trying to make me feel better.

Being here for almost a week was slightly difficult. I hadn't a clue what I was going to do. I was ignoring everyone and ignoring all the calls and messages. Amy—well, I didn't open any of her messages or calls. There was a lot of them, and it was well into the fifties altogether. I knew what they'd say, and I didn't want to deal with any of that shit.

I really needed to get a new number.

"Have you decided when you're going back to work?" he asked, making conversation.

"Nah, I'll probably take a while off to sort my shit out. I can't go back there just yet." The last thing I wanted to do was go into work and face everybody.

Tony nodded. "Agree with you there. Now, I say we go for a drive just around town and get something for dinner."

I hadn't been outside since I left Amy. Part of me was afraid to go out there, but I needed to break that habit. I needed to stop being afraid of her. She couldn't control me anymore.

"Where's Cass? I hate that I'm here taking up your space. I'll get my own place soon and let you be newlyweds and all." I smiled.

"You do know there isn't any rush. I think Cass likes having you here anyway. She's enjoying cooking so much for us." He tossed me a controller. "One round and we'll head out for a bit."

Kicking his ass on fight club, we got in the car and drove around the city, going nowhere in particular but just driving around. I sat back and stared outside at the traffic. Tony was acting weird, quiet and strangely weird. I noticed his jaw had a nice bruise on it from where Amy slugged him one.

"Did she ask about it?" I asked, referring to Cass.

He nodded. "I didn't tell her anything. I just said I hit it on the car door and she told me I needed to open my eyes more. Our wedding photos aren't too good. My eyes are half closed in a lot, and she's pissed."

I laughed. "You'll have to have a repeat then."

"True. She might make me dress up in a suit just to get some redone." He grinned. "It's not too bad. It doesn't hurt anyway."

"Where did you say Cassie went?" I asked.

"Baby shower. Sage had hers today and no guys allowed, apparently," he said.

I felt my heart quicken and stomach tied up in knots. "Oh, really? Is she doing okay?"

He sighed, shrugging. "Not sure. She's quiet. Won't say much, but she's excited about the baby coming."

How could she not be excited?

It was something I had always wanted, and finding out the real reason Amy never fell pregnant shattered me. I couldn't believe she had lied to me for so long about it, even faking her tears each month with the negative pregnancy tests. I hated her for it. She took the one thing away from me that I really wanted.

Now, I was going to lose probably my only chance of ever having that again.

I sighed. "I'm going to be a father," I said quietly.

Tony snapped his head to look at me, his eyes bright and wide with horror. "Amy? She's what? She's knocked up?"

"Nope," I muttered. "Good thing that never happened. Blessing in disguise."

He frowned. "How then? I'm not following."

"The girl from the club. She's pregnant." Sage. I wanted to say her name so badly.

171

He was silent a moment, giving the nod. "I see. Come on. Let's go get something to eat. I'm starving, and I take it you are too."

"Yeah, I am actually. Haven't eaten in a while." I hadn't eaten anything decent was more like it.

He and I headed in a small Thai place that probably had the best food in the city. We used to come here often and order a ton of shit we didn't need but still managed to eat it all.

We decided to eat back at his place and bought food to-go.

Tony started driving, but I realized he wasn't heading to his place. It wasn't until he parked out on the side of the road that I began to feel sick. My nerves were on edge.

"Do you need to get Cassie?"

"Nope. She's probably home now. Go in and see her," he said, giving me a nod.

I tried not to give anything away. My voice remained calm. "Who?"

"Don't who me. I know she's the girl you fucked, Oliver. I'm your best mate. I've known you my entire life, and I can tell when something's going on." He reached in his back pocket and pulled out a photograph, handing it over.

I flipped it over and looked at the image on the gloss paper. It was Sage and me at his wedding, sitting at the table and sharing our dessert together. It made me laugh. God, her halving the already small slice of cheesecake still cracked me up. It was as big as a teaspoon yet she halved the damn thing.

"Doesn't prove a thing," I said firmly, handing it back to him. "It's just a photo."

Tony snorted. "You're going to be a father. Go in there and fix things. She's the girl from the club. I didn't think anything of it until Cass said she wouldn't talk about the kid's father. You said you met a girl at the club we went to, and Cass was meant to pick her up from there that same night. It was her, wasn't it?"

172

"What are you now? A fucking cop?" I grinned, tilting my head back. I couldn't believe it. He knew. He damn fucking knew. "When did you find out?"

"Couple months back. Look, I know things with Amy aren't good, but mate, that girl in there is having your daughter. Go and try. I'm not saying ask her out or put a ring on it, and I know she won't force you into anything also. Just see if you can start up a friendship or something. She's alone too, and you need each other." He rubbed my shoulder, and I just stared out the window.

"They both can do better. They don't need my past brought into their lives. I'll only screw it up. That's all I do," I muttered.

He sighed. "No. You don't screw anything up. You're not a screw-up. If you don't go in there, you'll regret it. I just want to see you happy. This could be what you need. A new start and something to be happy about."

I grimaced. I hated that he was right, but I didn't want to burden her with anything. "I don't know."

"I've already messaged her and told her you're coming over. She's expecting you." He shrugged.

"You what? Are you fucking kidding?" I groaned, running both hands through my hair.

He laughed. "It was more of a cryptic message. Take dinner in. Cassie already got me some, so you can take mine to have. Eat and talk about whatever. I'll pick you up later…unless you sleep over." He winked, assuming something more would happen.

"Do I get a say in this?" I asked, shaking my head in frustration.

"Nah, you don't. Unless you don't really want to go in there. Then we can go and spend the night on the PS3 and getting drunk. The choice is yours." He shrugged, tapping the steering wheel.

Fuck. I hated when he was right.

I knocked on the wooden door of the guesthouse. Fuck, I was nervous. My palms were sweaty, and my heart was racing. I didn't know what the hell I was doing.

"I'm in the baby's room. I can't be bothered getting up, Cassie. You're going to have to come to me," Sage called out, and I could hear the tiredness in her voice.

Pushing the door open, I closed it quietly behind myself and made my way down to the second room. My heart was ready to explode at the sight of her on the floor and very pregnant. She glanced up and did a double take. I knew I was the last person she'd ever want to see.

"I, uh…I wanted to see if you'd talk to me. If not, I can just go."

*Well done, dipshit.* How fucking stupid did I sound right now? Of course, she wouldn't want to see me after what I had done to her.

I glanced around nervously, trying not to make eye contact. It was hard. She was so damn beautiful, pregnant and sitting on the floor like that folding up the pink blankets.

Sage just stared. I knew this was hopeless. I turned around and began to walk back to the door when I heard her.

"I've got a lot of Chinese, which I can't eat on my own. Are you hungry?"

I stopped and let myself smile a little. "Yeah. I brought some Thai over also."

My nerves soon faded away when I heard her soft laughter.

"Okay. Give me a moment. I need to put a shirt on."

I just hoped I wouldn't piss her off afterward. The last thing I want to do was hurt her in any way possible. She, though, held all the cards that meant the most to me. She had the power to really hurt me.

I was already fucked up. I just wanted to know if I had a slight chance at getting to know the mother of my daughter and my daughter.

A guy could only hope though.

174

# CHAPTER 15

SAGE

Holy shit. After all this time away, I thought I'd be immune to him, but it was not the case. I was trying to hide the utter shock and slight happiness I felt because he was here. Oliver was here, and he brought dinner over.

Another thought hit my mind. What if he wanted to take our daughter away and raise it with his wife? Over my dead body, that would never happen. I'd make sure to breastfeed for as long as possible with the excuse that she couldn't be away from me.

I quickly and shakily slid on a tank top and pulled it down over my stomach. I couldn't believe this was happening. Now I understood what Tony's text had been about.

I walked out and found him standing in the kitchen, leaning against the wall. Damn, he made something so simple and natural look gorgeous.

"Hi," I said, trying to find my voice.

He straightened up and my insides slightly melted with the smile that lazily appeared over his face. Walking toward me, he stood just a foot away and stared at me. "Hi."

My heart was going insane at being this close to him. I wasn't getting my hopes up though. The last time he had done that, he crushed them in an instant. I was still getting over that night.

"You're hungry, yes? Because I am. I just need to reheat mine."

"Sit. Let me do that," he said softly but not making any intention to move at all though.

A smile crept further across my lips. "I'm sorry. I'm still trying to figure out if you're real or a dream." I laughed nervously. Maybe I was half-asleep and dreaming this.

He chuckled. "I'm real, and you look good. Shit, no. I mean, beautiful. You look beautiful."

"So do you. Well, not beautiful but handsome and cute."

"Cute?" He raised a brow, looking amused.

I nodded. "Yes. Would you like a drink? I don't have alcohol though."

"Whatever you're having is good." He smiled and stepped aside as I walked to the fridge and grabbed the sarsaparilla. It was my craving and guilty pleasure. He spoke again, "Your parents won't come in, will they?"

I shook my head as I grabbed two glasses. "No, they're away for the week. Gone to see my pop who's not doing too well."

"Sorry," he said softly, making his way around here. "You're going to be alone?" He frowned for a slight second. "I don't know if I like that idea or not. When are you due?"

My breathing hitched at the mention of the birth. "Three weeks. I'm fine though." I couldn't help but laugh. "Ollie, I'm good. I've been alone before, and I can do it again."

He seemed pained for a moment. He blinked his eyes hard while he just nodded silently. He sighed and reached over, taking hold of the drink, or so I thought. He instead took my hand and pulled me a little closer to him.

"Sage, I'm really sorry for leaving you." I could hear the remorse and regret in his voice.

I kept my head down. I couldn't make eye contact, not with these hormones right now. "It's okay. I know I must have freaked you out somehow. It's okay. I don't blame you for leaving."

"What? Sage, look at me." His fingers brushed underneath my chin and tilted my head back. His eyes glassed over with his tears. "You didn't do anything wrong. It was me. I can't go into it, but please, trust me when I say you didn't scare me off. I wanted to

177

stay. It was just too hard. I don't want you to go through this alone. I want to know if you'd let me be in your life, in the baby's life."

My heart began to thump again. I opened my mouth to speak, but nothing came out. I closed it again and tried to keep my emotions in check. "Ollie, I want to say yes, and I can't stop you, but I need to know if you're going to take her away from me." God, I was starting to cry. My eyes filled with tears and my chest was rising and falling as my breathing picked up. "I get that you're married, but she's mine too. She's a big part of me, and I don't want to lose her."

"I left her. I'm getting divorced. She is not going anywhere near our daughter," he said, sounding panicked himself. "I promise I don't want to take her from you. I just want to be able to see her."

Divorced?

"What? Wait. I'm confused." I scratched my head, trying to process this new information.

He nodded. I felt his other hand sliding over my stomach, and his fingers spread out over the bump. "I'm staying with Tony and Cassie, just until I get my life on track. I don't really want to discuss things, but I left you before because things weren't good, and I didn't want you involved or hurt in any way with what was going on. I want to be here for you though. That's something I've always been positive about. You're important to me"—he began to slowly rub his thumb in a circular motion—"you both are."

I couldn't help but smile. His other hand slid up and caressed my cheek, wiping away the tears with his soft thumb.

"You're her dad. I want you to be there. I won't push you into anything though."

He smiled weakly and dropped down to his knees. "I don't mind a slight nudge from you anyway."

"Do you want to feel her kicking?" I asked, biting on my lower lip anxiously.

I watched his eyes light up. "Is she kicking now?"

178

I giggled, taking his hands and moving them underneath my top. "She is," I said and placed my hand over the top of his and gently pushed down.

A moment later, a hard kick pushed against his hands. I swear I could have seen the sadness in his eyes, but I had mistaken it for happiness.

"She's so strong. I've never felt a baby kicking before," he said. My insides froze when he leant forward and placed a kiss to my stomach, planting his lips firmly over the spot our daughter was kicking.

When he stood up, I was almost lost for words. He just pulled me close and wrapped his arms around my body. I couldn't wrap mine around him, so I just stood there with my arms pressed to his chest. It felt like an eternity, but when he pulled back, he realized what he had done.

"I'm sorry. I didn't mean to—"

I cut him off. "Don't be sorry. It's okay."

We sat down at the small table with our bowl of food and ate. Talking quietly, he asked about the store and if I liked the shelving. He had done them himself as the first guy fucked it up, as he so eloquently put it. I desperately wanted to ask him what was going on between us, but I got the slight picture that he didn't want anything serious, which was probably best for us both. After eating, I took the bowls to wash them up and made my way back to him. I found him standing in the spare room and leaning against the frame. I watched as he looked around.

Dragging his fingers over the wooden cot, he sucked in a sharp breath. He picked up the light pink blanket draped over the edge and put it back after. Then he made his way to the changing table. I wanted to laugh when he looked at the nappy and dipped his brows in confusion. It was so tiny.

He didn't seem to notice me as he slid the wardrobe across and looked at the mountain of clothing hung and folded in each shelf. Again, he sucked in a sharp breath then muttered a curse word. *Shit*, I think it was.

179

I stifled a giggle as he closed the door and his eyes then met mine.

"Well, fuck," he murmured.

"A lot to take in?" I asked softly as I walked into the room.

He shook his head, tapping his fingers against the wall. "Nope. It's exciting. I just kind of wish I could have helped you more. I feel a little useless that I didn't get her anything and just tossed it all on you."

"Ollie." My smiled faded as I noticed his limp posture and a defeated sadness in his eyes. "I didn't expect you to pay for anything. If it makes you feel better, you can buy the rest of the things we'll need."

His lips parted, eyes widening. "You mean you still need to get more than what is in here? Shit, how many things does a baby need?"

I laughed, shaking my head. I felt a warmth spreading through my insides as he cupped my cheek with his warm palm, caressing it with his thumb. I leant into his hand, welcoming it.

"I want to call her Olive and let her have your surname," I said nervously, looking up into his eyes.

Oliver's face was expressionless. He just stood there with his eyes on mine, and before I could grasp what was happening, he had his mouth against mine, kissing me as his other hand slid around and rested on my lower back. His fingers dug into my skin as he held tightly.

Stop.

We should have stopped, but I couldn't help it. I grabbed him back and fisted my hands through his hair. Hearing the deep groan from his throat as we kissed, I moaned. It had been so long since we last kissed and damn to hell if I wasn't going to enjoy it. I had no idea when it would happen again, and I wanted to make sure it lasted. I wanted him to know that I wanted him.

"Fuck, Sage." He pulled back slightly. "You're killing me, baby, and I can't move away."

180

With that, his mouth was back on mine. His tongue slid inside my mouth as I welcomed it with passion. Our teeth bumped, and we both smiled, but we never stopped kissing. My core was drenched in hormonal temptation. I wanted nothing more than for him to turn me around and take me here, hard and fast, but that wasn't going to happen. I was happy to just kiss him again.

"Ollie." A cry escaped my lips. I was pretty sure he felt it too.

The feeling between us was like he had said: a fucking fire, a raging fire that was burning up and spreading through my veins. As his hands moved, each touch was enough to make me melt.

Pulling back, we were both breathless. He was panting hard as his forehead leant against mine. His dark eyes pierced into mine, and I couldn't help but pull him closer. My hands rested on that toned ass of his as I felt his erection against my stomach. I wanted him closer, but our daughter was kicking and dancing around like crazy.

He smiled and looked down as he felt it against his own skin too. "She's worked up."

"You didn't answer me," I said, trying to hold in my blush.

He cocked his head to the side and narrowed his eyes. "I didn't? Hmm, do you need another reminder on how I feel about naming our daughter Olive Bailey?"

I was officially blushing. "Maybe." I tried to speak normally, but my voice was a breathy whisper.

"It's perfect." He smiled and lowered his head. He placed his lips to mine and bent his knees so he was eye level with me as he gently pushed me back against the wall.

I could feel his intense desire through the kiss.

Finally, I had to push him away. "Do you need to go soon?" I asked. The thought of him leaving left an empty feeling in the pit of my stomach.

"Not yet. We've got to cover a lot of topics tonight. It may take until the morning." He winked.

What was this? A playful Oliver? I didn't think I had seen this side of him, but it was welcomed.

I reached out and slid my arms up the front of his top. He sucked in a sharp breath as he watched my hands moving over him. It was almost as if I was hurting him, burning him with my touch, and I didn't know if he was afraid of me or not. I wanted to ask why he always did this, or why he jumped and pulled away or froze.

~

OLIVER

I reached out and touched her. This couldn't be real. There was no way that I finally had her in my arms again and that I was able to kiss her, touch her, and talk to her.

I had wanted this for so long.

She made everything feel better. She made me forget.

I forgot about the past year and the shit I went through. Just one look from her and I was completely fucked. All thoughts left my mind, and all I could see was her. Her eyes had me locked in some binding spell that I didn't ever want to come up from drowning in them.

I felt like a man with her. She made me feel like a man.

I was in complete charge. She never once questioned anything. I wasn't told to fuck off or get out. I was welcomed with a smile—a smile that shook the metal lock around my heart that I put up months ago.

"Are you okay?" I asked her. I didn't want to hurt her.

"Mm," she said sleepily while adjusting the pillow underneath her stomach. Then she opened her eyes.

I smiled and reached across the pillow, brushing a strand of hair behind her ear. "You're beautiful," I whispered, meaning everything bit of it.

She had a sleepy smile on her face, and she nodded. "So are you."

I laughed because I wasn't. "Okay." It was all I could manage.

"Oliver," she whispered. "Are we friends who kiss sometimes?" she asked.

I tensed up. I didn't know what we were. I couldn't give her a full-on relationship right now. I wanted to, but I was too mentally fucked up for that.

I just shrugged, sliding my hand over her stomach and leaving it there. "I don't know. Does it bother you if we're just friends for a while?"

"Who kiss occasionally?" she asked, still smiling even though her eyes were closed.

I leant forward and kissed her softly. I pulled back before she could kiss back. "Who kiss and have sleepovers."

Her eyes shot open, but she still looked tired. "You're spending the night?"

She didn't hide her shock when I nodded. "Yes. Does that surprise you?" I asked.

"A little. I know you've just ended things with your wife and I'm not expecting commitment from you. But when your daughter is born, please don't come and go and change your mind. It will kill me even more than it has done these past months."

It was my turn to try and hide my surprise. She had been that upset? Fuck. I hated that. I hated hurting her. I damn well wasn't going to hurt her again or our daughter.

"I'm going to be there every step of the way. You and Olive, you're going to be taken care of."

"Goodnight, Ollie," she mumbled and was soon fast asleep.

I lay on my side and just watched her sleep for a couple hours. She was peaceful and beautiful this way. My eyes ran down to her stomach that was resting over the bright green belly pillow that slid between her thighs. I was going to be here for her, for both of them. I had to. After what I put them through, it was the least I could do. My hand shakily reached out and rubbed her stomach. I smiled as I felt a strong kick. That was my daughter, Olive.

183

The vibrating in my ass stirred me from my almost comatose state, and I reached to check the message. Tony, of course, he was checking up on me.

*Where are you? You need a lift back?*

I should leave. Instead, I sent a message back.

*Nah, going to stay here. See you tomorrow. Make sure Cass doesn't kill me when she finds out about Sage and me.*

She was definitely going to kill me. I got her little sister pregnant then left her to deal with everything alone. It had to be done. The things that could have happened to her was causing bile to rise in my throat. Pushing those thoughts away, another thought hit me like a ton of bricks.

Fuck. My parents needed to know about the baby and Sage. Shit, of fucking course.

Sitting up, I pulled my clothes off, so I was just in boxers, and I climbed in beside her. I had no idea if I was going to be able to sleep. Probably not since my cock was straining against my boxers. I wanted her so bad. After kissing her, I needed her. I needed to get my fill of her. Once I had her again, I knew I'd never want to give her up again.

She made a noise in her sleep, and I froze. She just rolled over. I moved forward and wrapped my arm around her body. I rested my hand just under her bump and held her protectively in my grasp. She felt so right in my arms. It had been so long since I held a woman like this. Way too long.

"Ollie," Sage mumbled in her sleep.

I kissed her shoulder, hoping she'd soon fall back asleep. Her arm moved and went underneath my hand, moving her fingers, so I was holding them tightly.

"Don't go, please. I'm afraid to be alone," she whispered again.

184

My heart thudded hard. Closing my eyes, I forced the tears away. "I'm right here, baby. I'm not leaving."

~

When I opened my eyes, it was still dark out. I heard the rain bucketing down on the roof, and I knew that it was the main reason why it was still dark. A rainy day always used to be my favourite thing.

Rolling over, I noticed I was alone in the bed, and I frowned, sitting up.

I was about to call out when I heard her walk back in. "Hey, did I wake you?" she asked, whispering.

I shook my head, lying back down. "No. Is everything okay?"

"Yeah, just some cramps. They're gone now." She slid in the bed and pulled the covers up to her chin.

"Cramps? Labour pains?" I asked. That was one way to wake me up quicker.

"No, just like false ones. I get them every now and then." She hesitated and moved closer. "I didn't think you'd stay the night."

I couldn't keep away. I slid my hand over hers and pulled it close to my mouth, kissing it softly. "I told you I wasn't going anywhere. Are you hungry? I can make you something if you like?" I offered, surprising myself at how I really wanted to cook for her.

She well and truly took me up on that offer. Watching her eat was something else. She had maple syrup on her bacon, eggs, and pancakes. I scrunched my nose up at that. She laughed and told me it was really good.

My body agreed when I watched her lick the drizzling syrup off her finger.

"What time do you need to go? Is Tony picking you up?" she asked, her eyes widening. "If he knows, then my sister will know. Oh, god. I'm so sorry I put you in this mess."

I walked over and pulled her against my chest. "Don't apologize. He knows, and I thought maybe we should tell others as

185

well. If I'm going to be around a lot when she's born, then they're going to wonder why. Yeah?" I didn't want to push it, but I didn't want to get a fist to the face from her father when he found out.

"I guess so. Uh, are you, umm, are you planning to tell your parents?" she asked, looking cute as she blushed nervously.

I slowly nodded. "Is that okay with you?"

"It is. They should know, but I don't want them to think that I am like some whore. I know I'm the other woman in this, but I'm not a bad person," she whispered.

"The only woman." I corrected her. "There's no woman in my life apart from you now. I'm getting a divorce as soon as I can. I will make this right for you. Don't sell yourself short. You're amazing, Sage, nothing short of amazing."

She laughed. "Well, now you're just buttering me up and boosting my ego."

I grinned and sat on the bed, watching her as she tied her hair up. I lay back. "What were those other things you need for the baby? You said I could buy them so what is it?" I asked, smiling.

"Oh, I was kidding. I've really got everything," she said then bit her lip. "I guess, we could…I mean, you…you could go into a baby store and look around?"

I frowned. Why did she look so disappointed?

"How about we go? You and I? I'd like to go to the store and see what this body shop of yours sells also."

"You'd want to go there?" she asked. "Really?"

I nodded. "Sure, I do. How about we go to Tony's and talk to them and get it over and done with?" I knew it was going to be bad. To hell with it, the Band-Aid needed to come off.

"Ollie," she said softly. "One day, will you tell me what happened? Why you don't like me touching you?"

My insides stiffened. I didn't realize she caught on to that again. I squinted and sighed. "Sage, it's something that's not pretty. A fuck up. I don't want to drag you down with my problems. Okay?" I said, hoping she wouldn't push it.

186

She looked at me. Her fingers splayed out over her stomach. "Did I hurt you that day? Was it my fault that you were bleeding? That's why you left?" she said.

I could hear the tremble in her voice and the fear that she was the one who fucked it all up.

Shit. I didn't want her to ever think that. I sat up and leant over to her. "Sage, baby, you didn't hurt me, okay? I promise you didn't do that to me."

"Then who?" she asked, wide-eyed and looking for information.

The groan came from my throat before I could stop it. "One day I'll tell you about it. Let's just focus on the good things, okay? I just need you to be here and give me that reminder that there are good things to look forward to, okay. Please?" I begged her with my eyes, hoping she'd drop it.

Her lips were soon against mine, and I felt the smile coming on. "Okay. I can do that."

My mouth pushed back to hers. I laid her backward slowly, never breaking the kiss that rocked me to the bone.

The way she felt on my skin, her touch, and the simple kiss were all so much, too much. I couldn't think straight. I needed to slow it down and not rush it. This was all too new for me, for us.

I didn't want to hurt her.

As soon as I heard the soft moan coming from her mouth, I knew that I was the one who could end up hurt again. Friends— that was what we were.

Friends who just happened to kiss sometimes...Until it became something much more.

That time would soon come, and I wasn't afraid for the first time in months.

# CHAPTER 16

SAGE

"I'm so nervous. How do we play this out? Just walk in and act normal?" I asked, not sure what our next move was. It was awkward, and I wasn't fully convinced this was such a good idea.

We were on our way to see Tony and my sister, wanting to get it over and done with, but I had a feeling this wasn't going to go all smooth and easy. I was very much a nervous wreck, but I didn't want to show that to him and rattle him even more.

I could tell something was going on with him, and as much as I didn't want to pry, I really wanted to help him.

Oliver just chuckled, looking just unsure. "Uh, I don't know. I think we should just go in and see how it plays out." He shrugged, and I handed him the keys to my car. He frowned. "You don't want to drive?"

I pointed to my stomach. "I would prefer you to drive."

He gave me an odd expression, cocking his head to the side but just looked at me for a moment. "You're cute. You know that, right?"

Damn. This guy knew how to make me smile when I wasn't expecting it.

He got in the car and reached over, giving my stomach a rub. "Don't worry. Dad will take care of the driving."

My heart. Oh, my heart. It could have exploded right now.

I knew he was her dad, but to actually hear him call himself that...Holy fuck, that was unexpected.

My chest was rising and falling as he looked up to meet my gaze. I didn't know what to say. I literally didn't know what to say. I

188

didn't even know what I felt. It was a feeling of astonishment, happiness, and a tinge of fear.

I didn't fear him, but I feared what would become if this became more or what would happen if he left me again. I didn't want to be pulled into him and get myself too deep. We were jumping off the deep end right now, and there was no telling what could happen.

Before I knew it, the drive had ended, and we were walking into my sister's living room. It was very quiet. I looked at Oliver who sat on the couch. He patted the spot beside him. With a smile over his lips, he tugged my hand to pull me down beside him, and I did.

"Where are they?" I asked once I was seated, my voice coming out a raspy whisper.

"No idea, but I'm finding it difficult to keep away from you right now though." He leant closer, hand snaking over my stomach and around my waist. He leant into me as I lifted my leg and hooked it over his thigh.

The look he gave me was the same look I was giving him. It was a need to be with him right now, and I wanted him so damn bad.

"Ollie," I said coyly, biting my lip. I couldn't help myself, and I leant forward and pressed my lips against his.

I didn't think either of us was ready to stop, but voices at the front door made us pull apart. Moving not as fast as I would have liked, my leg was still over Oliver's lap, and my hand was fisting his shirt when Tony walked in.

"Oh, shit." His brows shot up, and he blocked Cassie's view, trying to distract her. "Babe, can you see if I left my phone in the car?" he asked.

"Ugh, you're so lazy," she grumbled, her voice fading as she walked back to the car.

Tony walked in and looked at us, his eyes flicking from Oliver's to mine. His voice was quiet and low when he spoke, "You better not have fucked on my couch. Cassie knows nothing, and I can only defend you two so much."

"We didn't do anything." I winked, not giving him any clue to whether he was wrong or right.

He let out a laugh. "Didn't do anything, huh? So, that baby just magically grew inside your stomach?" He winked at us and turned toward their room.

I didn't say anything as Cassie walked in and looked from me to Oliver. "I didn't know you were coming over." She looked at Oliver warily and directed her focus back toward me. "Maybe you should come over a little later, or I can come to you?"

"What?" I asked, confused. "Why can't I be here?"

She shrugged, and I could tell she was uncomfortable about something. "You can't just swing by unannounced."

I went to defend my actions and tell her to back it down a notch or three, but Oliver put his hand over mine, squeezing to silence me. "She's fine. I invited her here."

"You did?" she asked, looking at him confused. "Oh, I didn't know that."

He nodded. "I did. Plus, she's your sister and pregnant. She should be able to swing by whenever she wants. Being alone and this far along isn't worth the risk. She needs her family around."

When she went to walk away, she caught sight us of holding hands, and her eyes grew. It wasn't a happy look across her face as she called out to Tony. "Tony, get in here now!"

There was no denying that she was mad, and when Cassie became mad, there was no telling how long this could last. She had to win every fight. My throat grew dry as I pulled my hand back and placed it on my stomach. I was growing defensive. I was ready to justify our actions for sleeping together, and in my defense, I didn't know he was married even if I still hid it from them all.

"Cassie." Oliver stood, standing at six feet to her shorter frame. "Just hear us out—"

Her hand was the next thing we heard as it connected with his cheek. It was a loud stinging slap, and his eyes closed on impact.

His breathing began to increase as Tony cursed, stepping between them.

Something wasn't right. The way he reacted to her slapping him, it was as if there was more to it.

"Cassie." Tony gritted sharply. I had never heard him raise his voice at her before. "Don't."

"Don't? You cannot be serious." She glared back. "He is married. What the fuck am I meant to do?" Her eyes trailed over to me, and she shook her head. "What the hell, Sage? He's fucking married!"

"Cassie," Tony said again, warning her. "Not the time to do this."

With a scoff, she laughed bitterly. "Oh my god. You knew!" She gritted out, her words loud and full of hatred.

"Lower your voice," Oliver said very calmly. His cheek was a bright red where her hand had met his skin. I wanted to go to him, but I couldn't get up the damn couch.

"Don't tell me what to do, Oliver. This is my fucking house, and here you are hitting on my sister. Are you fucking stupid? She's pregnant, and you're married," Cassie bellowed out, throwing her arms in the air.

Oliver's body was shaking. He was still standing there, but his gaze dropped, keeping his eyes to the floor. I struggled but was finally able to stand up. I couldn't let him take the blame for this. Cassie looked ready to hit Tony as he grabbed her by the wrist.

"Stop," I said quietly. "What is your problem? He didn't do anything wrong."

"Bullshit. He is using you while he's here." She glared and continued with her rant about him being married and cheating.

She was about to find out just what was really going on. I couldn't take it anymore. I didn't want to listen to her accuse him of things he hadn't done or hear the names she called him.

Exasperated and annoyed, I threw my arms up and yelled, "Oh, for the love of god. He's the father of my baby."

It was dead quiet from the moment I stopped talking.

191

I reached out and grabbed Oliver's hand, pulling him to turn around and face me. He looked so sad. It hurt to see him in a type of pain I couldn't begin to understand. I didn't want him to be the one who got thrown shit at. This was both of us. It wasn't his fault at all. Maybe a little since he was married and slept with me, but I didn't care anymore.

Cassie shook her arm free of Tony's hold and crossed both arms over her chest. "He's what? You mean, you and he slept together while he was married?"

I nodded very slowly, highly ashamed of myself.

"I'm married, Sage. You're throwing this all in my face and saying that infidelity is okay. How could you do this to me? You're having a child with a married man." She wailed.

She didn't seriously turn this around to make us feel sorry for her, did she? My god. I groaned, running a hand through my hair.

"You don't know a damn thing about what happened. That's between Ollie and me," I said, trying to keep my voice steady. "I think I should go."

"Good idea," she mumbled. "You're going to kill Mum and Dad when they find out. I hope you're both happy with yourselves. I feel sorry for your wife, the woman you've hurt."

Watching her as she took off down the hall, I jumped a little when I heard the door slam. Oliver jumped also, and his grip on my hand tightened.

"I can't stay here," he said quietly. "I'm sorry. This was a huge mistake."

My heart dropped. Was he talking about us?

I looked up to see Tony nodding. He was looking at Oliver with sorrow. "I'm sorry. I didn't think she'd lash out. I know you don't need to be around that shit anymore, but you don't have to go. Let her calm down."

"Yes, I do. I can't. It's too much right now," Oliver said quietly. He let my hand go and walked down the hall. I saw him go into a spare room and heard the door close.

Tony stepped closer. "Take care of him. I'll sort your sister out, but whatever you do"—he glanced behind him and lowered his voice much softer—"don't let him go back to her. She's dangerous, and he doesn't need to be around that. Keep him with you. I'm begging you."

"What's going on, Tony?" I whispered back. I was confused as hell.

His shoulders sagged, and he shook his head. "Not my place to tell you. He will tell you when he's ready."

Oliver walked out. My head snapped up, and I noticed the bag over his shoulder. He didn't look like the broken man who had just left the room. Instead, he now looked calmer like a weight had been lifted off him. Whatever was going through his mind was nowhere to be seen. He just smiled and gave me a wink.

"Thanks, man." They both looked at each other, and Tony nodded. They hugged briefly, and he turned to me.

"Let's go for a drive. If I remember, I need to brace myself and face those baby stores."

I laughed, unsure what he was thinking, but I wasn't going to question it. "We don't have to go there."

"Well, either that or my parents. You choose." He shrugged. "I'm guessing we should ruin the day even more. So?"

"Your parents', I guess," I said, grinning back. "We may as well rip the whole Band-Aid off, right?"

He just laughed. "True. I don't know. Hopefully, my parents won't be worse."

That I could agree with. The entire drive, I was panicking increasingly. My heart was thumping through my chest, and Oliver hadn't said much. I wanted to ask what happened to him when Cassie slapped him, but I couldn't. He seemed slightly less pissed off right now but still on edge. Maybe going to his parents wasn't the best idea.

I'd soon find out just how much of a home wrecker I really was.

~

193

"Relax. You've got nothing to worry about," I said, leaning in closer to her. My hand was resting against her lower back as I walked her toward the front door of my parents'.

She gave me a pointed look and rubbed her stomach. "Easy for you to think that. I slept with a married man and fell pregnant because he wasn't smart enough to wrap it up. Your parents are going to think I'm a whore."

I laughed. "I wasn't thinking about anything when you dropped to your knees."

She blushed, rolling her eyes. "Wow, so it was my fault. Damn it. I am a whore."

My jaw clenched. "Don't," I said.

After hearing what her sister had to say, I wasn't in the fucking mood. I wouldn't stand and listen to her getting attacked. Fair enough, I was the married man and cheated, but that doesn't give anyone the right to attack her, and I'd be damned if I would sit by and listen to that.

"Ollie, can you stay with me just until my parents get back? I don't think I want to be alone, not right now with Cassie hating me," she said softly, so vulnerable.

I frowned and pulled her to a stop. She didn't look upset over anything, so of course, this surprised me. I gave her a smile and nodded. "There isn't anything to be worried about. I'll be here, okay? You don't need to go through it alone anymore."

"Thanks." She smiled, and I noticed a slight blush on her cheeks. "Something smells really good. Your daughter can probably smell it."

I laughed. "Oh, can she just? Hmm, well, luckily, my mother cooks a lot, so I think we can get little bunny something to eat." I leant in and pulled her closer, kissing her forehead.

My cock was stirring, which was welcoming. It hadn't been any use to me except for taking a piss.

I pulled away before the door opened and led her inside. "Mum? Dad?" I called out.

Sage was behind me walking slowly.

"Oliver? Is that you, honey?" Mum called out, and I tensed. Her tone told me this was about to get very real.

"Yeah, it's me, Mum," I answered.

She came barging into the room and wrapped her arms around me before I could move. She hadn't spotted Sage, which was good, although it wouldn't be too long.

Letting go, she reached up and looked at me the way I hated, with pity. "Oh dear, what's been happening. Amy called and is worried sick about you. She said you took off and hadn't been in touch since."

"Bullshit. She's a fucking liar." I scoffed. I was done with her games.

Her brows shot up, shocked by my outburst. "Oh well, your brother is here and his wife with the kids out the back. Join us for lunch?" She then noticed Sage behind me and raised her brows. "Dear, who's this?"

"Mum," I said quietly, warning her. "I need to talk to you. This is Sage."

"I remember her. She was at Tony's wedding," she said softly. "Oh, Oliver. What's going on? Have you gotten yourself into some trouble?"

"No, Mum," I said. I looked at Sage and pointed to the kitchen. "Hey, did you want to just go in the kitchen. I'll be in there soon."

She looked grateful for me getting her out of here. "Okay. Nice to see you again, Mrs. Bailey." She smiled at Mum and walked by us.

Sitting on the couch, Mum also decided that Dad needed to come in and have this talk. I didn't know what exactly to say or how to say it. I guess the truth was the best place to start. Neither of them was saying anything, but I knew they wanted answers.

195

"I left Amy. The marriage is over. I'm divorcing her." There was relief in the words as I told them both this. I was relieved to say it and actually meant it. "I don't love her, and I haven't for a long time. I won't stay there anymore."

"What?" Dad asked, his voice a small whisper. "Oliver, I knew things weren't good, but you don't mean that. You can work on this."

This was more than embarrassing.

"She isn't the woman I married. Our whole relationship has been a lie. I just can't stay with her anymore, especially since Sage is..." I paused, taking a break and sighing. *Here it comes.* "I slept with Sage, and she's pregnant. We're having a child together."

"How far along?" Mum asked, her voice steadier than I expected.

"She's due in three weeks. I cheated on Amy when things were starting to get rough, and now, well, now, I've made my choice. I know what I want, and it's the woman in there carrying my child. I wanted nothing more than to be a father, and Amy lied. She could never fall pregnant. It was all a lie," I said quietly, dropping my gaze down to the freshly vacuumed carpet. I could see the lines where Mum had gone over.

They never said anything. Mum and Dad shared a look, both mulling it over. I leant back on the couch and waited for the wrath they were about to unleash. Saying it out loud to them, I was mortified and gutted that I stayed with her for so long.

"Are you seeing her? Sage, I mean?" Mum asked, finally speaking after a good ten minutes of silence.

Good question. I knew I liked her, but I wasn't pushing anything.

I shrugged. "We're just friends."

"This is a lot to take in. You're telling us that you've left your wife and now shacked up with another woman carrying your child. How do you know it's yours? She could be saying that," Dad grumbled, rubbing his grey whiskers while sharing a look with Mum.

196

"She isn't like that. She gave me a choice to leave and stay with Amy. She's damn well worried about you two hating her. This isn't her fault."

After explaining in great detail that there wasn't a chance for Amy and me to start over, I had made it extremely clear that Amy was not to know about Sage or the baby. I didn't want Sage involved in any of that. Mum looked up toward the kitchen and laughed softly.

"I'm going to be a grandma again. Well, I guess that's something. Are you planning on living together or will you have the baby on different days to her?" she asked. "This is all new to us. I didn't expect you to come here and tell us this."

I sucked in a sharp breath. "I won't take her from Sage. I promised her that. Whatever she is willing to allow me, I won't fight her on any of it."

"You have rights, Oliver." Dad pressed quietly. "You have every right to go for custody."

Fuck. I just shook my head. "No. I won't do that. Sage and I will sort things out on our own. If we live together, then we will, but for now, I'm just trying to build up her trust. I left her once before, and now I need to prove she can count on me to be there for her and our daughter."

With that, I got up and walked toward the kitchen. I stopped and just watched her as I leant against the doorframe. Sage was sitting down and rubbing her stomach.

She closed her eyes, having a conversation with herself. "You're making me very tired." She yawned. "And hungry."

I laughed at the last part. "Does Mama want something to eat?"

She opened her eyes and looked like she was caught with her hand in the cookie jar. "Sorry. I was just rambling on about nothing."

"Yeah." I walked toward her, then kneeled. I rubbed her stomach. "It sounded like nothing."

197

She let out a soft moan, which did wonders for my neglected dick. "God, that feels good."

I don't think she realized just how sexy that sounded. It took me back to the night she sunk down on my cock and fucked me in the chair.

I pressed my lips to her belly as I kept rubbing. She looked absolutely exhausted.

"I should take you home. You need rest." I stood back up as Mum and Dad walked back in.

"How about you both stay for lunch? We'd like to get to know Sage. If that's alright with you?" Dad shuffled on his feet, looking nervous.

Sage smiled and nodded, and that was how our short visit turned into lunch.

Haddon and his wife, Julia, sat across from us. Their kids were making a mess eating and not taking any notice of us. Sage was quiet, and I didn't blame her. It wasn't the most comfortable lunch we'd had together.

"Oliver tells us you're due in three weeks. Are you nervous?" Julia asked her.

Sage looked up, offering a polite smile. "Very, but more so excited. I just want her out already."

Mum smiled. "I know that feeling. I take it you've had a baby shower with your family?"

I shot Mum a warning look. She was going to say something wrong. I could feel it.

Sage just nodded. "I did, and it was yesterday. It was lovely."

"Did you know my son was married when you decided to sleep with him?" Mum asked. "I can imagine your parents aren't too thrilled being pregnant while you're so young. You have your whole life in front of you, and now that's on hold."

Fuck, she just had to go there. "Mum," I said lowly.

"Oh. Uh, no, I didn't. We were drunk, and that's no excuse, but I don't regret it. I never have, and my parents are very

198

excited. Shocked at first, but they have never pressed to know who the father is. I know what everyone must think of me. It's okay," Sage replied with a shrug. "But it is what it is, and sometimes you can't help how you feel about someone. Even when you try and stay away, it's impossible to keep away."

"What do we think?" Haddon asked. "I met you at the wedding, and you seemed cool, but you also knew Oliver was there with his wife. You don't think it's low to screw him after that?"

"We fucked before the wedding. She was already pregnant at the wedding. We hadn't seen each other since that night, and she found out I was married that day." I glared at my brother.

Mum clicked her fingers together. "Oliver, mouth. Now, I think we can all agree this isn't easy on any of us." She paused and took hold of Sage's hand, squeezing it. "But we've got a new addition to the family. Two, actually. Sage and our granddaughter who will be here in three short weeks. Let's just try to all get along. We want Sage to feel welcome, which she is."

Julia frowned, opening a big trap. "What about Amy?"

I tensed at her name.

"Well, I don't think she's welcome in our home anymore. I never appreciated her anyway. If she can't treat Oliver with respect, then she's got none of ours," Dad spoke up. "Now, Sage, we were wondering since you and my son aren't in any type of relationship. Will you allow him to see the child whenever he wants to? Even allowing him to bring her here?"

God sakes. Why did they have to bring any of this up? They made her seem like she was taking the baby and running.

"You don't need to answer that," I said, rubbing her thigh.

"It's okay, Ollie. I don't mind. I'm not going to ban anyone. You're her family. Ollie knows this. There is one woman who won't be near her, but I won't deny you to see her," Sage said and smiled up at me.

I knew what everyone was thinking. The look on my parents' faces said it all. "Ollie?" Haddon grinned. "You hate being called that."

199

I nodded. "Yeah, but she's fine."

"Wait. You don't like being called that?" she asked, laughing. "You never told me. I've been calling you that for ages."

"Mother of my child, you get privileges." I winked, taking her hand and raising it to place a kiss on her skin. She smiled, and I soon forgot about the tense lunch we were having.

~

Sage was half asleep when we arrived back to hers. She was yawning, and I felt bad. It had been a long day, and an even longer afternoon when my parents decided to ask a lot more questions about her and the baby. Haddon's kids loved her, but Julia was still on the fence only because I knew she loved Amy. It wouldn't surprise me if she went and called her up.

Dad pulled me aside before we left. He was getting his lawyer to organize the divorce and wanted me to get a restraining order on Amy. It was something I wasn't sure I wanted to do. I knew it would be worth it, but that'd mean more people would know what happened between us. The thought of that worried me.

I was running her a warm bath and putting some bubbles in it when she walked in.

"What are you doing?"

"Running you a bath. You're exhausted." I stood up and turned the water off.

"That I am." She bit her lip and looked at me through her dark lashes. "Are you going to join me or is this a one person only bath?"

Damn, if I had this woman naked and lying against my body, then there was no way I'd be able to control the urge I had for her. I stepped closer and caressed her cheek, running my fingers over her soft skin while my other hand played with the hem of her top.

"Would you like me to get in with you?" I asked, low and husky as I began to lift her top up.

200

# CHAPTER 17

"This is really good. Thank you." I yawned again, covering my mouth with my hand as I lay back with my eyes shut. I was too busy enjoying the bath and the massage he was giving me.

Oliver ran his hand over my stomach with some body lotion gel and massaged it slowly. I could tell he was smiling wide.

"You're welcome. Are you comfortable?"

"I won't be able to get out." I laughed, slightly embarrassed. I looked at the tub and my body in it. I was going to be stuck.

"I will close my eyes. Don't worry, I won't peek." He winked. "Unless you want me to, then I can keep one eye open."

I giggled, covering my chest as I moved under the bubbles. I mumbled quietly, "I don't think you want to look at my naked body." I was bigger and not the same as when he had last caught sight of my naked body. I was definitely not thin like Amy.

Oliver must have noticed my sudden mood change. He lent over the tub and tilted my chin up to look at him. "Hey, stop it."

"Stop what?" I said softly, trying not to look at him.

I wanted to bathe with him, but I couldn't. I was so embarrassed about getting naked and sharing a bath with him that I chickened out and kicked him out of the bathroom until I was naked and submerged in the tub full of bubbles. The scent of berries filled the room—my favourite smell.

He shook his head and stood up, reaching for a large fluffy towel. "Sage, if you're self-conscious, then don't be. You, of all people, don't ever need to feel that way."

"Easy for you to say. You're all hot and muscles. I'm carrying around a ton of weight and bloating up. My feet feel like elephant hooves." I scrunched my face as I lifted a foot up out of the water. "See, they're huge."

He just laughed. "All in your head, beauty. Trust me. Now, up you go."

I just lay there watching him as he held a towel out and closed his eyes. I put my hands on the edge of the bath and tried to push myself up. Oh god, no. This couldn't be happening. I lay there while he kept still, but a smile was growing on his lips.

"Umm, I'm a little stuck," I said quietly.

His eyes shot open. He grinned and looked ready to help. "Oh, okay. Umm, hold your arms up," he said, tossing the towel on the towel rail on the wall by the mirror, and looked back at me. He closed his eyes again and leant down.

This was embarrassing. I held my wet arms up as he bent down and wrapped his arms around my shoulders to lift me up. My feet began to move, and soon, all was going according to plan. I was being pulled from the bath, but with his arms around me and moving to a ticklish spot, it didn't take long before I burst into laughter. It made him laugh, but his eyes were still shut tight. Before I knew it, my right foot hit a blob of gel and I slipped back down in the bath with water splashing harshly around me.

Oliver, who was fully clothed, fell as I clung to him tightly. I was still partially submerged in the water when I slipped, so it didn't actually hurt me. There was just a huge splash because Oliver went down with me.

"Oh, god!" I squealed.

He laughed loudly, soaking wet. "Christ." He went to move, but I held him down more.

"No. You will see me naked," I said with big eyes.

"I don't want to hurt you." He grinned, pushing his arms up to take the rest of his weight off my body. He was able to stop himself from completely crushing me, which was a good thing. "I've seen you naked before, remember."

202

The bubbles were long gone. I chewed on my lower lip and wrapped my arms around his neck. "Okay. Can you get up and then lift me up while in the bath?"

If I was going to get out, then I needed to just suck it up. He nodded and moved up. In a quick flash, I was being lifted and was soon standing in the bath as Ollie stepped aside and reached for the dry towel. I had no idea if he looked or not. I was too busy staring at his body. The outline of his muscles was prominent against his shirt.

I groaned internally. Oh, he was delicious.

~

Sitting up in bed after eating last night's leftovers, Oliver and I lay side by side while watching *Breaking Bad*. It was a show he loved, and I hadn't watched yet.

"Oh, god. That's gross." I cringed, covering my eyes with the blanket as a bathtub on the show fell through the ceiling and a man's body came falling.

Ollie was laughing. "You've got a weak stomach?"

"Yes." I sighed, peeking to make sure it was okay to look. I looked at Oliver. "Your parents are nice."

"Nice?" He grinned. "I guess so. They like you. I can tell."

That was a big relief. I was so worried about them not liking me and thinking I was just after him for money or to wreck his life and trap him. That wasn't the case. In all honesty, I felt something for him that I hadn't felt before.

I was terrified of him leaving again. I didn't want to go through it. It was awful that first time.

I asked him to stay with me because I was really terrified. I was scared to be alone and go into labour. My sister was still pissed. I knew that from the message she sent me this evening. Oliver just told me not to respond to her. She was acting petty and childish. Also, she was adding a lot of stress that I didn't need to feel at the moment.

Today was a huge day. It was god awful and emotional.

Julia hated me. She made no secret about that. I was close to breaking down, and all I needed for that to happen was for Amy to barge in here and throw her fists into my face or worse, hurt the baby somehow. It was what I was dreading: her finding out that Oliver and I made a baby when he was married to her.

Some time in the middle of the night, I woke up sweating. I slipped out of bed, taking off the long-sleeved shirt and flannel pyjama bottoms. I crept slowly to the bathroom. My thighs were aching, and my bladder was full.

I wanted her out. I was just over being pregnant.

Coming back to bed, Oliver was fast asleep. He was so cute when he slept. His hand was thrown over his head. The covers showed half his chest and the spread of hair that led down to his boxers.

I slid in the bed. Tossing my belly pillow to the floor, I lay down on my side.

It wasn't even a full minute later, and Oliver's body moved. I froze as his hand slid over my hip and rested on my bump, rubbing it gently. His warm breath hit my shoulder, and I stiffened. My heart beat faster as I felt his hard erection pressed up against my ass.

He was asleep.

*Just sleeping,* I told myself.

His hand began to slide further down, sending heat waves through my body. My core was heating up. The spread of enjoyable tingles surged through my body. I moaned unintentionally, which made his hand stop.

I didn't move.

*Shit. I blew it,* I thought.

That was until his fingers slipped into my panties and down the smoothness until they pressed against my clit. He kissed my shoulder, softly at first as he rubbed my hardened bud up and down. I pushed back against his hardness, and he grunted. His palm cupped me as I ground against him.

"Look at me," he whispered, his voice husky and sleep-laced.

My head tilted back, just enough to feel his breath over my lips before his mouth covered mine. Our tongue danced together as we slowly but still forcefully and passionately kissed. Oliver's finger slipped inside me, causing me to gasp and moan over his mouth at the same time. Reaching around, I found what I was feeling against my ass. I slipped my hand in his boxers and stroked him. The heavy groan coming from his throat had me clenching around his fingers.

He slipped his boxers down, and I rubbed his tip that was covered in his pre-arousal, lubing him up.

"Ollie," I moaned, stroking him faster.

"Shit." He broke the kiss as his fingers left my body.

His hand gripped my ass, pulling the panties down at the back and sliding them off my body. I kicked and tossed them somewhere with my feet.

His teeth bit down on my lower lip as he claimed my mouth once again. His boxers were already off as he pushed me forward. Lying on my side, I grabbed the sheets as he ran his hot length up and down my core. Pushing inside me from behind, he groaned. I tightened around him and moaned loudly. My god, I had forgotten how he felt.

Pure pleasure.

He kept a slow pace as he ran his hand down my thigh and lifted it up to get in deeper. I moaned again. His hand came back up and massaged my breast, gently pinching a nipple. A surge hit my core again, and I pushed my ass out against him. God, I had no idea if I was dreaming or awake.

For so long, I dreamt of this: to be with him again like this.

"I'm so close." I moaned, reaching around to hold his ass.

I kept my leg over his thigh, and he quickened his pace. Our lips crashed against each other, kissing desperately. The taste of him was intoxicating, delicious. I was drunk on him right now.

When his hand came around the front of me, rubbing his fingers over my throbbing bud, I gripped him. My eyes rolled as the feeling spread in my lower belly. I needed a release. All this pent-up emotional stress needed its release.

Our bodies crashed like waves as the tickling feeling began to roll and turn into something more intense.

"Oliver, oh my god!" I cried out over his mouth as my orgasm hit.

He groaned. "Yeah, baby. Let it go."

His thrusts hit me hard, shooting in and out as my body spasmed and I reached orgasm.

"Holy shit!" I gasped, my body hot with his slick sweat.

It wasn't long until he grunted and came, letting his own release out inside me. His strokes slowed down and finally came to a standstill. Our breathing slowed down, and the kisses turned to soft pecks.

As he pulled out, I let my leg drop back down on the bed and kept my body facing away from him. I was absolutely shattered. The man sure knew how to give a reminder.

"Sage, fuck. I'm sorry. That was what, sixty seconds?" He kissed my shoulder again and pulled me on his arm, turning me to face him more.

I smiled sleepily, in a post-sex slumber way. "You made me cum in under sixty seconds. Don't apologize for that."

His smile grew. I had no idea why he would be embarrassed. I wasn't expecting an hour or ten orgasms. What he gave was definitely enough for me, enough to make all my tension to sink away.

We fell asleep naked from the waist down and me lying half on his side. My leg draped over his as his hand wrapped around my back and the other possessively on my stomach. Our baby kicked more than ever after that fun, thrilling cardio exercise.

Oliver woke before I did. I opened my eyes to see him getting back in the bed with two cups: one coffee for him and a tea for myself.

"Good morning." He smiled. His voice was soft.

206

I brushed my hair to the side and smiled back at him. "Good morning. Sleep, okay?" I asked, instantly remembering our midnight romp.

A knowing look came over his face. "Best sleep in a long time, I'd say. What about you?"

"It was definitely good." I hesitated to touch him, unsure where we stood now that we were awake and the sex was over and done with. I wasn't sure if it was just a one-time thing or if it was now friends with sex.

"She was kicking a lot afterward." He ran his hand over my stomach, feeling her foot poking him.

"I want her out." I pouted as I lay on my back. "I dislike the heat and being so uncomfortable."

He looked up at me. "Is there any way to bring on labour?" he asked.

Biting my lip, I nodded. Of course, there was. "Well, spicy foods, castor oil, vigorous exercise, raspberry leaf tea…" I blushed thinking of the others.

"Tell me what else," he asked. "I can see your blushing, and it can't be that bad."

He was right. I was blushing. "Nipple stimulation and sex."

~

OLIVER

*Oh, wow.*

I kept a straight face as I slid my hand up to her breast and began to rub a finger over her bra, teasing her pink nipple through the fabric. "You mean like this?" I asked.

She laughed, covering her blushing face with her hands. "Oh god, I don't know. You're embarrassing me."

"You weren't embarrassed last night." I pulled away her hands one at a time.

Last night. God, my mind was blown. Well, it was more like my cock was blown. Goddamn, feeling her around me like that again was bliss. Pure and utter fucking bliss. I hadn't intended on sleeping with her like that, but I couldn't stop myself. Feeling her body and listening to her moans had me bursting to cum deep in her that second.

Her breathing picked up again, and I was hard again. It seemed impossible to stay soft around her. I unclipped the strap on her bra and pulled the material down, letting her breast out. Leaning down, I licked and slowly massaged her hard nipple with my tongue.

"Ollie, you don't have to." She sucked in a sharp breath.

I knew I didn't have to, but I wanted to.

Grinning, I pulled away and looked up at her sleepy face. She was struggling to hold back just as much as I was. I moved between her thighs, and she looked slightly panicked. I groaned as I realised she wasn't wearing anything.

"Sex is going to help this little monster come out, yeah?" I grinned and began to kiss down her neck, trailing it with my tongue and sucking lightly.

My cock got harder as she reached down between us and held me, guiding me to her. I then buried balls deep inside her, and it felt like fucking heaven.

~

Two days later, sex was becoming more and more frequent between us. It seemed as if we were both on a mission to fuck until we felt the sexual tension that was between us was gone. Like that'd happen. This woman brought out the horny teenage side of me, a side I hadn't experienced often at all.

"Ollie, I need to pack a hospital bag," Sage called out from the shower.

I walked in the bathroom and rolled my eyes, smirking when she tried to cover herself up. "You know, I've seen you naked plenty of times. Why are you still so embarrassed?" I asked, crossing my arms over my chest.

It was amusing that she was so shy. She wasn't shy when I made love to her. She was actually far from that.

"I don't know. I just get nervous when I'm naked." She shrugged.

Well, that was going to change. I pulled my boxers down and opened the door on the shower. "Move over, I'm going to stare at you until you're not shy around me."

"Please, don't." She groaned, trying to cover up again.

I laughed and pushed her hands up to the wall of the shower. "Your body is bigger, and it's more for me to enjoy. Why are you so afraid? Do you see how hard I am? That's just by looking at you, baby." I let go one of her hands and let her grab my hard dick. "This, this is what you do to me. Just one look and I'm stiff hard over you, Sage."

"But she's tiny, and I'm not," she whispered. Her eyes were filled with tears.

I frowned, wondering who the hell she was talking about, and it hit me. She was talking about her. Fuck, it never even crossed my mind that she'd worry about that. Sure, Amy was skinny, but she was too thin for my liking.

"Don't ever compare yourself to her. She's nothing. I promise you, your body is what I like, and all she is, is a crazy bitch who eats nothing but pills and smokes a pack of smokes a day. Don't ever think you need to be like that because you don't. You're so much better."

I wanted her to feel what I felt for her. I wanted her to see that I cared and that I loved the way she looked. I had enough of her doubting herself. It was time she felt what I felt for her.

"Turn around."

"What?" she asked. Her eyes opened wider.

I narrowed my eyes in on her. "Turn around, Sage. Don't make me ask again."

My hands were on her hips as I spun her around, pulling her ass back. I entered her, fucking her and stimulating her nipples. I squeezed her breasts, rolling the hardened peaks between my two fingers. Her gasps, moans, and cries filled the bathroom as I thrust. Every time she clenched around me, I almost came.

~

Sage was feeling more exhausted and tired. Her Braxton hicks were coming on stronger. Any day now, I had a feeling the baby would be coming anytime soon.

Of course, she didn't believe me.

Following behind her to the nursery, I looked at the bag she had sitting on the change table stand. Packing, god, it was crazy to think that in a short while I was going to be a father. It was exciting but nerve-wracking. I worried that I'd be a bad father and hurt them both.

This was the next step Amy and I were meant to take together. We'd planned it for ages, discussed it, and had all the doctor visits. At that time, I thought I was going forward. In actual fact, it was a trap, a step backward.

Now looking at the woman in front of me who was smiling as she read the list out and looking through the too many clothes for a child—in my opinion—I couldn't help but think that this was it. She and I, this could be the future I always wanted. The whole cheating thing opened my eyes to something else—something I had been so blind to see in the first place.

My wife abused me.

More than anything, I wanted to tell Sage. I knew she noticed the scars and marks. I knew she wanted answers, and I wanted to give them to her. I just didn't know if she'd leave once I told her the truth.

"What do you think? Do we need a dummy or not? I don't really want to give her one, but if she's a screamer, then maybe she would need one?" she asked, holding up this pink pacifier.

"Pack it, just in case. What else do we need? Throw up cloths?" I asked. "I don't know where anything is in here."

"You'll learn." She grinned. "Are you going to get up and feed her during the nights with me?" she asked.

My brows raised up. Was she asking what I think she was?

I just shrugged. "I will get up when you both do. Wouldn't be fair if only you did it."

Another thing I needed to decide on. I couldn't stay here forever. It was way too cramped up in here. The two bedroom was okay, but it was too small for two adults and a baby. This was a guest house, not a home.

She looked like she had only clicked in on what she meant. "I mean, you don't have to stay here. I'm sorry for assuming. I shouldn't have done that," she said, looking away.

I came up behind her and slid my arms around her from behind. "It's okay. I will stay here but only until I find my own place."

"Okay. Let's finish the bag. I'm so exhausted, and it's not ten yet." She yawned.

I laughed. "You're really over it, aren't you?"

She leant back in my chest, and I kissed the back of her head and rubbed her shoulders.

"It's getting painful to walk. I'm really tired. I want to get this done so I can go sit and put my feet up. Sorry, I'm so boring."

"Believe me, you have nothing to do with boring, baby." I kissed her again and grabbed the bag, heading to the closet to see what else we needed for this baby.

After making sure that we had everything we needed, we went to bed. I waited for her to fall asleep before I used her laptop to look up real estate. While on it, I also fired off an email to the lawyer my father had put me in contact with.

My sister-in-law, Julia, being the nosy bitch she was, sent me a text to ask why Amy and I split up. Instead of using her own phone, she used my brother's, thinking I wouldn't know it was her. My brother didn't put a kiss on the end of his texts and normally called.

My phone was on silent. Amy was back to her daily calls, demanding texts, and crying voicemails. I never opened any of them. Doing as my father told me to do, I saved them all for evidence.

Sage stirred, and I rubbed her stomach. She soon fell back asleep. She was definitely adorable.

"Ollie." She groaned, her eyes closed.

"Yeah, baby?" I closed the top of the laptop and looked at her, kissing her forehead.

"Ollie, I think it's warning signs." She groaned again. Her breathing picked up, and hands shot out to grip my back.

Warning signs. I read about this. "You mean?"

She finally opened her eyes and smiled. "It worked," she whispered.

I frowned. *It worked?*

I was about to ask her what worked, but then my smile matched hers. "Your body just responds really well to my cum inside of you. You're just made for me." I winked.

"Don't make me laugh. God, it hurts," she grumbled and sucked in a breath again. "God, we need to go, but I don't want to. I'm scared, and it's going to hurt. It's going to hurt so bad."

I lowered my head down and brushed my lips against hers. "I'm going to be right by your side. I won't go anywhere. Okay? Yes, it will fucking hurt, but you can take all that pain out on me. You've got full rights to scream, grip my hands, and call me any name you want. For now though, we need to get you up and dressed. The baby bag is ready, and I will call your sister and parents. Fuck, we haven't told your parents."

Her eyes widened. "Oh, god. Why would you say this to me now? I'm in labor. Don't make me laugh."

I grinned, ignoring my own nerves and putting on a brave face for her. She needed me. I just hoped her sister had calmed down and would accept that I was in this and wasn't going anywhere.

I got off the bed, helping her to sit upright. "Come on, beauty. It's go time."

# CHAPTER 18

SAGE

"That's it, baby. One more push. You can do it," Oliver spoke smoothly beside me.

His hand was holding onto mine, or more correctly, I was holding his tightly. His other hand was pushing my leg back as the midwife on the other side of me held me the same way.

We had been here for ten hours, and I was in so much pain. I was ready to get her out of my body, but she was fighting it. She was far too cosy in the warm bubble of the home I had kept her in. I just didn't have any energy left. I was tired and exhausted.

No drugs. I was fucking insane.

I shook my head, tears streaming down my cheeks as my chest rose and fell, breathing hard and heavy. "I can't, please. It hurts too much. God. Ollie, I can't."

"Yes, you can. You know you can. You're strong, baby. You're going to do this and have her in your arms very soon." I looked up at him as he spoke. He leant forward and kissed my sweaty forehead.

Too bad if I was still embarrassed about being naked in front of him. I was open and spread in a bed for everyone in the room to see. I was completely naked. The bra I had on got tossed off. Breaking out in a heat rash had me snapping and almost tearing it off.

The nurse, Mary, on my other side was what I needed to keep going. She gave my hand a reassuring squeeze as the doctor between my thighs looked up and nodded.

"Ready? On the count of three. One, two, and three…"

I don't think I had ever screamed so loud in my entire life. I gritted my teeth as I pushed with everything I had. I had two words to say: never again!

As I pushed, I gripped Ollie's hand hard, leaning forward and focusing on the positive. My daughter would be out soon.

I fell back to the bed and was panting hard as a loud scream filled the room. I did it. She was here and out. Oliver kissed me hard before I could take another breath. He cupped my cheek, and I tasted his salty tears as he pulled back. Both of us were crying.

"You did it, baby. God, thank you so much. I'm so proud of you," he said, kissing me hard once more.

"Congratulations, Daddy. Would you like to cut the cord?" the midwife asked.

He didn't hesitate to say yes. He grabbed the scissors and cut the cord. He stood there and just watched her being cleaned up. I lay there watching him. I couldn't describe how I felt at this moment.

I lay there after being cleaned up and dreaded what was going to come with my sister and my parents. Oliver had called Cassie and Tony, letting them know we were on our way to the hospital. He was going to call Mum, but Cassie insisted she would do it. I felt bad, but I made him call his parents. He didn't want to intrude, but this was his daughter. His parents had every right to meet their granddaughter.

When Cassie arrived at the hospital, she told Oliver he was fine to leave and wait with Tony. My god, he stood his ground and told her to get out. She refused, telling him that he couldn't turn up and act like a father after a couple days of us shacked up together. When Mum and Dad arrived, we were already in the delivery process, and I had told the midwife I only wanted Oliver in here. Too many people was going to cause unwanted stress.

"Hey, Mummy. You want to hold your daughter?" Oliver's quiet voice broke me out of my sleepy daze.

I opened my eyes and nodded. "Yes, please."

My heart was filled with so much love as she was placed in my arms. Oliver was grinning from ear to ear as he sat on the stool and leant over to the side of us. I looked up at him and just kissed him. He gave me something so precious and beautiful.

"A photo for the new family?" the midwife spoke.

We saw the flash before we looked up. Then she took another.

"She's perfect," he whispered, stroking a finger through her light spread of black hair.

Her were eyes closed, and long lashes fanned out over the top of her cheeks. She was utterly perfect.

I leant down and kissed her little nose. "She is that and more."

"Do you have a name?" she asked, snapping another photograph of us.

I nodded. "Yes, she does."

Oliver spoke up. "Actually, I was thinking that we call her something else. Olive is great, but it's not the first name you chose."

"What?" I asked, confused.

"I read your list on the computer. How about we call her Meadow instead?" he asked. "I'm not going anywhere, Sage. I know that's why you picked Olive in the first place. So she'd have a part of me with her, but she's always going to have me around. I won't leave you or her. You're both my life, you and her."

I didn't know what to say. I nodded, smiling and looking down at our daughter. "Meadow Olive Bailey."

It felt like five minutes, but it was almost an hour that we stayed there in that room, learning how to feed and soothe her. Oliver dressed her in a light purple suit, placing a little hat on her head. Meadow was fast asleep. She was snuggled against the corner of my chest and tucked neatly underneath my arm.

"Would you like a shower? To clean up?" Oliver asked, picking Meadow up and placing her in the small crib.

After taking a shower, I went back to our room. I felt somewhat better.

Meadow was still asleep. Oliver was holding her, and I could see he was already protective of her, not wanting to let her out of his sight. He had been like that with me too, getting up and helping when I wanted something. I was grateful that he was here. I really was.

The bedroom door opened, and Tony and Cassie entered along with Mum and Dad. Setting a bunch of flowers down on the table, their eyes went directly to Oliver. Cassie went over to them and was about to hold Meadow from Oliver's arms.

"She's sleeping," he said quietly, not showing any signs of letting her take Meadow.

I could see a smile on Dad's face. I was a little confused about that.

He kissed the top of my head. "Congrats, princess. I heard you screaming from outside."

I laughed quietly. "And I did it all without pain meds."

"She was amazing," Oliver spoke up. He reached over and held my hand, stroking my palm with his thumb.

It was time to get the elephant out of the room. I could see my sister throwing daggers at Ollie while he wasn't looking. I didn't want him to feel like an outcast.

I sat up a little more. "Um, as you may have guessed, Oliver is Meadow's dad."

Cassie scoffed. "He's married!"

"Cassie!" Tony growled. "Don't start. We've spoken about this."

"Married?" Mum asked. "I thought he was getting divorced?"

"I am." Oliver cut in. "I have no intention of leaving, so please, if you're pissed, then let it out. It won't change anything though."

Dad sat down beside him and sighed. "Well, we figured you were. You two weren't good at hiding him sneaking over months ago."

"What?" I asked the same time as Cassie. She looked more pissed than surprised though.

Mum shook her head, sighing. "You never remember that we have cameras around the house and yard. One night, we were heading to bed and noticed him coming in. Then, again the next night. It's not a problem. You two were awfully cosy at the wedding, feeding each other and barely leaving one another's side. We just assumed something was going on."

Well, heck. I didn't expect that at all. I looked over at Oliver and bit my lip. He looked equally shocked.

"Wait. You two were cheating while at my wedding?" Cassie gasped. "Oh, god. I feel sick."

"Cassie, not now. Your sister just had a baby, your niece. Stop being so dramatic." Mum sighed then looked over at Meadow and smiled. "She's a lot like you," she said to Oliver, trying to break the tension.

"You think?" he asked. "She's so small."

I agreed. She looked just like him with my dark grey-blue eyes.

The door opened, and Oliver's parents walked in. "Sorry. I hope we're not interrupting. We heard a little girl came early." His mum smiled, placing her bag on the floor beside the chair.

Meadow was passed around to everyone. Her face had been kissed so many times, and her photo was taken over and over again. The exhaustion had caught up with me, and I fell asleep during the visit with everyone. The last thing I remember: Cassie was begging Oliver to let her hold Meadow. I thought Ollie liked her grovelling back to him.

~

A few days later and Oliver walked in the room with a big grin on his face. I was feeding by the window in the chair and

217

feeling completely and utterly worn out. I felt like a sleep-deprived zombie with the amount of times Meadow fed during the night.

"What are you smiling like that for?" I asked. It was impossible not to smile back at him.

"You two get to come home today. What's not to smile about? How are you feeling? I picked up those salts for the bath they recommended with your, uh, healing down there." He scratched his jaw that had a dark stubble, looking at me awkwardly.

I avoided eye contact. My god, how embarrassing.

"You didn't have to do that," I murmured quietly.

He sat in the chair opposite me and shrugged, reaching over and pulling the blanket back to see Meadow's face clearer. She was still drinking away. Her eyes were wide open, looking up at me. I could sit and stare at her all day. Just like I had been doing these past three days.

"Hey." He rubbed my knee and got my attention back. I raised my brows, and he continued. "I don't mind getting you things like that. It's the least I can do. Trust me. My mother's already been in my ear, and she gave me a list of everything I need to do to make you feel comfortable when you're home. I don't know. I feel useless. You've just given birth, and all I did was stand there and watched."

"She has?" I was definitely interested in hearing this. "She's sweet, so is your dad."

His parents were great and loving people.

I squeezed his hand as Meadow stopped drinking. "You've done more than stand around doing nothing, Ollie. You helped a lot and you being here is all I need."

Oliver just looked at me, but finally, he nodded. "They like you. Anyway, I have your bags in the car. Whenever you are ready, we can head off. I can't lie. I'm pretty stoked to get her out of here."

"Well, she's finished feeding. Are you sure you're okay?" I asked, biting my lip nervously. "I mean, you don't have to come back to the house with me if you don't want to. You won't hurt my feelings if you say no."

"Sage, I promised. I will come back. I'm staying regardless if you want me there or not. You won't be alone." He stood up and kissed my forehead.

That seemed more natural for us now, kissing and holding hands. It wasn't forced or for show. It just felt nice, and maybe we were just in the newborn bliss, but having him here with me and seeing the way he was with Meadow made my heart ache in a very good way.

Carrying Meadow in my arms, we walked out of the room.

I should have known that she'd find out. I mean, it wasn't a huge secret that Oliver and I just had a baby and were kind of shacked up together. We weren't in a relationship, but we were basically living together. I didn't know what was going to happen if she found out or when, but it was a no-brainer that she'd come looking for answers and most likely give me a black eye.

Out of all the scenarios, I never expected her to come to the hospital, holding a small package in her hand with a pink ribbon and smiling right at me as Oliver and I walked out with our daughter.

My heart was pounding more than ever as Oliver froze and I clutched Meadow in my arms tighter, pulling the blanket up so Amy couldn't see her.

~

OLIVER

"You need to leave," I growled, keeping my eyes dead on Amy's smiling face.

I had no idea what she was smiling for. She was up to something, and like always, I had no fucking idea what.

She began to step forward, and I moved, blocking the pathway to Sage. Amy rolled her eyes. "Can't I see the child that was created while we were still married? You owe me that much,

Oliver. I've played nice and haven't made a big deal about this. I could, and you know that."

Something flickered in her eyes, and I swallowed hard. I knew what she was playing at. She was referring to all those months of hell with her.

Shaking my head, I said, "No. You've nothing to do with her. You need to leave before you get in any more trouble, Amy."

"I can't believe you filed a restraining order on me, Oliver. How fucking rude can you be! I didn't deserve that. I'm the victim here. You had an affair and lied to me about it. What's worse was after you screwed her, you still went and saw her. An emotional affair is what you and she had!" She snapped.

Pulling my phone out, I took a photo of her as proof that she violated the order. It only added to her fury. She began to walk closer, and Sage spoke up.

"You need to leave. I don't know what the hell is going on between you two, but don't do it here. Not today, and not in front of my daughter. Ollie, let's just go."

"So she speaks. Hope you know he'll only fuck around on you, just like he did to me. Trust me, honey, you're not the first woman he's fucked while we were married. Take your bastard child and leave him before he hurts you again." Amy snickered. "Just wait until he moans another woman's name in bed, just like he did to me last week."

*Fucking bitch.*

I wanted to wrap my hands around her neck until she was limp and dead. All I needed was Sage thinking I was some cheating prick who kept fucking my wife after leaving her. Amy sure as hell knew how to screw me over.

Amy pushed the pink wrapped parcel to my chest and winked. "You'll be back. You always come back to me, baby."

Sage didn't say anything on the drive back to her place. I didn't know what to say to her. She was going to wonder, and I wanted to put all those questions to rest. Today wasn't meant to start off like this. It was meant to be a good day. We were bringing our daughter home, and that was all I cared about.

Meadow yawned but fell back asleep when I lay her down in her bassinette. Sage turned her monitor on and bent down, kissing her forehead. I left her in the bedroom and went to the kitchen. Her mum had been cooking, and the fridge was stacked full and the freezer just the same.

I heard Sage walking out, and she went to the couch and sat down. "What now?" she asked.

I turned around and shrugged. "I don't know what to do next. You hungry or thirsty?"

"Not really. Did you want to come over here and talk to me? I kind of want to ask what that was at the hospital," she said quietly, pulling the blanket up on her body.

A cry from the bedroom and she went to move. I shook my head. "Stay. I'll bring her out. She may just want to be closer to you."

Meadow fell back asleep in the rocking swing once she was laid down. I took a seat beside Sage and sighed. How to start. I had no idea what to begin with. Well, I did. It was just that I needed to say it and get it out there.

I was afraid she'd look at me differently once I did.

"Are you and she getting back together?" she asked softly.

I looked into her eyes. Shit. She was worried that I was really going to leave. Running a hand through my hair, I groaned and shook my head. Amy was really fucking wrecking things before they could stay good.

I grabbed her hand and cupped it with both of mine. "No, I'm not. I just didn't want to tell you this. I thought I'd have a bit more time, but you went into labour earlier than expected."

"Sorry," she whispered.

"You have nothing to apologise for. I'm the one who needs to be saying sorry to you. For the rest of my life, if I have to, I will. I just need you to listen to me before you speak. This isn't easy, Sage. It's something that I'm very ashamed of, and if you want me out of your life, then I completely understand," I said quietly, my voice shaking.

I wasn't this nervous when I told my parents about what happened. Sage, she could take Meadow away. She could want nothing to do with a man who couldn't do fuck at all to protect himself from his wife.

She sat up more. I could hear her breathing picking up. "Ollie, you're scaring me. Are you okay? You can tell me, and I'll be here for you."

I smiled weakly. She was the most selfless person I knew. Hopefully, it was going to stay that way while I relived a past that I wanted nothing more to stay that way: in my past and out of my future.

"Amy and I met in college, around eight years ago. Coincidence, or so I had always thought. She was perfect in my eyes. I don't know. I just always thought she was smart and beautiful. Now, I don't find anything about her smart or beautiful. She's an evil bitch who lies. Turns out, she planned to run into me one day. It was all in her plan to get me to notice her. It was some fucking bet to see who out of her friends could tie me down. I'd dated before her, but it was never serious. I was just too polite to tell them I wasn't interested." I let her hands go and leant forward, watching my daughter.

"We were engaged and married two years later. I never fucked her last week. I haven't done since before I met you. I just couldn't do it anymore. She wasn't a sexual person, but it never bothered me. We went months without sex, almost a year once. Then after a while, the topic of babies came up, and I was all for it. It was on her terms. Everything was always on her terms." I muttered the last part slower, more so to myself.

"After a year of trying to get pregnant, it wasn't happening. She had me tested and all that bullshit to see if I was healthy enough. She thought my sperm was low, but it wasn't. Funnily enough, she said she was all good as well. I should have insisted on coming to her appointments. It would have saved me months of stress and worry that something was my fault. So, we began to take shots to help her conceive. Sex was pretty non-existent. Once a month when she said she was ovulating. She wasn't though. She never ovulated once.

"The year after we got married, she went away to her parents' place. They live around six hours away, and I couldn't get time off work. She ended up staying there for two months when it was only meant to be a couple weeks. Again, I didn't think anything of it.

"She recently told me she'd gotten her uterus taken out. She didn't want kids at all but couldn't risk losing me. The fucking shots she took were just water, and her friend was the doctor, so she got them easily enough. It was a relief when she told me. Of course, I was pissed off. She lied to me, and if I had known she did that, I would have divorced her then and there.

"This all goes back to her bet in college with her friends. Also, they bet for how long it would take before I married her. They all knew I was from money and wanted a piece of it. I never proposed to her. I was going to, but she just said let's go get married, and we did it that day. It's something I will always regret.

"It was also the first sign. She liked to control me. She likes power and has me do as she says on a whim. I'm not a pushover, but after six years of her nagging, complaining, and always telling me what to do, I began to give in more and more. She liked to make me feel like shit like I wasn't good enough to do anything. I began to believe her. I was more or less a failure in her eyes.

"That night you and I met, she and I had gotten into a fight, and I was sick of listening to her calling me an asshole. She loved to tell me I was useless in bed and unable to get a woman off. God knows how many times I'd been told my cock was too small to give any pleasure. She didn't touch me. She just laid there and made it miserable.

"I told her I cheated. I admitted it to her, and she looked at me dead in the eyes and said she didn't believe me. She then threw the biggest fit of her life, and it stunned me. She was throwing chairs and snapping the legs. Then when I thought she had calmed down, she put a knife into my stomach. I was just lucky that she was a nurse and could stitch me back up. She loved to hit me with anything she got her hands on. She has a temper, a wild temper."

"Oh, god." I heard Sage gasp, but I kept talking. I was going to lose my nerve if I stopped now.

"I've had three cracked ribs, a fucking hair thing stuck to my stomach, and books pegged at me so hard that she gave me a concussion once. That's why I left you." I shifted on the couch, turning my body to face her. "You felt blood on my back, and I panicked. I was furious at myself and pissed off that I let you see that. It was humiliating. I never wanted you to have any of that in your life. Our daughter doesn't deserve to be around any of that. I figured leaving would be better.

"I've got a restraining order on her. My lawyer is drawing up divorce papers, and I want out of that marriage. If it weren't for Tony, I would probably still be stuck there with her, listening to her daily abuse and being on the receiving end of her constant abuse.

"Pretty fucked up, isn't it? A grown man too fucking scared to leave his wife in fear for what she'd do if I left her. Today, she was warning me to come back to her," I grumbled, looking back down at the floor.

My eyes were clouded over with tears. I didn't want to blink. I didn't want her to see this side of me ever.

She sat there for a long time, and I didn't dare look at her. I was trying to control my own breathing. I was trying not to damn well cry. This wasn't something I wanted to tell anyone, but now it was out there for her to judge me.

Her hand slowly slid along my arm and down to my hand where she gripped her fingers with mine. "Ollie, I won't let her touch you ever again," she said with determination. She was shaking and her voice uneven.

I glanced to my right and looked at her. Her eyes were big with and full of anger. She was biting down on that plump lower lip of hers.

I cupped her cheek, leaning forward until my forehead was against hers. "You're more than I deserve, Sage," I whispered softly. "You deserve more. More than I'm afraid to give. I don't know if I can give you what you want from me. At the moment, the label freaks the shit out of me. Maybe one day…"

Relationship, that was what I wanted to give her. It was what she wanted even if she didn't tell me that. It was written all over her face. It was in her hopeful eyes.

Just when I thought she couldn't surprise me anymore, she did. "I don't need a ring or a promise to love me from you. I understand a little better with what you went through. It's going to take time for you to heal, and I will help. I won't ever make you feel less worthy than what you are. I will never push you to be with me. I'm honestly happy being as we are, friends."

"That kiss." I smirked slowly, correcting her.

She smiled. "We're family, Oliver, and we have a beautiful daughter that's brought us together. I won't push you for anything more than you to be in her life." She looked over at Meadow then back at me. "Just promise me that you won't go back to her and that she won't be near Meadow."

"I promise you that I won't go back there. I will never let her touch you or her. We have a daughter, and we're always going to be family, Sage, and I won't hurt you. I will always protect you both," I said quietly, bringing my arms around her waist and pulling her in closer.

"Thank you for telling me everything. Thank you for trusting me like that. I know it must have been hard to say. I promise you it will stay with me, and I won't bring it up again. I'm really proud of you though. I can't begin to imagine how hard it was for you," she whispered. "I'll never hurt you like that, Oliver. I won't ever treat you badly. I like you in control, in charge, and in me," she said, her fingers running up my sides. "You're the man of the house, and it'll stay that way."

I couldn't help but laugh at that. She knew how to make me feel in control, giving me back the dominance I once had.

"Man of the house, ay?"

"Yep. Also, I must say. You're very good in bed. I enjoyed it a lot." She blushed.

"You're talking in past tense. You mean now that the baby's born, the great sex stops too?" I faked a groan, and she laughed, giving me a playful grin and shrug.

Finally, I kissed her and held her close. Lying back, I pulled her down to lay on me as well.

Grabbing the blanket, I covered her body with it and rubbed circles on her back until she fell asleep against my chest.

Noticing the parcel on the table, I carefully moved from underneath her body and made my way over and picked it up. God knows what Amy brought, probably a tracking device. I opened it and looked at the pink romper suit, tossing it to the table. I ground my teeth together when I read the card with her handwriting.

*My darling daughter, your second mummy will love you and see you soon. We'll be a perfect little family soon, my precious angel.*

# CHAPTER 19

I was breathing hard as I glanced in the mirror. Watching the roller door close as I sat in the garage, I tried to calm myself before I went inside and saw anybody. My breathing was hard and heavy as I sat in the seat, shaking. I had never been so freaked out in my entire life.

Unclipping my belt, I headed through the door toward the main house where Mum was watching Meadow for me.

Oliver was going to lose his shit when he found out.

"Hey, that was quick. How did you go?" Mum asked, looking up and smiling as she rocked my daughter in her arms.

I had a fake smile on my face, hiding any evidence of worry. "All good. Everything looks well."

"That's good. Did you go on any type of birth control?" She raised a brow.

Oh, god. She just had to go there.

I gave her a pointed look, taking my daughter from her and smothering her tiny head with little kisses. "Mum, that's just not even cool to talk about with you. We don't need to discuss anything like that."

She chuckled at my embarrassment. "You have been living with Oliver in that guesthouse. I'm just assuming you and him are safe. Unless you want another little surprise to come along like this possum."

"Oliver and I aren't together. We're just friends." *Who make out heavily and fool around.*

227

"Keep telling yourself that. What time is he home from work tonight?" she asked, changing the subject swiftly.

Oliver was at work. He went back three weeks ago after much hesitation.

It was very weird to see him leave and then come back in the afternoon. I found myself missing him during the day, but when he came back, he doted on Meadow until she went back to sleep for the night.

"I think five tonight. You're not bothered that he's here?" I asked nervously. I didn't think they would be after insisting that he stay and make himself at home.

Mum just looked at me with a smile. She was up to something. "Not at all. He's a great guy. I wasn't too sure about him after Cassie called and let us know that it was a married man who was the father, and not to mention, you had her banned from the delivery room."

"She what!" I snapped my head up, looking at her incredulously. "She slapped him across the face, and I asked him to be in the room with me. God, she annoys me sometimes." She annoyed me a lot, trying to baby me, telling me how to look after Meadow, and trying to tell Oliver he needed to sort Amy out then come to me.

I wasn't letting him anywhere near that crazy bitch.

The second Oliver told me Amy had been physically and emotionally abusing him, I wanted to hurt her just as much as she hurt him. It explained so much as to why he was closed off with me, flinching when I touched him at times.

The mark on his stomach from the straightener and the other small scars over his chest and back were almost faded, thanks to my anti-stretch mark oil rub. He was hesitant at first, but I knew he didn't want any reminder of what Amy had done to him.

I sat on the chair and laid Meadow across my chest to feed her. "She's growing. I don't want her to grow anymore."

Mum just smiled, looking away as I unclipped my bra and latched her on. "I used to say the same thing about you. But there's

228

nothing you can do to stop it. Oh, Greyson called before. He said he would be home this weekend and wanted to visit. Just text him back. I have a feeling he feels left out."

"I spoke to him yesterday," I spoke to him almost daily. He was far from neglected.

"You're playing house, Sage. Before, you had all the time in the world to do things together. Now you've got a child and a boyfriend to spend time with." She winked at the boyfriend part, and I just rolled my eyes.

That wasn't entirely true. I just had a baby and going out without Meadow just didn't sit well with me. "Whatever. I'm going to finish feeding then go take a hot shower until Oliver is back from work."

~

Meadow was on my bed with nothing on. She was kicking her legs about and squirming when Oliver walked in. He took one look and playfully covered his eyes.

"Oh, no." He laughed. "Daddy doesn't want to see that." He grinned putting his hands back down.

I smiled, reaching for the fresh diaper, but he took it from my hands to change her himself. He was always happy to help and didn't complain, no matter the time. Kneeling by the bed, he began to dress her.

"She's very alert tonight."

"She is." He grinned back. "She looks happy and full from her dinner."

I laughed, nodding. "She loves her milk."

I didn't miss the hint of a smirk, and I glanced at him curiously.

"So, how was your appointment? All good down there?" he asked, giving me a brow wiggle.

I blushed, laughing at his choice of words. "Yes, it's all good. My vagina is ready to go, and I'm on the mini pill." We hadn't spoken much about sex, but we both were eager to go for it again. I wanted him. "Anyway, you're home early. I didn't think you would finish until later tonight."

"I was thinking…How about we take a drive?" He laid her down beside me then got off the bed and unbuttoned his navy shirt, showing off his tanned and toned chest.

I could see the light spread of hair trailing below his work pants, and my eyes wandered down.

God, he was gorgeous to look at. As always, he noticed me checking him out.

"Where do you want to go for a drive to?" I asked then I remembered what happened earlier today. I sat up, bright-eyed with eagerness. "Oh, god. I need to tell you something. It was weird and really scared me."

He frowned, tossing his shirt in the basket by the door. "What happened? You found a spider or a mouse somewhere in here?"

"This morning, at my appointment, Amy was in there at the doctor's also," I whispered. Just the image of her sitting opposite me was enough to make me shudder.

His smile was long gone as he stopped and stared. "What?"

I nodded, continuing. "When I came out, she was still sitting there. Then, when I was driving home, she followed behind, really close. I wanted to brake so she would slam into the back of me, but she's not worth it."

The look of anger on his face was close to erupting. "She's following you? Did she come here?"

"No, she didn't. I took a few too many wrong turns, then came back here. Why is she following me?" I whispered. I had chills down my spine, fearing the worst.

He grabbed his phone, and with the blink of an eye, he was gone and out of the room. The front door closed, and I sighed. I wanted this woman out of his life. She was driving me insane. There was no way in hell any of us would know what was going to happen next.

I picked Meadow up and carried her out to the kitchen. Oliver walked in and went past us to the bedroom. My heart wanted to go and ask him what was going on, but my head told me to leave it and not suffocate him.

The day he showed me what Amy had left, I was seething. Bitch had gone crazy. She was not Meadow's mother, nor would she ever be. I wouldn't allow her to be anywhere near her. Oliver's restraining order wasn't working too well. She was coming to me in hopes to rattle him. I just hoped this divorce happened sooner than later. There was no telling what would happen if she refused to sign.

Lost in my own thoughts, I felt a body press against my back. Then his arms wrapped around me, holding me to him. It was a moment's warmth that eased the worries deep within my body.

"My parents called. They want to know if you would like to come around for dinner," he asked, kissing the top of my head.

I hadn't seen his parents since Meadow was born. His mum usually called, and we spoke. I think they were trying not to overstep and to ease their way in. Oliver told me Amy hated his parents. She was always rude, and his mum was worried that I was going to hate her too.

I shrugged, unsure what he wanted to do. My parents gave us space for our own meals, and we usually ate in here unless they invited us over there for a Sunday roast. "If you want. It doesn't bother me."

He turned me around, cocking his head to the side. "If you don't want to, then we don't have to. I know its short notice. She only called this arvo."

"No, I didn't mean it in a bad way. I would like to go for dinner. They haven't seen Meadow for ages unless you wanted to go alone with her. I don't know. I'm just nervously rambling." I blushed, looking away from him. "I don't want them to feel like they need to invite me just because of her. I get it if they think that's the only way they'll see her."

"No, baby. No." He sighed, puffing his cheeks out with a hard breath. "Shit. It didn't come out right. My parents want you, Meadow, and myself to come for dinner tonight. My brother may be there with his kids also. Mum didn't say."

I just nodded. It didn't bother me to go there. "Okay, we can go. Did you still want to go for a drive?"

"Yes. We're going to go for a drive. How about you take a shower before we leave?" he asked. "Don't you need to change?"

I frowned, looking down at myself. "You want me to change?" I wasn't dressed up or anything. I was just in a tank and sweats.

My appearance didn't really get much of a makeover. I wasn't too focused on contouring on mornings when I had a little girl to tend to. I was too wrapped up in being a mother and enjoying every moment I had with her.

"No, uh, you're fine as is. I just didn't know if you wanted a shower while I'm home and can watch her for you." He lifted Meadow who gripped his shirt and face-planted into his chest. Startling herself, she let out a loud cry.

"Aww." I pouted as Ollie wrapped her in a hug and rubbed her back. Settling down sooner, she nuzzled against him. "Daddy's girl," I grumbled and walked off, ignoring his laugh as I headed to the bathroom to shower, which I did need to do.

~

Oliver held my hand, lacing our fingers together as he drove to wherever we were headed, which I had no idea. He just said he wanted to go for a drive. Pulling up in the drive of a two-story home, I looked over at Oliver, confused.

"Is this your brother's house?" I asked, looking around.

"Nope. This is my house. I spent the past two weeks finalizing the paperwork, and I picked up the keys today." He grinned, pushing his car door open.

I didn't know why, but it hurt. He was going to be moving out and starting off on his own, the thought of Meadow taking turns being with each of us separately.

232

It began to break my heart.

~

OLIVER

She was smiling, but I knew she wasn't really smiling. Sage looked on the verge of tears.

Shit. I had no idea what I had done or what was wrong. I sighed nervously and leant against the doorframe of the back door while she looked around outside. Walking past the pool and spa, she gave me another fake smile.

"I know. It's not the flashiest place around, but it's a fixer. It'd be good, yeah? I'm going to build a better deck and put in a veggie garden. The inside will need a coat of paint, and I'll rip the kitchen out and redo that," I said, watching her still. "You don't like it, do you?"

Her eyes widened. "What? No. It's great for you. This is like a man's dream house. It's really nice, but you're right. There are lots that you can still do to improve it. Honestly, it's great, Ollie."

"Why do you look so sad?" I asked when she walked in the back laundry.

"No, I'm not sad, just hormones. I cry at anything lately. I'm happy for you," she said, and her voice came unevenly again.

I grabbed her forearm, pulling her to a stop. "Baby, what's wrong? What did I do?"

"Nothing, Ollie. I promise. It's just me, and I'm ridiculous. Show me upstairs again." She bit her trembling lower lip, swallowing and breaking eye contact to look down at Meadow who was asleep in her arms.

"Tell me why you're upset, please?" I asked softly.

She leant into my palm as I caressed her cheek and stepped closer. After giving birth, I didn't think she could get any more beautiful, but she did. Every day, I would just watch her, whether she was sleeping, focusing on cooking in the kitchen, or just lying in bed with her top off and feeding Meadow. She was just completely beautiful.

233

She sighed, blinking her tears away. "You're moving. It's great, Ollie. I just got used to you being around. I guess this is where it gets real."

"What?" I whispered, confused.

She rolled her eyes, looking at me as if I should know what she was thinking. I didn't.

"You and me. The thought of Meadow coming to stay with you...and it's not like I don't trust you with her because I do. It just hurts to really think about her coming here and then back to me, however we decide to do it."

*Fuck.* "No. No, stop. Just stop." Holy fuck. She was crying. She was going to send me into my own panic attack. God, did she not even realize what I had been trying to ask? "I want you here as well."

"What?" she asked while using her free hand to wipe her tears.

I bent down and held her face with both hands. "Sage, I'm not going to take her from you. I promised you that already." I frowned, concentrating on making sure she understood me clearly. "Your parents' place is great and all, but it's their place. The guesthouse, it's too small. Every time we get into bed, I'm worried your dad is going to barge in and lecture us about safe sex. I'm a grown man, and I want space and privacy. I really want you and Meadow to move in with me. Fuck doing part-time parenting. We're in this together, and I want it to stay that way."

"But you said you can't do this. I'm so confused." She sniffed.

"There are four bedrooms. You can have your own room if you want. I like how things have been, and I want to keep it that way. I also like sleeping with you at night. It's a nice feeling." I smiled. I loved having her in my arms during the night.

"Let me think about it. It's a huge step, and if I move in, I have to pay rent. I can't just live here for nothing. We'd be like roommates, yes?" she asked.

That was a kick in the gut, but I nodded, knowing it was my fault for putting the relationship status off limits and she was just following what I thought I wanted.

"Roommates." I agreed.

The tension was gone as we walked into my parent's place. I wasn't expecting her to say yes to moving in with me.

I wouldn't lie. It did hurt when she assumed I wouldn't want her around. How the hell was I meant to look after Meadow on my own? I had no idea what I was doing half the time. She was the natural. I just read book after book, trying to catch up on what to do with a newborn.

~

"Sage, look at you! You look wonderful. Are you thirsty? Hungry? We have dinner almost done, and I can get you a glass of wine or something else if you'd prefer?" Mum gushed, giving her a kiss on the cheek. It was nice to see, but she was trying too hard to be liked by her.

If only she knew that Sage wasn't Amy. She never would be.

Amy had one hell of a nerve following Sage to and from the doctors. I had no idea how she knew, but I was determined to find out. If Meadow had been with her, I would have gotten in my car and drove over to her instead of calling the lawyer to inform him what she did. He suggested a restraining order on Sage as well, and I had him handle it.

"Juice is just fine. I'm not much of a drinker." Sage blushed.

We both knew what happened the last time she got drunk. The result was wrapped up in my arms with her grey-blue peepholes open and tiny pink tongue poking out at me.

A snort came from behind us. "Isn't that how you both got in this mess in the first place?"

I spun around, facing Julia, and laughed sarcastically. "What mess? If you're talking about my daughter, then I'd think very carefully before you respond to that."

235

"Julia, don't." Haddon warned, passing her. "Where's my niece? I want first cuddles."

"Oh no, you don't, Haddon. Grandma has first cuddles on her." Mum warned, shooing him away as she went to the kitchen and brought out a beer and a drink for Sage. "Here you go. Now let's sit and catch up."

Mum was grilling Sage about everything possible. Haddon and I exchanged glances and Dad just chuckled when she went onto another question. Julie was sitting there quietly. I knew she told Amy about the baby and where she'd given birth at. For the life of me, I couldn't understand why she'd do it. The only reason I came up with was her being jealous and petty, trying to cause drama for no reason. She and Amy went hand in hand for that bullshit.

"Tell me. What is your favorite thing to cook? Are you a baker?" Mum asked.

I groaned. "Mum, seriously. Let her breathe."

"Oliver, watch your tone. I just want to get to know her better. It's been a while since we last caught up." Mum narrowed her eyes back at me.

"I'm not much of a cook. Honestly, I can't cook very well. Oliver eats all my burnt food though." Sage blushed. The way her cheeks changed made me smile. She was adorable.

I grinned. "You rarely burn anything, and it still tastes good when covered in sauce."

Sage laughed. "You're sweet. You do eat anything though."

"Are you two together?" Julia asked, staring at my hand on Sage's thigh. It was a habit, and it was hard not to touch her when she was around. "You're not even divorced yet. Isn't that a bit disrespectful to Amy? You know she's struggling, Oliver. I can't sit here and be happy and pretend everything is all okay when your wife is at home waiting for you to get over your cheating."

The timer on the stove went off and thank fuck for that.

"Dinner." Mum stood up, avoiding eye contact with anyone as she and Dad rushed off the kitchen.

236

"Julia." Haddon snapped when they'd left. "Stop it. Just for fucking once, be quiet."

"Well done, father of the year. Swearing in front of the kids again, Haddon." Julia gritted, sitting back and crossing her arms over her chest. "Sorry, Oliver. I didn't mean to state the truth."

I shook my head at her. "You've got no idea what shit you caused by telling her about Sage and the baby. Things you don't understand, and you never will. Go back and spill your guts to Amy. I don't care. I don't give a shit about her, and while you're there, tell her that." I growled. Standing up, I picked Meadow up and laid her in the small rocker Mum had brought out. "What Sage and I are, is none of your business, Julia. None of anyone's goddam fucking business except hers and mine."

"Ollie," Sage said quietly.

I looked to where her eyes flickered and saw my nephews staring at me. Fuck, just what I needed.

"Daddy, Uncle Oliver said a bad word." Six-year-old Toby grinned. "Does that mean we can say that too?"

"No." Julia snapped. "Your uncle has bad manners. Ignore him."

Max, who was three, just laughed while playing with his trucks. He repeated the word *fuck* and giggled. I bit my tongue as Haddon did what any parent would do when you hear your child swear. He ignored it and then left the room, laughing.

"Come on, kids. Let's go and eat. If anyone of you repeats words like that again, you'll have hot sauce in your mouth and sitting in the naughty chair all night." Julia warned, and they nodded.

When we finished dinner, Mum loaded us up with leftovers and gave Sage a ton of recipe books to go through and look over. Then she offered her cooking lessons. She was no longer fawning over her, which was something shocking. She was not trying to get on her good side anymore. Mum and Sage were really getting along, laughing and talking more and more. Julia didn't like that one bit. I think her being so pissed made my night.

237

Driving home, I noticed her behind us, right up my ass, tailgating basically. Meadow was screaming. She was hungry and tired. Sage was trying to hold her dummy in to keep her settled, but she just spits it out again.

"You want me to pull over? I can." I offered.

"No, keep going. It's only a few minutes away anyway. We'd be sitting on the road for an hour if she fed now." She turned her body around and gave up trying to settle her. She'd pass out. I hoped.

Almost home, the car behind us flashed its headlights. I didn't want to pull over, and I hoped Sage didn't notice, but she did.

"Who's that?" she asked. "Are you speeding? Jesus, Oliver, you can't speed."

"Amy," I said. "I could try your trick and slam the breaks on if you'd prefer."

"What the hell? God, she is really pissing me off. I'd tell you to slam the breaks on if Meadow wasn't in the car," she muttered, sitting back around.

I couldn't help but laugh at how serious she was. She looked too sweet to have an angry side most the time, but I did remember the first time I saw her angry. It was at the wedding, and she gave me the finger.

Reaching over, I rubbed her thigh reassuringly. "If you weren't in the car, then I would." Amy wasn't giving up. Sighing, I grumbled, "Fuck this. I'm done with her shit."

Pulling over, I had enough. Amy was doing my head in. No way in hell was I going to put up with her following us around like this. Sage grabbed my arm and pulled me back, but I shook her off. I had to do this. Obviously, the restraining order was worth jack shit. I kissed her cheek and got out of the car.

My feet hit the gravel as I walked towards the yellow Volkswagen beetle. Yes, she couldn't have chosen a less obvious car.

I got to the front of her door and crossed my arms.

238

"What the fucking hell do you want?" I said venomously at her smiling face.

"How's Meadow? Beautiful name. Did Sage do well in labor? She must be torn up down there. Sucks for you now, huh? Bet you're regretting leaving a nice tight woman." She snickered.

I ground my teeth together, trying not to slam her face into the steering wheel. Leaning down closer to her open window, I narrowed my eyes at her. My fists gripped the roof as I lowered my voice, trying to stay calm but partially failing.

"Don't ever, and I mean ever, talk about them again. I've never been happier, in fact. I'm done with you and your games, Amy. Now what the hell do you want and what the hell do you think you're doing following us? I'm about to call my lawyer yet again since you love to violate court orders."

She shoved over a large yellow envelope that sat on her passenger seat, pushing it hard against my chest. "I have a gift for you. Something I know you'll be very happy with, my love."

# CHAPTER 20

Oliver got back in the car and slammed the door, startling Meadow and waking her, which made her continue her screaming fit. I bit my tongue and kept my eyes on the road as Oliver started up the car and drove us home.

I was in a hurry to get Meadow out and feed her. Sitting down on the couch, it took all of two seconds for her to latch on and feed. This girl could drink and drink.

"Hungry sweetheart," I whispered, stroking her cheek.

Her little hands wrapped around my pinkie finger and squeezed tight. Sucking down the milk so fast, she coughed and splattered it over her face.

"Well, someone is just in too much of a hurry," Oliver spoke, walking out from the bedroom.

I definitely agreed with him there.

"Yep." I smiled.

I wanted more than anything to ask him what Amy gave him. I couldn't believe he had been so careless to get out and walk over to her. She was insane, crazy, and frightening. The way she smiled when she sped off made my skin crawl. He didn't say anything, and it wasn't like I had rights to ask about it. For all I knew, it could be some naked photographs of her to keep him company.

"I'm going to put her to bed then have a shower." I yawned, standing up.

Oliver sat on the couch with the envelope beside him. "Want some help?"

"No, it's fine." I smiled over my shoulder at him as I walked away with a sleeping child in my arms.

Thank god, she didn't have a full nappy. I wasn't looking forward to changing her then waking her up and having her screaming all over again. Her arms flailed out above her head as I turned the monitor on and walked into the other bathroom, closing the door and undressing.

Each time I showered, I tried to avoid looking in the mirror. It wasn't that I was ashamed or embarrassed of my body. I was just shy about it. I no longer looked pregnant, and it was a little sad. I loved being pregnant. Well, not the last week.

As I rubbed conditioner in my hair, the sliding door opened, and Oliver walked in. The steam of the shower window only gave me an outline view of him as he put the lid on the toilet down and took a seat.

"I don't know if you're mad at me or not," he said quietly, stretching his legs out in the small room. I agreed. It was getting cramped in here.

What? Since when was I mad?

Ignoring him until I rinsed my hair, I wrapped the towel around my body and slid the door open. "I'm not mad. Should I be?" I asked, grabbing another towel to dry my hair.

Oliver shrugged. "Amy used to say fine a lot, and I knew that was code for I'm pissed off at you."

"I'm not her." I snapped with a glare. "Don't ever compare me to her."

I never would be like her. That woman was something else, and he had to get it through his skull that I was nothing like her, nor would I ever be. She was evil, pure evil.

My eyes softened. Turning away from him, I left the bathroom. Him and I, these feelings I felt for him were so much clearer and real. I loved him, simple as that, and not just because he was Meadow's father. He was amazing. He was just perfect in my eyes.

I loved him so much.

241

"I didn't mean you were like her. I'm sorry. I know you're nothing like her, Sage. I've never once thought that or compared you to her," Oliver said quietly, following me into the bedroom.

"Well, you just assumed I was mad because I said the word fine," I said and cocked a brow. "I need to change. Are you going to stand and watch?"

A smile formed over his face, shaking his head. "Yes."

His eyes drifted down, and my body began to ache. Heat pooled between my thighs at the way he spoke.

I shook my head and nervously said, "You make me nervous."

Oliver walked closer to me. My hands were at my sides as he lifted his hand up and tugged on the piece of towel tucked into the front of my body, loosening the towel and letting it drop completely. I was too shocked to move as I stood bare naked.

"You're so beautiful. I've seen you naked before, and I told you I plan on seeing you like this again," he whispered, tracing a finger from my collarbone to my fuller breasts and tracing over the soft pink nipple that began to harden from his gentle touch. "I want you so bad. I need you, Sage."

Oh, god. Those words.

Finally, I reached out, pulled on the hem of his shirt, and began to lift it up. After taking it off his head, I worked on his belt. Dropping to my knees in kneeling position, I pulled his jeans down and ran my hand over the large hardening bulge in his boxer briefs.

He was caressing my cheek as I leant forward and nervously pulled the tight material lower and let him spring out. Both my hands wrapped around him. God, he was such a beautiful sight, glistening in pre-arousal as I opened my parting lips and tasted him.

I heard the sharp hiss of breath he took in as I ran my tongue around his lush head.

"Oh, god."

Taking it as a good thing, I parted my lips further and began to slowly suck him from hilt to head as I used my hand to stroke him into blossoming pleasure.

As he neared, he began to thrust in and out of my mouth. I kept going, wanting him to feel the pleasure that was taken from him far too often and he received far too less. He needed it. He needed to regain that control again, and I wanted him to give in. I wanted him to be greedy and to take it as I willingly gave it to him.

He deserved to feel like a man and a woman on her knees worshiping him.

With a curse and deep throaty groan, he came, throbbing harder with each shot of fluid he blasted down my throat. I swallowed quickly, unable to spit it out and risk gagging.

I stood up, and he stood there panting hard, looking ready to collapse, but he wasn't in the mood to stop. He licked his dry lips and looked down at me with hunger, desire, and lust.

"I need to be inside you."

"Take me" was all I managed as his mouth took mine furiously.

Oliver was taking his sweet time, kissing my body. I wanted him to make love to me desperately. I needed it, but he wasn't rushing things though. In a way, I was grateful. It was going to be the first time since giving birth that we'd be intimate, and my anxiety about him not liking me anymore disappeared from my mind.

My body jerked as his wet tongue slithered between my core. He began moving up and down, round and round. Then he pushed hard over my pulsing bud as he wrapped his arms around my thighs and waist and pulled me hard against his face.

*Shit.*

I was losing it. I was seriously losing my mind with what he was doing to me right now.

"Oliver." I clamped my hand to my mouth as I jerked and withered against him.

He pushed his tongue so hard as he ate me out, and well, when I say this, I mean, he really fucking ate me out like a starved man who hadn't eaten in years.

My hands were in his hair as I tried to pull away to recover from the blinding orgasm he sent me in, but he wouldn't loosen up. He was going just as hard and fast, taking me to a new height as another orgasm rippled throughout my body.

He knelt but still bent forward as I tried to buck him off me. He held my waist down to the bed as he continued with his mind-blowing skills. I had no idea where this was coming from. He wasn't anywhere like this before. The first time, he was slow, gentle, and not at all aggressive.

"Oh god, please. I need you in me." I moaned, wrapping my thighs around his head as I bucked up and down.

Taking the not so subtle hint, Oliver released me from his mouth and looked up. Licking his lips, he hovered over top of me. He kissed me.

He was kissing me hard and passionately that I was lost in a trance as he slowly slid inside me.

I gasped as he fully entered and stopped. He felt so damn good, so snug. It hurt but not as much.

"Shit. You have no idea how incredible you feel, Sage. I want to bury myself in you and stay here forever," he murmured as he slowly started to move. Reaching up, he skimmed his fingers down my arm until his fingers clasped mine, and he held me the entire time we made love.

This was slow, tender, and passionate.

~

When I rolled over, the sun shone through the window and hit my bare back as I lay against Oliver's warm chest. His arms were wrapped around my body, and he pulled me closer. Feeling his lips press against my forehead, I smiled.

Then my eyes flew open.

"What time is it?" I whispered, not wanting to move.

"A little past eight," he replied back quietly. "She's still asleep. I just checked on her."

I sunk back into him and relaxed. Meadow had slept the entire night without waking once. I take it she was completely exhausted from last night.

Stretching, I ached deliciously in my lower area. Oliver and I spent a better part of the night getting reacquainted with each other.

"What time do you start work?" I whispered.

He shifted his body, so he lay on his side and faced me. "I'm not going in today. You know, you still haven't answered me."

Grinning, I tried to pretend I had no idea what he was referring to. "What do you mean? Did you ask me something?"

He laughed. "You know I did."

The thought of moving in with him was scary. It was a huge step, and we weren't dating, so it would still be a little awkward, but I guess it was just the same as him staying here. This place was small, and Meadow was only going to get bigger.

"I will pay rent and have my own room, so we have our own spaces," I said, looking at him.

My heart was beating a million miles an hour. I didn't want to suffocate him, and he still needed his space.

He gauged my facial expressions. I didn't care about what he would say. I would still be paying rent.

"Okay."

"Okay?" I asked, wary of him giving in like that.

Oliver smiled. He looked so sleepy and cute with his dark hair all over the place. "You can pay rent. Unnecessary, but if it makes you feel better, then okay."

"It does." I assured him.

I was pushed to my back, and he moved over my body.

He couldn't seriously want to go again, could he?

I ran my hands up and down the side of his body and locked his legs under my thighs. He was ready to go.

"You didn't ask me what was in the envelope," he whispered huskily.

Major turn off.

I raised my brows at him. "I am not sleeping with you if you mention her name, Oliver."

"I'm not that much of a jerk. I was just wondering why you didn't ask about it," he questioned, kissing my nose as he lay against mine.

Shrugging, I glanced away then back up at him. "It's none of my business."

"You'd like what was in it," he whispered, bringing his lips closer as his hard part pushed against me.

I moaned. He was teasing me so bad right now. I tried to push against him, but he raised his hips and moved away.

"Ollie." I groaned.

"She signed," he said and sunk inside me with a deep thrust. His words didn't register until he stopped moving again and cupped my cheeks. He looked me dead in the eye. "I'm not going to work today because she signed the divorce papers and I'm going to file them."

I just stared at him. "That's really good news. You should have told me sooner." I pinched his ass, and he just laughed, kissing me as we continued with our sleepy morning sex.

~

OLIVER

"Should I be worried at all? Her signing so fast and without a fuss?" I asked Clayton, my lawyer.

He shook his head and closed the grey filing cabinet. "No. You're a free man. She didn't fight over anything. This was a quick and easy divorce. I think she knew if she fought you on the money part, then it'd turn ugly. She had a change of heart."

Change of heart or change in her plans.

I didn't know why, but after Sage asked if there was any chance Amy was playing at something else, I became wary of Amy.

246

It was quick, and I had been expecting a long, drawn-out fight with her. For someone who promised she'd never give up, she was giving up very easily.

"Oliver, this is a good thing. Try not to stress about it. She's broken the AVO more than once. She's setting herself up for nothing but more legal trouble. Soon, she'll be held in contempt," he said, "You gave her the house and everything in it. I think she got a fair deal."

"What about Sage and Meadow? What if she goes anywhere near them?" They were my main concern. I could take the hell unleashed on myself, not so much for them.

Clayton sunk back in his chair and drummed his fingers over his desk. "Oliver, go home and be with your family. If Amy goes near them, then call me, and I will go straight to a judge myself and organize a hearing."

I left the lawyer's and headed to the mall where the mother of my beautiful daughter was working, much to my dismay, but I couldn't stop her. She wanted to work. Then she'd work.

It was hard to think that I spent a good part of the year building this place. Her shop, as soon as you walked in, smelt of everything good.

Avoiding the looks of the group of women who were walking out and giggling, I walked inside and found Sage sitting with Meadow in the baby sling carrier behind the counter. She smiled and turned Meadow more upright.

"Look. It's Daddy! He's come to visit us."

I grinned, picking my daughter out of the sling just as Cassie walked in with a coffee in her hand, looking run off her feet.

"My god, some people are assholes." She snapped, sitting down and frowning.

"Language." I warned, teasingly. "My child's first word better not be *a-hole.*"

"Like you're one to talk. All you do is drop f-bombs." She grinned. "What are you doing here anyway? Can't leave my sister alone for ten minutes?" She wiggled her brows.

I looked at Sage who just blushed and looked away.

If only she knew how hard it was to not be near Sage all the time. I just laughed and walked to the men's section of the store, which was a quarter the size of everything else.

"I need shaving stuff. Do you sell that? Nothing too smelly, just manly."

"Nope," Cassie called out the same time as Sage said, "Yes."

"So you two are shacking up for real? Not that we didn't see it happening. Mum's going to be heartbroken now the house is empty. She'll want Meadow for sleepovers soon," Cassie said.

I sighed. She could want sleepovers all she wanted. They all could, but I wasn't letting her out of my sight. "Cass, you tell your mum the day she gets Meadow is the day my daughter will come up to me and ask, 'Daddy, can I sleep at Nan's?'"

Sage laughed, walking over to us. "Oh, yes. I agree. She needs to be at least six before anyone has her. She's too little for now."

Ignoring Cassie and her calling us overprotective parents, Sage grabbed a tub of men's cream and undid the lid. "This smells good. Not too girly, and you should get the after shaving balm as well." She picked that up and the small shaving brush. I'd normally just use an electric razor.

Sage put the brush over Meadow's cheeks, and she tried to eat it.

"She's hungry again?" I asked. *How much can this girl drink?*

"Oh, no. I fed her like half hour ago." She ran the bristles over my jaw. "Soft, isn't it?"

I nodded, locked in her spell.

She grabbed that and three other products and bit her lip, chewing on it before asking. "How did this morning go?"

Finally, she was getting used in asking me whatever was on her mind. "Done. I'm divorced and done with her. I asked what you mentioned, and he said not to worry. I think something's up though. It was too easy."

"Maybe she sees that you're actually happy and living without her?" she said.

"Hope so. Now, I need to talk to you about us moving. I wanted to get in there this weekend. I'll stay there and fix things up before you come though. Are you okay with being apart for a night or two?" I asked. I wanted to get this house sorted with furniture before she moved in. This was pretty huge, and I wanted to make it nice for her and not just a guy's home, but somewhere she'd feel at home as well.

She hummed but nodded. "It'll suck but should be fine."

"I'll make it up to you." I smirked.

Last night, she was utterly amazing. It was pure bliss being with her. I couldn't get enough of her body, her soft moans, and frustrating growls as I brought her over the edge again and again. She was perfect, and staring at her now, I wanted nothing more to take her home and have her back in that bed again.

"Ollie, stop looking at me like that," she whispered, playing with my shirt's hem.

~

I took Meadow back to her parents and left my work ute for Sage to drive back home. It was almost three when she walked in, and she found Meadow and me lying down on the floor, playing with rattles. She sat down beside us, and without saying anything, she leant in and kissed me.

Dinner was quick and easy, Chinese. We ended up soaking in the tub for almost a good hour. We were both too lazy to get out, and we kept adding more hot water to it. Going back to bed, I pulled her body against mine and held onto her close.

"Cassie asked if we were banging," Sage said with a soft laugh.

"Do people still call it that?" I winked, laughing myself.

"Apparently, she said the sexual tension was very noticeable between us the other day, and today she reckoned we were about to screw against the wall." She smiled, running her fingers up and down my chest.

Her sister had nothing better to do than worry about everyone else. I shrugged. "If we were alone, we would have, but your sister can think what she wants. Let her mind wander, just like everyone else's does."

"I'm happy that you're divorced, Ollie," she whispered. "Really happy."

I smiled. "Me too."

My life had changed so much in the past year. Never did I think I'd be divorced at twenty-seven. Then again, I never expected to find another woman and feel things for her that I had never experienced. I thought I fell in love and felt that. Now, I realised it wasn't love. It was something else. Maybe lust but definitely not love.

When I looked at Meadow, I was in love.

When I looked at Sage, I was definitely feeling love, but I wanted to make sure of it before I told her.

"Ollie," she whispered, and I knew she was up to something.

I raised my brows, looking down at her as she tilted her head back and looked up toward me. "Yes?" I asked.

"I was thinking you're going to get a present. Something that you will enjoy, and it's just for you." She began as she sat up, moving between my thighs. I raised my brows about to ask what it was when she pushed a finger to my mouth. "Tonight is just for you."

My hands slid down her arms as she took me in her mouth and began to suck. Damn, this woman was giving. I lay back, enjoying the warmth of her mouth wrapped around my cock as she sucked me up and down. She'd use her tongue, hands, and then change it up again, sending me near the edge each time until she stopped and started again.

My thigh tensed up and I came hard, unable to hold off any longer as she sucked harder. Groaning her name and flexing further into her mouth, she moaned loudly, and that only turned me on even more.

I pulled her against my chest as she moved up from the bed and kissed her, ignoring the taste of myself on her tongue as I kissed her deeply. She might have said no to her receiving pleasure, but there was no way I'd lay here and not feel her body underneath mine as I made love to her until we both became exhausted and fell asleep.

~

Meadow woke up screaming through the night, which jolted me awake fast. Sage was up and breathing heavily while I jumped out of bed and picked up Meadow, trying to settle her as I handed her over.

"Ollie, she was really screaming. My heart is still pounding," she whispered, pulling the covers up over them both as she lay down with Meadow beside her.

I got back in the bed and rubbed Meadow's back as she fed on Sage. "She definitely knows how to give people a scare. This is probably her nighttime cry for us."

The three of us all fell asleep in the bed. Meadow was between us and sleeping quietly when I woke up. She was letting out soft snores as Sage had her close against her body. I got up and pulled on some sweatpants. Giving them both a kiss, I got on the laptop to do some work.

I opened my email only to see email after email from Amy. They were random shit from her asking if I would come help fix the TV or tighten a screw on the cupboard. Did she think I was that stupid to fall for her drama again? Ignoring them all, I forwarded them to my lawyer and sent him a message of my own.

*Fix it, or you're fired.*

He was too laid-back. He should be taking all this more seriously. Much more serious than he had been since he wasn't too worried about Amy's stalking tactics.

Divorced or not, my instincts kept telling me the same thing. This was far from over with her.

# CHAPTER 21

I missed him, and it was crazy. We'd only been apart for two days, but I still missed him. Oliver called, texted, and sent me photos as I did the same to him. It would be worth it in the end once the house was ready.

He decided to rip the kitchen up and rebuild it before we moved in. In that way, it was done and over with. He was worried about Meadow getting bothered with the noise, so he said it was easier to do it this week before we moved than to wait a few months after we moved in. A true builder.

Greyson crashed at the house while I packed some of my things up. I think Oliver was most excited about setting Meadow's room up. He was looking forward to rebuilding everything himself. He missed out on it the first time, so now he said it was a chance to do that.

Greyson picked up Meadow and tickled her stomach. She didn't smile but just dropped her lip.

"She hates me." He sighed.

I laughed. "No. She's just fussy and getting to know you."

"Yeah, right." He grinned and kissed her cheek. "She's cute. I guess that makes up for it all. So, when do you want to head off?"

"I don't know. I need to get out of my sweats and change her. Then we can go." I got off the couch, and Greyson handed Meadow over for me to get her ready.

We were going to pick out some appliances. Oliver told me to pick whatever I liked, and I honestly had no idea what to get.

Mum wrote me a list, and I was going to follow that or at least try to. I knew the basics, but there were so many brands to choose from. It was daunting.

Greyson decided to take it upon himself to pick out my clothing for the day. How I should have known that he'd pick out something that I'd use to wear. I wasn't comfortable wearing my tight clothes. I was happy with the maxi skirt and baggier top.

Greyson raised his brow and held out some navy washed out boyfriend jeans. "Put these on."

"Grey, they're too small for me," I grumbled. "Why can't I just wear a skirt or dress?"

"Why are you wearing big loose clothing? You don't need to." He laid the jeans on my bed and went back to the closet to look for a shirt.

He was pushing me.

"I'll wear them with a jumper."

"Nope. I found something else for you to wear that you can't wear a jumper with." He grinned, taking the jeans back and then handed me a pair of pink-cream shorts and a light grey top. "Tuck the top all the way in. Show off your MILF body."

He was going to kill me.

I took them and scowled. "They won't fit!" I called out as I headed for the bathroom. "Go dress Meadow since you're so into dressing other people."

"Oh god, dressing a baby is going to be better than dressing you," he called out, sounding eager.

Once we were all ready, we got into the car and went to the mall.

Walking through the mall and pushing my sleeping daughter in the pram, I ignored the smug look on Greyson's face as I was wearing the outfit he had chosen with some brown chunky heel sandals. I felt nervous. My legs were all out for everyone to see. Normally, it wouldn't bother me, but I'd just had a child seven weeks ago. I felt like everyone was staring at me and thinking I was too big to be in mid-thigh length shorts or a more fitted top.

Walking into a store with kitchenware, I immediately got a little excited.

After paying, we carried the bags to the car.

"Do you even cook?" Greyson laughed.

I nodded. Indeed, yes. "I'm getting better slowly. Oliver eats what I make, so that's a good thing."

We put the bags away and made our way back to the mall, getting ready to look around again.

Greyson had asked me what was going on between Oliver and me. It was hard not to tell him exactly, but I didn't really know myself. After sitting down to eat, I decided to answer him.

"We're friends. Ollie and I are just figuring things out. So there is no pressure with labels or anything. It's good that way. He's a great father, and we get along well. I don't want to push him into a relationship so soon after just being divorced. I'm happy as we are." And I really was. Sex, that was amazing with him, and we both expressed feelings out that way.

"What about his wife?" he asked, digging into his sushi roll.

I hated even talking about her. "Ex-wife." I corrected. "She's his ex, and I don't know about her. She is insane, crazy, and very freaky. I mean, she dyed her hair jet black and looks scary and fudge." I giggled, making sure not to say the f-word while Meadow was around. Both Oliver and I were trying to make sure we didn't swear as often as we normally did.

"Does she want him back?" he asked.

"Yes, she does. I know that for a fact. She's emailing him and sending texts. It's annoying me, but I can't do anything about it. Oliver gets angry, and his lawyer isn't doing anything about it either, so he fired him. The whole house is a filler for him. It keeps him busy and takes his mind off her." I grabbed a sushi roll and took a bite. Eating was helping me deal with all of this.

~

My phone buzzed on the drive back to the house, and Greyson read out the message, "Come straight to the house. Your dad dropped off the last of your things."

255

*Oh, okay. Well, then.*

I pulled over and did a sharp U-turn, heading back the other way.

Oliver's work ute was in the drive along with Tony's. Both had the trailers filled with scraps of wood and a heap of carpet. Tony was helping around. It was going to be interesting to see what the place now looked like.

Carrying Meadow inside, I slipped my shoes off and looked around. The house was already set up, and I was shocked at what good taste the man had. I was expecting a two-seater with a throw over it. Instead, I was met with a large charcoal L-shaped lounge with a huge matching square foot seat in front of it. On the other side were two large matching chairs that rocked if needed to.

Greyson abandoned me, heading over to Oliver's father and brother to chat and help them out with some lifting. I stood there feeling a little out of place. It was surreal that this was my new home.

"Hey." His voice held excitement as he walked over and took Meadow from my arms. "Welcome to your new home, baby girl." He kissed her head. He smiled down at me, lowering his voice so no one else could hear. "I missed you."

"I missed you too. We both did. The house looks good." I smiled. "I didn't think you'd have so much done."

"This is my job. It's what I love doing. I ripped the carpet out. The floorboards look better. That doesn't bother you, does it?" he asked, placing his hand against my lower back and pushing me towards the stairs. Leading us up, he stopped in the large hallway. "The bedrooms are up here. Master is down the end. Then there are two next to each other and another to the side here." He gestured with his hand. "Which one do you want? I don't mind."

"I'll take the one down the end next to the other. Meadow can be in the middle room if you want. But you should take the master room. It's your home."

I was so nervous right now. This was it. It was us living together, along with our daughter.

256

We were so messed up and doing this all backward.

"Babe, this is your home also. If you don't like something, we can change it. How was your shopping?" he asked. Taking a step back, he dipped his brows low and looked at me. "I'm extremely hard right now looking at you."

I blushed, feeling less self-conscious than I did. "Don't. I didn't want to wear this."

"Why not?" He frowned. "You look very hot. If we were alone, I'd have you naked and in the bed right about now."

He sure did have a way with words. "Not on your new couch?" I teased.

Leaning forward, he kissed me softly. "Don't worry. We'll get to the couch and every other surface in this house."

If we were alone, then yes, I'd definitely be naked with him right now.

I walked in the room I chose, and there was a bed already in there. It didn't take too much longer until the rest of the furniture was in.

The kitchen was actually done and completed. Now, it had a large, sleek white modern island and matching benches and cupboards on the other side with a pantry. There was a sliding door across from that with an alfresco sitting area that was overlooking the swimming pool and outdoor yard. There was also a large family room with a separate meal area.

The laundry was a decent size as well.

Oliver had already set up the study. Then in the living room, there was another room off the side of that where we were going to have Meadow's toys and play area. It was a big house, much bigger than I last remembered.

After six hours of unpacking, cleaning, and setting things up, it was complete by 2:00 AM.

I slumped down on the couch and fought to keep my eyes open. Meadow was fast asleep in her bedroom. I think she was exhausted after being passed around everyone during the day and taking everything in.

Tony and Cassie were still here.

Cass came and sat beside me, yawning loudly. "My god, I could so go for a can of Bundy right about now."

"You're going to drink?" I asked. "How can you think of doing anything other than sleeping?"

"The boys are drinking outside. They finally got the BBQ built," she said. "You sure you're okay being here? No one would hate you if you didn't live with him."

I shot her a confused look. "Cassie, it's better than the alternative. I don't want to pack a bag each week and say goodbye to Meadow."

"And you won't have to do that." Oliver's voice startled me. "It's easier this way. We're both able to parent together, and no one is packing bags like we're two estranged parents who can't stand each other. This is what's best for our child. She's with us both."

I stood up when our daughter began to cry. I yawned. "I'll go. I think I'm going to head to bed. I'm exhausted."

~

OLIVER

I watched Sage walk off and turned back to see Cass and Tony staring at me with grins on their faces.

"What?" I asked.

Tony shook his head and shrugged. "You two are so fucking weird."

"Living together but in separate rooms," Cass added. "You're obviously screwing. Why not share a room?"

I shrugged my shoulders. "It is what it is, and I'm not going to deny or confirm your imaginative thoughts."

They both burst out laughing.

Tony patted my shoulder. "Mate, you've been getting laid. It's pretty obvious when you come to work, smiling from ear to ear. Or when you have to go home for lunch, which you rarely do, but

258

there's no judgement here. Do what works for you both. Now, let's go crack a few open and celebrate your bachelor's pad."

"My gir..." I stopped myself when I realized what I had almost said. Clearing my throat, I corrected him. "Sage and my daughter live here. It is definitely not a bachelor's pad nor will it be. So keep your piss up house party to yourself."

Cassie grinned. "Aww, Daddy's gone all old and boring. Maybe he's not getting laid after all."

I was definitely getting laid more than ever. "Don't you two need to be somewhere?" I asked, sighing.

"Oh, buddy, no way in fucking hell. We're celebrating. Now, let's celebrate." He smirked. "And I want answers."

~

Walking up the stairs after another hour of sitting outside and drinking, I went down to Meadow's room and opened the door quietly. God, I had missed her so much these past two days. Not being able to see her each morning and night was utter pain and hell. If Sage hadn't wanted to live with me, it would have ripped out my heart. I couldn't even imagine doing what she had mentioned, weekly visits and then not to see her for another week. Not to see them both, it would break me.

Kissing her cheek, I stroked her soft hair and then left the room. I made my way down to Sage's room where she was steadily breathing, sleeping quietly and on one side of the bed.

I went and had a shower, washing the dirt and dust off my body and then climbed into bed. I couldn't sleep. It'd been okay these past two nights. I didn't have to overthink it. I worked, slept, and got up early to work again. Now, I was lying here and staring at the ceiling. She was down the hall, asleep and alone. Somehow, this separate room thing seemed crazy stupid, but I didn't want to push her into something she wasn't ready for.

"Screw it," I muttered to myself. I tossed the blanket off my body and walked down to her room again, sliding in beside her. I wrapped my body around hers and kissed the base of her neck.

She wiggled, turning in my arms and facing me. Her thigh draped over my hip as I cupped her ass. I kissed her, and she began to kiss back, sleepily, lazily, but needily. Within a quick moment and in the same position, I pulled her panties aside. My cock, free from the slip in my boxers, was buried deep inside her, slowly thrusting in and out. I wasn't going to last long. It was hard not to blow within seconds of feeling her wrapped around my dick like a tight fist.

Her breathing picked up as I kept a slow, steady pace until we both came together.

~

I woke before she did. Meadow was awake, and I could hear her restless cries. I jumped out of bed before Sage woke up. I walked down to my daughter and saw her kicking her legs up in the sleeping bag she slept in each night.

"Hey, little girl. You ready to get up?" I whispered, turning the monitor off. I picked her up and laid her down on the change table. I passed her a tube of cream to hold onto while I changed her.

Sage walked down and into the living room an hour later. "I'm sorry." She yawned, covering her mouth.

"For what?" I asked, pulling her down onto my lap and kissing her cheek.

"Sleeping in. Did she wake early?" she asked, her arms wrapped around my waist and she melted into my side. A perfect fit.

I shook my head, looking at Meadow who was in her rocker swing fast asleep. A bottle of milk and she was out like a light. "No. She didn't wake that long ago. I don't mind getting up to her, but you may have to pump some milk into a couple more bottles for me. She was really hungry this morning."

"Can I ask you something? I don't want to put you in a bad mood at all," Sage whispered. I tensed up slightly but lay back and kept quiet as she kept speaking. I could feel her nervousness in her

260

body as she played with my hair. "If she keeps writing to you and begging you back, would you go back there? To try again with her?"

I didn't hesitate to answer. "No." I definitely wouldn't. "Our whole relationship was built on lies from the start. The trust is gone. I wouldn't ever go back and try when I know that it wouldn't work. It would end badly."

Badly, meaning one of us dead.

Her body stiffened as she realized what I meant. Relaxing, she slid off my lap and smiled. "Good. Because if you did, I'd come and kick your ass out of there."

I laughed, watching her walk out of the room. I had no doubt that she would do that as well.

After a lazy morning, we decided to head into town and stock up on groceries. After almost two hours of walking around slowly and filling the trolley, we headed back to the house. There was a red wrapped package on the doorstep. Sage picked it up and brought it inside while I grabbed the other bags from the car.

"What's that?" I asked, nodding towards the gift.

She opened it and held up a recipe book. "Did your mum stop by?" she asked, confused.

"I don't know. Probably." I laughed. "She goes a little overboard with helping out. We'll probably be getting books each week now."

"That's nice of her. I hope you're ready to be trying new foods each night. Weeknights I am going to try and cook dinner, since you brought all the furniture and everything else here." She grinned. "Which by the way, you have a very good taste."

I looked at her, hungry for something other than food. "Of course, I do."

"Ollie, stop staring at me like that. Oh and tell me why you were in my room instead of yours last night?" She wiggled her brows.

I laughed as she tossed me another empty bag. "I got lonely, and my bed was too big and cold."

"I know. I prefer snuggles too." She grinned and sat on the bar stool, starting to flip through the cookbook. "Remind me to thank your mum for this. It's got some good recipes in here."

"Well, I look forward to trying them then. No take out then?"

Her eyes widened. "My god, no. Well, Friday and Saturday nights are good, but not weeknights. We can cook together if you're home early enough, but since I'm only working on and off until I go back, then I can do it." She shrugged.

"Nope. We can cook together. Anyone hear us talking right now, and they'd think we'd been married for years." I winked, teasingly.

She looked up at me and blushed. "I'm sorry. I don't want you to feel that way."

"I was joking, Sage." I winked. Maybe I was a little hurt, but I didn't show it. "So Meadow is asleep. You want to go, and you know?" I wiggled my brows at her.

"Ooh, take a nap? Yeah, I would love too." She wiggled her brows back. She looked at her watch then back up at me. "We have around two hours until she wakes up."

"Two hours. Well, I only need a couple of minutes." I smirked, grabbing her by the waist and pulling her against my body.

I lifted her up and began to carry her to the stairs when my phone rang. I groaned and pushed her hard to the wall using my thigh to hold her up as her mouth and hands roamed over my neck and waist as I checked my phone.

God, she was a mood kill.

I tossed the phone to the floor and turned my attention back to the sexy woman wrapped around my waist. We didn't make it up the stairs. I laid her down and bottoms off in a quick flash. I tugged my jeans down. I grabbed hold of the stair behind her head and thrust in hard. My knees slipped on the hardwood. This wasn't that comfortable.

I lay down and she immediately straddled me.

"Fuck. You feel so tight." I grunted, holding her by the waist as she kneeled above me.

She was not holding back as we went fast and hard. Her breathing was loud, face flushed, and hair tied up as she grabbed my hands and kept moving wildly.

My ass was numb, and her movements weren't slowing. "God, I need you to just fuck me, Ollie. Hard!" she cried out. "I can't." She bit her lip in frustration.

I held her waist down and lifted her shirt. My hands slid up her slim stomach to her full breasts and grabbed them. Seconds later, she spasmed and came. Her slick wetness covered me as she bounced up and down.

With my cock throbbing harder, I released inside her, shooting a few times until we were both spent and breathing hard. I didn't anticipate it when she slid off me and stepped over my head, giving me a good view of what I just dived into.

God.

She giggled. "Come and find me, lover. If you want more, that is."

"Hope you're ready for more, baby. We've got a whole house to cover!" I called out laughing, getting up and chasing after her.

Oh, I planned on giving her more. Definitely more.

# CHAPTER 22

"There was another book. This one looks really expensive, too," I called out, staring at the Donna Hay recipe book. I almost had the whole collection now, and they weren't cheap. I made a point to Google them last week.

His mum was very generous with the cookbooks. I received one every week since we moved in and we'd been living together for three months. It was a lot of books, and I felt a little bad. His parents had gone on a cruise, and we couldn't contact them to say thanks.

I threw the wrapping paper in the bin and read over the book. I looked up when I heard a loud giggle coming from Meadow. She was so adorable. The little sounds she made were cute and so little.

Meadow was just over five months old and rolling around like crazy. She definitely had us both on our feet and following her about.

The months had been so fast. Oliver was working more and more, but it didn't bother me. I was now back at work for a couple days a week, and Meadow went to either my mum's or Oliver's mother for the few hours. They loved having her around.

Oliver walked downstairs with a towel wrapped around his waist. Water droplets were over his chest from his hair. I couldn't help but look at the bulge pressed underneath the towel. That man was such a tease. He was sexy as hell.

I smiled. He was comfortable going shirtless, and he already forgot the scars and marks that Amy had put there.

264

"Another one?" He frowned, gesturing to the book. "Do you think she subscribed them for you? I don't see why she doesn't just knock on the door and give them to us herself. But if she's away, maybe someone from the post is bringing them over."

"Maybe she's trying not to be too forward?" I suggested. Going over to the large bookshelf he had built, I slid it in a slot next to others.

Meadow was biting her teething stick and watching cartoons on the floor. She loved the bright colours on the screen.

"She's going to be crawling soon. God, she's growing so fast. She's not little anymore. I do love how she giggles when you tickle her. It's the best thing in the world," he said, actually looking a little sad.

"Clucky already?" I teased, laughing.

He just shook his head and grinned. "Can you imagine another one? God, I'd be grey before I was thirty." He laughed and made his way back upstairs. "I think you're the clucky one, Sage," he called out.

"Clucky, my ass," I muttered to myself, hating that I was unable to stop smiling like an idiot.

I sat on the floor with Meadow. She was playing with a rattle and making more noises when Oliver came back down and sat opposite us. He leant over and kissed me.

"Do you want to go over to Haddon's today with me?" he asked.

His brother was alright. It was Julia who hated me and made it her mission to make me feel uncomfortable when I was around her.

"Do you mind if I stayed here?" I asked. "Sorry. I just would rather not go there."

"No. You were up most the night with her. Why don't you sleep? I can take her with me," he said, fingering Meadow's dark hair that was covering her eyes. "If you don't mind?"

"I would love that." I lay down on my back and stared at the ceiling. "She was so fussy last night. Just didn't want to sleep."

Meadow was up and down a lot lately. Although, if she slept in the bed beside me, she would sleep almost all night. "I think she is going through a clingy stage."

"You should have woke me up. I didn't hear her at all." He got up on all fours and crawled over, leaning over the top of me. He kissed me and rolled us, pulling me on top of his body.

Looking down at him, I propped myself up with my hand. "You've been working hard. I don't mind sitting down here with her so you can sleep. I do miss you though."

"Same." He wrapped his arms around my lower back and pushed up against me. "It's been too long, baby."

"It's been a week, but it feels like months." I pouted.

With Oliver and me in separate beds due to Meadow's weird sleeping pattern, we weren't getting it on as much as we used to. Not that it really bothered me. I had been on my period this past week, so it was kind of a blessing.

He pushed his head up and planted his lips against mine. "We should do something. Just us for one night."

Like a date?

I held in my excitement. Even though things had been really good between us, we were still under the friends category.

Amy had gone complete AWOL on everyone. We hadn't heard a thing, which was good. She was finally leaving us alone. Hopefully, she had moved out of the country and vanished.

Oliver was also talking to someone about what happened. It was starting to give him nightmares and making him jumpy some days. I didn't know how he would respond to it when I brought it up, but after a few days of thinking it over, he said it was probably a good thing.

Answering him, I nodded. "We should. We could order in and veg out on the couch."

"Now that we're boring." He chuckled. "Or we could go see a movie?" He shrugged casually. "Grab dinner somewhere?"

I liked that idea.

Meadow began to cry when Ollie moved so he was back on top of me and tickling my sides. Living with him, I learnt that Oliver was very playful at times and loved to stir me up. He moved off me and picked Meadow up, sitting her on my stomach as he still knelt over my knees.

"What do you say, Mummy? You think Daddy should take little miss for a while and let you rest?" he asked.

She responded by lying down and slobbering over my chin.

"Oh, I take that as a yes. Yes, you do want to go with Daddy and see your big cousins." I grinned and wiped my chin and neck. She started jumping and clapping excitedly. Oliver just grinned and picked her up. "What's for dinner?"

I looked at him like he was insane. "Ollie, it's not even ten in the morning. I'm not even thinking of dinner, so please tell me what you would like to eat."

"I'll get something. Don't worry about cooking or anything. Just go to bed and sleep." He let Meadow back on the floor, and she rolled to get back to her chew stick. The front bottom teeth were almost through.

Finally, he got off my body. I stood up and headed for the kitchen.

"How long will you be gone for? I have bottles in the fridge. Do you want me to feed her before you leave?"

"Yeah, that may be a good idea. What else do I take?" he asked, leaning against the kitchen counter while I turned the Nespresso machine on.

I grabbed a cup and made him coffee to help keep him awake for today. Oliver was watching me closely. He often did this, just sit and watch. It'd make me nervous at times, but now I was used to it.

"Christmas is coming up soon. How do you want to celebrate that?" he asked quietly.

I turned and looked at him. I hadn't really given it a thought. "Uh, I don't know. What do you normally do?" I asked then regretted it. "I mean, what do you want to do?"

"You, Meadow, and I. Here and doing whatever." He shrugged. "I just want a relaxed day if that's okay with you? Unless you have plans with your family?"

"Nope. Nothing. Here sounds good." I smiled and slid his coffee over.

Oliver kissed me goodbye as he and Meadow headed off to his brother for a visit. I headed up the stairs and decided to take a long soak in the bath, enjoying the peace and quiet. I did feel a little bit guilty about being here and not doing anything but worrying about myself.

Finally sinking into bed after my relaxing bath, I enjoyed the fact that I could lie down and just stretch out. I enjoyed having the whole space to myself. Just as I fell asleep, the doorbell rang.

Oh god, you're kidding me.

Throwing on some sweats and a shirt, I raced down the stairs to get to the door. My mum probably decided to come over and visit, or Cassie if they knew Ollie took Meadow.

When I unlocked the door, I was met with nothing. No one was there.

I closed the door and locked it again. I was about to walk up the stairs when the bell rang again. The loud noise made me jump. I turned and went back to the door, opening it, and again, I was met with nothing.

Standing there, I waited in case it was some kid messing around.

When I finally closed the door again, I locked it and waited for a moment. Nothing went on again, so I left and went upstairs. I lay in bed with the blankets tucked up underneath my eyes. My heart was pounding like crazy and my skin covered in goose bumps as the doorbell rang over and over again.

I grabbed my phone and sent Ollie a message, wishing he never left because I missed them.

*I miss you both. XO.*

268

I was too petrified to move from the position I was lying in. I couldn't tell if the pounding in my ears was from my heart thudding loudly in my chest or footsteps running up the stairs.

~

OLIVER

I smiled and fired back a message to Sage.

*Miss you more, baby.*

I hated being away, but she needed it. She looked exhausted as hell. Her eyes were fighting to stay open, and she was constantly yawning. It'd do her good to have a break for a couple of hours.

Haddon was outside with the kids, pushing Jade on the swing when I walked out with Meadow in my arms. He grinned, and the other boys ran over. Max was bouncing up and down at my feet.

"Uncle Oliver, can we push Meadow on the swing?"

I grinned, squatting down low. She was looking at them curiously with her big eyes but clung to my shirt. "She's a bit too small, buddy. How about when she's bigger, then you can?"

He sighed. "Alright," he said sadly. Then his eyes lit up again. "Can she play on the grass with us? With our cars?"

"Sure." I rubbed his mop of hair and set Meadow down on the grass. She looked around and then fell to her side and just rolled. She loved the grass and tried to pull it out. "Keep an eye on her," I said to the boys and stood when Haddon walked over.

"You're a sight for sore eyes." He grinned. "Where's Sage?"

"Home. Tired so she's sleeping," I said.

He looked down at Meadow and picked her up, getting groans from his sons as he took her away from them. She grabbed his nose and tried to eat it, which just made him laugh.

"She's cute. Are you enjoying fatherhood?" he asked.

269

We walked over to the deck and sat down. Leaning back in the deck chair, I looked out at the boys, then over at my daughter. "Love it. She's amazing."

"She is. She's definitely a little looker. Just wait until she's older and has all the boys after her." He winked, giving me a nudge in the arm.

I threw my head back and laughed. I was laughing, but on the inside, I was dreading it. Nope. Definitely not happening. "She will be homeschooled and kept in the house until she's thirty or sent to a school for nuns."

"Yeah, whatever you say. She'll have you wrapped around her finger, and I bet you give in to her every demand." He smirked. "Like you are with another woman in your house."

"Don't know what you're on about." I shrugged, keeping a straight face. "She doesn't make demands. It's weird. She's very different." I frowned slightly. The more I thought about it, I realized she was different and hated making decisions. "She's more submissive."

"Likes you being in control?" Haddon asked, bouncing Meadow on his knee.

I nodded. I guess she did. She always asked and never told me what to do. "Sage likes me to do a lot of things. She cooks, cleans, and does all that without complaint, but there are times where she'll ask what I want and says she likes it when I tell her what I want and like."

"She sounds good for you. Nothing like that psycho bitch. What about in bed? She calls the shots?" he asked.

I groaned. "What is it with everyone wanting to know if we're screwing? Yes, we are, and no, she doesn't. Unless she's horny and just wants to be fucked hard. She's good for me. I feel in charge and like a man. Not sitting in silence waiting to be yelled at or have something thrown at me. I don't regret cheating at all now. Yeah, it was wrong, and I would never do it again." I reached my hand out and stroked Meadow's soft hand. She pulled away and grabbed my little finger, trying to eat it. My heart was filled with love, nothing but deep love for her. I smiled. "Not since she's the outcome."

"I wish I knew what you went through. I had an idea, but I didn't ever think it would be true. If I ever see her, I don't know what I'd do to her. My fist would probably do the talking." He grunted. "Julia thinks the fucking world of her. She won't believe a word I try to tell her."

Typical. Amy would have gotten in her ear and made up some bullshit.

I shrugged it off. Not wanting to strain my brother's marriage with my mistakes and problems. "Don't worry about it, man. She'll come around."

*Hopefully*, I added in my mind.

I slid my phone out again. Meadow was on the deck with some of the boys' stuffed animals and playing with them. She already had those three fawning over her like crazy. They loved it though, talking to her and trying for her to speak. All she'd respond with was something unpronounceable.

I sent Sage a text, hoping she wasn't asleep.

*Will be back soon.*

I received her reply almost instantly.

*Good.*

I read that one word over and over. She wasn't pissed that I wasn't there, was she? Fuck. Well, I hope not. I didn't want her to worry.

Amy was nowhere to be seen for the past few months. It was pretty damn good. She was gone and out of our lives. I now had a new lawyer who actually seemed to know what he was doing. The last one was fucking useless and too lazy to file any paperwork. The restraining order was up, but I wasn't able to get another in place. Not when she'd left us alone.

271

"You should come on the camping trip next fortnight. It'll be down on the beach with the guys and us," Haddon said.

"How long for?" I asked, wondering what Sage would think. Maybe she'd not like the idea of taking Meadow out and camping with others. She could be too young. I didn't know. I had no clue about what age kids could and couldn't do anything.

"Just a weekend. Go ask Sage if she'd want to come as well. I'll bring the boys, so definitely bring Meadow. I've got the outdoor sun tent to keep her in. She won't get out or anything. Could be a good weekend away," he said.

It did sound tempting, and it would be fun to get out and do something together.

~

Heading back home, I pulled into the drive and noticed that all the blinds were closed. Walking up the stairs, I put Meadow in her cot with a bottle and laid her down under a blanket. She could hold it now, which was a plus.

I opened Sage's bedroom door, and she was under the doona and breathing heavy.

"Sage," I said quietly. She jumped and pushed the covers off her face. Her eyes were red and swollen. Fuck. I rushed over to her and slid in beside her. "Baby, what's wrong?" I asked, brushing her hair off her face.

"Oh, god. Please don't go again," she said, crying into my chest. "I didn't want to worry you."

"Worry me?" I asked. "Baby, what happened? What's got you so upset?"

"Someone was here," she choked out.

My body tensed. "What do you mean? Sage, tell me what happened. Who was here?"

She shrugged. "I don't know, Ollie. The doorbell, it just rang and rang and wouldn't stop. I checked the first couple times, but there was no one. I was so freaked out I stayed up here, and for ages, it kept ringing."

272

"I wished you had called me. I would have come back immediately," I said. In the back of my mind, Amy's name came up, but I didn't say anything. If she were messing around with Sage, I would find out and rain hell on her. This was definitely not okay.

"I didn't want to bother you. I'm sorry," she whispered. "I'm so tired. I just can't sleep."

"I'm here now. Sleep, baby. I'm here, and nothing will hurt you," I whispered back, kissing her head gently as I stroked her cheek.

She leaned on my chest. Her body was rising and falling softly while I watched her. I knew it. I knew it was too good to be true with her being away. She'd be the only one capable of fucking up our lives with some mind game bullshit.

I felt her lips against my chest, and she looked up. "How's your brother? Was Meadow good?"

"She was very good. The boys love her. Haddon is good. He invited us to go camping with him and the others in a couple weeks. What do you think?" I asked her, stroking her back up and down.

She fisted my shirt and snuggled in closer. "Is Meadow going to be okay camping? She'd have to sleep between us if we shared a tent," she mumbled the last part.

"We will be sharing a tent," I stated. Like hell, she was sleeping alone or with someone else. "I think she will be alright. She can go swimming, and your sister and Tony will be there. It could be fun to get away and do nothing, yeah?" I suggested.

"Okay. That sounds nice. If Meadow is cranky and sooky, I can just go stay with Mum with her so you can stay and have a good time." She yawned, arching her body into the bed more and then shivering.

I shook my head, pulling her close to me and laying my leg over her. "Not going to happen, baby. I'm not going if you two don't go."

"We can go." She yawned again. "I'm going to fall asleep."

273

As her eyes closed shut, I lay there and kept looking at the ceiling. How could she be so perfect without even trying? Her body was tight against mine while I played with her hair. I loved her long hair. She thought about cutting it short, and I had said an outright no.

I needed to tell her how I felt before it was too late. I wanted her to know that this was more for me, and I didn't just look at this as a "friends with benefits" type of relationship. I loved her. She was the mother of my daughter, and I couldn't think of being with anyone else.

Sage was it. She was the one I wanted, yhe one I would fight to keep no matter what.

I pressed my lips to her forehead and softly whispered like I had done every other night that she was asleep in my arms and unable to hear me.

"I love you."

# CHAPTER 23

I was sitting in the car while Ollie drove us to this camping spot. I couldn't say I wasn't nervous as we passed all the trees along the dusty dirt road. If I said that, then I'd be lying.

This was a huge deal. We were staying out in the middle of nowhere with our daughter who wasn't going to sleep in a cot. She'd be in a tent, and god knows what I'd do if she decided to scream all night long and annoy everyone else who were obviously here for a lot of drinking and relaxing.

Oliver turned down another road, and I looked over at him. He was in black board shorts and a grey top with turquoise *Hurley* written on the chest. His hair was a little messed up, and he had a few days of stubble, but he looked nothing short of hot.

Figuring there would be more of his friends than mine, I was a little worried. We hadn't discussed the ins and outs of our relationship, and everyone now knew he was single. So, what if some drunk girl made a pass at him and offered him a hookup. He and I hadn't had sex for three weeks. Maybe he'd take her up on that.

Jealousy was seeping through my skin.

Women in tiny white bikinis were walking up, obviously just coming up from the water. They were all stick thin and Amy-like. Of course, he'd be attracted to that.

"We're here," he said, breaking me from my green-eyed monster thoughts.

I forced a smile and nodded. "Cool."

Cool? Oh god. Could I have been any more stupid?

275

He just laughed. "Alright. So I'll get the tent set up. Meadow's still asleep, but when she wakes, we should take her down to the water for a paddle."

"I can help with the tent if you want." I offered.

How hard could setting one of those up be?

In no time at all, Oliver had the tent set up by the car where Meadow slept in her car seat. The window was down so we could keep a close eye on her until Ollie pulled me in to "test" the mattress. We weren't really kissing in public, so when he attacked my mouth with his, I wasn't surprised.

I slid my hand over his boardies, and he groaned and flexed against me. I needed him so bad.

"Ollie."

"I know, baby. I know," he murmured and pulled back. "I don't think we're going to be able to fuck even for a couple minutes this weekend."

I giggled. He was so cute when he got frustrated. I slid my hands up his back and underneath his shirt. "Such a hard life," I whispered. "Don't worry. I'll make it up to you when we're home."

He smirked. He lowered his body back down and ran his hand up under my thigh, kissing me hard with passion and grinding against my body as I clung to him desperately. "You're so fucking gorgeous, Sage." He ground out between kisses.

My smile grew bigger. He knew how to make my heart explode. I almost let those three little words slip out.

Almost.

Cassie popped her head into the tent. Her eyes widened as she looked at our position and climbed in beside us, zipping the tent down. Oliver and I just lay frozen, confused and stunned.

"Umm," he said. "We're busy."

"No, you're fucking not. You're lucky you have clothes on. You're going to die when I tell you this," she whispered. "Get off her, please! I need to talk seriously, and I can't when you're both dry humping in front of me."

He couldn't move. I could feel the reason why because it was pressed against my groin. "Just talk," he said, strained. "I'm not moving."

Her face scrunched up, realizing his reason for staying still. "Please, when I tell you this, promise you won't leave. Please stay here."

Now I was worried. "What?" I asked, my voice low and serious. I had a million different thoughts going through my mind right now.

"Promise me." She urged.

Oliver's body tensed up, and he sat up, kneeling over me now instead of lying. He unzipped the tent and let some air inside. Cassie was still staring, but Oliver wasn't waiting around.

"Fucking say it." He snapped, growing impatient and annoyed with her.

"Amy's here," Tony whispered or more stated as he poked his head through the open zip flap.

"We're leaving," Oliver growled, running both hands through his hair. "Who the fuck invited her to come? If I had known, I wouldn't have agreed."

I didn't know what to do. I was just lying here, and then I panicked. "Get off me. I will not have her out there with my daughter."

"Our." Oliver narrowed his eyes at me, and I immediately blushed. I didn't mean to offend him.

Oliver and Tony stayed in the tent. They were talking silently while I got out with Cassie to check on Meadow. She was still contentedly fast asleep in the car seat. The warm air was nice, and the waves could be heard from the beach, which was just a minute walk away from where we were.

"She turned up with some other woman," Cassie said quietly. "I think Julia invited her. Haddon looked pissed as hell with her."

I sighed, glancing around and spotting Daniel and Greyson. I hadn't known they were going to be here too. It really was a friends' catch-up weekend. My eyes lingered over to where a large tent was with two pink chairs. Amy walked out wearing heel sandals and a short dress, laughing as she held a wine glass in her hand. The other friend, I had no idea who she was. She was pretty though, tall and slim. Typical.

Cassie rubbed my shoulder, and I looked up at her. "He loves you. You know that right?" she said softly.

I smiled sadly. "I don't think he loves me like that. How I want him to love me."

"But you love him? Like really love him?" she asked, keeping her voice soft.

All I could do was nod. I loved him completely, but I didn't think anything was going to go further with us. If all I got were what he and I had now, then I'd settle for that just to keep Oliver in my life that way. I'd always have him, thanks to Meadow, but I wanted more. I wanted more than he said he could give me, and that was okay.

Oliver came out of his tent and looked ahead to where she was. She didn't deserve to be called by her name. I could see the anger seeping off his body. He looked around and spotted Julia. She looked at him, and her eyes widened.

Yes, love. Fear him.

"We're going to stay if you want," Oliver said, walking towards me. "She won't screw our weekend up."

I wasn't too sure how I felt about that. I nodded slowly. "Umm, okay? Are you sure?" I asked.

A laugh escaped his lips. "I talked to Tony. If she tries anything, then there are people to witness what she does. I am hoping she fucks up and gets herself locked up. I'm just going to make a quick call, okay?" he said and kissed my cheek.

I watched him walk away, sighing to myself. I hoped he was going to be okay with this. I didn't want him to cower. I was proud though, proud that he wasn't backing away and hiding from her. She was playing him, trying to get to him, and I wouldn't let that happen.

278

Meadow let out a yawn, and I thought, *Finally. I could go and do something other than sit and try not to stare across the ground at Amy, drinking and laughing away as if her being there wasn't a problem in the world.*

"We're going down to the beach. Did you want to come swimming with us?" Tony asked, tossing his can of Beam in the garbage bin.

"I'll come. Should we wait for Ollie?" I asked, glancing over at him. He was still on the phone, and the argument he was having looked heated.

Tony and Cassie shared a look, then Cassie spoke, "Tony can wait. Did you bring your bikini? Or are you wearing it?" she asked.

My god. I wasn't expecting to be wearing one in front of everyone.

My cheeks heated up. "I need to put it on. I'll change Meadow and then meet you down there."

I stripped off in the tent with Meadow. She was already changed in her swimmer's diaper and this cute one piece frilly bather's outfit that was in the colours of a watermelon. She had a pink hat on and looked absolutely adorable.

I slipped my own bikini on. It was a pastel green strapless. There were cut outs in the side of both the top and bottoms, showing off my tanned skin. When I carried Meadow out, I was met with a set of legs in my view. Oliver's legs.

~

OLIVER

I stared at her as she stood up. My dick was hard, and I was begging it to go down. Looking at her body in the scant material that covered her, I couldn't help but groan at her. She was fucking gorgeous. I knew being here was going to be a challenge.

"Isn't she cute?" Sage smiled and held up Meadow in my view.

279

I had to finally smile. She was damn cute with her swimmers on and kicking her legs out like a frog and looking around. I took her and stepped back.

"You think she's going to like swimming?" I asked, carrying her against my chest.

"I hope so. Are you going to come in with us?" Sage asked, putting a thin beach dress over her head and pulling it on.

I shrugged. I had no idea. "Do you want me to?" I asked, stopping until she began to follow and catch up.

"Yes, I do. Sharks may be out there, Ollie. You need to protect us." She grinned.

Well, it was settled then. I was going swimming. She had a way with words. How could I deny anything she'd ask of me?

Haddon walked over, and I avoided him. I was fucking pissed. He knew damn well what Amy being here would do to me. The fact that Julia invited her...well, fuck. I just wanted to rip her apart and lay into her bad. She was starting shit up that she had no idea about.

Amy spotted us, and I made sure to keep my eyes ahead. I didn't want to talk to her or even look at her.

I wrapped my arm around Sage's waist, steering her down to Tony and Cassie. She leant into me, and her arm slid around my back. I didn't know if she was feeling possessive or worried, but when her hand went into the top of my boardies, I did nothing but kiss the top of her head. We were here together. Sage, Meadow, and I were all here together. If Amy thought I wanted her, then she was going to see that she was nothing to me—nothing but the biggest regret of my life.

"Ollie, look. She loves it!" Sage beamed, grinning from ear to ear as Meadow giggled and got all excited sitting on the sand in the shallow part of the water. That was until she took a handful in her fist and tried to eat it. She scrunched her face and wiped her tongue with her hand, only getting more sand in.

I laughed, pulling my shirt off and wiping her mouth clean. "She shoves anything in her mouth." I picked her up and tossed the shirt on the beach. Sage walked up and put that and her dress on the towel and came back down.

Daniel made it no secret that he was checking her out. She looked good for someone who'd had a baby five months ago. If anything, her body now was even better. I loved the way her hips curved into her perfect arse and went down to her long thighs. She was a man's dream.

"Stop staring." She laughed. "I'm nervous as it is."

"What for?" I asked, frowning. "Sage, don't start this self-conscious stuff. You're perfect as is. Now get your ass out here so we can go out deeper and get Meadow used to the ocean."

Meadow held both her small arms up, signalling she wanted me to lift her.

Fuck, I loved that.

Meadow loved the water. She was kicking and splashing and got more than excited while we were out deeper. Sage and I shared kisses now and then, forgetting about everyone else. I still needed to tell her about some things. I'd leave it until later.

Walking back to the shower block, I pulled Sage, who was holding Meadow, into the men's one and in a separate shower cubicle. We took turns in washing the sand off ourselves and Meadow. She was getting hungry and tired.

Sage lay down in the tent and fed her. I lay beside them and closed my eyes, the heat making me completely exhausted. My body wanted to sleep, but my mind wanted to go and ask Amy what she was playing at.

My lawyer wanted photos of her here, which I happily took and sent.

Our tent zipped open, and I quickly pulled a blanket up and covered Sage's breast just before Greyson popped his head in. Just because he was gay didn't mean he could see her. She wasn't for other men to stare at.

"She sleeping?" he asked.

I hadn't realised she was until I looked at her. She was asleep with Meadow half sucking and sleeping.

"Yeah." I sat up. "What's going on? You all drinking now?" I asked.

He smirked. "They are. I won't be able to keep up. Just wanting to see if you wanted to come out for a few."

"Alright. Get me a cold one, and I'll join you." I couldn't be fucked, but he was Sage's friend, and I was going to make an effort for him. I'd be happy to just lay here and sleep, but I might as well get up and do something other than brooding in silent anger.

Walking out and over to the fire pit we'd made, I took a seat and silently sat, watching the flames. All the things Amy put me through was starting to come back. The heat of the straightener rubbing my side had unintentionally crept back into my mind. The scar had faded greatly, but the pain of what she inflicted was still there.

Greyson started talking about going fishing early in the morning. It'd been years since I'd picked up a rod and cast a line in.

"Count me in." I grinned.

"Me too." Her voice turned my inside cold.

"Guys only." Haddon snapped. "Just like this is guy time."

"Oh, Haddon." She giggled. "Relax. We're all adults here. Don't start something that's not there."

"Not there? You weren't even invited here, Amy." He hissed. "You two are divorced, so why not leave him alone. You're insane if you think anything is going to happen again with him and you."

"Look, you all need to lay off her. She's done nothing wrong. How is she meant to react after her husband cheated on her and got another woman pregnant?" Julia snapped.

Oh, for fuck sake. I was sick to death of hearing it.

*Don't react.* All I kept hearing was Sage's voice telling me this was what Amy wanted.

She wanted a reaction. That was all she was after to prove she could still get to me.

She couldn't. Not anymore. I drowned them out and got up, sitting over with Tony and Greyson as Haddon and Julia got into a fight. I talked about anything that would distract me from the two women who utterly pissed me off right now.

I jumped up without hesitation after an hour when I heard Meadow. She was up, and I was relieved. After Amy tried to play the victim, she took off and hid over the other side of the camp with Julia and Simone. Neither of them was winning. I thought it took Haddon every bit of self-control he had not to drive home and leave his wife there.

I stopped just outside the tent, listening to them having a little conversation together. My heart was bursting. She was a perfect mother, and Meadow was more than I ever expected to have.

Meadow was babbling, learning new sounds.

Sage laughed softly. "Go back to sleep. Mama is tired, and Daddy is having a rest with his friends."

Meadow didn't stop as she talked to herself again.

"Are you hungry? Do you want some fruit?" Sage yawned. "Apples or pears? What about cuddles? Come and cuddle Mum?" Sage laughed softly. "Or do you just want Dad?"

I thought she wanted her dad.

I laughed, opening the zip up and undoing the tent. I looked at them both lying there. "Daddy is here. How'd Mummy and little bunny sleep?"

"We slept well. We missed you though." She smiled, patting the bedding beside her. "Having fun?" she asked.

I raised my brow and scoffed, climbing inside and zipping the tent so Meadow couldn't escape. I lay down and pulled her up so she was on my chest.

"Amy's starting shit," I said quietly. I knew she would do this.

Telling her that wasn't easy, but she was someone I could talk to and feel no judgement. Even talking to the shrink was harder than talking to Sage. I couldn't trust him enough to fully open up to him.

Sage lay on her side and played with my fingers. "What did she do? You know, if you want to leave, then we can go. I don't want you here if you feel uncomfortable."

"No." I sighed. "It's not that. I think she thinks she's getting me back. I feel like she will try something when no one's around."

"You mean like try and sleep with you?" she said quietly.

I shrugged. "She's crazy. Who knows what she's up to?"

"You're not screwing anyone except for me," she said sternly. "I don't care what she does. I will drown her in the ocean if she touches you."

"Can I watch you do that?" I asked, smirking at her. I loved her jealousy at times.

I leant forward and pressed my lips to hers. When I pulled back, she smiled—a smile that made all the problems dissolve.

The air in the tent was hot and humid. I wanted more than anything to make love to her, but right now, it wasn't going to happen. Not with our daughter around.

Sage sat up and brushed her fingertips through her hair. "Come on. Let's not sit in here while that whore is out there. These are your friends, not hers, and be damned if you're doing anything wrong. So let's get up, take our daughter to play with her cousins, and you can cook me a steak for dinner because I am starving and want to eat that. Then we will go for another swim, and when Meadow falls asleep, you and I will sit out there and roast marshmallows. If people fall asleep before us, then you're going to give it to me in your car because I am so horny and just need you badly."

It was a good plan. I sat up and cupped her cheek, the words on the tip of my tongue. Instead, I chickened out and said, "We don't have any marshmallows."

# CHAPTER 24

SAGE

I kept my eyes shut as a little hand played with my face. A set of slobbery lips were on my mouth, and my eyes opened. Oliver was holding in his laugh as Meadow gave me morning kisses.

Our first night camping went well. Meadow slept between Ollie and me, only waking once for a drink and then she went back to sleep.

"Morning, love," Ollie said huskily. When Meadow lay down, he lifted his head and gave me a kiss.

I loved the mornings with him. Him and her.

"Morning to you too. Sleep well?" I asked, kissing him back.

He nodded, sliding his hand up over my waist. "I did. Although, I had a foot in my stomach and hand over my face most the night." He chuckled.

I laughed softly with him. "She's not very still. I missed having your arms around me. You keep me warm."

"You were cold?" he asked.

"No. I'm warm right now," I whispered softly.

Meadow was trying to eat my boob. Her hands were pulling the straps and whinging. Oliver kissed her cheek and reached over, undoing my bra strap after someone flicked it with her hands to get her morning milk. She was going to hate it when I stopped feeding her this way soon. I didn't want her teeth biting into my skin.

Oliver let out a yawn. A grin broke across his face as well as a soft laugh when the little girl between us let out a loud blast of pops from her behind.

"Well, good morning to you too, thumper bum," he said, kissing the back of her head.

"What's the plan for today?" I asked. "Sunbathing and swimming?"

Ollie's eyes widened. "Shit. I forgot to mention. Greyson wants to go fishing, so he and I and the other guys except Daniel are heading down the beach a bit. You don't mind?"

"Not at all. Going to catch me a fish for dinner?" I asked, loving that he was asking me if I minded.

"I hope too, baby. Are you going to be alright back here?" he asked.

Ugh, Amy was still lurking around and playing more mind games. Last night, she ate alone in her tent. I didn't even think she ate. I thought she just stuck to her bottle of wine.

Daniel was acting weird, giving me lots of playful smiles, and Julia wasn't talking to anyone. My god, her and Haddon got into it big time last night. Oliver and I took the boys down to the beach while they tried to sort their argument out and built sandcastles. They were adorable. I did blush when they called me Auntie Sage. Oliver just kissed my cheek and smiled, making me feel relaxed about the whole thing.

"I will be. Cassie and I might go for a walk or something. There's a walking track." I smiled. "I like it out here apart from the obvious person who won't leave."

"I know, babe. I'm sorry. I know you must be uncomfortable and annoyed."

Keeping silent, I stared at the side of the tent, avoiding his gaze. I was annoyed. Spending a weekend with his ex-wife wasn't something I would volunteer doing. When I looked back at him, I just broke the gaze again. He knew it wasn't enjoyable for me.

"We should leave today. We could go and stay somewhere else."

"No. I don't want to make you do that. We shouldn't have to leave, Ollie." I looked back at him, keeping my voice down so we didn't wake others. "Why is she here and doing this? This isn't right. Why can't you make her leave? As well as her friend?"

"You don't think we've tried? That I've tried? We fucking have tried to get her out of here, and she won't go. I'm so close to losing it, Sage, but then that's what she wants. She wants a reaction, like you said, to get me on the wrong side, so it looks like I was the one abusing her. Fuck, Sage. You think this is easy for me to spend this weekend here with a woman who made my life hell?" He snapped. "You have no idea what hell I went through. You may know what happened, but you don't know how it felt each day, Sage."

I looked away, hiding my hurt from him. He said my name so many times. I knew he was mad with me. "Well, you make sure of that, don't you, Oliver?"

Scoffing, he gritted. "Don't do that. Don't Oliver me like I'm a child. You had the option of leaving, and you said to stay. I was ready to leave the day we got here, but you said stay and show her you're not afraid. Easy for you to say. You've had it easy."

"Yes, because getting pregnant to a married man is what I always dreamed of. If this was all too much for you, then you could have left." I shot back. "I gave you the option of leaving, and you took it to start with."

Fury was evident. His jaw ground together. "I did that to protect you. Don't ever throw that back at me again, Sage. That's a low fucking blow."

My eyes burned with tears as he got up and pulled his shoes on, unzipping the tent and climbing out. I lay there. Everything he said was right. I had no idea what he was feeling. I tried to understand, and I thought I could understand, but I didn't. He was angry with me, and I hated that. I felt awful.

I lay here as I silently cried and wanted the day to go away. I wanted to leave and go home.

We'd never fought before, and I hated it.

Meadow finished, and I couldn't lie here anymore and take the uneasy air that was left in the tent. Grabbing her things and mine, I stepped outside and picked her up. Oliver was sitting in front of the fire with Tony, talking over something. He looked up as I stood with Meadow, and I looked away, heading to the shower block with her.

This was awkward, holding her as I tried to get us both washed. It was a warm day, too hot for heavy clothing. I put on my bikini with mint green shorts and a coral tank top that was low and loose. My hair was all up in a messy bun.

Meadow looked gorgeous in a lemon coloured tie up romper. She had little thongs on her feet. I couldn't wait until her hair was longer so I could do more than just put the fringe part in a soft side braid and clip it up.

As I walked out with her, Oliver walked toward us. My heart was pounding hard. I had no idea what to say, and I didn't want to cry again.

"Hey," he said softly. "I shouldn't have spoken to you like that before."

"Don't," I said, shaking my head. "You were right. I have no idea. I don't want to fight, so let's just forget about it."

He sighed, tilting his head to the side. "The last thing I want to do is make you cry," he murmured.

I looked over to Greyson and Tony. They had the fishing gear ready to go. Keeping my voice normal, I said, "You should go fishing. Enjoy the time with the guys."

"Sage," he said, merely a whisper. "I don't want to go when we're like this."

I blinked back the tears and sucked in a deep breath. "I'm not mad or upset. We both said things, and I'm sorry for what I said to you. I know you didn't just leave me. I understand your reason. I just want to help you. I never meant to snap. I don't want to fight you, Ollie. God, this whole thing here is stressful, and it's only making us both edgy. We can't even get two minutes alone to screw."

Two minutes alone and I would love to just fuck the frustration out on him that I felt right now. I was sure he felt the same. We were both on edge and bickering at each other. It wasn't doing either us of any good. The only couple who hadn't been fighting was Cassie and Tony.

Oliver took Meadow from my arms and put her down to play with her toys.

He stepped closer, tilting my head up with his hand under my chin. He bent down and kissed me on the mouth. His lips were cold, and I could taste sauce over his tongue. My legs began to feel weak, and I grabbed his arm with one hand, kissing him back and savouring this small intimate moment.

"She does anything, text me, and I will come back and sort her out myself," Oliver said sternly as he grabbed his fishing gear. "Think of somewhere you want to go. We'll go."

"Anywhere?" I asked, raising a brow.

He nodded. "Yep. Snow or sun. Anywhere and we'll go there just the three of us."

I liked the sound of that a lot. I smiled. "Catch us some dinner, baby. Your girl is hungry."

I was relieved that he didn't do anything but smile at my little slip-up. He walked back to me and wrapped his arms around my waist. "Oh, Daddy will bring home dinner. Don't you worry about that."

"Daddy? That's kind of kinky." I bit his lower lip as he kissed me and pulled away.

I pouted, which only made him grin. "You want it kinky, baby? You want Daddy to fuck you and show you who's boss?"

Oh, god. I ran my hands through his black hair, tugging as I fisted it. "Hmm, I don't know. I think Mummy's the boss."

"In the house, yes. The bedroom? Not a chance in hell." He winked, spinning me around and pushing me forward.

I laughed loudly as he began making thrusting motions from behind me and into my ass. He held my hands behind my back as he went harder. I was just relieved no one was near us to

289

see this playful banter we were doing. It wasn't uncommon for Oliver and me to fake having sex like this. He'd often do it when I was in the kitchen, bending me over and making thrusting motions as I lay over the counter and just laughed.

"Ollie." I laughed. "God. You're hard, and your daughter is probably watching you fornicate her mother."

A growl escaped his throat. He turned me around to face him. "She's busy playing in the shade with her toys. Now give me a kiss before I leave. I need something to miss while I'm away," he said huskily. Dipping me backward, he squeezed my ass and kissed me hungrily.

His tongue swept through my mouth. I relished it from him. I craved him so bad. Ollie pulled away, leaving me wanting more. I could never get enough of him. He looked sexy as fuck in a pair of boardies and a tank top. His muscled arms were on show with the black tattoo on his shoulder. He was hot, damn sexy as anything.

I wrapped my arms around him, and he smiled sadly. "I have to go. Greyson is heading over and making throw up motions."

I nodded, not bothering to look at my crazy friend. "Go and catch some fish. I'll be okay here. I promise."

"Ask Cassie to watch Meadow for thirty minutes when we get back," he said. His eyes burned into mine, saying I need you.

I grinned, wiggling my brows at him. "I need you too, handsome."

~

Cassie and I ventured off with Meadow in the sling sitting against my hip. Haddon's boys, Max and Jade, came with us, walking ahead but still keeping close. They were on the lookout for wild animals and hidden tracks.

It was an eventful walk as Cass tripped and then almost walked into a low branch. It was just like old times with us, two sisters, laughing and giggling like crazed idiots. She soon began telling me that Tony and she wanted a baby. They were hoping to fall pregnant by the end of the year.

I couldn't wait for Meadow to have a cousin to play with.

When Cass asked if Oliver and I were going to have another baby, I laughed. Hard.

"Yeah, I doubt that. We're not even dating. Could you imagine what Mum and Dad would say?" I grinned, not that the thought of another baby was bad. I just wasn't even thinking about that now.

She smiled, taking a sip of her water bottle. "I think you will."

Once we reached the lookout, we stood for a while, taking the sight in. We took a couple of photos and went to walk back to the campsite.

The boys were having heaps of fun though they were starting to get bored, as nothing was exciting at the end of the walk. I didn't know why Julia let us take them. I was surprised she didn't refuse them to come with me.

"Auntie Sage, can we go swimming now?" Max groaned.

Cassie smirked as the little boy held my hand, and she mouthed *auntie* to me. I poked my tongue out and ignored her.

"Yep. We're going to go swimming if your mum says you can."

Their eyes lit up as their energy came back, and they raced us to the camp. I came last. Running with a sleeping child on my side was kind of impossible.

Once in the camp, I checked my phone for any messages. There was one from Oliver with a photo of a crayfish he caught. They were obviously having a good time.

I put my phone back in the tent just as Meadow woke up. We went down to the beach after getting our bathers on.

Amy, Julia, and Simone weren't around. An empty bottle of wine was though.

We walked in the water with Meadow. She was squealing in excitement and looking forward to going swimming again. She was a water baby, and she loved every moment of this. I already wanted to come back, but maybe next time, it would only be with Ollie and Meadow, just the three of us.

After some time, we decided to head out of the water. Cassie took Meadow so I could shower and dress. Walking back up from the beach, I went to the shower block and rinsed all the sand off myself. As I came out of the cubicle, I was behind Amy who was putting some makeup on. She looked at me through the mirror and smirked.

I wrapped the towel around myself tighter, and she snorted, sending my heart thumping hard. "I'd be covering myself up too."

*Ouch.* "Well, maybe someone has a spare paper bag to put over your head. I'll ask around for you."

She laughed, but her laugh was thick with sarcasm. "You have no idea what you're playing at, little girl. Take your daughter and get the hell away from him. He's going to leave you eventually."

Was she really threatening me? She had to do it hidden from everyone else.

"Amy, really? You beat the living shit out of him daily. Your emotional abuse may have gotten him down, but he's stronger than you think. He wants nothing to do with you anymore, and if you even think of hurting him in any way, then I will kick your ass myself."

"He's so weak he needs a woman to fight his battles, huh?" She laughed. "A typical weak man."

She wasn't going to stop. She really thought she could control him still.

I rolled my eyes. "Grow up, Amy. You need to be locked in a room with nothing but padded walls. You're insane, crazy, and a fucking psycho."

She bit her lip and narrowed her eyes.

I hit a nerve. Good. I hoped it struck her and knocked her down a peg or two. Unfortunately, I never ever anticipated what

292

she was going to do next. She let her eyes rake up and down my body, making me shiver with disgust. Her hand came forward, and she caressed my cheek, holding it tightly in a strong grip so I couldn't move my head as her other reached hand up and ran down the bare skin of my stomach. I was frozen, sickened and too disgusted to move.

"Mm, so soft. Ever been with a woman, Sage? I'm sure he's not as gentle as I could be," she asked softly, looking aroused.

I stumbled backward. The other toilet door opened, and I was met with a body into my back. Hands were on my waist and a hot breath over my nape. Her friend, Simone, was here as well. God, this was sick. I felt disgusted. What they were doing was horrible. They were taking it too far.

"Mm, you are so beautiful, Sage. I bet you've never been with a woman before." Simone purred, licking her tongue slowly down my neck. They were touching me, and I hated it.

Amy's fingers got the top of my bikini bottoms as her mouth neared mine. Her breath hit against my skin, and I found my feet again.

I pushed her off me with a hard shove to her chest. "Don't come near me. Keep your hands to yourself." I snapped, glaring at them both with water filling my eyes.

She sighed. "We don't care what other women look like, but unfortunately, Oliver loves a slim woman. I notice your thighs touch against each other. Little on the chunky side, aren't you? If you worked out, then you'd have a thigh gap, which is far more attractive, Sage." Amy snickered, turning to face me.

"Yes, I agree. Oliver loved to fuck us both at the same time. God, the way he managed to make us both explode together." Simone smiled, leaning against the stall. "You should ask him about it. Ask him what he really got up to those two days he was away from you. He will lie and say he was at your home, but he wasn't. He isn't into your chunky thighs and gut as much as he makes out to be."

Amy giggled. "Agreed! I bet he isn't even screwing you. Well, not with us around, he isn't. He's seeing what he's missing out on, and what he's stuck with."

*Mind games. Don't believe them. Don't believe a word they say. He wouldn't do that to me.*

I wasn't going to let her get to me. I shot back with my own response. "Actually, Oliver loves my body, and I normally do have a thigh gap." I gave her my own smirk as I kept talking, keeping my voice steady while stepping closer to her. She was forced to take a step back, pinned to the bench sink. "It's normally when Ollie's between them, and for your information, he loves my legs tight around his head when he's devouring my pussy."

The look on her was priceless as I turned and walked off, leaving the bitch to think that over. My back hit the brick wall of the building as I shakily dressed in shorts and my tank again. How on earth could I tell Oliver or anyone what just happened? Being felt up by two women I hated had humiliated me, and I was shaking so bad.

What had me frozen on the spot were her next words to me. "You may not be replaceable to Oliver, but you are to Meadow. She's too young to remember you, Sage."

That was it. I was done.

~

OLIVER

"Hey, you catch anything good?" Haddon asked, coming over to Tony's and my bucket.

"Nope," Tony grunted. "Unless you count a piss ass tiny fish then I got nothing."

I chuckled. "Well, we got some crays for dinner and fish. I'm doing all the work as usual." I grinned, stirring up Tony while he sat on his rock and cast another line out.

Tony chuckled. "Yeah. The fish are just attracted to your pretty face. That's the only reason why they're jumping up at you."

I let out a loud laugh. "Well, no wonder they're hiding from your ugly mug then."

"We both know I'm the prettiest out of us all." Tony grinned. "I just haven't showered today."

Haddon grinned, taking a spot beside Greyson. "What do you think the women are up to? Fighting?"

"Probably. Hopefully, they have driven the bitch out of here," Tony spoke up. "Fucking dogs."

"Got that right," I muttered. Hopefully, they were leaving.

The guys and I were fishing for a good couple more hours, a bucket full of fish to Tony's one, and we were all happy. It was a good morning's effort. Greyson was oddly quiet. I didn't think he knew how to take us all. We were older and probably less mature than him.

Washing up, we put our fish in the Esky and grabbed a cold beer to sit and drink. I yawned. I was about to close my eyes when a hand was on my shoulder. I jumped. I was startled and I looked up to see a sorry looking Cassie.

"Sorry," she said quietly.

I nodded, relaxing again. "It's okay. What's up?"

She held her finger up. "Tony, can you take Meadow for a bit? Don't drop her." She warned and took my daughter over to her uncle.

I frowned. I stood up when she tilted her head to the side. "What's going on?" I asked. I wasn't up for any more surprises.

"Sage," she said low. "Amy and that crazy friend of hers must have cornered her in the bathroom when she was showering."

"Is she okay?" I managed to ask, looking around. "Where is she? Why didn't she call?"

"She's in the tent, but Amy is still in the bathroom. I locked her in there from the outside. They were full on fighting, Oliver. Daniel had to pull them off each other. I don't know why or what happened. Sage won't talk. She just asked me to keep Meadow until she calmed down."

"Is she hurt?"

295

Cassie hesitated, and I gritted my jaw. "What the fuck happened?"

"I don't know." She threw her hands up. "All I know is that Sage slammed Amy's face into a mirror or that is what I assumed since Amy is bleeding and the mirror is smashed, and her friend was freaked out. You should go in there. She needs you, Oliver. We'll watch Meadow. I will let you deal with crazy who's locked up in there."

I hurried back to the tent.

Zipping it back up, I lay down and pulled Sage to my body. She was shaking but not crying. She was awfully quiet.

"Baby?" I said quietly. "Do you want to talk about it?"

"Those two days you were gone rebuilding the kitchen. Were you really there?" she asked, her voice firm. "Or were you with Amy?"

"What?" Why would she even think that? I was nowhere near Amy.

"Did you fuck them both? Have you? Her and Simone?" She gritted, fisting my shirt tightly. "Answer me, Oliver!"

"No. I've never been with Simone, and I definitely haven't been with Amy since I last told you. Where is this coming from? Why the hell do you think that? I've never even had a three-way, not something that interests me," I said sternly.

Sure, every man would be lying if he said he didn't want a woman on his face and another riding his dick, but I wasn't interested in that anymore.

She sniffed, slowly breaking. "Have you not slept with me because I'm too fat now? You don't like the way I feel, or you prefer thinner women?"

"Sage, where the fuck is this coming from?" I snapped. "You know why we haven't slept together. It's because some little girl cock blocks me constantly. God, you want to fuck, then I will fuck you right now and let everyone hear it. Is that what you want?" I asked, holding her tighter.

296

She shook her head and began to cry. "I'm sorry. I'm so sorry, Ollie."

"Baby, what's going on?" I asked, trying to soothe her. I hated seeing her crying. Her tears were breaking my heart. "Tell me what happened. No secrets, remember? We talk to each other all the time. Let me in to help."

"She...They..." She gasped, crying harder. "Touched me."

My eyes narrowed. I pulled her back and held her by the face with a firm grip. "What?" I asked, fuming. She looked away, and I shook her slightly. "Tell me what the fuck happened, and don't lie to me. Talk. Now."

She opened her mouth and told me how she came out from showering, and Amy was in there. Simone was there too, and then she broke eye contact when she began talking about how they touched her and everything they said to her. They were taunting her with nothing but a load of bullshit. My blood was boiling when she told me what Simone had done, licking her body. I was shaking with furious anger. Amy was pushing it. She was going after me through Sage.

I needed to find something else out. "Cassie said something about a mirror and you pushing her face into it. Did you do that?" I asked, stroking her wet cheek. "I won't be mad. I just want to know what made you so angry to walk back in there after leaving."

Her eyes narrowed, and her breathing picked up. "She threatened Meadow. I left and was walking away until she said that I was replaceable to her. I couldn't help but go back in there. She doesn't get to talk to people that way. She was awful, and how they touched me made me felt sick. I won't ever let anyone tell me I was replaceable to her. She's my daughter. Mine. I'm her mum, Ollie. No one else. No one will ever take my place as her mother."

"You're her mother." I assured her. "Only you, baby."

I kissed her. It was the only way to get her to stop talking herself into a panic attack.

I gripped her ass hard and rolled on top of her. Our bodies were the ones doing the talking. Her hands were rushing to get my shirt off. I stunk of fish and saltwater, but she didn't care. She moaned, lifting her hips as I pulled her shorts and panties down and tossed them aside.

"Keep quiet, baby. We both need this," I said, pulling my boxers down. "You do this to me. No one else. There's never going to be anyone else, Sage. Just you."

My cock was hard. It was harder than it had ever been as it was throbbing, standing straight up almost against my stomach. The pulsing veins were prominent as I knelt over her. I was turned on as fuck while I looked at her half-naked body.

She noticed my size. She stared at me as she reached up and stroked, rubbing the wetness that was seeping out of me. My eyes rolled slightly as her hands slid around, grabbing my ass and pulling me forward. Bending up, she took me in her mouth, licking and sucking hard. She moaned, and I pulled out with a sharp hiss before I came.

"I need to cum in you," I whispered, too wrapped up in the pleasure to even think straight. I was sick of holding back. "Fuck, I love you."

Her eyes went wide when I thrust inside her. She let out a loud gasp. She wasn't fully wet, but I didn't care. I needed to feel her. Her body was meeting each of my thrusts, and I knew I wasn't going to last long with her doing that.

Thinking of her pleasure, I rotated my hips against her clit and moved faster and faster. The pleasure started building up inside me, increasing with each thrust. My thighs tensed up too quickly. It'd been too fucking long, but I was going to give her what she needed first.

"Oh god, yes. Ollie, keep going. I'm so close." She moaned, bucking against me wildly.

I stopped. She ground against me, and I shook my head, pulling out before I blew. "Just a sec, baby. I'm going to cum so fucking hard if you keep that up."

Starting up again, I went slower. I kissed her passionately as I increased my pace. My balls slapped against her ass as I fucked her into an orgasm.

"Oh, fuck, Ollie. Yes, I love you too!" She moaned out, wrapping her thighs tighter around me, grinding up into me as I pumped hard and fast.

Hearing those words, I lost it. I spurted deep inside her. I'd never came so hard in my life. I knew if she weren't on birth control, we'd have just made another baby. The idea of her pregnant again with my child only had my orgasm coming on stronger. I grew harder as I kissed her. Neither of us was quiet. It was impossible to be anything but that right now. I came, still shooting deep inside her until I finally finished.

"That was amazing. Best sex ever," she whispered back as her breathing calmed down.

"I'm sorry. I didn't even last thirty seconds." I breathed hard, leaning and wiping my forehead covered in sweat on the pillow beside her. "It was. You are, baby. You make me lose control like that."

"I like it when you lose control and manhandle me. God, I came for what felt like multiple times at once. I'm leaking already." She giggled softly, squirming underneath me. I didn't care. I wasn't moving just yet.

I loved hearing that sound coming from her. "I love you, Sage." She opened her mouth, and I pushed a finger against her lips. I was going to do this right. "No, I really love you. I have for a long time. The moment I laid eyes on you, I couldn't stay away. Then, the day you gave birth, I fell in love with you. You're not just Meadow's mother. You're my girlfriend, lover, and the only woman I want to be with. I want you pregnant again, baby. The thought of you swollen and in our home...fuck. It drives me wild."

"I want more babies, too." She smiled. "With you, and I really love you as well."

Pulling out, we both gasped. I grabbed a shirt of mine and wiped her clean. She was gorgeous lying there, post-climax, glowing, flushed, and filled with me. I tossed the shirt aside and lay down. Both of us laughed when we heard Meadow. Cassie was trying to tell her to open wide and eat her pureed fruit for lunch.

It felt good like a weight had been lifted from my shoulders. I loved her, and she loved me.

"I didn't push her face into a mirror," Sage said quietly.

I looked over, not saying anything. I wanted her to talk, to let me know what else had happened. Taking her hand in mine, I lifted it up and kissed it.

She kept talking. "You won't believe me. No one will. Those two are insane. Amy, when I walked back in, was standing there, and I did slap her on the face. I couldn't help it. Her friend screamed and grabbed my arm trying to push me into a wall, and then Amy screamed. She went absolutely crazy and head-butted her face into a mirror. God, she just turned around and smiled."

I stayed quiet. I wasn't shocked at all. "I believe you," I said, wanting her to know that I believed her. Without a doubt, I believed her.

"You do?" she asked, her eyes tearing up again.

"Of course, I do. Baby, you're talking to the man who she hit and abused for years. I know exactly how mental she can be. She did that to try and get you to be blamed. I won't let that happen," I said, fixing my shorts up and sitting up again.

Sage sat up and grabbed my thigh. "Where are you going?"

"To fucking get rid of her. I'm done with her being here. She doesn't ever attack you and then get away with it." I warned. I was angry, and Amy was going to experience just how much I was done with her.

"Ollie." She looked panicked.

I leant forward and kissed her. "I love you, just keep thinking that. I am, and nothing else will hurt us, and I'll meet you out there. Keep my chair warm, baby." I winked and climbed out of the tent.

There were a few odd looks from the others as I started heading for the toilet block. I shook my head at Tony and Haddon

300

as they went to stand, letting them know not to follow. I was sorting this out myself once and for all.

Daniel was walking toward me, looking like he just woke up not long ago. He slipped his sunnies down over his eyes when he blocked my pathway. "I want to talk to you soon, mate," he said, looking at me.

I shook my head. "Not a good time right now."

I kept walking, stopping when he called out. "I'm going to ask her out. Just wanted to give you a heads up."

I spun around, cracking a grin. "Sage? You're going to ask out the mother of my daughter? You do realise we're here together?"

He just shrugged. I wanted to wipe the smug look off his face. "You may be here and fucking every now and then, but that's all you two are together."

"You're joking, right?" I wasn't in the mood for this. "You fucking cheated on her. Like she'd take you back, Daniel."

"No. I just wanted to let you know that I'm going to ask her out. Anyway, like you can talk. You screwed her when you were married. She'll never trust you completely." He held his hands up and smiled. "No hard feelings, bro. Just warning you that I'll be making a move on her soon. I'm not looking to be called Daddy or anything. She's your kid, and I respect that."

My jaw tensed, and I curled my fingers into a fist as I fought the urge to knock him flat on his ass. I walked away before I did just that.

I could hear her talking when I unlocked the door. They both raced over and froze when they saw my murderous glare. I stepped into the bathroom, trying to stay levelheaded and trying not to smirk at Amy's cut forehead and nose. Simone opened her mouth, and I shook my head. It was just the three of us, and I was out for revenge.

"What the hell do you think you're getting at?" I said, taking hard strides as I kept my eyes on her. I grabbed Amy by the face in a tight grip and pushed her hard back into the wall.

301

Simone went to move, but I grabbed her by the wrist. She shook, looking at me as I kept my eyes on Amy but spoke to her. "Sit your fucking ass down now! Or you're next!"

"Oliver, calm down," Amy said, muffled through her mouth as Simone slumped to the floor.

My brows shot up, fuming even more. "Calm down? You're fucking telling me to calm down after what you just did to Sage in here? Touching her? You've got to be bullshitting me. What the hell do you think you're getting at?"

"We were just messing around," she said quietly.

I dropped my hand and laughed, scoffing. "Messing around? I'm sure my lawyer is going to love that one. I must admit, slamming your face into a mirror was clever, but Sage isn't like you. She's not a violent bitch. She's my girlfriend, Amy. No matter what you say, she and I are together and if you ever"—I lowered my voice, stepping closer so my face was almost against hers—"if you ever, and I mean ever touch her, look at her, and ever mention my daughter's name again, I will fucking kill you with my bare hands myself." I snarled.

Grabbing Simone by the hair, I yanked her up hard and wrapped my hand tight around her throat. I had never been so angry in my entire life. I was furious. Everything I was thinking was going to land me in jail. I wanted to hurt these women and make them pay.

"If you ever touch Sage like that again, I will rip your fucking tongue out of your throat. You never fucked me. You're both too fucking disgusting, and yes"—I snapped my eyes back at Amy—"I may have been married to you and fucked you a few miserable times, but it was the worst time of my life. You were like a lifeless body. My cock barely stayed hard." I gave her a grin. "You taking away the chance to fall pregnant is a blessing to everyone."

"Oliver." She laughed. "Obviously, I hit a nerve. You grew your balls back after I took them off you. Don't worry. What you go through next will be your own fault. It'll be your own stupid fault for not listening to me. By the way, how's Sage's cooking? She

302

like the cookbooks I brought for her?" she asked. "I know the way you eat, and well, I'm helping you out by showing her what you like. I am the only one who knows what you like, Oliver. I was hoping she'd have run off when I rang the doorbell. Who knew the bitch would stay. It'll take more to scare her off than I thought. She'll realise soon. Yes, she will. Then you won't have anyone. You'll be alone and back on my doorstep." She smirked, talking as if I wanted her like I somehow needed her.

I punched the wall behind her head, slamming my fist into it hard and through the plaster. They both jumped. My voice was loud and getting raspy. Spit came from my mouth and over her face. "Do not fuck with me, Amy! Pack your shit and get the fuck out of here now and leave us all alone. Don't fucking test me anymore. I'm not yours to control!"

A stall door opened, and I dropped my hands and stepped back. Julia looked pale as she walked out, frightened.

Just what I fucking needed.

She tried opening her mouth to speak, but nothing came out. She looked absolutely petrified.

"I'm sorry. Oh god, Oliver. I had no idea." Julia broke into a sob of tears. "I was here the entire time. They were awful. God, I've been too frightened to move after what they did to Sage. She didn't do anything to them. They said so many horrible things to her."

I didn't say anything. I turned around and walked out.

Judging by the looks over everyone's faces, they all heard. I wasn't quiet, nor was I trying to be. Sage was sitting in the chair with Meadow asleep over her chest. I took my daughter, which woke her up. I lifted her up carefully and walked to the tent with her. I needed a moment to cool off and collect my thoughts. I was shaking. I was so angry. Never had I spoken to Amy like that. It took every inch of control not to break down and hide like she tried to make me do.

When Meadow was back asleep and I calm enough to go out, I kissed her forehead and made my way back to the others. I tugged Sage's hand and lifted her out of the seat. She stood, only for a moment, until I sat and pulled her down on my lap. I wrapped my arms around her waist, holding her close.

"You okay?" she asked softly.

I nodded. I kept our conversation private as others were talking loudly. "We're both going to the lawyer when we get home. I'm done, Sage. I could have snapped her neck in there."

"I know. We all heard you and her. Haddon had no idea Julia was in there," she said, kissing my nose.

Pulling her closer, I slid my hand up her back and rubbed her bare skin with my fingertips. "The books, they were all her, not Mum. Throw them out. No, actually we'll take them to the lawyer as well. I will do everything possible to keep you both safe."

"What about you, Ollie? You need to keep safe as well." She rested her forehead against mine and sighed. "Let's not talk about this now. Wait until we're on the way home."

Good idea.

Amy walked over. "Uh, we're going to leave."

"Good fucking riddance. About time." Tony clapped. "I'll drink to that!" He was pissed off, and it showed.

Simone glanced over at us. She was rubbing her throat. "Sorry," she croaked, looking at Sage. "I'm really sorry for what happened. It was wrong."

Sage didn't say anything. She took the beer from my hand and took a long mouthful, avoiding eye contact with anyone. The two girls must have known they were fucked.

Daniel offered to take the girls' tent down to get them to leave quicker. After taking it down, he sat back with the group and winked over at Sage. His eyes were glued to her.

I slid my hand up Sage's thigh and kissed the side of her neck, sucking a little as she tugged the base of my hair, causing an uncomfortable look from Daniel who shifted in his seat. Everyone was going to know.

"Can we take a moment to talk about what happened in the tent earlier? With you two?" Haddon smirked as he winked at Tony. "Because we all heard you."

I shrugged, smirking. "What is there to tell if you all heard it?"

Tony winked, wiggling his drink at me. "Just curious what this means?"

Sage was mine and not up for anyone else to have.

There really was only one way to make it known just how much she was mine. Probably not the best way, but fuck it. I didn't care. I was done sitting back, letting people walk over me and telling me how things were going to go. I was calling the shots, letting them know that what was going on between us was serious as all fuck.

"Sage and I are going to have another baby."

Everyone stopped and stared at us. Daniel's face went from a smug smile to instant blank stare, unable to hide his shock as his beer sprayed from his mouth. His eyes watered over as he coughed loudly.

Tony was the first to speak, stuttering and finally getting his words out. "You are? Wow. Shit. That's great. When?"

"We are?" Sage whispered, trying to hide her confusion. I gave her a look to tell her to play along. She grinned. "We're trying all the time. Day, night, and all hours in between."

We weren't, but we would be. Her barefoot and pregnant in our home was something I wanted to see more than once if I had it my way.

I smirked, shrugging and pulling her closer, our mouths nearing. My mouth was against hers, and she was glowing with happiness. I whispered one word between each possessive kiss. "You. Are. Mine."

# CHAPTER 25

SAGE

I was his.

That was all I could think about since we had been home. Oliver claiming me like that, in front of everyone, was just unexpected, and wow. The whole getting pregnant again part almost knocked me off my feet. Good thing I was sitting on his lap. Otherwise, I might have just fallen over.

Meadow was so cranky today. She was crying over the smallest things. I was exhausted as hell. Being at work with her clinging to my body was difficult. If I put her down, she screamed. If I held her, she'd be okay until I wasn't focusing on her, then she would get crabby.

When the door slid open, I smiled. "Please take her for me."

Oliver smirked. "She unsettled?" he asked, placing a kiss against my lips.

I nodded. "Very. She's really sooky today."

Ollie picked her up from the pram and held her out in front of him. "You giving Mummy a hard time? I don't think I believe a little angel like you would do that."

Rolling my eyes, I laughed. "Believe it, stud. She did."

Meadow giggled as Ollie kissed her and tickled her tummy. He winked. "See? She just wanted Daddy to play with."

"I think that's it then. You get her all revved up each morning and then leave for work." I sat down and stretched my legs out. "How has work been anyway?" I asked.

He shrugged. "Much the same. Just sorting over contracts. They keep changing the design, and it only costs them more money, which I don't care about, but it's wasting a lot of my guys' time. What about you? Busy morning?"

"Yes and no, in bits. It gets really busy for a while. Luckily, she didn't scream. Did you want to get lunch?" I asked, checking him out in his work gear.

He was very gorgeous, tall, and muscled. His tan was coming out more, and his hair was neatly parted to the side. I loved that look on him. It was so professional, but he still had the "fuck me and love it" edge to it.

I did fuck him, and I loved it.

"I'll go get it. You wait here, babe. I'll take her with me," he said, walking back over and kissing me once more.

Ever since we came home, he had been very in charge. I did like it a lot. I liked him telling me what was happening and how it was going to happen. Just sitting here, I watched as he took Meadow with him out the door to get some lunch.

I was so lucky.

I decided to do some tidying up. I had been thinking about hiring another girl since Cassie and Tony were busy with their own baby making. I hoped she fell pregnant soon. Oliver was so excited for them when I told him on the way home.

I knew he wanted another baby, and we talked more about it, but we're going to wait until Meadow was one and the whole mess with Amy died down. He didn't want stress to take a toll on me if I was carrying his child again.

He also informed me that he got very turned on at the idea of blowing inside me while I'm unprotected. I blushed at the memory. I also got very turned on as well. We were turning into a pair of horny kids.

"Hey. Do you have anything for dry skin?" someone asked. I turned around and saw Julia standing in front of me.

She and I hadn't spoken since the camping trip. Now that she realised just how awful Amy was, she was trying to make up for being a horrible bitch. My words, not hers.

I nodded, not sure what to say. I was kind of out of it. "I do. Is it for your face or body?" I asked, still not moving.

"Face. More so this area," she said, gesturing to her T-bone.

I walked over to the moisturisers and pointed to a couple. "Well, this Aloe Soothing Night Cream is really good. It hydrates skin that needs more gentle care, so that could be a good option for you. There is also an Aloe Facial Cleanser, which is really refreshing, and then you'd put on an Aloe Soothing All Day Cream, which leaves the skin soft and smooth all day. I'd probably recommend all three. That way, you get the most protection possible. Even adding the face restoring mask to do once a week if your skin is really sensitive also."

I held them out for her to test some on her hand. She leant down and smelt it. "That's not as strong as I expected. It's actually really nice and feels so soft."

"I know. It is fragrance and alcohol-free as well. There is another type. It's new and smells insane." I smiled and reached up for the Vitamin C skin reviver. I held it out and let her smell it.

Judging by her eyes, she loved it. "That's good enough to eat."

I laughed, putting it back. "Tell me about it. I could walk around all day and just smell each one of these. The perfume oils are the worst. They all smell delicious."

"Which would you think I should try? I'm not really into all this makeup, facial cleaning stuff. It's very confusing," she said, and I swear for the first time ever, she looked embarrassed and ashamed of herself.

I felt horrible. She had her hands full with the kids and probably didn't get the time to just do something for herself. I smiled and put the others away, picking up a small makeup bag. I handed it to her. "I'd suggest you try the aloe creams. There is a smaller pack which had the Aloe Calming Facial Cleanser, Calming Toner, Soothing Day Cream, and Soothing Night Cream. That way, you can see how it works before you go out and stock up more of it."

We were chatting at the counter after she brought her moisturisers and a lip balm when Ollie and Meadow walked in with lunch. His brows shot up, looking surprised as she hadn't noticed him yet. I smiled when Meadow held her arms out to me, and I took her.

"Hello," Oliver said formally. I could have rolled my eyes at him.

Julia smiled up at him. "Hi, Oliver. Sage here just talked me through some skin care regimes."

He broke out into a grin. "Ah, you should see what she makes me put on each night and morning, and here I thought the water was doing me good."

"You don't complain at home." I smiled, talking as Meadow put her fingers in my mouth and giggled when I pretended to bite down on them.

"True. My skin's never been softer," he said and rubbed his cheeks.

Julia laughed. She looked at us hesitantly and then lowered her voice. "I went to see your lawyer, and I made a statement with the police as well."

"What?" Oliver asked, his voice so soft. His face was back to the formal stare.

She nodded. "I told them what happened." Julia glanced over toward me. "Everything except for when you came in and—" she whispered, stopping herself. We all knew which part she was referring to.

I hadn't thought she would go and do something like that. When Oliver and I instantly left on Sunday morning, we met his lawyer in town. A restraining order was slapped back on Amy as well as a pending sexual assault charge. Oliver did tell his lawyer about wrapping his fist around her throat and pinning her to a bathroom, not wanting that to come back and bite him on the ass. His lawyer didn't note that down. He said don't even admit to that. It would make him look abusive, and that was the furthest from the truth.

~

After an exhausting day, I slumped on the couch and put my feet up.

"I'm so tired." I yawned.

Ollie was walking around the living room with Meadow in his arms. He raised his brow. "She's going to be up all night, isn't she?"

She wouldn't settle unless in her father's arms. I yawned and rolled on my side. "Do you want to put her in my room?" I asked.

"I'm sorry. Who's room?"

I couldn't hide the huge smile growing over my face. "Our room."

Oliver moved me into his master suite. We were now sharing a room. My old room was a spare room for visitors.

He looked pleased with my answer and winked. "Good. What do you think about Julia inviting us for dinner tomorrow night? She's done a full 360 with you."

"I know. It's odd. She hated me, and now she wants to hang and get coffee. I'm wary, but I will go and be friendly with her," I said, sitting back up. I walked over to him and rubbed Meadow's forehead. "She's getting sick, maybe?"

"I'm not sure. She could be teething, and she's cranky over that," he said and bent at his knees. "I'm proud of you, baby. You didn't have to agree to tomorrow night, you know."

"I know, but she's your sister-in-law, and there isn't any point in holding a grudge." I leant closer and pressed my mouth against his.

He kissed me back and whispered against my lips, "I love you."

~

310

I woke up to Sage spreading kisses on my body.

"Oh, god. I love you." I moaned.

"Mm. I'll never get tired of you saying that to me," Sage whispered. "Tell me again," she said, kissing down my chest.

I groaned. How could I not say it? I'd been saying it every day since I first told her. "I love you, Sage. I love you."

"Ollie." She sat up and positioned herself above my hips, slowly sinking down as I filled her. "I love you so much. God, I can't get enough of you."

She began to move slowly using her thighs as she came up and then back down. Her hands planted firmly against my chest. I rested mine against her thighs, stroking slowly up and down then sliding them around and gripping her perfect ass, wanting her to move faster.

She shook her head and moaned softly. My cock throbbed at that sound. "It's 2:00 AM, and she's finally asleep. I'm going to enjoy this baby," she whispered with another moan. "Enjoy it, Oliver. It may not happen for a while again."

I grinned, smirking and lying back to watch her. "It will happen again. She can cry. I need my fix of you as much as I can get it."

When I felt her tighten, my breathing picked up, and I held off blowing as she climaxed. Her cheeks were flushed, and hair fell down the left side of her shoulder. She was moving faster and shaking. My turn. I wrapped an arm around her waist and moved quickly. I pushed her off me and onto her back. I got between her legs and gave a deep thrust. The bed moved with me as I drove her into another orgasm. Her moans were loud and legs spread wide apart as I lost myself in pleasure.

The sheets were a sweaty mess as I thrust once more and stopped, unable to keep going after filling her deeply.

Both of us were breathing heavily as I pulled out and lay on my back. "Good enough?"

"Think you can go again?" she asked, her naked body covered in my sweat as she looked over at me.

I laughed. "Baby, I'm not a machine or a man in one of those porn books you read. I can't blow and go. Give me a bit to recover from that."

She giggled. "So if I did this, you wouldn't like it?" she asked.

I had my eyes closed until I felt her. My eyes flew open, and I jerked upright. Fuck, her lips were wrapped around me, sucking and licking, both of us mixed together. I was glad tomorrow was a weekend. I didn't think I could make it into work.

"Ollie, do you not like that?" she asked with a pout as my hard erection lay pushed against her face.

That sight, wow. She was incredible.

I reached down and stroked her cheek. "You drive me crazy. Get on me, wench. I can't move."

She giggled. "I'll give you wench." She knelt between my legs and used both her hands as she began to stroke me.

I waited for her to ride me, but it wasn't happening. She was going to jerk me off. I was extremely wet from her already. Now I was slick as she cupped my balls with one hand and used the other to massage me up and down. There was nothing for me to do except lay there and enjoy.

My stomach was rising more quickly as I got nearer. My eyes shut tight as I focused on her and her beautiful face in my mind. Her hands were both working in different directions, which was different but definitely good. Her movements were slow, but she squeezed hard.

"Sage, baby. I'm close." I warned her, my voice ragged and hard as she kept rubbing me.

"Oh god, Ollie. Cum for me. I want you to cum loudly." She moaned and began to stroke me faster.

As my orgasm neared, my eyes shot open from something I hadn't been expecting. "Oh god! Christ, Sage! Fuck!" I gave a loud, guttural groan and cried out loudly as I blew. The first shot of thick cum spurted up over my chest. The next load was just as hard, and the third, my fucking god, was just as strong. The fourth, well, fuck me, I could barely see straight when that hit the back of Sage's throat as she surprised me even more and sucked me.

I just stared at her, completely stunned. Never had I done that, and never had I fantasized about it either. But goddamn, that was instant and intense. Fucking intense.

"Wow," she whispered. Biting her lip nervously, she broke into hysterical laughter. "It just flew through the air, and there was like lots of it everywhere."

"Sage," I said quietly, loving the look of happiness over her face. "A little warning next time would be appreciated."

Her giggle died down, and she sighed. "Like you would have agreed. You would have said no. It was a heat of the moment kind of thing. I've never done that before though I have always wanted to. I heard it's really good and extremely pleasurable for a man."

"Can't say I ever complain about the other orgasms you've given me, but that was different," I said. I was actually a little embarrassed. That had brought a whole new level of intimacy for us. I looked down at my chest. She was right. I came hard and strong. "Shower with me?"

"Wait. Are you mad? I didn't mean to make you mad," she said, getting up off the bed and following me into the en-suite.

I shook my head. "No, baby. I'm not mad. I just didn't expect that. I've never had that done before. In the future, let's just discuss spontaneous ass fingering first, yeah?" I smirked with a chuckle. Then I narrowed my eyes seriously at her. "And don't even think of mentioning it to your sister. God, Tony raves on and on about it all the time. Like I need him cheering me on for that. It was a once off thing only. Not again, baby."

She broke out into a loud laugh. "Oh god. I don't talk about our sex life to anyone. It's just between us." She pushed her hand over my chest and rubbed the dripping load into my chest hair. "You never asked my permission before you tried it on me. Isn't that right?"

"You've never said no." I winked. "Also the words you screamed out were definitely no indication that you didn't like it." I grabbed her wrist and pulled her against my chest, covering her too as I led her into the shower. "I love you."

"I love you too, Ollie." She smiled, pushing her lips up to meet mine.

~

The next morning, I woke up to an empty bed and groaned.

"Not how I wanted to wake up, beautiful," I called out, hoping she heard me.

I glanced over at the clock. Shit. It was almost 11:00 AM. I jumped out and found some boxers and pulled them on. Sage walked in as I pulled on a shirt.

"Look who finally woke up. Tired?" she asked.

I nodded. I couldn't believe I slept in for that long. "I'm sorry," I said a little sheepishly.

"Don't apologise. I kept you up late. Anyhow, breakfast or your case brunch is in the oven. We'll have roast pork tomorrow, so that's what is defrosting in the sink. Please don't touch it, and Meadow is happily playing in the living room with her toys. She only woke up half an hour ago. I think she may have just needed to sleep after the camp trip," she said in a big rush as she began to strip the bed sheets.

I smirked with my eyes on her ass. "Anything else?"

She groaned, reaching over as she put fresh sheets on. "Your lawyer called. He said to call him back, and can you pass me those dirty work clothes behind you please?"

I grinned. She was fucking adorable. "Yes, wifey," I said inadvertently.

We both just stood there. What the hell did I say that for? I didn't know what to say. Sage just looked at me stunned. Then her eyes went wide, and she looked anywhere but me.

314

I stepped forward. "Sage." I said quietly when I gained composure again.

"Do you hear that? I think Meadow is crying," she said coolly.

"I don't hear anything," I muttered, trying to listen, but still I heard nothing.

She grabbed the clothing and the sheet from my hands and backed away, leaving the room in a hasty rush.

I sat on the edge of the bed and rubbed my forehead. What had possessed me to say that to her or refer to her as my wife? God, I was a fucking idiot. I freaked her out, and it wasn't half obvious that that was what I had done.

I knew I told her that marriage wasn't on the cards for me. I just couldn't commit to her in that way, but I was hers fully. I loved her and wanted to be with her, but marriage was just so soon. That wasn't something I could give her.

I fucked it up royally. I grabbed my phone from the dresser and dialled my lawyer. He answered on the second ring.

"Oliver. Good. Glad you called back." He sounded panicked. I sat back on the bed and listened as he kept talking. "I did some digging around for you. I have a guy following her over the next few weeks just to see what she's up to also. The books and doorbell, that's hard evidence just how far she is willing to go. The camping trip, as bad as it turned out, is good for us. We're building a strong case. Your sister-in-law came by yesterday and gave her statement. If Amy oversteps, then we've got her. She's been warned of the fine, and since this was multiple breaches on her behalf, then she will serve jail time. The magistrate has issued the double order covering everything. We don't know how far she is going to go."

I sighed. This was all a head case. Amy was doing my head in. "Hopefully that knocks some sense into her then. She'll be pissed scared if she knew going to jail was a definite possibility for her."

In a way, I hoped she would fuck up and come near us just so she would be locked up and out of our way.

315

"She could plead insanity to try and play the victim and say that years of living with you lead her to this. That is the worst case." He sighed.

I could tell he was worried that was going to happen. I didn't want to hear it.

"No. Worst case is if Sage or my daughter get hurt because of her. I know you're doing all you can, but make sure she stays the fuck away from us. This has gone on too long. I showed you the photos and messages. How can she plead that if she were the one to cause me all that pain?" I gritted.

After ending the call, I headed downstairs. Before she could turn and back away, I pushed her body into the refrigerator and cupped her between the thighs. The contents of the fridge rattled as I pressed my body to her.

"What I said, it's just a title."

"It's okay. I understand," she said as her breathing picked up.

I shook my head. "No. You don't," I said, pushing my palm harder into her. "You mean more to me than she ever did. You will always mean more. You and Meadow are the love of my life. Maybe someday I will be able to ask, but having that band on my finger only reminded me that I was trapped, like I was in a death sentence and not wearing it makes me feel sane."

"Ollie, trust me. It's okay. I wouldn't ever pressure you to do anything. I'm happy as we are. We're good. It's only a piece of paper and a ring. It's not going to mean we're any less committed to each other. I love you, and you love me. That's all that matters. Don't feel bad or guilty over it. If you tell me you'll never leave, then that's enough commitment from you to make me feel safe and secure here," she said, taking my hand and running her fingers over my left-hand ring finger.

She pressed her lips against it, and I squinted my eyes shut hard. "I promise to never leave you. Never, baby." She was everything to me.

316

"Oliver, you don't need to wear a ring, and I don't need to wear a ring. You don't ever need to feel trapped because I won't ever make you feel anything less than what you are: a man. A strong and incredible man who has all of my love. I'm yours, and maybe if you break up with me, then I will follow and drag your hot ass back home to where you belong." She took my hand and placed it against her chest. I could feel her heart beating hard. "This is where you belong, with Meadow and me and our future babies to come."

"I like the sound of that." I rested my head against hers and sighed. "I don't deserve you. You're too good for me, baby."

"Maybe, but I don't deserve you either," she whispered. "I do need you though."

My eyes met hers, and I ran my free hand up and around the base of her neck, kissing her against her forehead. I pulled back, moving my hand from her thighs and pulling her tight against my chest. I held her closely and relished the love we felt for one another. "I need you too."

I needed her more than she could ever understand.

# CHAPTER 26

"Oh my god. Ollie, quick! Come here!" I squealed out excitedly.

Oliver came running into the living room where Meadow was on all fours and rocking back and forth, blowing spit. She was talking to herself in a language neither of us understood.

Bending down beside me and across from Meadow, he grabbed a teddy bear and set it in front of us. "Come on, little girl. Come to Daddy and Mummy."

The excitement that filled me burst as she took a shaky move. She began to move slowly at first. She giggled as she became aware of what she was doing. She soon came charging towards her daddy and squealed excitedly as Ollie picked her up and kissed her.

His eyes were just as teary as mine were. He smiled and pulled me to him and kissed me hard. I laughed over his mouth, trying to breathe, but he wasn't letting up.

"She's on the go now, baby," he said to me as Meadow squirmed in his arms, wanting to get down and go.

I pouted while watching her. Suddenly, just like that, I burst into tears. She wasn't a baby anymore. She was a crawling child. Oliver had me in his arms in an instant, pulling me down onto his lap and asking what was wrong. I just wrapped my arms around his neck and clung to him tightly. My tears were probably silly, but it was saddening.

Oliver kissed my forehead and wiped my eyes dry when I finally calmed enough to speak.

"What's wrong?" he asked softly.

I sighed, rolling my eyes at how crazy this was going to sound. I shrugged a little and sniffled. "It's just she's no longer small and little. She's even trying to get out of your arms, and it won't be long until she doesn't want us around and doesn't need our help. She's not a baby anymore, and I don't want her to get any bigger."

He smiled a smile that could make my heart race and stomach flutter instantly. "Sweetheart, she can't stay little forever, and if you're so upset…" He looked at me darkly. I knew what was coming, and it was hot. "Then, there is one way to get you another little baby in your arms. Then another after that, and as many as you want afterward."

"Oliver." I blushed, glancing away with a smile.

"I'm dead serious, Sage. Say the word, and you'll be pregnant again," he said and stroked his hand lightly up and down my back.

I wanted another baby. There was no doubt about it. "Maybe."

"Maybe?" He laughed—gorgeously, might I add. "I'm taking that for a yes."

I fingered his hair and massaged his scalp, earning a low groan from him. His eyes were dark and full of desire. I could feel his hardness pressed underneath my ass. He was always hard and ready for me just as I was ready for him.

Leaning forward, I pressed my lips against his. "I might have forgotten how we got pregnant in the first place."

He smirked. "It was on a floor, and you were underneath me."

I rolled my eyes, slapping his arm playfully. "How romantic. Our daughter was conceived illegitimately and in a nightclub while we were horny and drunk."

Oliver's features hardened, and he held onto my waist with both hands, a little too hard. I didn't say anything as he clenched his jaw and swallowed. "Don't ever say that again. She was made with love and won't know anything else until we decide to tell her anything different."

I just nodded, hating that I had upset him. I didn't think my words through, and I cringed at how I said it. "I'm sorry," I said softly. "You're right."

He smiled, shaking his head and sighing. "Just don't do it again, or I will throw you over my knee and spank that pretty ass of yours."

I giggled. "Yes, sir."

~

Meadow was crawling around after her cousins who thought it was hilarious at how fast she was getting. She had a toothy grin, and her little fists were pounding into the carpet as she let out a string of slobber and giggled loudly then charged after them again.

Haddon turned back to us. It was clear that he had missed those days when his boys were young and learning how to do new things on their own. "She's a terror. Wait until she climbs in her cot."

"Don't remind me," Oliver muttered.

After my breakdown about Meadow being not so small, he had his own one when she wouldn't sit on his lap and watch the TV with him.

It ended with him almost begging me to let him put his rod in my pond and let the fish swim out. I had fallen on my ass laughing hard at that description. It ended with me saying no again and him telling me that it would happen and would be much easier if I consented to it. Otherwise, he would be forced to take this matter into his own hands.

I rubbed his thigh and kissed his arm as I snuggled up to him on the couch. "Don't pout. She's still your little girl."

"For now, until she's too embarrassed to be seen with her dad." He scowled. He was guilt-tripping me, and it was almost working.

Julia walked in and sat beside Haddon. They looked much happier, more in love and not bickering. I could tell the revelation of what really went down between Oliver and Amy had made her feel god awful. It should because Amy was a bitch who wasn't giving up easily.

The sooner she left us, the sooner we could have another baby.

I wasn't going to fall pregnant with her lurking in the dark shadows of our life. I didn't want the fear of her doing something crazy to us and then an innocent child suffering. Oliver knew that was the only reason as well.

"When is Mum dishing up dessert?" Ollie asked, stretching out on his parents' couch.

"Oh, you never change, and it's ready, young man." Jean, his mum, appeared with a smile. "Come into the dining room and eat before it goes cold."

"What is it? Oh please, tell me it is sticky date." Haddon jumped up, grinning.

Ollie was next. "Nah, that other one. The rolled pav with cream and berries."

Julia and I looked at each other and laughed at how eager these boys were for their mother's cooking. Jean just laughed softly. "Sorry, boys. The girls wanted rhubarb and apple crumble."

Oliver gave me a look. "Traitor." He smirked.

I giggled, swatting his backside as I walked with him. "You still love me though."

"True, baby," he said, taking my hand and leading me into his parents' dining room.

Needless to say, when they heard Oliver and I were officially dating and together, we were cheered on with a loud "Finally!" I admit we did take way too long to stop pretending that we were just friends. We were never going to be just friends. It was impossible to be anything but what we already were.

A family.

321

Heading home, the three of us were exhausted and tired. Meadow was snoring lightly in the back seat when we pulled up home. I vaguely remembered getting out and letting my feet drag up to bed. I was tired, and Ollie wasn't getting lucky tonight.

When I woke, I woke with a sudden moan and bucking of my hips. My eyes hazed over with sleep and my throat was dry as I licked my lips and tried to focus. I couldn't see or think straight. His tongue was giving me a good lashing as he went slowly up and down. His fingers curled inside me as he sucked and bit my throbbing clit. I moaned again. My hands slid down my chest toward him where he looked right up and me.

He growled, letting me know he wanted me and he wanted me soon.

"Oh." I felt my eyes roll as I kept them on his.

He held my waist tightly and pulled me down into his open mouth. He was licking faster and faster as I was overcome with a bursting pleasure that rippled throughout my clenched core. Keeping my eyes on his, I shook and bucked.

I was shaking hard from the sensitivity as he hurried up to thrust his ready arousal into me. I let out a cursing moan, as he didn't start slow. He was hard and deep, being relentless with my body until we both came and clung our sweaty bodies to each other.

Lying and basking in the after glory, I was too tired to move. I was aching all over.

Oliver ran his hand over my bare stomach and whispered, "All the good stuff just wasted."

"Are you seriously still pouting?" I asked. Surely he wouldn't want another baby that bad.

His face scrunched with distaste. "I'm not pouting."

I closed my sleep eyes. "I think you'll be pouting until you get your own way, Oliver. I'll make you wait longer, years even before I'm possibly ready."

"Like fuck, you will." He snorted and tossed the covers off his naked body.

I opened my eyes long enough to see his toned back and ass as he walked into the bathroom and turned the shower on. He was so pouting and extremely cute doing so. When I opened my eyes again, he was getting dressed. I didn't want to get up out of bed. It was so warm and comfortable.

Yawning, I asked, "What time is it?"

He checked his watch. "Around 9:00 AM. Lie in bed. I'm going to work for a bit and will take Meadow with me. She's having a bottle now."

"You sure?" I asked. "I can get up if you need to go to work."

"Nope. Relax and sleep for a bit," he said and leant over, kissing my forehead gently. "I love you. Be back soon."

"I love you too. Thank you," I whispered and closed my eyes again, rolling onto his side of our bed.

I snuggled down and enjoyed the moment I got to spend sleeping and being lazy. Little did I know that evening, I would give anything to be up and to be with my daughter.

~

OLIVER

"Hey, want to sit on Daddy's chair?" I asked in an embarrassing excited voice as Meadow crawled around my office floor.

She just looked at me and took off. I laughed. Typical.

I was sorting over some new files and contracts when Tony walked in and spotted Meadow. Bending down, he held his arms out for her in hopes she would come toward him.

I sat back and grinned. "You won't get anything from her."

"Must run in that family," he grumbled and stood up. Taking a seat opposite me, he sighed. "Cassie's gone crazy."

Knowing exactly what crazy was, I raised a brow. "What's going on, and define crazy. Amy crazy or normal crazy?"

"Oh, not Amy crazy. Just enough that we're on a sex schedule and it's only when she wants it. I have to time blowing a load just before her orgasms in hopes it shoots up just as she gets off. Who knew it was so complicated." He took his hat off and set it down on his knee.

I couldn't help but laugh. I'd been there and done all that. It was not the best time of my life. It was a waste of my damn life. That was what it was.

"I don't know what to tell you. Sage and I weren't trying, and she got pregnant. Maybe you should get Cass to just relax about it. How long have you been trying for?" I asked, trying to sound helpful, but I had no clue.

"A few months. I think she is pregnant, but she won't take a test." He sighed. "When are you having more?"

"When Sage lets me." Which would be soon, hopefully. "I'm wasting the best loads of my life lately."

He shook his head, grinning. "Charming. Just charming."

Meadow crawled over. I bent down and picked her up. Finally. "Coming to hug Dad now, have you?" I smiled and kissed her cheek.

She snuggled into my chest, and I loved this feeling. I looked at Tony. "Daniel told me he wants Sage back."

"He what? You're kidding me. When?" he asked, incredulously.

"Camping," I stated. "I almost wiped that smirk off his fucking mouth." I gritted out.

"He's got no chance. Like she'll go back. I think he's realised what he threw away with her. Have you asked her about him?" he asked.

I shook my head. I wasn't keen on bringing that up. I didn't know if I could take hearing about them two. "No. I don't think I should. I will just leave it."

He laughed, swivelling in his seat and cocking his head back with a knowing look. "Don't you dare leave it. Go home and tell her. She will be pissed if you don't."

He was right as always. "I hate you," I stated.

Loud laughter echoed around the room. "Yeah. I know you do. Don't worry, Meadow. Uncle Tony still loves your dad."

I headed home. I grabbed some dinner for us on the way to give my girlfriend the night off cooking to woo her into seduction or charm her into staying with me. I didn't have a doubt that she wouldn't go back to Daniel, but a voice in the back of my mind was telling me otherwise. *"Yeah, but Daniel doesn't have an Amy lurking around at every hidden corner."*

Scowling, I set Meadow on the floor, and she took off. Some help she was going to be.

"Sage, you up?" I called out.

"Boo!" a voice called out from behind me, then she wrapped her arms around my waist. "Missed you."

I wasn't going to tell her that she scared the utter fuck out of me. Her laugh was loud and contagious as she kissed my backbone. I pulled her around to face me and crashed my mouth against hers, unable to stop myself.

I growled when she bit my tongue and refused to let go. She was in a very playful mood today. Her hand slid down the front of my jeans and cupped me. Releasing my tongue, she moved her hand back. I swear the number of times this happened would have given me blue balls already.

"I love you," she said with a beautiful smile.

"I love you too. Is everything okay?" I asked, slightly worried.

Giving me a sharp nod, she walked off, leaving me hanging with a stiff cock and no release.

"Damn, woman," I grumbled under my breath. I opened the freezer door and stuck my head in it to give me a distraction.

I decided to prepare the food while Sage and Meadow sat up at the table. She fed her while I kept going with the stir-fry.

Meadow made one hell of a mess in the process of scoffing her food down. Her hands and face were covered in mashed veggies. Even dried bits stuck her hair together. Sage picked her up and took her for a bath. I knew once she came back, we'd have to talk about the Daniel situation.

~

"Ollie, I need to tell you something and please don't be mad," Sage said softly, rubbing my wrist once we sat to eat at the dinner table. Meadow was already asleep in her room.

I glanced up at her with raised brows. "Yes?" I asked, hoping it wasn't something that would tear me apart.

"Daniel texted me," she said quietly.

I wasn't surprised. I gave her an amused look. "Hmm. Did he? And what did Danny want?"

"Now, now. Don't be like that." She giggled.

"What did he want?" I damn well already knew what he wanted. He made that quite clear. With her and I together or not, he was going to have her.

What I wouldn't give to pound my fist into his face this very moment.

Sage squeezed my hand, and I looked at her again. "Don't worry."

"Tell me," I pressed. Letting out a sigh, she moved her hand from mine. I didn't like the coolness I felt right now. Reaching over, I grabbed her hand and pulled her from her chair and onto my lap. Stroking her cheek, I said, "Open and honest, baby. Tell me what's got you so anxious."

"He asked me out," she murmured.

Well, I gave him props for going all out and not beating around the bush. I nodded. "What did you write back to him?" I asked.

"Obviously, I told him it wasn't a good idea." She looked away and then back toward me. Her eyes bore into mine. "We're in a relationship and have a child together. I'm not going out with other men."

I sighed, placing a kiss against her temple. "He told me he was going to ask you out again when we were camping. Just before I went hell for leather on Amy."

326

She pulled away and looked slightly pissed off. "I'm sorry. What? Why didn't you tell me?"

"Because I didn't know how to," I said with a shrug. "It's not something I wanted to hear, especially from a guy I consider one of my good friends."

Sage stood up, straddled me, and wrapped her arms around my neck. "Daniel and I are over. We were over the moment he let that woman feel him up in front of me. I don't care what he says. I have my eyes on one man and one man only."

"He sounds pretty hot." I smirked.

A smile came over her lips as she began to slowly roll her hips against my groin. I groaned, sliding my hands down over her ass and splaying my fingers out.

"Oh, he's sexy." She let out a breathy moan. "Extremely hot, and I mean fucking gorgeous."

"Language." I warned, huskily.

"Yes, Daddy." She moaned again and let her head fall back as she began to move off me.

Oh, no. Not this time, she wasn't.

I stood up and pulled her back to my body, lifting her up and setting her down on our dining table. Our tongues slid over one another's. She tasted so damn good, so sweet, and soft. I grew harder. I needed her now. I didn't give a fuck what she had to say about it. I was going to damn well have my woman.

Pulling her back down off the table, I spun her around and pushed her face forward. Her head was down low as my hand worked relentlessly as I tugged on her shorts and slid them down.

I let a sharp hiss out through clenched teeth. "Shit."

No panties.

She wiggled under my hands as I gripped her ass, spreading those gorgeous cheeks and looking at her wetness from behind her. "Ollie, please." She moaned.

Giving her ass a swift slap, I growled huskily with my own impatience. "Patience, girl. You've teased me all evening. Now it's my turn."

327

I bent down. Just like the night at the club, I let my tongue do the talking. She wasn't quiet. Her moans increased when she clenched around my fingers. I stopped and pulled away, denying her that pleasure.

"Oliver." She gasped. One of her thighs trembled as I stood again.

After lowering my jeans that almost burst at the zipper, I grabbed myself in my hand and stroked a few times. I was hard and ready for her.

I slid in, and she moaned loudly as I groaned and pushed in as deep as possible. Holding her hips, I started giving her a steady pace. I was losing control quickly as I dug my fingers into her hips and continued fucking her relentlessly. One of my hands slid up her back, and the other snaked around to her low ponytail that I pulled back. Her body moved with my force as I kept thrusting into her. Harder.

My hand was still wrapped around her hair as I gave it another sharp tug. My other hand on her hip slid around the front of her smoothness, and I began to rub her. Her moans increased as she pushed her ass out into me.

Like wildfire, we both came.

It was the quick, hard fuck that we both needed to take the edge off and to get the sexual tension back to its normal rate before we needed each other again.

~

"Thank you for dinner. I enjoyed it immensely," she whispered while curled up against my side.

I wrapped my arm around her, holding her closely, and stroked her back up and down lightly. "Let Daniel try and win you. It'd give me great pleasure in seeing that prick fail."

A deep chuckle came from her chest. "Such a guy."

We dozed on and off after dinner. We both actually had been able to sit and eat at the table where I had bent her over and made her scream.

Waking up in the early hours of the morning to the TV on, I nudged Sage awake. "Baby, go to bed. I'll go and turn everything off," I said, kissing her forehead and sitting up as she sat up also.

"Meet you in there." She yawned, standing up and sleepily took one step at a time as I switched the TV off and checked the locks on the doors.

Heading upstairs, I passed by Meadow's room, and her musical mobile was on above her cot. I walked in the bedroom where Sage was sliding into the bed.

"Was she awake?" I asked.

She looked confused. "Meadow? Oh, I didn't hear her, so I left her," she said, getting back up.

"Did you turn her mobile on?" I asked. "I thought you did, so I didn't check on her."

A soft laugh escaped her, but a saddened pain was still there as she sighed. "Oh, god. Please don't tell me she's standing and playing with that. I swear she's growing in advance to these books."

"My offer still stands, baby." I wiggled my brows and kissed her gently.

She pushed back from my chest and rolled her eyes but still smiling as she tugged on my shirt. "Fine."

"Fine?" I raised a brow. "What are you saying fine to?"

She smiled, biting her lip. "Like you don't know. It could take months anyway. Let's have another baby, Ollie. You wore me down with your cooking and amazing sex tonight. I give in. Knock me up with another baby."

I couldn't contain the grin on my face. I knew it. I had her hooked on me. "I'll throw the damn pills out."

Sage walked down to Meadow's room, and I began to strip my shirt off, getting it just up over my head when I heard a blood-curdling scream coming from Meadow's room.

Sage.

"Sage!" I yelled, racing down to her. My stomach knotted up at every possible thought.

Sage was standing over her crib, looking panicked and shaking as she cried hard tears, trying to talk. She couldn't get the words out, and I was about to shake her. "Oliver, she's not breathing. She's turning blue!"

Every parent's worst nightmare was happening right before our eyes right now.

# CHAPTER 27

Panic.

Anger.

Devastation.

Heartbreak.

Guilt.

It all consumed me and ate me from the inside out.

I sat in the waiting room with Oliver pacing holes into the sterile floor of the hospital. I felt helpless and useless sitting in the emergency waiting room. I should be in there with her, doing something or at least holding her hand. I should be kissing her and telling her everything would be alright and that we were here.

Oliver stopped walking and froze. He ran his hands through his hair. Then he spun around and curled his fist and slammed it into the plaster wall of the waiting room, startling others and making them jump as they witnessed him losing it.

Loud curses came from his mouth.

White paint and cracked pieces of the wall fell to the ground as he pulled his hand back and slammed it into the wall again.

I jumped up and rushed over before security could come and throw him out.

He tried shrugging me off as I placed both hands on his arm. It only made me hold him tighter. "Please. Just come and sit down." I practically begged him.

His eyes were wide and glazed over. He swallowed but didn't reject my offer. He came over and took a seat beside me.

331

Both of us had been here since 3:00 AM. It felt like five hours, but in reality, we had only been here for thirty-eight minutes. Every moment of it was pure hell.

"Mr. and Mrs. Bailey?" A woman in navy blue scrubs came out, wearing a light blue net over her head.

I ignored what I felt when I was called Oliver's wife. We both stood up and rushed over, anxious to take our baby girl home and never let her out of our sight again.

Oliver's hand was on my waist, holding me close against him.

The doctor glanced at the wall and frowned. Shaking her head, she diverted her attention back to us. "Please, come with me."

My heart rate was increasing, and I was trying not to fall and lose it.

We followed her to a small room. I felt my chest lighten when our daughter came into view. Oliver's hand tightened around my body, holding me possessively close against him. He was calmer but not for long.

"Is she okay? What caused this?" Oliver asked, sounding impatient.

The doctor glanced at both of us. "Do either of you take drugs?"

"What?" I asked angrily with a scoff. "Is that a joke?"

Oliver was just as pissed off as I felt. "No. Christ. What the hell is going on? Is our daughter alright?"

"Your daughter needed to have her stomach pumped. There was a significant amount of morphine mixed with a type of cough syrup in her system. They're running a toxicology report at the moment," she said, looking at us.

I felt as if I was being accused of the imaginable. I was so mad. "Neither of us have any of that in our home. She's never even been sick. There's no need to give her that, and how the hell did morphine get into her? We're not a fucking drug couple if that's

332

what you're thinking. We'd never hurt her. I wouldn't even know where to get morphine from."

Tears were leaking from my eyes as Oliver squeezed my hand. "We didn't do this to her. Get me someone else who will actually talk to us, instead of looking at us accusingly." He snapped loudly.

Another doctor close by, who was wearing a white coat, overheard Oliver's rant and came over. "Everything okay here?" he asked soothingly.

"No. She's accusing us of drugging our daughter on purpose." Oliver hissed, pointing and giving her a dirty look.

"Sir, please," the doctor said softly. "Let's go into the room and talk about your daughter. Mandy, I've got this," he said, glancing to the woman beside him. "Meet me in my office in ten." The way that he said that to her, she knew she'd done the wrong thing.

Our daughter was hooked up to tubes, way too many for a precious little girl who'd done nothing wrong. I walked over and stroked her finger lightly. I wanted her to open her eyes and wake up, to say the word *mummy* or *daddy*, even to let out a giggle, anything. I would give anything to hear her right now.

"Hi. I'm Dr. Alderson. I'm one of the doctors who rushed to your daughter. She doesn't have any kind of needle marks over her skin. We thoroughly checked for those. I take it she still drinks milk? Or is she breastfed?" Dr. Alderson asked, glancing up from his clipboard.

I was unable to speak. Oliver did it for me. "She was breastfed. We'd only just put her to the bottle a couple weeks ago. Are you saying it was fed to her through her milk?"

"I'm afraid that's how it looks like. Now we did pump her stomach, but there was a significant amount, as Dr. Hawkins mentioned, enough to kill a grown man, unfortunately. You got her here before the worst outcome could happen, but I'm afraid, it's a waiting game. I would highly recommend that you both get a blood test to be on the safe side. We don't know if either of you has also

333

been poisoned. Sometimes the symptoms don't come on immediately." He set his board down and took his glasses off. "Your daughter's breathing stopped while she was being examined. We had to perform CPR twice. Her brain began to swell, and we won't know just how bad the internal injuries are until the scans come back."

"What does that mean?" I asked, finding my voice. The doctor looked between Oliver and me, and then I knew. I understood what he was going to say. "How long?" I asked.

Oliver frowned. His eyes widened as he sat down and shook his head. "No. Don't even think that."

"I'm sorry. She's on a ventilator to help her breathing as she's not breathing on her own. If she wakes, there's no telling what type of damage there has been done. I stress when saying this, if she wakes, which isn't a high possibility due to her age and the amount that was consumed by her body. You need to think about making a decision: if you would like to keep her on, or switch the life support off and let her go," he said sadly. The reality hit me like a tonne of bricks crashing down. "I'm sorry."

Oliver looked panicked. His eyes were wide, and he kept shaking his head, repeating the word over and over again. "No."

My breathing became hard as the doctor left us alone. I bent forward and fell to the floor, clutching my stomach and gasping, trying to let anything out. This wasn't possible. She wasn't brain dead. There was no way our little girl was not able to wake up from this. I couldn't let her go. I would never say goodbye to such a sweet innocent gift given to us.

"Oh, god. No!" I screamed, letting the tears fall.

Sobbing hard, I sat bent over with my hands and knees on the floor. I couldn't stop the scream. It burned, and it hurt. I wanted to take the pain from her. I would do anything to make this go away.

A set of strong arms wrapped around my waist and hoisted me up. I clung to him tightly, never wanting to let go. My legs were weak, and I couldn't stand on my own.

"Baby, I know. I know."

Oliver was crying, harder than I had ever witnessed a man cry. His bloodshot and tired eyes didn't open as he hit his head to the wall and held me tight. His body shook with a raw rumble, a heartbreaking pain as he broke down and cried with me.

I didn't know how long we were there for. Neither of us didn't try to move. We just sat, crying and holding each other.

I looked up, and he reached up and wiped my eyes, wiping my streaming tears which were uncontrollable.

"Baby," he said softly.

"I can't let get go, Ollie. I can't," I whispered. I wouldn't give up on her.

He nodded. "I know. I can't either."

The thought that should have been the first in my mind finally came up, and I pulled back. "How did she get that in her body? Neither of us would hurt her, ever. So how did it get into her blood? We make those bottles of milk ourselves. I don't know how it got into a bottle of hers."

His jaw tensed. It was now on his mind as well. A sharp click of his tongue and all of his featured darkened, saying just one word. "Amy."

"She wouldn't hurt her. Surely, she couldn't go that far?" I said, shocked.

Hell, he'had to be kidding. Meadow was a small child, still a baby in my eyes.

"She threatened me. Said whatever happened next would be my fault. She did this, Sage. I know it." He ground out. "I'm so sorry. This is all my fault. All of what's gone wrong is my fault."

I didn't say anything. I knew it wasn't his fault. Leaning forward, I placed my lips to his and kept them there. The feeling of comfort was there.

When I pulled away, I took his hand and shook my head. "Oliver, you were a victim of hers for years. None of this is your fault. All you have done is try to move on and live your life. She is the one who wouldn't let go. Do you really believe she did this?" I asked but knew she would have.

"She's a nurse. She can get her hands on morphine without a problem. I know she did this," he said in barely a whisper.

After I sat in the other seat, he stood and walked to the small hospital bed. Reaching over, he stroked his fingers through our daughter's hair and began to shake as he cried silent tears. Leaning down, he kissed her little forehead.

"I love you so much. You are and always have been the love of my life. You and your mother are my life, baby girl. Just sleep, and I know you can get better, princess. Please just wake up soon so we can take you home and keep you safe," he whispered.

How could I not break down again after hearing that?

The door opened, and I looked up to see two police officers walking in. "Oliver Bailey?" the younger one asked firmly.

Oliver stood up straighter. Relief flashed through his eyes. "Paul," he said, walking over to the officers. "She did this. It was her."

"We've got a couple officers heading over to her place now with a warrant to search the premises," the older officer spoke. It seemed as if Oliver knew them. I just sat there.

"Shit. Uh, Sage. This is Paul, and this is Tyson. They're family friends of Dad," he said, urging me to stand. "This is Sage, Meadow's mother."

Both their eyes softened. I had heard his father, Theo, speak about them before at the family dinners, but I didn't know they were police officers.

I managed a soft smile. "Nice to meet you."

"We wished it was under better circumstances. We're deeply sorry," Tyson said, nodding in respect.

All I wanted to do was shake my daughter awake. The moment I walked into her room, I knew something was wrong. My eyes widened. "Her cot mobile. It was on. She didn't turn it on herself, Ollie," I said. "It was on, remember?"

He seemed to get where I headed with this. Fingerprints.

336

Leaving me alone, Oliver went out to make a formal statement while I stayed in the room and held my daughter's hand. The machine beside me helped her breath. I hated that thing already.

A nurse came in to take my blood. I was numb the entire time.

How could I have let this happen, let my child be a victim to a horrendous crime? She was fighting for her life. I should have checked on her sooner. That musical should have been my first warning. Of course, she wasn't able to reach it herself, and it couldn't fall down. Someone turned it on. It was neither Oliver nor myself.

Goosebumps formed all over my skin as I realised someone was in our home while we were sleeping. Some parent I turned out to be. I couldn't protect my daughter, and now she was hurt.

My phone rang and stopped me from my thoughts, and I looked down at the number. Cassie.

"Now's not a great time, Cass," I said quietly.

"I'm pregnant!" She screamed. "I couldn't hold it in. I needed to tell someone other than Tony."

"Hi, Sage," he called out with a chuckle.

I tried to fight off the tears. They were gaining a child. We were losing one.

"That's great. I'm happy for you both," I said quietly.

"Oh, thought you'd sound more excited, Sage. Don't be jealous. You can't be the only one having babies," she said, her voice making me flinch as she tried to pull authority over me.

I was happy for them. I was just not in the mood to talk.

"I need to go," I said softly.

"Here. You fucking talk to her then," I heard my sister snap, and then Tony's voice came through my ear. "Sage?" he asked.

I couldn't stop it. I couldn't stop the tears as they flowed. "What's going on? Are you okay?"

337

I shook my head as I spoke, "We're in the hospital. Meadow's, she's—" I stopped myself. What was she? Was she dead or alive? "Ollie, he's going to need you."

I hung up.

Of course, I was beyond happy for my sister, but I couldn't give a fuck about them right now. I had something more important to worry about. Our daughter was still fighting for her life.

The door opened, and Oliver walked back in. His shoulders slumped and eyes drooped in defeat. "The doctor wants a decision," he said. I went to speak, but he beat me to it. "I told him no. We're not giving up on her. She's going to wake up, baby. I know it. I can feel it."

Relief filled me. "Good. Me too. I can feel it too."

"Her heart is still beating. Until that stops, then she's not going anywhere," he said, kissing my temple hard.

I clung to him even tighter. Tony and Cassie were most likely almost here, and I didn't want him to find out the way I had done. I swallowed the lump in my throat and tilted my head back. "Cassie's pregnant. She just called."

Oliver stared at me, not uttering a single word. I didn't even hear a breath. He just nodded.

"So she just rang at this hour and said she's pregnant? What did you say?" he asked. I could tell, and it was not hard to see that Oliver was upset and pissed off.

"Just that she and Tony are having a baby," I said quietly, looking away. I didn't want to say how she attacked me. It wasn't that big of a deal.

I felt both his warm hand on my cheeks. "What else? What are you hiding?"

My eyes brimmed on edge with tears. I shook my head, not wanting to tell him, but the look in his eye told me to spill it now. "She said I was jealous. That I could have sounded happier for her. I just couldn't jump up and down when our daughter is lying in a bed like this." I gripped his hands and held him tightly. Tears ran down my cheeks, spilling onto my neck and the fabric of my jumper. "She could die." I was sobbing so hard. My heart ached at that very thought. "She could die, and I know if that happens, I'll never want another baby again."

Oliver nodded. "Same. Another child is the furthest thing on my mind right now," he said quietly.

There was some relief in my body. We just needed to focus on our daughter, hoping she got better.

Time passed us by, and every excruciating minute, we sat and held onto our daughter's hand. We watched her as she looked so peaceful, so quiet and still. I didn't like it. I hated the machine and all the needles stuck into her skin. Her tiny body was covered with blankets as she just lay there, so still.

Tony and Cassie hadn't said a word since coming in. My sister did let out a loud gasp and held her flat stomach as she looked at Meadow. I almost slapped her across the face for that. If she dared make this about her, I would lose it.

My thoughts were on revenge. I swear to god if Amy had anything to do with hurting my precious child, then I would hurt her back myself. I would hurt her until she was dead and gone.

A mother's revenge is something no one wants to experience.

~

OLIVER

Sage was awfully quiet.

The look across her face said it all. She wanted whoever did this dead. Just as I did. I would kill to protect my family. Man or woman, I would end their life with my bare hands.

If Amy had any part in this, in hurting my daughter, then I would rain hell on her parade and end it once and for all.

I knew it was my fault. I blamed myself for letting this happen.

I was warned, and I should have listened. I shouldn't have brushed what Amy said off with a shrug. It was personal, and it now had my daughter fighting for her life.

What kind of woman tries to take out a child? A child that I had always wanted. A baby that Amy would never give me.

She was punishing me for leaving her. It was my fault.

"Do you want something to eat or drink?" I asked, finding my voice, rubbing Sage's thigh gently.

Her hand was on Meadow's small one, and her fingers ran over her tiny ones—the little fingers that had yet to hold my hand as we walked across the street.

She shook her head, eyes exhausted, and said, "I'm fine."

Fine. That word I hated. It had been a damn long time since I had heard that word used in a context like that. I knew better. She wasn't fine, and it was okay. I wasn't fine either.

I leant over and kissed her cheek. "I'll get you something. You need to eat and drink something."

"Thank you." She smiled, not a real smile, but it didn't matter.

Tony got up with me while Cassie sat in the same spot and sighed. "Could you get me something? This baby is making me so hungry."

"Not the time, Cass," Tony said in a low warning tone.

Her eyes widened, and I didn't give a fuck if she was offended or not. "Cassie, it's fantastic you're pregnant and all, but if you ever speak to Sage the way you did before, I won't fucking sit still and let it slide. Watch your mouth and respect that our daughter is in here on life support."

She flinched at my look. I didn't care. I honestly didn't care that she was my best mate's wife and now pregnant. I hated that she used her older sister status to treat my girlfriend like shit.

We went out and grabbed a couple of coffees. Tony finally opened his mouth to talk. He'd been holding off a damn long time. "Let's sit before we go back. Just talk to me without the girls around."

Nodding, we sat in the corner of the cafeteria, and I ripped the top off the sugar packets. "She's going to die." The words came out flatly. I felt nothing.

Tony's eyes widened, looking shocked that I was so blunt about it. "What? Don't say that. She's going to be fine."

"No. I spoke to the doctor without Sage around. Her organs are fucked. They'll start to shut down soon, and then it'll be over. Amy wins," I said, keeping my head down. "She always wins."

"Amy did this?" he asked, looking pissed.

"Yep," I said, seething.

I was more than seething. I was livid. My fist could punch as many walls as I put it through. It was all a vent for where I wanted to land my fist: Amy's face.

I needed a distraction, something else to think about. "So"—I sat up straighter—"you're going to be a dad? Congrats, man. That's great. I'm really happy for you."

He smiled but not for long. He sighed. "Thanks, but let's not talk about that right now. I called Haddon. He was going to call your parents. Cass was calling her parents. They'll probably all be there by the time we get back."

That was a relief. I didn't want to make that call.

"Did Paul and Tyson find anything? Any signs of a break-in at your place?" he asked, glancing around the room to keep prying eyes out of earshot.

"Not that I know of. They're there now, taking prints and photos. If she got in, then I have no idea how it happened. I know she did it," I said, trying to stay calm. I could only stay calm for so long though.

Knowing that our family was on their way, we decided to go back.

I needed to stay strong. My girl was breaking away slowly, and I needed to keep it in check for her. I wouldn't let her see how crushed I was right now and how utterly fucking devastated I was at what happened.

Seeing my daughter gasping for breath earlier was the single most terrifying thing I had ever witnessed. Sage was frozen, screaming and shaking. I'd pushed her out of the way and pulled my daughter from her cot, lay her on the floor, and stuck my fingers down her throat, thinking something had gone down and blocked her airways.

Next move was CPR. Sage called for help, and within two minutes, the ambos arrived. Our daughter wasn't breathing until they took over and she was slowly breathing again. I knew if she ever opened those perfect little eyes of hers that she'd never be the same.

~

We were almost at the room when my ears pricked up. I heard Sage crying loudly, and Cassie stood out of the room pale as a ghost. Her parents were beside her while my brother and parents sat in the opposite chair.

"What happened?" I wasn't asking. I was demanding.

Cassie looked from Tony to me, nervously shaking her head. "I don't know. I didn't mean it," she whispered.

"Mean what?" I snarled. "What the hell did you do this time?"

Tony's hand was on my arm, holding me back from tearing into his wife. "Mate, calm down."

I shrugged him off. "Don't tell me to calm down. My child is in there, and she did something." I looked back at Cassie with a murderous glare. "What did you say to her?"

Her parents kept quiet, obviously having no idea themselves. Cassie sobbed. "I didn't mean to upset her. I didn't mean anything by it. I swear."

"Cassie, what did you say?" her mother asked softly.

She wiped her eyes on the back of her sleeve. "I just suggested that turning off her life support would be easier. I don't know. How do you know she's not suffering? She's dead. Why draw it out any longer? It's only hurting you both."

My mother's loud cry was hard to ignore. My chest tightened at my sister-in-law's words.

"Are you really that coldhearted?" I gritted, walking closer toward her. Everyone was silent. Cassie's tears ran down her face as I narrowed my eyes and pushed a finger to her chest. "Miracles do fucking happen, and until that's your child lying in that bed, I suggest you shut your fucking mouth or get the hell out of here."

Sage clung to me tightly as I walked in with her coffee and sandwiches. I set them aside and pulled her to me. Her sobs were hard, and her breathing was shallow.

"Tell me you love me," she whispered once she managed to calm herself long enough to talk. "Tell me you love me."

I pulled back just enough to draw her in for a deep passionate kiss. I let her know I loved her. Today, always, and I'd never stop loving her. She was the mother of my daughter and always would be. My tongue slid over hers, and my hand reached up, fisting her hair harshly. I wasn't breaking down or crying, but I was letting her know how broken I was right now. She was the only one who could calm me, who could make everything better for a mere moment. I didn't want to lose what we had, but if it came to it, I would let her go to protect her.

Her hands dug into my sides—a feeling I used to hate—but now it was what I needed.

I needed to feel pain and to be inflicted with it. A punishment that I deserved for putting her through this, for killing our child.

A seven-month-old innocent child, who had her entire future to look forward to, may not even make it to her first birthday. All because of me and my past—a crazy woman who was hell-bent on delivering her revenge until it tore my family apart.

The one thing I wanted to do was fuck her in a closet or bathroom and to think of something else for a few minutes, so I didn't have to think about all the what-ifs surging through my mind. I wanted to thrust my dick down her soft throat and gag her with it. It wasn't the time to be thinking this, but I needed to control my anger. I knew it was only a matter of time until my hands were wrapped around someone's throat, crushing their windpipe. I had no hesitation about doing that.

Sage looked up and broke my thoughts of her. "Tell me. I need to hear you say it." Her voice sounded urgent and on the brink of losing it again.

"I love you. I fucking love you so much it hurts." I growled over her mouth as I kissed her again.

She started sobbing. I tasted salty tears that spilled into my mouth through our kisses. It wasn't long until she pulled away, and I realised they were my tears. Her fingers wiped them away. "I love you, too. I love you."

We stood in silence, holding onto each other. I was well aware that she and my family could look in and see us both crying and kissing, holding each other and hoping that our daughter woke up. I hated what her sister had implied.

I walked over to Meadow and kissed her little cold nose. "What Cassie said…She had no right to suggest that."

"No," Sage said harshly. "Oliver, if she wakes up. If she's not the same and needs more attention or has any complications or brain damage, then she's still our little girl. She's the same person," she said, wiping her tears as she walked over and ran her fingers through her dark soft hair.

I agreed. "Your sister just doesn't think. I don't give a fuck if we spend every cent we have on her recovery. I won't ever love her any less, and it doesn't change a thing. The doctor said she's not suffering. She's just sleeping."

*Permanently.* I didn't dare utter that word though.

"We'll get through this," she whispered. She reached over and squeezed my hand softly, reassuring me of something we both knew was going to be a hard road to recover from.

"How can you be so sure?" I asked dryly.

"We have each other." She didn't miss a breath as she answered.

344

# CHAPTER 28

His fingers dug into my thighs as his thick erection charged into me deeply. I let out a strangled scream as Oliver fisted my hair, tugging and grunting with each thrust. Our bodies were hard against each other, clinging needily and hungrily. His breathing was heavy, heaving as the muscles in his chest contracted with every breath.

No words were being said. Maybe the occasional "oh god" or "fuck, yes," but other than that, we had nothing but raw passion to live in. It was something we both needed, well and truly needed.

Our teeth knocked against one another, but neither of us cared. We continued with our furious kissing while Oliver drove his cock in and out, the speed picking up. The bed head banged into the wall as his body raised off mine. The only thing touching me was his groin while my hands slid over the thin layer of hair spread over his chest, soft fur spreading down to his trimmed pubic region where we connected as one.

My eyes watered as I felt an increasing pleasure, not just from the burning sensation beginning to trickle through my lower belly but from my heart. How I loved him so much. I loved him more than words could describe, and nothing could take that feeling away.

Oliver's knees nudged my thighs farther apart. My breasts were now pink and swollen from his fingers pinching the hardened nubs. He flicked his tongue over them as he had done, biting and teasing.

Flinging my hands up to his shoulders, I rocked against him, creating friction as I pulled his body back down. Oliver's breath was hot over my face as his eyes burned into mine. Our eyes were wide open, staring into each other's soul.

There was no hiding here.

A loud moan escaped my throat as my orgasm rippled throughout my body. I tightened and contracted around his slick, wet cock as he spurted deep inside me at the same time. His cock pulsed with each deeper thrust. I moaned his name over as my name escaped his lips. His body tensed with his last thrust until our sweaty bodies lay connected with each other and we passed out.

Sleep was rare. It wasn't something either of us had wanted to do, but it was needed.

Oliver and I were crashing, burning, and dying slowly.

We spent all our time at the hospital, watching over our precious daughter who was still fighting. We didn't want to go home. It wouldn't be the same if we did. I refused to go back when she wasn't there.

My father came to the hospital tonight at nine o'clock. He waltzed in with his briefcase and laptop. He told us to go home, back to my room at their house and rest. When Oliver and I tried to object, he said he had no intention of sleeping tonight and was going to stay up and work, keeping a close eye on her. After a heavy promise to call us if anything happened to her, any big or small changes, we reluctantly agreed to leave the hospital so we could finally shower and sleep.

I didn't realise how much I had missed sleeping until I lay my body down and fell asleep.

Oliver's heavy snore woke me up, his arm tightly around my waist as his cock lay over my thigh. We were still in the same position we were in after our lovemaking.

Fifteen days.

It was torture. It was the worst hell I had been through and so much had happened in those days. Luckily our blood test results came back negative, and we were all clean.

A pregnancy test had been done, and no, I wasn't pregnant. I didn't miss the slight flash of disappointment in Oliver's eyes. A tinge of disappointment was also in mine. I loved him, and I did want another baby but not like this. Neither of us was capable of dealing with something like that right now.

Amy. Oliver was convinced she had played a part in this, but when the police went to question here, she had a rock solid alibi. I knew Oliver didn't believe it and he was determined to prove the truth. He wasn't letting this rest.

Leaning forward, I kissed his lips gently. Stroking my fingers through his hair, I inhaled his scent. His eyes fluttered open, and I blushed, caught out.

"You're not sleeping," he said a husky whisper.

"Thinking," I whispered back as he pulled me closer against his body.

He pressed a kiss to my temple, letting his lips linger a moment longer as his hands held my waist. He pulled me on top of him where he was thick and heavy, erect as I sleepily lifted my hips and slowly slid down on him.

Soon after making love, I lay against his chest. His soft fingers caressed my hair. I fell asleep, warm and protected against the man I was deeply in love with.

The next day, we grabbed a quick shower. We both were eager to get back to the hospital. It was almost 9:00 AM. It was the longest we had ever spent sleeping, but it was needed. We both felt better, and the dull headache I had been beginning to get was gone.

"Do you want to grab something to eat on the way, or get something from the kitchen?" I asked, rinsing conditioner through my hair.

Oliver took over doing that as he stood behind me. "Here will do. We can make some coffee to take with us."

His hands slid down my sides, holding my hips where he slowly rubbed. He'd left bruises against my skin, and immediately he felt guilty. He made tender love to me when we woke, and now, his erection was pressed against my ass. We'd fucked so many times through the night that it was impossible he could want more, but he did, and so we did again.

~

Walking into the hospital, we spotted the doctor walking out of her room. Oliver clasped my hand tighter and led us into her room. Mum was sitting there beside Dad who was looking directly at the wall.

"What did the doctor say?" I asked breathlessly.

My parents stood up, giving us both a sad look, and my heart dropped. Mum stepped forward. "I'm sorry, dear. Still no change."

*Don't cry.* I couldn't cry again.

Every time the doctors told us this news, my hopes faded a little more, and I couldn't help but just cry. It was devastating, and I hated this type of heartbreak.

Oliver strode to his daughter and bent down, giving her a kiss. "Morning, beautiful," he whispered softly.

He spoke to her every chance he got. We both did, telling her about things during the day. She would just lay there though. No movement, no nothing. Just silence apart from the breathing.

"Did you sleep well? You look better. Both of you do," Dad said, sitting back down again.

"Slept good," I said. My eyes went to Oliver, and he nodded too. I knew what he was thinking without needing to ask.

Tony came in shortly after my parents left. They went home to get some sleep, and Mum was going to do some cooking for us. The cafeteria here wasn't cheap, and the food sucked. Cassie hadn't been back for three days, not when Oliver kicked her out.

I expected Tony to defend Cassie, but he took Oliver's side and sent her on the way after demanding she apologise for saying such harsh things. I loved my sister, but it wasn't the right thing for her to say, not when she wasn't in our shoes.

She was extremely inconsiderate, reading pregnancy magazines and then talking about names. I was on the brink of losing it. Oliver did lose it when she brought up the subject of Meadow waking and being in a vegetative state.

God, if Meadow could be woken up by the thundering of Oliver's voice, she would have done so. He was ropeable, and I was disgusted that Cassie had made it sound like a dirty word.

Oliver and I had no problems at all in taking care of our daughter if that were the case. Hence the reason she was still on her life support.

We didn't care. We loved her either way.

Tony and Oliver were talking, quietly chatting about work and anything else to take our minds off the present situation.

I sat and read to her. Every day, I would read her storybooks, hoping for the slightest reaction to anything.

"Do the police have any new leads?" Tony asked. My ears pricked up to listen in as I turned the page of *Peter Rabbit*.

Not that I didn't already know. Oliver told me whatever he was told and vice versa.

He sighed. "Nothing. I don't know. We were both put in the clear and thank god for that. I wasn't going to stand being accused of something like that."

"What can you do?" Tony asked.

Oliver shrugged at him when I glanced over. "My lawyer is working on it. I have no idea who'd want to do this and hurt her other than Amy. Simone, I don't think she'd go that far. Not after being pissed scared by me when we were camping."

"Whoever did is one fucked up bastard. Poisoning a child is beyond sick, and if they ever find out who was behind it, then they're lucky if they get to stay alive." Tony groundout. He then sighed sadly. "I'm really sorry about Cass, man. She's not herself."

I scoffed. "Yeah, right. You've not known her as long as I have."

Tony grinned as he looked up at me and shook his head with a slight laugh. "True. But Cass...well, she was pretty pissed when you two hooked up and were having a kid together. She's got it in her head that she's the eldest, so she needs the wedding and baby first. I don't know. I tune her out most the time."

"She needs to get over her jealousy. She's coming off like a stuck-up bitch," I muttered and looked back at Meadow. "She needs to be supportive and realise there is a time and place for everything. I am happy, but her pregnancy is the last thing on my mind right now."

I stroke my daughter's fingertips after I placed her little plush Jellycat bunny beside her. I just stared, hoping and praying that she would wake up and give me a toothy grin.

~

OLIVER

"How do you feel about animals?" I asked out of the blue.

Sage gave me a curious look. "I love animals. What are you thinking?" she asked.

"We should get a pet. A dog maybe or even a cat." I suggested, playing with her fingers.

A pet would be good. Meadow would love a little kitten, but they scratched. Maybe a dog, but then she would scream when he licked her. I grinned. "A bunny. She'd loved a couple fluffy bunny rabbits, yeah?"

"Oh, we can call them Flopsy and Mopsy. We've been reading books about bunnies," she said, her eyes lighting up with excitement.

That seemed to be the only way we were coping right now, talking about our future and making plans—plans that would involve our daughter when she woke up and we could take her home.

The police were useless. I didn't dare tell Sage what they had said. The son of a bitch laughed in my face and scoffed at the idea of a five-foot woman beating up a six-foot man. How could a full-grown man let a woman do that to him?

My fist almost went into his jaw. If it weren't for my father, it would have.

Fingerprints had been taken, but the house came up clean. There was no forced entry anywhere, and they had no suspects. I couldn't believe it. I knew Amy was behind it all. She had some genius plan that was playing out.

I could see her now, sitting back with her wine glass and smiling evilly.

Sage broke my thoughts and nodded toward the door. Haddon walked in alone. "You feel like coming out for a quick beer and smoke?" he asked.

I could sure as hell use one but couldn't.

I shook my head until Sage rubbed my thigh. "Go. It'll help until we're back in bed again."

Haddon groaned. "Seriously. Don't talk like that you two."

"Oh, didn't you know? Ollie here gives quite the tongue lashing. He's very well hung and skilled." Sage winked.

God, I loved her. She knew how to break the ice and put a smile across my face.

My brother covered his ears. "Nope. I don't believe it. Little Oliver has never done that before."

Standing up, I slapped him on the back. "Only to one woman. Unlike you, brother, who's had every woman's thighs wrapped around your head. Then again, I hear you're not getting lucky anymore. Unlike us, we're still going strong."

"Boys, seriously. Child in the room." Sage growled, but still, she was smiling.

~

We sat in a beer garden across the street. Tony was also here. They'd planned this right from the beginning. I wondered if my woman knew about it. I felt guilty for leaving. I wanted to stay and be there in case Meadow woke up, but I was losing my mind.

The doctors came in every hour to do checks on her. I didn't give a shit how much her bill was going to be. I just needed her to be in the best care possible. Money was no object for us.

"Daniel got in a fight. His eye is pretty fucked up," Tony said, swigging back on his beer.

351

Now that made me smile. "Yeah? 'Bout time someone did that to him. Who was it so I can thank them personally?"

"The woman's husband." Haddon laughed. "Serves him right for going there."

True. He had it coming to him after always being like that. I just grinned, and here he was trying to pick Sage back up. Let him try. She'd really fall for a man like that again.

We sat back and had a couple of drinks until Cassie wanted Tony to come home. He was pissed and venting on her. Apparently, she had been more hormonal than usual. I missed out on that one, but I didn't think I could ever see my girl throwing fits of jealousy the way Cass had done.

When she had brought up Meadow being a cripple for the rest of her life, all I said was, "It's a damn good thing you're pregnant right now." I would have thrown her out on her ass.

Sage was ballistic. She was on the verge of hitting her. Her fists were clenched and jaw set in a hard line as she walked up to Cass and threatened to hit her if she didn't walk away.

Making my way back to the room, I was greeted by my parents who were leaving. Everyone had been more than supportive, and although the decision would still be made, no one ever brought up turning that switch off.

I wouldn't watch her die that way.

"Dear, can we get you anything?" Mum asked, pulling me in for a hug.

"No, I'm good. Sage might use some more magazines maybe?" I suggested. "Or food. That makes her think of something else."

Dad chuckled loudly. "She just took a bag full of them in there. She's teaching her how to crochet so that'll keep her mind occupied."

Ah, Mum with her sewing. Julia hated it. No wonder she loved Sage so much now. Number one daughter-in-law. I just laughed. God, these two were starting to turn into best friends.

Speaking of best friends, I'd left a message on Greyson's phone. He needed to get his ass down here for her. I didn't know what was going on between them, but she rarely spoke to him anymore.

"Hey, you. Relaxed?" Sage asked when I walked in. She was a beautiful sight to see, standing there and dressing Meadow in some clean clothing after giving her a sponge bath.

It was hard to watch, especially since Meadow loved the water. She loved swimming and the beach, and baths were a fun time for her too, the three of us in the tub together filled with bubbles. Her laugh, or more so squeal, was contagious. I wanted that back. I'd give anything to hear her make those sounds again.

Yeah, she was getting a bunny.

Sage walked over and wrapped her arms around me, breathing against my chest. I kissed her and held her close. "I had an alright time. You two were on my mind though. You okay?" I asked. She was so strong—stronger than I had ever imagined.

Sage was my rock, my safety net, the one person who when I looked into those grey-blue eyes, I knew things would be okay.

"You never leave my mind, Oliver. That's how I know I'm okay," she whispered, her words tugging at my heart.

Fuck. How do I respond to something like that? She was never afraid to show her feelings, letting me know just how much she loved me. I was a lucky man.

"My parents visited you. Does that mean you're going to make me a blanket?" I asked.

She smiled, pulling away and sitting down where she pulled out books and some purple wool. "I'm going to make Meadow a blanket for her bed. It's too white over there. Oh, and your parents are coming back later. They're just going to have dinner first."

I sat down and smiled, listening to her every word as she told me all about this blanket she was going to make. She even promised to learn how to knit me a beanie for winter time. She was focusing on this to take her mind off the real world, just as I used her body to make my mind off it. I should feel like a prick for

353

taking her the way I did, not letting her have a break, but she didn't care. She told me to use her when I needed it, to take all the stress out of her and that she wouldn't mind. I couldn't just use her. I couldn't, so I made sure to love her each time.

My phone buzzed in my pocket. I was exhausted and tired. Pulling it out, my body woke up.

*Please meet me down at the park. I need to talk to you.*
*Amy.*

What the ever-loving fuck did she want? I hesitated. Did I *r*eally want to go and meet with her? I didn't know. I did know that I wanted to wrap my hands around her throat until she was dead and limp. If she did hurt Meadow, then I was going to find out.

I began to text back. Sage was reading a magazine and didn't look over as I hit send.

*No.*

I couldn't do it. I didn't want to see her. I was right where I needed to be. Seconds later, my phone buzzed again.

*Please. I really want to talk. Only talk.*

Talk. Yeah, that was all she wanted to do. For all I knew, she'd brought a gun to come and finish me off. I couldn't sit here and just wonder. If she wanted to talk, then fine, I'd go listen and then tell her to fuck off. I knew when she was lying, and I'd soon be able to tell.

I stared at Sage, and I knew what I had to do. This was for us.

"I'll be back soon. Okay, baby," I said, getting up from where I sat.

She frowned slightly. "Where are you going?"

354

"Just getting some dinner. I was thinking Chinese or Thai?" I asked, hoping to God she believed me.

A smile spread across her face, lighting up those sad eyes, and I felt like shit for lying to her. "Oh, yum. Get both. I feel like being lazy and eating heaps tonight."

I chuckled as I bent down and kissed her forehead. Maybe she was pregnant and didn't know it yet. "Anything for you, baby. I love you."

"I love you too, Ollie, more than you love me."

"Not possible, pretty. Stay here with our girl, and I'll be back soon." I assured her. I kissed her lips once more and then walked over to Meadow, bending down and kissing her forehead before I walked away and left.

I pulled out my phone and sent a quick text back.

*On my way.*

A reply came in almost immediately.

*I'm here, waiting. See you soon.*

Getting in my car, I drove. This wasn't what I wanted, but it needed to be done. I parked over on the side of the road and got out. I walked to the park bench where she sat.

She turned around before I spoke. She looked the same as the last time I had seen her. Only now, she was blonde again, resembling the girl I met in college with a big smile.

"Oliver, thanks for meeting me," she said softly, standing up.

I narrowed my eyes. "What the fuck do you want, Amy?"

Nothing was going to fool me this time. She might think I was easy to be played, but I wasn't.

Amy blew out a breath, rubbing her shoulders from the cool air. "I...I heard about Meadow. I'm so sorry. I can't imagine anyone wanting to hurt a child. I know you think it's me who did this, but I promise you, Oliver, I would never harm a child."

I scoffed. "You didn't seem to mind hurting me when you got the chance."

Her eyes widened and tears formed. "I know. You have no idea how much I regret what I did to you. I'm so sorry, and I can't apologise enough." She paused, hesitating. "I've been seeing someone, a councillor, three times a week, and she's helped me so much. I've been taking meds, as well. I know I went a little crazy, and I know you'd never forgive me. The things I said and did are horrific, but I want to try to fix this."

My heart began to race. She seemed so normal. I hadn't seen her this way in years. "What?" I asked in a dark mutter.

"I still love you, and I want to know if there is any way you'll try again, slowly?" she asked, her eyes flickering with a glimmer of hope.

She had to be fucking shitting me. "I'm with Sage. I love her."

It wasn't what she had hoped to hear, but she didn't let that show. "Will she love you if your child dies? I can tell she blames you, Oliver. She thinks I did this and that you didn't protect them. Can you honestly say that you don't want to try with us again?"

I shook my head. "No, Amy. I don't want to be with you. You blew that chance long ago. Only I was too blind to see it. I'm not blind anymore. I have a family, and you're not going to take that from me."

I turned around and began to walk away. I wasn't falling for that. No way in hell would I go back to her.

I felt a hand on my arm and nails digging in slightly. Freezing, I turned back and shook my arm from her grip. The look in her eye, the way she smiled, and the way she spoke were all too familiar.

"Are you sure, Oliver?"

356

# CHAPTER 29

SAGE

Oliver was acting weird, strange, and almost a little distant.

I tried to talk to him, but he wasn't in the mood to talk. In the end, I just sat there, eating dinner quietly and reading a magazine on celebrity gossip. That could always cheer me up.

Sighing, I looked back over at Ollie, and he was sitting in the chair with his eyes closed. He opened one eye and looked at me.

"You're staring," he said.

"What's wrong? Are you mad with me or something?" I asked, confused by the shift in his mood when he came back with dinner.

Oliver reached out, and he pulled me up and over to sit on his lap. "No, baby. I'm not mad at you. I could never be. I'm just tired and stressed. I hate waiting. I want her to wake up so we can leave this fucking hospital."

"I know. Me, too," I said quietly as I leant my head down against his chest.

His heart was thumping loudly. I sat up and looked at him again. Leaning forward, I kissed him and wrapped my arms around his neck. How we weren't out of the honeymoon phase was beyond me. We couldn't keep our hands off each other.

"What were you like growing up?" I asked, placing low kisses against the stubble of his jawline.

His arms slid down over my ass, and he pulled me against him. "I was smart, focused, and loved to play sports."

"Did you have a lot of girlfriends?" I asked, getting to my main point.

Oliver chuckled, the grumble vibrating off his chest. "Jealous, baby?"

"Absolutely." I pulled back with a grin. I wasn't really, but it was cute to see the smug smile over his face.

"I didn't have many at all. None compared to what I feel about you. I think I went through hell to get to you," he whispered.

Tears filled my eyes, and I smiled. "I'm not going anywhere. I'm all yours." I was so happy right now as I leant closer and pressed my mouth against his.

Meadow hadn't made any new progress. That was the devastating part. Each day we'd sit here and stare, hoping to find any type of sign that she was improving, yet there was nothing. My hopes were starting to fade.

When I looked back at Oliver, he looked lost in his own little world again. Something was up, and I wanted to know what. "Ollie," I said quietly.

He raised his brows. "Hmm?"

"What are you not telling me?" I asked hesitantly. I was nervous to hear the answer.

He swallowed and uttered the words I never expected to hear. "I went to see Amy."

My mouth dried up. I went to get off his lap, but he held me down tightly. I struggled. "Tell me you're kidding. How could you do that?" I asked angrily.

"Sage, I had to see what she wanted. She wrote, and I went. I know it was fucking stupid, alright?" he muttered, looking dissatisfied with himself.

"You got that right. You should have told me. God sakes. What if something happened to you? What if she hurt you or worse?" The thought of her taking Oliver away from me broke me in half. I couldn't cope, and I sure as hell wouldn't be able to deal with that pain on top of everything else.

Oliver sighed. "I'm sorry."

"What did she want?" I asked quietly, not sure if I wanted to know the answer to this question.

He paused a moment, just sitting there and thinking it over before he spoke. He loosened his grip on me, and he kissed my cheek gently. "Me. She wants her and I back together."

He wouldn't do that. He couldn't leave me again, especially now. "Ollie," I said, my voice breaking.

"I love you. Just let me hold you. Let me love you like this, Sage. It's all I can do right now," he said, his voice cracking slightly.

Then I knew. I knew his answer, and it broke my heart.

~

I woke up when the door creaked open. I kept my eyes closed as Oliver spoke. "She's asleep," he said softly.

"I can come back. I don't want to interrupt," my sister said. "Do you want coffee?"

Oliver moved, but he didn't speak. He just kept me to his chest, stroking his fingertips down my back and then up again. He and I had slept in the recliner chair, not very comfortable, but being snuggled against him was all I wanted and to be near if our daughter woke.

"Sweetheart," he whispered beside my ear, brushing his lips softly over the skin.

I clung to him tighter, not letting go. "No," I said quite calmly.

"Cassie is here. She's coming back to see you. I'll go have a smoke outside. I just need to walk about a bit," he said, kissing my skin again.

Sitting up, I cupped his cheek. He hadn't shaved in weeks, and I was beginning to love his scruff. He was sexy and intense to look at. I hadn't ignored the way some of the nurses ran their eyes over him as they did their daily rounds. Oliver didn't take notice, only holding my hand and making it known that I was his and he was mine.

We were together. For now.

Oliver reached the door, and I suddenly panicked. "You'll come back, right?" I asked, trying to hold my tears back.

He walked toward me and slid his arm around my back and pulled me flush to his chest. "Of course. I will be back. I'll get you something from the bakery." He winked and then kissed me gently, igniting a spark of desire burning through my skin. "I love you."

"I love you," I replied, not wanting to lose this moment with him.

Oliver left, and I sunk back in the chair where we lay moments ago. Picking up my needle and thread, I began to go over the design. It was confusing, but I was starting to get there. I couldn't wait until I finished it.

Cassie walked in and closed the door. She looked a mess. Her eyes were red and blotchy. My guess was she'd just had words with Oliver.

"Sage," she said quietly as she walked over to Meadow and looked down at her small body with wires and tubes still coming out everywhere. She covered her mouth with her hand as she held in her tears. "I am so sorry. I don't know what came over me. I swear. I didn't mean to offend you. I wouldn't try and hurt you that way."

"But you did," I said softly. "Suggesting we turn her support off after twelve hours, how could you say that, Cass? She's my daughter, and I wouldn't dare say something like that to you if you were in this situation."

Tears were running down both our cheeks. I couldn't stop myself from crying. The thought of saying a final goodbye to Meadow was utterly heartbreaking. I set the needle and thread down and cried some more. Bringing my knees up, I curled my arms around them as I sobbed my heart out.

My sister wrapped her arms around me, pulling me into her chest. She kissed my forehead and stroked my hair. "She will wake up. I know it."

"What if she doesn't?" I asked sadly.

"She has the two best parents ever. They love her and show her strength. I promise everything will be okay. We're all here for you." She assured me.

Having my sister here lifted a weight from my shoulders, but the thought of Oliver agreeing to do something reckless and stupid brought heaviness in my chest. I needed to talk to him once he got back here.

Finally, I was able to bring myself to ask about Cassie's pregnancy. She and Tony were eight weeks along. She was hesitant to tell me at first, but I promised her that I wanted to know all about my little niece or nephew and Meadow's cousin.

When Oliver finally came in, he was wearing a bright smile as he handed over a paper bag filled with mixed lollies, something that I had taken to eating most days. The candies were going to rot my teeth, but they tasted too good to care about that.

"So, I spoke with the doctor. He wants to put her in another room with other children," Oliver said as his smiled faded. "I said no."

"Okay. Is that what you think is best?" I asked him as Cassie walked over to her and began to brush her hair.

Oliver nodded. "Yes. I don't want her in a room with other children who are ill. The doctor made some remark about the cost being heavy, which isn't even on my mind. I don't care how much this costs. She's staying in here."

"Ollie, are we able to afford this?" I asked softly. I knew having her in here each day wasn't cheap. It was expensive as hell.

He just nodded. "I've got it covered. Don't worry about a thing. How's work going? Have you thought any more about hiring someone?" he asked me.

I did, but I wasn't sure. The business had been closed ever since Meadow had been admitted. Working was far from my mind. My parents, of course, offered to help us out in any way possible, but it wasn't money I was after. I just didn't want to be away from her in case she woke or worse.

"I'm going to hire someone. Maybe in a couple weeks when things settle down here," I said, reaching over and holding onto his hands, giving them a squeeze. "What about you? Are you okay to be off work?"

"Dad got it covered, and I have men that I pay to do things for me. Don't worry, beauty. Now, hand over that bag. I want a black cat." He grinned, digging through the bag in search for his own lollies to eat.

~

When the night began to fall, I had a visit from the man who pissed Oliver off more than once—Daniel.

Striding in with a blank stare, he looked and realised I was alone. A small smile formed over his lips. "Hey," he said softly.

I smiled back nervously. "Hi. How are you?" I asked him.

He gave me a look that said, *"Really? You're asking me how I am."* He took a seat beside me and reached my hand. "I'm good. Now, how are you doing?"

"Not good." I admitted.

It was the truth. I wasn't doing well at all. Everything was turning to shit, and I knew it was only a matter of time before Oliver left.

Dan sighed. "Sweetheart, have you eaten?"

"No. I'm not that hungry. I'm just tired," I said. The days here were getting longer, and my ass was aching from sitting in the chair most of the day.

He chuckled, giving my thigh a rub. "Still no news? I wanted to come sooner but thought I better give you both some space."

My eyes wandered over his face, a faint bruise forming near his eye. "Did you get into a fight?" I asked.

He laughed. "You could say that. Just a rowdy guy at the bar."

"What happened? Tell me some gossip. I don't know anything except about celebrity gossip at the moment." I laughed. He knew everything, so he'd have to know what was going on around town.

"Nah, pretty boring. I was drinking, and a guy just got into a fight and his elbow connected with my eye. All an accident," he said.

362

Something changed on his face. He was lying to me. Daniel forgot that I knew when he lied. It was how I found out about him having sex with that woman he apparently didn't sleep with.

To Daniel's dismay, Oliver walked in and narrowed his eyes, but he didn't say anything. He sat down and picked up one of my trashy magazines. He gave me a wink as Daniel looked ready to start sweating. What was going on with them? Were they having some type of pissing contest that I didn't know about?

Lifting his arm, Daniel checked his watch and sighed. "I need to go. I just wanted to come and say I was thinking about you. If you need anything, you have my number." He leant forward and pressed his lips to my cheek.

Oliver's jaw hardened as he stared daggers into Daniel's skull. I loved that he could get as jealous as I could sometimes.

As soon as the door closed, Oliver was up on his feet, pressing his mouth against mine. "You're mine, Sage. Never forget that."

I moaned. "I won't."

I whimpered as his tongue darted into my mouth. His hands held me tightly as he sucked on my lower lip, biting down. I grabbed his ass and pushed myself into him. We had a bathroom connected to the room, and that was where Oliver was leading me to. His cock was bursting at the seam on his zipper, ready to get out and take me hard.

~

As I cleaned myself up, I noticed something on the floor that had fallen from his pocket: his phone.

I shouldn't, but I didn't care. After making sure the door was locked, my fingers shakily unlocked his screen. I smiled as I saw the photo of Oliver, myself, and Meadow all lying down in bed as his background.

I pushed the button on his phone to read the text messages. I saw one number that wasn't saved, and my insides churned. These were her messages to him.

And then I read all his replies.

Reading them one by one, I felt my heart break all over again.

~

OLIVER

Sage walked out from the bathroom and kept her eyes diverted from mine. The mood had shifted greatly, and the air was colder and tenser. She was stiffer and alert. Normally, after a quick fuck, we were still all over each other. Now, she was distant, pulling away just as I had been doing.

She handed something over. I looked at her palm then realised it was my phone. "Here. You dropped it," she said quietly, shoving it into my hand.

Instantly, I knew. She knew.

"Sage," I said, standing.

It didn't bother me the slightest that she had gone through my messages. I didn't care.

I didn't want to hide this from her, but I did hide it from her. I lied to her and kept it hidden. I fucked up. I needed to explain and tell her that what I said meant nothing, but I couldn't. A part of me wanted to hurt her and push her away before she was hurt even more, more than I could ever handle.

"I'm just going to lie down. Can you hold me? I just want you to hold me," she asked, her voice cracking. She sniffed loudly and wiped an arm over her face. I noticed her eyes were watering.

I was up in an instant. I sat down and pulled her down on my lap. My hand was on the lever to recline the chair. "Baby, you don't have to ask me to hold you."

She sighed. "Do you love me? Really love me, Ollie?" Her voice broke as she started to cry. "I don't understand. Am I not enough for you?"

"I love you more than anything. You're impossible not to love, baby," I said, smiling as I pulled her head back. Laying her down against my chest, I kissed the top of her head and pulled the blanket up over her body, keeping her warm.

When she fell asleep, regret filled me.

How could I do this to her, to us?

I was pushing her away. I was going to hurt her badly, and I didn't know if we could ever come back from this. She was going to hate me, blame me, and never talk to me again.

For some reason, the only reason, it was the only way I knew how to save her and my daughter from any further pain. Amy had threatened them. She threatened my girlfriend by telling me, as I stood with her in the park, that there was a man in the room pretending to be a doctor. He could easily kill my daughter for good then hurt the woman I love with a single shot in the head.

Quick and quiet. No one would know a thing.

That was when I agreed to come back to her. I practically screamed it at her.

The messages, I had to play along and tell a woman I despised with everything in me that I loved her and couldn't wait to see her. The messages that Sage had read said I couldn't wait to feel her body against mine again.

It was a wonder that she was still here on my lap, holding me tightly and telling me that she still loved me. I didn't deserve her.

I felt like the biggest asshole. I was no better than Daniel, but I hoped she'd understand that I was doing this for her, for them, to protect them.

My brother and my lawyer were the only ones who knew what was happening. My lawyer hated this idea, but it was the only way to reveal to the world who Amy really was: a coldhearted monster. He had everything drawn up in case something happened. Sage would get it all: the house, money, and anything else I owned if I wasn't around for her and Meadow anymore. I hated that thought and that I wouldn't be able to give her more children like we had both wanted.

Fuck. I would give anything for her to be carrying my child again. I wanted to watch her grow and to be there for all the mood swings. I wanted to be told there was no sex tonight or to be woken up in the middle of the night for a food run. I wanted to make something insane like bacon and maple syrup, which Sage told me she craved badly while pregnant with Meadow.

I wanted to do all that.

I wanted to marry her. I loved her so much that I would marry her just to make her completely mine. I'd do it tonight at the church in the hospital, but that would be selfish of me. I couldn't leave her married to me and expect her to stay faithful and wait for fuck knew how long while I went back to my ex-wife.

Pretending to be happy was all I could do.

I was going to fake it.

Amy thought she had me wrapped around her fingers again. Little did she know that I had a plan of my own. Live or die, I would get my revenge on her.

I would make her pay and suffer.

Revenge was all I wanted. It was all I needed. It drove me to make it through until the next day.

Sage stirred in her sleep, and I rocked her gently. She was too good for a man like me, but again, I was a selfish bastard. I couldn't let her go. Daniel wasn't a threat anymore. She figured out his lies again tonight. Good thing. It was one less thing I had to worry about while I was gone.

I had no idea how long this would take.

The next morning, I was going to break her heart and regret it every single second for the rest of my life. I had to do this to protect them.

I could tell her. Sure. But she'd want to help me, and this was something I couldn't have her mixed up in. I needed her to be here with our daughter, taking care of her for me. The thought of Sage being anywhere near Amy broke my heart. I knew what Amy would do. She'd kill her.

She wouldn't hesitate to kill her.

~

When I woke, my body felt lighter. I jerked up, slightly panicked when I didn't see Sage anywhere. Bile rose in my throat. I

366

hadn't planned to fall asleep. I wanted to look at her all night and hold her closely.

I got up, walked over to my daughter, and kissed her forehead. "Good morning, princess," I whispered. "I just want you to know that Daddy loves you so much and he always will. I need you to get better and wake up for Mummy. Can you do that, baby? Please just wake up and make sure you take care of Mummy for me. Never forget that Daddy loves you both so much."

Sage walked out from the bathroom and gave me a sleepy smile. "Do you want to go to my parents'? I'd like to just go home for a bit. Tony and Cassie are on their way here to watch her for us."

Home—that was the place I had brought for us, not her parents' house.

I nodded slowly, my eyes stuck on hers. She deserved at least this. "We'll leave as soon as they get here."

~

I drove us to her parents'. They were both at work. The rain poured as we ran to the door to the guesthouse. Lost in the moment of her white shirt clinging to her body, I spun her around and pushed her against the door. Her lips parted, and her hair was a damp mess from the rain. I leant forward and kissed her.

She had told me being kissed in the rain was a fantasy and the most romantic thing possible. I couldn't think of being anything less of romantic right now. I wanted to make this moment last.

Her hands slid up my sides as our tongues dived into each other. I flexed my hips against her body and reached around her, cupping her ass and then gripping her tightly. Lifting her up, she wrapped her legs around me as I got the door unlocked.

Once inside, I kicked the door close and went in the bedroom. I couldn't wait to make love to her. I removed my clothes and pulled her panties down and quickly thrust into her as she screamed in pleasure. We were wrapped in our own bubble, moaning each other's name as I pushed deeply inside her, ignoring the world around us.

I made love to her until I no longer could, and we spent the time cuddling one another. Being close to her like this was all I needed to keep myself sane. After a while, I stood up and lit candles around the bathroom as the power was out. As we lay in the large tub, her body was on top of mine, and I rubbed her shoulders soothingly. She was starting to relax even more. I wanted her to be relaxed and loved.

I had stripped her naked and kissed every inch of her body. No skin left not kissed and made love to with my mouth.

There were no sounds except the water around us. Sage moved and straddled me. I held her soft flush skin to mine. My fingertips grazed up her back to her shoulders as my breathing became heavier. She stared into my eyes, burning into my soul as I pushed her slowly down and filled her completely.

A loud breathy moan came from her lips as I claimed them again. Her mouth softly responded as every hair on my body stood upright.

I never believed people when they said you could make love. I didn't see the difference between that and fucking. Maybe I had never felt anything other than just the pleasure going to my cock to notice, but that had never happened with Sage. Each and every time, I felt it, the pounding in my chest and the squeezing of my heart. I loved her, and I felt her love right back with each slow movement.

I could have her fucked and spent easily, but it wasn't what I wanted. I needed her to feel the pleasure she gave to me even with just a look or a smile. She made my life different, and I didn't want to lose that.

I pushed her up, and I stepped out of the tub. I helped her out and dried ourselves with the towel. Pulling her to the room with me, I lay her down and climbed on top of her. As I continued making love to her, I felt tears streaming down my eyes.

She reached up and rubbed underneath my eye. "You're crying," she murmured as I kept the steady pace against her.

"So are you," I whispered back, kissing her tears away.

Her hair splayed out in the pillow as her legs slid up mine, locking me in tighter. Our bodies moved in sync, knowing what the other needed and automatically adjusting.

I had come inside her but didn't stop. I didn't want to stop no matter how tender the head of my cock was right now. I just needed to keep her close. She was made for me, to fit me.

Our mouths crashed as our breathing became hard and ragged. Her hips met my thrusts. Her moans increased as she trembled underneath me. Pushing my pubic bone against her, I rubbed quicker until she was panting and crying out loudly. She tightened and spasmed around me. I ignored that all too familiar sensation to unload again and just focused on her. I wanted her to come and come until she was exhausted.

I'd make love to her until she felt all the love possible from me.

"You're so beautiful," I whispered, placing feathery kisses to her skin.

"Mm," she mumbled sleepily. "I love you, Oliver."

I was glad she couldn't see my eyes right now or feel the pain in my chest. She held my heart in her hands, and until she let it go, I was hers.

Blinking back my emotions and swallowing, I kissed her temple. "I love you more than anything in this world, Sage."

"I don't want you to leave," she whispered. "Please, whatever you're going to do, don't do it."

Shit. Not what I wanted to talk about. "Baby, I love you. I will always love you. Remember that, okay?"

Her body began to shake, and I soon felt the warm tears against my chest. Holding her tighter, I cupped her cheeks as I pushed her against her back. Her tears shouldn't have made me hard, but they did. I kept my eyes on hers as she cried and moved into her.

"Feel this, Sage." I groaned softly. "You feel it, don't you? The love?" I asked as I stayed still.

I didn't dare move. I was rock hard inside her as she gripped me firmly. The feeling of her velvet warmth was enough to make me come on my own.

"I feel you, Oliver. God, I love you so much. Just love me. Don't stop."

"Never, baby. I'll never stop loving you." I growled huskily over her mouth as I went from slow lovemaking to hard, passionate lovemaking.

~

Slipping out from the bed, I went to the living room where my clothes were. It was still raining. Sage had fallen asleep in my arms after we spent most of the morning making love and holding each other.

I sat down at the counter and rubbed my temples. She was right. I didn't have to do this.

No one was forcing it on me except the woman who tried to take out my daughter.

This was all me. This was my plan. The big build up that would finally come to an end.

Grabbing a piece of paper, I scribbled a note and went back into the bedroom. I pulled the covers over her body and bent down, placing a kiss against her soft pink lips while trying my utter hardest not to fall to my knees and cry. I blinked back the tears and stood up.

Placing the note on the pillow beside her, I turned around and walked out the door. I didn't need a car. I called a cab and gave him the directions to where I was headed. The last time I had been here, shit went down.

The memories of hell that Amy put me through, the torture, and abuse resurfaced. I was strong enough not to fall into the weak man again. I was, and I knew it.

God, I hoped this would work out the way I had played out in my mind. I silenced my phone and slid it in my jean pocket. Amy was going to think all was forgiven and that I was here to make amends and fix what I apparently fucked up and left.

Bile rose in my throat as I stared at the white door. Trying not to retch, I forced myself to walk forward and make this happen. I kept myself from turning and running back to the woman I wanted to be with, the woman I had left moments ago with a note.

What a fucking coward I was. I couldn't even say it to her face.

Amy knew I was out here. She'd probably be watching for all I knew.

I lifted my hand and knocked twice on the door, hard so she would hear through the rain. Within two seconds, the door swung open, and there stood Amy on the other side, looking the same as last night when I had left her.

"I'm glad you're home," she said with a growing smile. "Come in. It's freezing out there."

I could have laughed. *Yeah, it's nothing to what a coldhearted bitch you've been.* Instead, I just nodded and stepped inside the house.

This was all going to end. One way or another, this was going to be the last time she hurt my family and definitely the last time she hurt me.

Revenge. It was what it all came down to, and sure as fuck, I was ready for it.

# CHAPTER 30

He left me.

He wrote me a note and then left me.

I was walking numbly through the hospital. My legs carried me forward. There was no way I could do this and go in there and face everyone. I wondered if they knew.

Tony would have known. He'd have to.

Anger was now charging through my body.

Storming into the room, Tony and Cassie whipped their heads up. They were both sitting in the chair and reading papers. I narrowed my eyes on my brother-in-law and glared.

"Did you know?" I spat.

He frowned, standing up and taking a hesitant step toward me. "Know what?" he asked quietly.

He knew I didn't take shit from anyone and that I hadn't been this angry since Daniel broke me after cheating. I wanted to bare my teeth and charge at him, but I wasn't that crazy. I threw my hands up, and instead of screaming, my anger was overcome with the start of loud sobs as I tried to get the words out.

"God, Tony. Did you know he went back to her and that he left me?" I asked, finally letting the emotion I had been holding back take over.

Both Cassie's and his eyes widened. Tony leapt forward before my body gave way and fell. His arms held me up as he shook his head. "No, Sage. I didn't. God. What the fuck did he go back to her for?"

I clung to his chest and let my head fall as my sobbing became erratic bursts of heartbreaking cries. I couldn't tell him the answer to that, especially since I had no idea myself.

Oliver told me the reason, but I didn't believe it. Not for one second and not after we'd made love like that. If I had known that was just a goodbye lovemaking session, then I wouldn't have fallen asleep. I would have tied him to the bed and kept him there beside me forever. That was where he belonged.

When I managed to stand on my own, I grabbed a handful of tissues and wiped my eyes and loudly blew my nose. Cassie was rubbing my thigh, waiting for me to fill them in on the details. I reached in my pocket and pulled out the piece of paper I had found before coming here.

> *Sage, don't hate me. I love you, but this is what's best. You need to be safe, and this is the only way I can keep you and our daughter safe. Don't come to try to bring me home, and don't call me. I need you to stay away from me. If Meadow wakes, I'll support her and you. But that's all I can do for now. Don't make it harder than it needs to be. I need to be with my wife. It's where I belong, and it'll never end otherwise. Don't forget what I told you. I love you, and I always will.*
>
> *Oliver*

I handed it over to Tony and my sister. They both stood, reading it, and Cassie was the first to speak. "I don't understand. He just up and left you?"

I nodded. "He went to see her last night."

Tony's voice hardened. "I'm sorry. What? What the fuck is he doing? How is he protecting you? Did she threaten him?" he asked, tossing the note back to me and running his hands through his hair. "I don't fucking understand what made him do this."

"He said he needs to protect you, but why? Amy must be behind this, Sage. You should go over there, or Tony. You go and see him," Cass said, sitting back down in the seat beside me.

373

"Oh, yeah. The last time I went there, she almost broke my fucking jaw. I think I will stay here and keep out of her swings." He sighed. "I don't understand. If he needed help, then he knew he could come back to us and ask."

"Maybe he's too embarrassed. I mean, if I was abused for years and a man, then I'd be really embarrassed to ask for anyone's help. He knows none of us judged him any differently for it. He's stronger now. He changed his life around and put her in the past. He even stood up to her at the camp," Cassie said, sinking back into her chair and sighing. "Maybe he blames himself for what happened to Meadow." She added quietly.

I looked over at her and shrugged. "He told me he knew Amy did it. I don't know. I didn't think he'd leave me and go back to her. Maybe he just realised he missed her and did not want to be with our sick child and me."

"Bullshit." Tony hissed angrily. "I don't fucking believe any of it."

He took off, slamming the door, making both Cassie and I jump. I just sunk back in my chair where I spent the night wrapped in Oliver's arms and let more tears fall.

"I'll give you some space. I'll be back soon," Cassie said softly, kissing my forehead.

When the door clicked shut, I stood up and walked over to Meadow. She had no idea what was going on around her.

She was so innocent to experience the pain of her first heartbreak. I wondered if she could hear us. I imagined she would be able to. I wanted her to grow up in a home filled with love and happiness and to see her parents showing affection toward each other. That was how I grew up, my parents showering each other with love.

It was all I wanted, deep down. I wanted to be loved and to be fought for.

I had no idea if I would see Oliver again, and I had no idea if he was happy. I just hoped he knew what he was doing. The last thing I wanted was for him to fall back and be abused again.

Time seemed to just stand still. All I did was stare down at my sleeping daughter. I'd often place my head close to the large tube coming from her mouth and pray that I could feel her own breaths coming over the top of it and that secretly, she had been breathing on her own all this time.

It never happened.

I didn't eat. I didn't want to sit with the others in the cafeteria and join them. I knew they were there to just cheer me up, and I didn't want any of that. I wanted to do what Ollie and I had done every day, sit here and eat together as a family.

Were we a family, or was I now just a single parent?

I sighed. I had no idea. I had no idea about anything anymore.

"I heard you could use a friend?" It was Greyson.

I spun around. My eyes blurred with tears almost immediately as I rushed over and wrapped my arms around the tall man who clung to me tightly. "I missed you," I said, sobbing.

He held me tighter, comforting me even more. "Oh, baby. Don't cry. It's okay. I'm not leaving you again."

Pulling back, he brushed his thumbs over my cheeks and wiped the tears away. I smiled, still crying while trying to sound stern. "Don't ever leave me for that long again."

"Yes, Mother." He winked. "I'm sorry. I had exams and finals. I'm all done, sweetheart. I've finished school."

I grinned. Somehow just having Greyson here with me made this all better. I stepped back and looked at him, taking his slightly muscular body in. "Working out?" I asked.

He chuckled. "I have been to the gym once or twice. Are you okay?"

"No. I'm a mess. My boyfriend dumped me, and all I want to do is shake my daughter so she wakes up, but that'll do more harm than good. I don't know what to do. I'm so frustrated. I'm really broken. I feel numb. I want to go and find out what the hell is going on," I said with a strangled scream. "I mean, who the fuck just takes off like that? He could have told me."

"Maybe in his head, what he is doing is the only way to protect you? He's a smart guy. I don't think he went into this blind," Grey said as he came over to Meadow, pulling out something from his back pocket. He slipped a deep purple headband with strands of silver around her head. He grinned. "I got that for her last week."

I smiled at him. He was always so good with her.

"She loves it and so do I." I crossed my arms over my chest and bit my lip a little. "Do you think he had a plan? That he knows what he is doing?" I asked quietly.

Maybe Oliver did, and the whole idea was for me to trust him. I knew he'd never do anything to purposely hurt me. If he wanted to hurt me, there were worse ways he could have done it. Cheating was the main one, and he always promised me that he would never ever be with another woman.

The text messages that I had seen shattered me, but I knew Oliver never spoke that way.

"Okay. Come on. You need a shot of anything that will get you smiling and then we can talk more about all the sex you and hot baby daddy had been having. Don't think I didn't hear you while camping." He nudged me in the side with a cheeky grin.

I groaned. "You heard that?" I asked, feeling my cheeks flush.

He bent over and burst out laughing. "Babe, we all heard it. My god, it's a wonder you could move. Also, the shadow in your tent gave it away. I don't even want to know why you bent forward when he was sitting on you. It was pretty fucking hot."

Oh my. "That's embarrassing. No one said anything about being able to see us. We didn't know." I slapped my palms over my face and groaned. "That's humiliating."

Oliver was gone for now. I was determined to see what was really going on with him, and I hoped he wasn't getting himself in any more trouble. All I wanted was for him to be safe and come home to us.

For now, I was glad to drink the ache away with my friend.

I kept my eye on Amy and smirked. She was fucking deluded and stupid if she thought I was back for whatever she wanted: to play a happy family.

I turned around from the spare room that she had turned into a nursery filled with pink and Hello Kitty shit and walked away without a word. Sage would have had a fit if she saw all this pink cat crap. She was persistent in letting everyone in our family know that animals, fairies, and butterflies were in. Anything else wasn't going in her room.

Of all the things, she thought I was going to bring Meadow back here and take her from Sage? No fucking way.

"You don't like it?" she asked, following out after me.

I laughed. "No, Amy. Did you forget my daughter is stuck in ICU and hooked up to a breathing machine? She's basically comatose." *No thanks to you.*

"She will get better," she said quietly. "I'm sure of it. She has to. I think she will love her room."

I was on boiling point. Ever since I got here, I had barely spoken two words to her. I was testing her out just to see how calm she really was or so she claimed to be.

In the four hours that I had been here, not much had happened. I sat on the new couch and watched TV. Amy was silent. I think she was trying to ease me into her trap. I wasn't falling for anything. I was here, reading and waiting.

*Bring it, I say.*

Tony had called nonstop. I knew Sage would have gone to him and showed them the letter. I hoped they realised that I didn't go back to Amy for love. No one believed that she could hurt anyone. Amy had the police wrapped around her fingers, and that fucked me off.

Of course. Why would they think she'd want to harm a child, let alone a grown man? It didn't make sense to them. No one could completely understand what it was like being here, and if they thought I was weak for coming back here, then fuck them all.

*I'm not the weak man you all think I am. I'm not the boy who was too afraid to leave out of fear anymore, and I damn well make my own choices now. I decide what I want to do. So sit back and judge me and think I'm a useless and cowardly prick for leaving Sage and my daughter.*

This was the only way to get what I needed to prove that Amy had done this to Meadow.

I was here to save Sage's life. I had never felt so panicked when Amy told me Sage could have her brain blown through her skull at any second if I didn't agree to come here. I couldn't give a shit about my safety, but I would do everything I could to protect the ones I loved. Plus, the one woman who was causing that pain was now in the room with me. That gave me a slight relief that my girls were safe and alive.

I knew Tony and my brother would protect them. Haddon wouldn't take his eyes off Sage.

"What are you thinking?" Amy's voice broke me out of my thoughts.

I glanced over and shrugged. "Nothing much. I think I might take a quick shower to warm up a bit more."

She jumped up and headed toward the kitchen. "Okay. I'll make a start on dinner. What would you like?" she asked.

Dinner? Like I could even think about eating right now.

I just scratched the base of my neck and shrugged. "No idea. Anything you'd like to eat is good with me."

"I will make tacos then. You love those still?" she asked, her eyes beaming.

"Yeah, I do." I forced myself to smile. "Thanks." I added just for good measure.

I turned the shower taps on, and the water blasted out. I checked the door, making sure it was locked and then quietly opened up all the cabinets and checked the shelves. It had to be in here. She normally had her medical supply bag at the back. Peering in and pulling out all the towels, I sighed.

*Fuck. Where could it be?*

I scanned the room for something else—anything to hide a syringe or a vial of morphine in. I thought I heard footsteps nearing, and my heart skipped a beat. Quickly putting everything away, I closed the cabinets and kicked off my shoes. Her footsteps disappeared, and my eyes landed on her small perfume bottles.

I unscrewed each one and sniffed them all. I felt like a creep, but this was serious. I was about to give up when I reached up for the last one. I recognised the bottle. Sage had them in her shop.

I knew exactly what they were like. It was thick oil that was so good you could eat them. Amy had the vanilla one, and I always told Sage whenever I smelt it at her work that it was like walking into a bakery. Then, I'd head to the bakery and get my fix of the pastries.

Sage started wearing them at home, and not long after the sweet scent filled my nose, I was kissing her skin, trying to get a fix of her.

I tilted the bottle from side to side, but it was watery. Not thick and oily. My heart rate was picking up rapidly. I unscrewed the cap and lowered my nose to sniff it. My god, whatever the hell that was wasn't perfume. It was a bitter, sour-smelling water.

I was pretty sure this was what Amy gave to my daughter.

"Oliver, are you almost done? Dinner is ready."

I froze, almost dropping the small glass bottle. "Almost," I called back out to her.

I put the bottles back to where they were originally, and I stripped and got in the shower for a quick wash. My mind was raging. I knew it. I knew all this time that she had played a part in this. Screw waiting things over. I was ready to fucking murder her myself.

After showering, I quickly changed into a shirt and some pants and went straight to the dining room.

Sitting through dinner, I was hesitant to eat anything she cooked. Not wanting to draw suspicion to what I had planned, I sat and ate while making pleasant small talk with her. She kept talking about her counselling sessions, and like a robot, I told her that I was proud of her for taking steps to get healthy again, earning myself some brownie points.

I cleaned up the dishes, not wanting a frypan around the back of my head. I told her to sit and relax while I cleaned since she cooked. At home, Sage and I did this together, along with the odd bubble fight and a fuck over the counter if we were horny.

"What do you want to watch?" I asked, taking a seat on the couch.

"I don't want to watch TV." Amy pursed her lips and slid over to the spot beside me on the couch. I watched as her hand came up and rested on my thigh.

Not going to happen.

I pushed her hand off and shook my head. "No," I said firmly.

One thing I had no intention of doing was fucking her. One woman owned my cock, and that woman was the mother of my child.

"Ollie." She purred. "We should at least try."

I ground my teeth together. "Don't call me Ollie. I hate it, and I said no. Why would I need to try and fuck when I'd just spent most my morning inside another woman?"

She froze. I was pushing her, and I didn't care. She had to have known that I was in love with Sage and that I had no fucking intentions of screwing her. That'd be cheating, and cheating wasn't something I would ever do to Sage. No way in hell could she think my cock would get hard for her. Only one woman had that effect on me, and it was going to stay that way.

"You could pretend I was her if that helps." She shrugged, standing up and walking in front of me. "I know I wasn't sexual before, and that was my fault. I want to be everything you need, Oliver. Let me make it happen."

She went to bend at the knees, and I pushed her aside and stood up. "Get on the bed," I growled. "Now."

"Oh, I like you in control." She winked and took off excitedly.

I followed her into the bedroom. She was sitting on the bed, and I walked toward her. I pushed her, so she was face down. I pinned her arms above her head and sat on her. I bent down closer and snarled against her ear. "I fucking said no. Don't push me!"

I quickly got off, feeling disgusted for even touching her. She hurriedly climbed off the bed and spun to face me. Her hand flew between us, and she smacked me across the cheek with the back of her hand.

Before, weak Oliver would have stood there and taken it.

Not now.

This Oliver wasn't about to get walked over. As her hand came down, my own hand flew up, and I smacked her in the mouth, hard, not flinching for hitting a woman.

"You hit me." She gasped, holding the right side of her face. Her eyes were wide and watery.

I smirked at the fear in her eyes. "Oh, yes. I hit back now."

# CHAPTER 31

SAGE

"You're miserable. You should try and sleep," Greyson said. "I will watch Meadow if that's what you're worried about."

I sighed. I wanted Oliver to hold me so I could fall asleep. I didn't want to go to sleep. I had this sinking feeling in the pit of my stomach. "I don't know. I want to go over and see him."

"Sage, are you out of your fucking mind? Have you met Amy?" Tony said. "God, she's insane. I don't know what the fuck to do. He won't answer my calls, and Haddon won't either."

I groaned. "Well, what can we do? Sit here and just see what happens?" I asked.

He was mine. Oliver was my man, and I was damned if I would sit and let another woman hurt him.

I once told him that if he ever left me, then I would go out, find him, and bring his ass home where he belonged. That was exactly what I planned on doing. Oliver was mine, not hers, and Meadow needed her daddy.

She needed us both here to get better.

"I don't know. Maybe we could call the police or his lawyer? Do you think Oliver told him what he planned on doing? It just doesn't make sense, and I can't concentrate without food."

Both men shrugged, going quiet. Clearly, they didn't like my idea.

Giving up on the fight, I rolled my eyes and shrugged. "Okay, let's go and eat. I'm hungry."

Everyone in the room just stared at me.

"You want to go and eat?" Greyson asked slowly.

I nodded with a soft laugh. "Yes. God, I don't care where. Just get me out of here before I take off to Oliver and that crazy wench's place."

Within seconds, everyone was off their feet. Mum and Dad stayed put. They were going to keep an eye on Meadow. I loved them for that. Dad tugged on my hand as I began to walk out with the others, and I looked at him with a frown.

"Here," he said quietly. "Take it."

I looked down at my palm, and there sat a couple of rolled up hundred dollar notes. I went to protest, but he gave me a stern look. I just smiled and leant down to kiss his cheek. "Thanks, Dad."

"Go and eat something decent. I don't want to see you back until you're so full you can't eat anything else. Got it?" he said sternly. Mum just smiled, keeping her eyes down at the novel she was reading.

I nodded slowly. "Yes, Dad."

We didn't venture far, just down to the steak and grill we went to for Tony and Cassie's pre-wedding dinner. It was packed as usual. Only this time, I wasn't pregnant. I took a seat beside Greyson, and he slid his arm over my chair when Daniel walked over.

He knew Danny boy was trying to get back in my pants. It was amusing how possessive Greyson could get at times. He made up for the possessiveness I missed from Oliver right now.

Just thinking about him put a damper on my mood. I hated that he left the way he did.

"What do you want to eat?" Grey asked, leaning in closer against my ear.

*Oliver.* I almost actually said that. Instead, I replied with the usual. "A big well-done steak, chips with pepper gravy, and maybe a side salad. I need to fatten up."

He laughed, poking me in the stomach. "I should have known. I'll go order for us. You want a drink?"

After the shots he and I had after lunch, I didn't want a drink. They were still burning in my throat. "Uh, just Coke is good. No alcohol for me."

"You're not knocked up again, are ya?" Daniel winked from across the table.

*I wish,* I thought to myself. I just shook my head. "Nope. No baby in my belly."

He just licked his lips and put his head back down, looking at the menu as he glanced up and mouthed the word *good.*

What in the hell did that mean? If he thought just because Ollie wasn't in the picture right now that I'd spread my legs and let his piddly dick inside me, then he had another thing coming. Until Oliver came home, I was still his and only his.

The thought of being with another man made my stomach churn.

If it took a year, then so be it. I wasn't just pushing him aside and out of my mind because that was what he thought was best. No. Oliver was going to realise that I knew what was best as well, and that was making the choices together.

I knew why I never begged him to stay when I read the text messages. If I asked him, I knew he would stay and do the right thing. He was that loyal of a man. Maybe my subconscious knew he was really trying to put an end to what Amy was doing. The letter was bullshit. After staring at it most the day, I threw it away. I didn't need a fake goodbye from him.

He pushed me away in hopes that I would leave.

Amy had fucked with his head for far too long. If he believed that he was doing this for our family, then I believed him. I was that secure in our relationship to know he wouldn't go back to her just out of love or misery.

He hated her, despised her.

It made no sense.

He had a plan, and I wanted in on it.

We were a team. We were partners, and we did things together. We talked openly and honestly. There was nothing off-limits.

Okay. Well, anal was off-limits even though he thought he could convince me. No way. He couldn't convince me enough to let him try that.

Dinner was probably what I needed to take my mind off everything. There was no mention of hospitals, children, and Oliver. I felt like I could smile for the first time today and really mean it.

After dinner, Greyson drove me back to the hospital. It took every inch of self-control not to get my phone out and call Oliver or his parents. His brother had spoken to me and told me that everything would be alright. Somehow, when he said that, he didn't look like he actually believed it himself.

I grabbed Greyson's arm and pulled him to a stop. "Hey, I need to use the bathroom. I drank too much Coke." I groaned. "Meet you in the room?"

He laughed. "Yeah. I'll meet you in the room. I'm going to keep going with the blanket you're making, Granny." He teased. He was actually a better knitter than I was. I swear he needed to be in design school or something like that. He was amazing.

Wrapping my arms around his body, I hugged him tightly. "In case I hadn't told you this, thanks for being here. I love you."

"Love you too, and I won't be going anywhere. Count on me. We're going to be okay," he said, planting his lips firmly to my cheek, and then pulled back. "Hurry back."

Skipping on the bathroom, I should have felt guilty for lying to him, but I didn't.

I practically sprinted to my car in the deserted car park. My hands fumbled to get the door unlocked, and the engine started before someone came out after me. I was done sitting back and pretending all of this was okay. It wasn't, and I was going to haul my man's hot ass home to where he belonged.

I couldn't believe what I was doing right now. This was borderline crazy, and I was probably going to get my ass flogged or head cut off. I pulled my black hoodie up over my head once I reached my destination. Yes, I was actually wearing black like someone on the neighbourhood prowl. I stole it from Greyson before I left the restaurant, faking being cold.

My eyes scanned the dark street. I had no clue which house belonged to him.

Shit. How could I not think of that in the first place? My stalking skills were very basic.

Then there it was. The VW Beetle that belonged to her. Bingo.

I quickly ran across the street, hoping I wasn't spotted by anyone. I walked until I was at the front of their house. All their blinds were closed, but the lights were on. I was going to march up to the front door, bang on it, and demand to see him.

Their grass was overgrown, and I was shocked at the difference between the house they had lived in and the one he brought for us. Ours was much nicer. It was a proper family home. This, this wasn't a house you brought kids home to.

Beginning my walk of confidence, I got to the bottom step of the front porch. A noise had my bones jumping out of my skin. I quickly lifted a foot to take the first step unto the house of horror.

Then Oliver's voice had me frozen. I raced around to the side of their house. My god, my heart was pounding like crazy. I walked down until I saw a window. I leant in and pressed my ear to it, trying to listen in.

"You fucking killed her! Admit it!" he said. "You tried to kill her!"

"I will kill you if you don't shut your trap, you pathetic bastard!" Amy's voice was next, screeching loudly over the top of his.

Oh, god. *Oliver, what did you get yourself into?*

I wasn't thinking. I was reacting on basic instinct. Survival mode. I ran toward the back of his house and hoped to hell the

386

back door was open or unlocked. I didn't know what I was going to do if there wasn't a way in. I did know that I wasn't going to let her hurt him. He'd been a victim far too long, and tonight, that would stop for good.

But then it clicked in my mind. I was walking in unarmed, open for attack.

I looked around for anything I could use, and my eyes landed on a fire poke. Shit. Was I really going to do this? Go in there and start swinging? Of course, I couldn't. God, I would wait until I figured something out.

If I went in there, it was to save his life.

I heard a crash inside, and I jumped. My breathing picked up as I slowly undid the back door. I held it, so it wouldn't creak and slowly closed it. Then up on my tippy toes, I crept inside.

The inside of the house was just like my opinion of the outside. It was very different from ours. It was what I had first expected Oliver to live like. Nothing was nice. Everything seemed worn and old. Then again, if my wife threw things around the place, I wouldn't buy nice new furniture. It'd all be cheap and replaceable.

Hearing a loud scream, I bit my hand and ran into the first room I could see. Shaking hard, I glanced around to see where I was. Unfortunately, it was a small shoe closet that stunk of dead feet. I tried to keep quiet and still. All I could do was hope that I wasn't going to get caught, hope that the man I loved would be okay and that he wouldn't get hurt or much worse.

~

OLIVER

"You have no idea what you've done!" Amy hissed, rubbing the side of her hair where I pulled on it awfully harsh after she tried to fling her foot into my groin. "You're an abusive asshole!"

I chuckled. "Oh, yeah? I know. It's not fun being smacked around, is it? Although, I do think you've got a set of balls on you.

387

You were right. You're as manly as they come. Except you're in the body of a fucked up woman."

"Fuck you!" She spat in my face.

I didn't flinch. I wasn't backing down, and I hadn't since I first slapped her. She went wild and drove her fists into my chest. I didn't care. The pain I felt from her was nothing I wasn't used to. I was immune now.

"Tell me why you did it? Why you went after Meadow? No. Better yet, tell me how you got into my house," I asked, walking down the hall and into the living room with Amy hot on my tail.

She laughed. "You still didn't figure that out, huh? Well, since you and that whore of yours are always too busy screwing, it was easy to get inside and go up to her room. Which by the way, really, Oliver? You spend that much on a child? Spoilt much."

"Get on with it." I snapped, ignoring the comment about Sage being called a whore.

With a sigh, she rolled her eyes. "I climbed through the laundry window. It was open. I guess your whore was doing the washing. I snuck in and noticed you two asleep on the couch. Very romantic, all cuddled up like that. Remember when we would cuddle, Oliver? Anyway, I stalked up the stairs and found her room. She was fast asleep but began to wake. I spotted her bottle, put the mix in, and handed it to her. She was too hungry to notice a damn thing. Little piggy. You're going to have a fat daughter if you're not careful, but then again look at her mother. So I put the musical thing on and took off. Not even ten minutes later, she was being hauled out in the ambulance."

I stared at her in shock. I grimaced at her as she just spoke to me like that was the most normal thing to do, to sneak in and try to kill a child.

Was she that fucking crazy?

I snapped and hurled my fist into her face. Blood spurted out from her nose as she screamed in pain. Falling down on the couch, she began to wail loudly.

My fist uncurled, and I stretched it, ignoring the shooting pain in my wrist. Fuck. She had a head like steel.

"You're an asshole," she proclaimed.

I smirked. "I know. You told me that for years. Just thought I'd show you a fraction of what it felt to walk in and see my daughter fight for her breath."

Standing up, she wobbled on her legs for a moment and then dropped her hand. Her nose was uneven with a large bump. It was definitely broken. She just laughed and charged toward me. She pushed something into my sides, and I cried out in agony as the stings of electricity seized my body from side to side. I fell down to the ground as my eyes rolled from the Taser she sunk against my skin.

I hadn't expected that.

"I will fuck you up badly. I should fuck you right now, tie you up, and force you to fuck me! Just so that bitch would never want you again!" She dropped to my level, attempting to straddle me. I flung my knee up, cracking her head back off my body. She fell backward with another loud yelp.

"You'd resort to rape to get your own way. Not even a box of Viagra would get my dick hard for your beastly face." I shed bitter tears while trying to ignore the throbbing pain in my side.

She heaved, swallowed, and blew out a breath. She stood up, giggling. "You're not giving up as easily as I thought. Tell you what, let's take a breather and get back into it. I'm nowhere near done with you."

"Just fuck off and leave me alone. That's all I want!" I said with every ounce of my strength and forced myself upright.

Amy spun around. Her lips parted as she licked her lips. "I want you. Is that hard to believe?"

"You fucking had me until you went batshit crazy," I said exasperatedly.

Her anger reached a whole new level, and she looked like a cat ready to hiss and pounce. "You cheated on me. You broke a marriage vow and cheated. I watched you for weeks, and it took you more than a month to admit it to me. God, I knew you fucked her that night you came home. I followed you. I watched you two fuck, and I watched her suck you off, and you just let her do it. There was no mention of a wife, and then you had the nerve to do her again and again! You were kissing her on the mouth."

She always managed to floor me with shock. "You followed me there?" I asked. I was completely astonished. I had no words for it.

"I could forgive the fuck, Oliver. It was the fact that you kissed her. You kissed her like you loved her. It was like watching two long lost lovers reunited. That broke my heart, and you didn't care," she said, defeat in her eyes as they glassed over.

"I felt like hell for weeks. I was guilty, Amy," I murmured.

She shook her head. "No, you weren't. If you were guilty, you wouldn't have eye fucked and flirted with her at Tony's wedding. In front of everyone, you two acted like you were together and then you went and slept with her that night."

"I didn't sleep with her that night."

"You spent the night cuddled up in a bed with her. I know. I fucking came to get you and walked in on that. I should have strangled you then." She gritted through clenched teeth. "I thought it was wonderful that you left her when she fell pregnant. That was the icing on the cake."

This was mind-blowing. I was stunned beyond belief that she had followed me and watched it all. I didn't have a clue that she knew all of this. It should make me feel like a prick, but it didn't. I was more relieved that she knew and the secrets had all come out. There was nothing left to hide from her.

"I kissed her like that because I was already in love with her. You were my wife, but I was never in love with you, Amy." I let her know, showing that there was no regret at all.

She strode across the room and lifted something. "You know how to really fuck me off, Oliver. God!"

I ducked as she threw a vase at my head. Fuck. Where do all these things come from? She was pulling them out of her arse.

390

I coughed and stood up, stumbling as I caught my breath. "What do you want from me? What the fuck is it that you need apart from making my life a living hell?" I asked, breathing hard.

"Oliver, you broke my heart when you fucked that whore." She gritted. "Do you know how embarrassing it was to go into my parents' church and have people talking about us? That my marriage was over, and you had another pregnant woman?"

Oh, fuck. She was back to this. God, this woman loved to rehash everything from the past. "If you walked into a church, it'd blow up in flames. You're the person they all despise."

She threw the glass candle holder that was sitting on the coffee table. I wasn't expecting her to hit me again, and it smacked into the side of my head, the red glass shattering. I fell backward again.

Fuck. Fighting with her was like being in a boxing match for three straight days. I was fucked if I could get up and bring her down. I just rolled and lay on my back. My chest was rising and falling as I breathed heavily. Warm blood trickled down from my eyebrow.

At last, blood was shed.

"You compare me to Satan?" She hissed menacingly.

"Fuck, yes!" I threw my hands up. "You're the goddam devil. I was a fool to ever marry you. I regret it immensely, and I regret ever agreeing to go out with you. All I can put it down to is being drugged or fucking brainwashed."

Her eyes were like slits out of anger. "Don't, Oliver. I will hurt you."

I scoffed.

"You've already hurt me, Amy. Can't you fucking see that? You kill me every day." My voice was as normal as it came. I didn't have it in me to yell at her anymore. It got us nowhere. She didn't give a fuck about me, never had.

"No, but I will." She stood at the end of the couch where my feet was. She kept her eyes on mine as she reached in a cushion down the side of the couch. I froze as she pulled out a black pistol.

391

My life flashed before my eyes as she held it up. "You're going to shoot me? This is how it ends?" I asked quietly.

Fuck. I knew she would pull out a gun eventually. I just didn't realise how I would feel in that moment.

Sage and Meadow were the only two people in my mind, and the thought that I wouldn't be around for them anymore almost felt like a bullet to the heart. I'd never watch my daughter grow up. I'd never get to make Sage my wife, walk my daughter down the aisle, or warn her boyfriends off. I wouldn't get to see if my daughter would wake up from her coma and that killed me. Sage would have to go through it alone. She'd move on, and someone else would get to put children in her stomach that I desperately longed to do again.

Amy grinned. "Quick learner. Of course, I was going to shoot you. If I can't have you, then no one will. I promise you that. Although, maybe you'll see your precious Sage and Meadow in hell where you belong, you adultering cock-sucking asshole!" She screeched. Her cheeks and neck were flushed, and she pulled her blonde hair out of her face. The blood from her nose already dried up. She swallowed and took a deep breath. "I want you to die slowly. Maybe shoot you in the stomach or chest. Where would you prefer? Tell me, and I'll make your wish come—"

Amy's body jerked forward. She yelped as the gun went off. My whole body jerked in fear.

Who else was in the fucking house?

There were footsteps, and I stayed still on the floor behind the couch. Amy groaned as she moved. I looked down so I could see her. She was blinking, and a look of horror spread across her pale face.

The footsteps stopped, and there was a loud thud as something fell to the floor. I noticed the fire poke from outside.

Well, at least that took her down. Then I heard the safety on the gun click, and I stopped breathing, almost.

"No. No. No. Please, don't shoot me. Please. I swear you can call the police. Take me in, and I will admit everything. I have the drugs. They're in the bathroom. Just don't shoot me. Please don't do this to me. I promise I'll leave you alone. I'm sorry. I'm so sorry for what I've done to you." She was begging and sobbing hysterically. Never in my life had I seen this woman beg like that before. Tears were running down her face as she lay there. There was real fear in every word she spoke, and her eyes were glued to the person standing over her.

All I heard were Amy's sobs and a shaky intake of breath.

When I finally took a breath, thinking it was a cop, I heard a loud bang. My eyes shut hard. I was expecting to feel pain or just nothing but darkness. I expected to be shot as well and killed, but when I opened my eyes, I was staring at my ex-wife who was gasping and choking as blood began to seep from her neck, then her ears, mouth, and nose.

"I hear that a bullet to the throat is worse than being shot in the heart and that you will choke on your own blood and suffocate. Now, you know just how she felt after you tried to kill her when she lay there and couldn't breathe in her bed. So lay there and suffer with every last breath, Amy."

I jumped upright, ignoring all the pain and the ringing in my ears. There stood Sage, holding the gun with her trembling hands as she watched Amy lying there, holding her throat as she tried to breathe.

*Fuck.*

# CHAPTER 32

"Sage."

Oliver took a hesitant step toward me as I stared at a very dead Amy. Her face was a bloody mess. There was so much blood everywhere. Blood oozed out of her neck, coming from the disgusting gash that I had put there. My arms were still held up, trembling, as the gun I was holding was still directed at her.

"What did I do?" I asked, barely able to breathe.

He took the gun from my hands and set it on the table beside us. "Sage, I need you to get out of here. Run. Just fucking get out of here now."

My eyes snapped up to his face. His forehead was bleeding. "She was going to kill you. I had to do it. I had to do it," I said. I didn't even recognize my voice. It was steady and too calm. I was certain that I had done the right thing.

"I know, baby, and right now, you need to go before the police turn up. I don't want you involved in any of this," he said, his voice urgent and forceful.

I couldn't leave him. "No. I can't go. I just…Oh god. What did I do?" I couldn't focus. I was beginning to fall into a panic attack. I stared at him and slapped his cheek hard. "You could have died. Then what? What about me? What am I meant to do without you, Ollie? Fuck!"

I clasped a hand over my mouth, feeling the bile rise up in my throat. I was ready to vomit.

"Down the hall. The bathroom is to the left." Oliver's hand went to my back as I went to where he led me. I knew where it was.

I passed it on the way, just before I shot the woman who was seconds away from killing the man I love.

Falling to my knees, I began to throw up. I had a burning sensation in my throat as I vomited. I felt as if I had swallowed blood. My whole body felt sick as it shook.

When I looked up, I saw my reflection in the mirror. Blood splattered across my face, her blood.

That was when panic really set in.

I wasn't screaming or crying. I just went silent as if time stood still.

Oliver had called someone. He was more panicked than I was at this point. Not even four minutes later, a car pulled up, and heavy footsteps came through the front door.

His lawyer.

Oh god, I was going to be arrested. I was going to go to jail and be prosecuted as a heartless murderer. Amy had begged me not to do it, but I did it anyway. I just pulled the trigger without a second thought of guilt. It was self-defense, but they'd want to know why we didn't just cuff her or call the police.

Instead, I shot her.

"Sage, I need you to listen. Can you do that for me, baby?" Ollie said, holding my face in his hands.

My eyes flickered at his. I nodded, listening to him, but I didn't hear the words. His mouth was moving, but I just kept my eyes on his face. There was a bruise forming on his cheek and a cut that needed to be stitched up. She had really hurt him, and I wanted to ask him so many things. I just couldn't bring myself to talk.

His lawyer then began to talk. He and Oliver were in a deep conversation, and they were speaking at a rapid pace.

The gun was still on the table. His lawyer picked it up and began to wipe the prints off it. He then walked over to Amy and lifted her hand, putting her fingerprints back over the gun. Then he passed it to Oliver, who also then began to put his own prints over the weapon.

What was going on?

"Sage, don't say a word when the police arrive. They're on their way, and I stress this desperately, do not confess to shooting her," his lawyer said again. "Don't talk. Just let me do the talking."

Mere seconds later, a loud siren rang through my ears. The police.

I hadn't even noticed either of them call anybody.

Slowly, I sunk down to the couch. The police walked in and looked at the scene in front of us. One officer shook his head and made a call on his radio, asking for an ambulance and that there was a causality.

Oliver was being interviewed, and when the female officer took over, introduced herself as Officer Stokes, and asked the next question, my hearing came back.

"Can you tell us exactly what happened here? A fight broke out, and you just shot her?" she asked him.

Oliver's lawyer nodded for him to answer. "Yes. I shot her."

"No, you didn't," I said, panicked. What was he doing? I couldn't let him go to jail for this.

The officer's brows raised. Oliver shot me a glare, and his lawyer shook his head, motioning for me to shut up.

"Can you explain, Miss?" she asked.

I swallowed, shakily starting to tell my side of what happened. "She was going to shoot him. She was asking where he wanted to be shot and was about to pull the trigger. I hit her, not hard. Just enough to make her fall and the gun went off."

"Where did you hit her and with what?" Officer Stokes asked. She was writing on the notepad as she asked these questions.

Sighing, I pointed to the fire poke. "I just hit the back of her legs. I came to see him and heard fighting. She was screaming at him. I knew she'd hurt him, and she was. She was about to kill him." I went back to a state of shock.

"And the gun went off? Okay. Then what happened?" she asked.

Oliver spoke before me.

396

"The gun was knocked down to the floor. Amy went to lunge at Sage, and I shot her. She was going to kill us both if she had that gun in her hands. She already tried to kill our daughter. This woman wouldn't stop at anything," he said sharply with every bit of confidence. "She even admitted to injecting the mix into her bottle and breaking into my home. I told you all this before, but no one believed me."

I couldn't believe what I was hearing. Oliver was taking the blame for me. He was owning up to killing her when he hadn't done that at all.

The minutes seemed to drag on forever, and I just wanted to get out of this house.

The coroner looked over Amy's body. There was no way she would have recovered from that bullet. I didn't even aim right. I just pointed and shot. The bullet hit her spinal cord, severing it instantly. She was paralyzed, and she bled out from the carotid arteries. She had no hope in hell at surviving. By the noises she made, I think she suffered in a bad way. I should feel awful, but I didn't. I was just relieved. When forensics swept over the house, they found a box full of medical supplies that had been reported stolen weeks ago. They found photos of Oliver. She had been keeping tabs on him, stalking him.

Getting the approval to leave, Oliver wrapped his arms around my body and kissed my temple. "Let's go home, baby. It's over."

"Huh. Strange. I guess you were right. Although, I still find it astounding that a woman could take out a man and abuse him." The officer who Oliver had gone to months ago let out a heavy chuckle.

The bastard.

Before I could stop myself, I spun around and curled my fist up into a ball and drove it into his chubby face. He stumbled back, dropping his paperwork and blinking in utter shock. A look of anger spread over his features, and our lawyer pulled me away.

Oliver cursed at me loudly. I just shook my head at the officer in front of me and ignored the blistering pain in my hand.

"He was abused, and you didn't believe him. He came to you months ago for help, and you laughed at him. This is your fault. He could have been killed tonight and then what? Would it finally click through that narrow-minded skull of yours that yes, men can be emotionally and physically abused just as much as women can!" I yelled at him. Everyone else stood still, unsure what to say to me.

"Miss, I suggest you leave before I charge you with assaulting an officer." He warned, rubbing his reddened cheek. "Now."

I almost laughed and told him to fuck off. "Yeah, because I can assault an officer but not a male. That woman deserved to die. She tried to kill my daughter and then him. You didn't do anything to help us. Now, you finally have your evidence."

Oliver dragged me out of the house he once called home.

No charges were pressed. He only had to go to the station tomorrow to give a formal statement, but it was self-defense. With the lie he told, he was protecting himself and another person from a woman who was willing to shoot him dead.

His injuries, the stolen supplies, plus a small jar they found with morphine in it was enough proof that Amy had tried to kill our daughter. She would have been taken in on manslaughter charges along with attempted murder if all had survived.

"Where's your car? How did you get here?" he asked once we were at the end of his driveway.

"Oh, it's down the road," I said quietly, pointing to where my Jeep was.

We walked in silence. Oliver kept his arms tightly around my body. He refused medical treatment, but he let them stitch the gash on his forehead and remove the glass out. He refused to be taken into the hospital.

I grabbed his hand and pulled him to a stop. "I'm sorry," I whispered through tears.

He shook his head. "No. I'm the one who is sorry. I should have never put you in a situation like that. Fuck. What were you thinking coming here? Do you have any idea what I would have done if she shot you? I would have died, Sage."

"I would do anything to protect you," I whispered, looking down from his face. "I told you. I wouldn't ever let her hurt you again."

Oliver stepped forward and took my cold, blood-splattered face in his palm and gave me a sad smile. "There is nothing I wouldn't do to protect you. What really happened back in that house goes to the grave with us. I will take the blame for shooting her. Never talk about it with anyone, Sage. I don't want anyone to know what really happened. Okay?"

"Are you sure?" I asked shakily.

He nodded. "You saved my life. I'm going to spend the rest of mine taking care of you. Let's go home and clean up. We can talk more there without the prying eyes watching us."

I looked around and noticed neighbours in their sleepwear coming out to see what all the commotion was about. "I want to go home. Our home," I whispered.

~

OLIVER

We stood in the shower, naked with the hot water spraying down over our skin. Slowly, the red faded into nothing until it was just pure water. Her hair was wet and tangled, and I began lathering in the shampoo to wash it clean.

Sage's shoulders slumped as she quietly sobbed. I felt awful. I hated seeing her in so much pain, and after what she did tonight, I knew it was going to be a long road ahead, a long road to recovery.

I took the blame. There was no way in hell I would let her go down for a crime that she walked in on and did just to protect me. I was stupid not to be prepared for a gun, but after being electrocuted in the side with a Taser, I was ready to give up.

Amy was a woman who wasn't ready to stop.

The way she died, she deserved it, and if she suffered badly, then that only made me strangely happier.

I didn't want to know if Sage had shot her there on purpose, but it made no difference. Now, I knew that my girl could shoot and that she was a keeper. If tonight told me anything, it was that I had a woman who loved the fuck out of me and she would keep her word when she said she wouldn't let anyone hurt me.

If anyone laid a hand on her, I'd do exactly the same.

No one hurt what was mine, and Daniel had a very sweet reminder coming to him.

I felt as if I could breathe again. I was able to relax and not feel the need to constantly worry or glance over my shoulder for her. She was dead and gone. There was no coming back from that shot.

"Tilt your head back, baby," I murmured softly, bringing my hands up to help her.

She leant her head back under the stream of water, and I began to rinse the soap out. "It feels nice. I like it when you wash my hair."

I smiled. "I like doing it. You ever think about cutting it off?" I asked. It was so long, and I often wondered what it would look like shorter.

"Sometimes. I like it long. It makes me feel pretty," she whispered back.

Sliding my arms around her waist, I turned her, so she now faced me. Her naked body was pressed against mine in our shower, in our home. I leant in and kissed her soft pink lips. She gave in and kissed me back.

I wanted her to forget what happened, to give her something more to think of.

Pulling away, I rested my forehead down to hers. "I think you're the most beautiful girl I've ever seen in my life. You're extremely pretty."

"You're pretty too," she said, and a smile finally formed over her lips. "I love you. Just take me to bed and love me. I don't want to think, Ollie. Make me not think."

If this were what she wanted, then I would give it to her.

Drying her body off, I led her into our bedroom with slow kisses against her lips. Laying her body down gently, I moved between her thighs. Her silky soft skin was against mine as I ran my hand down her stomach and then over her thigh. I kissed her hard and with all the love that I had in me.

Fitting inside her caused us both to moan loudly. She was heaven wrapped around me like a silky warm glove. My hips rocked back and forth into her, grinding against her gently. I was taking my time with her.

"Oliver." A sweet moan escaped her lips as she closed her eyes and ran her hands up my back.

"Open, baby. I want to see you," I said, trying my hardest not to blow already.

In a flash, her eyes opened, and she stared at me. I watched as they filled with tears and my heart tightened. I stroked her forehead and kept my pace as her lips parted and she began to whimper and quiver underneath me. Letting all her tension go, she melted.

Groaning, I let go and joined her in a pleasurable release.

Her thighs wrapped around my legs, and she shook her head. "Don't stop."

Oh, fuck. I was already going soft. I definitely couldn't fuck my way into another instant hard on.

"Baby," I said, the tenderness of my head throbbing.

"Please. Don't stop," she said and pushed up.

I was already half slipped out by now.

"Five minutes and we can go again," I whispered, trying to soothe her by lying to her side and pulling her close against my body.

In that five minutes, she fell asleep and curled into my side. I reached and tugged the blanket over our nakedness and held her closely. I wasn't sure if I was able to sleep, probably not. I just lay there and stared at her, keeping my eyes on her and kissing her forehead now and then when she stirred. She needed to sleep after the hell I put her through today.

Trying to forget everything that happened today, I passed out.

Morning came, and we hadn't really said much. I think the shock was still there, and now it was news to the community. Our families were going to know Amy was dead and that she had been shot. The details were left out, and we weren't going to mutter a word of what happened in that house.

It was our secret, one that we would carry to our own grave.

"This is what I needed. I'm so hungry." Sage let out a moan as she sunk her teeth into the sausage roll as we drove to the hospital.

I grinned. "You know. I love it when you eat like that."

"Pervert." She laughed. "Oh, god. Ollie, this is really good. You want a bite?"

She thrust the sausage roll in my face as I drove. Trying to keep my eyes on the road, I opened my mouth as she pushed the savoury food inside my mouth. It was hard not to laugh, especially when I bit down, and she growled at me for almost taking the whole damn thing.

Yes, because the two others in her paper bag weren't enough.

"How was Meadow yesterday?" I asked.

"The same," she said quietly. "She's just the same," she said a little more defeated.

I reached over and rubbed her thigh. "She will get better." She had to. Amy was gone, and our daughter could wake up to a fresh start. I hoped.

~

When we walked into her room, our parents and friends were all standing and talking. It wasn't hard to guess what they were talking about.

"Oh, Oliver. Your face. Are you okay?" Mum asked, rushing over. "My god. What happened? Sage, are you okay?" she asked then turned her attention onto my girlfriend.

I pulled my arm around her tighter. "Mum, we're okay. Now, where is my daughter? I want to see her."

That was all I wanted: to hold her close and kiss her little cheeks. She was our ray of sunshine through the dark nightmare we'd been through. Everyone was quiet as we stood over our daughter and kissed her.

The news of Amy was hot on everyone's mind. I knew people wanted to know what happened and hear the gory details, but I just didn't want to dive in and tell anyone. Amy was a monster.

Did I really want to let them all know how my ex-wife beat my ass crazy until my girlfriend blew her throat out? No. I didn't want to even think about it.

The vivid image was still fresh in my mind.

"Baby, I need to go for a little bit. Are you okay here?" I asked.

She knew I had to make a formal statement. I didn't want her to be there for that. She'd been through enough. Rehashing and talking about it in greater detail wasn't what I wanted to do, but it needed to be done to go on with my life.

This was the part where Amy was out of my life for good.

A big part of my mind wondered just how long Sage had been in the house for and what she had seen or heard. Did she know that Amy was following us all this time and knew about our affair? It was sickening.

I blamed Julia. Maybe Julia really didn't have anything to do with it, and Amy was just keeping tabs on me like she had said. The proof was unknown. Only one woman knew the answer, and she was long gone. It didn't matter anymore.

I had my girlfriend and my daughter. My main focus was getting them both better, making sure Sage was going to get through this, and having my daughter wake up. I needed Meadow to wake up.

Truth be told, I didn't know if Sage and I could survive it if she didn't.

"You'll come back right?" she asked, her eyes wide with slight fear.

I leant down and kissed her softly. Brushing my fingers through her hair, I nodded. "I will always come back for you."

# CHAPTER 33

Decision day.

This wasn't going to be easy at all. Oliver and I were going to sit down and talk seriously about what we were going to do: continue Meadow's care or say our goodbyes.

We didn't want to turn the machine off, but it had almost been a month, and it was torture. It was growing harder and harder each day to come in here.

Were we just hurting her even more?

All of our time was spent in this room.

The hard realization was now sinking in. She might just never wake up again.

Were we hoping for a miracle that was never going to come? I had no idea. I hoped she would, but with no changes, we were slowly letting our hopes die.

A hand rubbed my shoulder, and I sighed, leaning against the warm body that pulled me into his embrace. My hand was still stroking her small cheek as tears streamed from my own eyes. Ollie kissed the top of my head and tightened his hold on me, making me turn in his arm.

He looked broken, so sullen and sad.

"Did you get any sleep?" he asked quietly.

I pretended not to notice the stares from my parents as he asked me that. Sleep was something I had been struggling with. The nightmares were awful. I thought things would get better. Truth be told, I wasn't coping at all. I killed someone, and Oliver had taken the blame for it. Even though it was taken as self-defense, I felt so guilty.

"A little," I murmured back to him. He knew that was code for *"No, I hadn't slept at all."*

The only time I had been able to fall asleep was when he was beside me. If I began to wake, Oliver would gently rock me back and forth, kissing my forehead and stroking my cheek to comfort me enough until I was back asleep again.

He nodded in understanding and gave me a weak smile. "If you want to see someone, let me know. The guy I see is really good."

I hadn't thought about going to his shrink to lie on a couch and spill my thoughts to him as he sat and wrote on a notepad then nodded thoughtfully. I wondered if Oliver lay down or smoked a pack of cigarettes to get through the anger and resentment he felt toward the woman whose name would never be mentioned around us again.

"I can talk to you. Why talk to anyone else?" I shrugged it off. He knew, and I trusted him more than anyone in this point in my life.

"Okay. How about"—he paused, and a smile began to twitch on his lips—"why don't we go and get some breakfast, talk, and then come back before the doctor does his checks?"

Taking his hand and giving it a squeeze, I looked around. I went to Meadow and leant down, kissing her forehead. "Food sounds good."

Instead of the usual cafeteria here, we went across the road and down the street to a small café and sat outside in the sun. Oliver looked nothing less than sexy sitting back, reading today's paper as he kept his Ray-Bans on. I found myself catching glimpses of him and thinking to myself how lucky I was to have him in my life.

The women eyeing him as they sat across from us had me wanting to glare and possessively shout out, *"He's mine bitches. Back the hell off."*

406

He was mine.

There was no way I would ever let him go again. Not a chance.

Oliver peered up and grabbed his energy drink, pausing as he went to take a mouthful and looked at me. My insides flipped as he smiled. "You're utterly beautiful, Sage."

Swoon.

"I think you are also and so does everyone else for that matter." I added the last part dryly.

He scoffed. I knew he was rolling those gorgeous orbs of his. "I'm here, and my eyes are only on one woman, the woman who has me entirely."

I leant forward and looked down at my bowl of cut up fruit salad. Smiling, I looked back at him. "You are just too romantic for your own good. Tell me, what do you think about Greyson working with me in the store?" I asked, taking a forkful of watermelon and popping it into my mouth.

"He would fit in extremely well."

I raised a brow, and he shrugged.

"He knows all about that beauty crap, and you and he get along great. You trust him, and as do I. Hire him, then you can stay home and grow our babies."

I almost choked as I swallowed my food. "Grow our babies?"

He nodded, although his eyes were back on his paper. "Yes, dear. You're going to be pregnant and a lot if I have it my way."

"What if I only want one more?" I asked, testing him.

A grin was ticking the corner of his lips. "Whatever you think, sweetheart."

My eyes narrowed. "Oliver, you're not deciding how many times I will be pregnant."

"Okay, beautiful. If that's what you say," he said again, but I knew by his tone that if he wanted ten kids, then I would be pregnant a lot. I loved that he was so sure of this. It made me happy and giddy on the inside.

Back to reality, my mind was all over the place. In the hospital, Meadow lay in her bed, still and unmoving. It broke my heart. I couldn't tell our parents the news about turning her support off.

The tears were prickling my eyes. I tried to focus on the small spot on the wall that was slightly chipped away, willing myself that I could do this and move on. Oliver was the same. He just stood there beside me and said nothing.

It was when an arm touched my shoulder that I snapped back and broke my determined stare. "I think...I...umm. I'm not sure what I am thinking," I said in a breathless whisper.

Mum looked at me, confused. Even Dad sat up straighter and focused on what was going on. "Sage, what's the matter? Are you alright?" she asked me, looking from my expression then back to Oliver.

"We're going to say goodbye to her," I said again. I didn't recognize my voice. It was too soft, too dizzy.

She nodded. "Are you two going home for the night?"

Frowning, I shook my head. Feeling Oliver's hand bunch up into a fist at the base of my back, I bit my lip. I shook my head firmly. "No. We're—" I couldn't say it.

"We are turning her support off today," Oliver spoke clearly even though his voice was soft.

Over the next few hours, we watched our parents come and say goodbye to the precious angel who changed our lives. She made us stronger, happier, and more in love than ever. Of course, there were lots of tears and quiet sobs. We were never frowned upon for making this choice. I think everyone knew in the long run that Meadow wasn't going to wake up.

She was gone.

Cassie and Tony, along with Haddon and Julia, were the last to leave. Greyson was quick to leave after coming in the room.

I didn't want to be here any more than everyone else. From here on out, I would despise being in a hospital again.

"You sure you're both okay to do this?" Haddon asked, rubbing Oliver on the back.

Ollie just nodded. "No. She's not going to wake up, though, is she?" he mumbled and walked away, going over to our daughter's bed and stroking her cheek.

Alone. It felt so weird that the next thing we would be doing was planning a funeral and organizing where she was to be buried and the type of flowers we would use. I didn't want to think about it.

We had signed all the paperwork needed to discharge her from care. Our hands were shaking as we signed.

"Can I hold her?" I asked hesitantly. "I want to hold her when it stops. I need to hold her."

"Dear, I think it's best if you both wait outside," the elder nurse said, her eyes giving us a warning that what would happen wasn't going to be a memory we should have.

Oliver cleared his throat. "Put my daughter in her mother's arms. She will hold her for as long as she damn well wants."

Doctors and both nurses were shocked that the normally easygoing man they had come to know was now furious. His Adam's apple bobbed as he swallowed and clenched his jaw. The nurses scurried across to the bed and nodded, pointing to the chair beside her leg.

"Please, sit down."

I fought back the loud cry I needed to make and sunk against Oliver who was also sitting. I couldn't do this without him. This was going to be the hardest moment of our life. Amy was nothing compared to what this felt like. She was a bad person and a horrible woman, and our dear innocent little daughter was a beautiful soul. She was too little to learn to hate. The only selfish bone in her body was the one that wanted her milk and food.

As Meadow was lifted, I held my arms out to cradle her. Holding her after so long was the best feeling ever. She looked as if she were sleeping. Oliver tightened his grip on my hip as I leant more against his chest, glancing up at him. He was crying. The tears weren't full on thick, but his eyes were glassing over.

I pressed my lips against his and smiled. "I love you. We'll be okay, right?" I asked, needing to make sure that we could get through this.

The one thing I was afraid of was the possibility that our relationship wouldn't go on.

He stroked my cheek, wiping away a tear. "You and I can get through anything. We have each other. We fight for each other with a fierce love. You won't hurt alone. I'm right by your side, baby. I'm here with you."

God, he was amazing.

We sat there, reading her one more storybook and showering her with kisses. But the time came for both of us to say our own goodbyes. We told Meadow just how much we loved her. "You know, baby girl. You're so strong, and I knew the moment you came into our lives that everything would be okay. You made us a family, and we're still going to be a family. You'll be here in our hearts forever, Meadow Olive."

I shook, clutching her as the doctor came over with a sad supportive smile. "Are you ready?" he asked softly. "It's never easy."

Oliver nodded. Neither of us could speak as they muted the machine and began to withdraw her tubing. My eyes stung from the tears. She lay there in my arms, unmoving.

No more little breaths.

No more hoping she would wake.

We knew it was because there would be no more.

No more Meadow.

Or so we thought.

A small and very quiet cough came from the little human in my arms, and my entire world froze as I looked through my blurry eyes and down at her.

~

Three weeks ago, I was saying goodbye to my daughter.

Today, I was lying on the bed with her in my arms as she slept. Her bottle was firmly in place as her little chubby hands held it after she had a big drink and then passed out immediately.

There were no words to describe what I felt when I looked down and saw her eyes slowly opening as she coughed stronger and louder.

Sage was in shock, and our daughter needed water. I had never seen the doctors move so fast. They immediately got fluids down her dry throat. Our daughter was waking up, a possibility we gave up on.

Did removing the breathing machine help her breathe again? No fucking idea.

I was glad to have done it now. It brought her back to us.

Our family, who we thought had left us to head home, were all there when we both walked out of the room in tears. They surrounded us with comfort. Then Sage and I had looked at each other, and both busted into laughter because our day had been nothing short of fucked up.

We explained to our parents that she woke up and was being checked out. Dad almost passed out. He was shocked, and Mum was struggling to talk. I hadn't felt that happy in a long time. To be able to go in and see my daughter who was screaming and kicking the doctors away was pure bliss.

For now, all her checks came back normal. She responded normally, and nothing was evident that she had any type of side effect from the drugs she was given. Our sleeping beauty had come back to us, healthy.

Sage walked in the room with a lazy smile across her lips as she hugged the towel tighter around her body. "She asleep?" she asked.

I nodded. "I don't want to let her go. Can she stay here forever?" I grinned, glancing back down at my daughter.

She let out a snore, and my heart leapt at the noise. I didn't care if she snored the house down, just as long as she was alive and well.

"She can stay here forever. I don't mind," she whispered, sliding in the bed and onto her side after putting some pyjamas on.

Neither of us had let her out of our sight. The only time we weren't watching her was when we passed out. Meadow slept in our room. The cot, which had been built for the third time, was at the foot of our bed. Call us overprotective, but there was nothing that would stop me from making sure she would be okay.

"You okay?" I asked, taking my hand from Meadow's pink flannel pyjamas and reaching over to stroke my girlfriend's cheek.

"It's hard to believe that she woke up. I'm waiting to wake up to the nightmare that we were in," she whispered.

I agreed there. This felt too good to be true after everything we went through. It seemed as if we were going to have all this happiness taken from us. "You ever think about that night?" I asked hesitantly.

Her eyes snapped to mine, wide with fear, and I instantly hated myself for bringing it up. We never spoke about that night. "All the time," she whispered on the edge of fear. "She knew about us. I hate that it was time we could have spent together. It feels like we wasted most of a year."

"If I had known that she knew, I would have left sooner," I mumbled quietly.

"Ollie, you said Tony came and got you. Do you think that you could have left on your own?" she asked, looking extremely nervous.

It was a question I had been avoiding. The answer was easy, and it wasn't a lie. My stomach ached at the thought of still being with her. What she had done to me—she took away my life and masculinity. I was afraid, depressed, and ashamed. The worst part: I believed everything she said to me. I had made her crazy. I did that to her.

I knew my marriage wasn't perfect. Maybe I was to blame in some parts.

I knew cheating and being in love with another woman did help. It didn't make things easier—that was for sure—yet if I hadn't gotten Sage pregnant, then I still would have been in love with her. It made no difference. All it had done was show me what love felt like.

The sex, unbelievable.

The love, even better.

All I could do was give her a small smile and said, "No. I don't think I had the strength to leave. I was weak, Sage. There are no excuses."

"Oliver, you're the strongest man I know. Just because you stayed, it doesn't make you weak. You survived that. What she did was inexcusable, and I know she hurt Meadow. But, Ollie, when I pulled the trigger, all I could see was how she had hurt the man I love," she said softly.

That night, after putting our daughter down to bed, we made love and connected even more than ever.

The days that soon passed us were spent the same as when we had come out of the hospital with our daughter: lying around the house and being hermit crabs. There was nothing wrong with it. We wanted to block the world out and enjoy what we had while we had it.

A loud knock on the door and I looked up from the floor where Meadow was rolling around and going from toy to toy. She giggled and got up on her knees, crawling fast to her mum who was lying on the couch and reading a book.

"Door?" I asked.

"Thanks, babe." She winked.

I groaned as I got to my knees and walked past her. Stopping, I came back and kissed her forehead. "You're lucky I love you."

"And you're lucky I love you and put up with your snoring." She giggled and groped my ass as I walked away.

I was fucking lucky.

My brother and Tony decided to pay us a visit. Cassie was behind them with a bag of chips in her hand and eating a handful at a time. I knew it was wrong to think, but fuck, she needed to stop eating. She was barely four months pregnant and looked awful as hell.

"Can I help you?" I asked, leaning against the frame of the door.

"Yes." Tony grinned. "We have an idea. You going to let us in or what?"

I laughed. "I don't think I want you in here. Tell your wife if she touches my white walls with those orange fingers, then she can scrub them all clean."

"Whatever," Cass grumbled with a mouthful. "I'm pregnant."

I rolled my eyes as Tony sighed and turned around to face her. "How can we all forget that? You tell us every goddamn five minutes."

Ah, looked like those two weren't getting along as well as they made out. I knew things were hard. Tony was worried about the money side of parenthood, as Cass wasn't working.

I sighed, rubbing my temples. "Just make sure you wash your hands and don't pick my daughter up or give her those," I said, nodding at her bag of Cheetos.

"Paranoid much." She snorted, wiping her mouth on her sleeve.

How the hell does Tony get a hard-on around that?

My eyes narrowed. "Cassie, I am paranoid. Don't fucking joke about that in my house, and don't tease Sage about it. She's been through enough."

"Ollie, who's at the door?" she called out along with a giggle. "Meadow, don't suck on my toes."

414

Haddon was first in and held his hands up. "Clean. I get first hold."

Before either of us could say anything else, he was off and lifting Meadow up.

She giggled and clapped her hands. "Bub. Bub. Bub."

Yes, our angel was also getting better at talking as well.

Sage was watching Cassie as she gulped down a big thick shake and then burped. "Oh my god. I want to vomit. I hope I wasn't like that," she whispered, leaning into me.

I didn't know. I wasn't there.

"Don't worry. You weren't. Remember those last days? We lay in bed, and all you wanted to eat was my co—"

She elbowed me in the side, and I groaned.

"I was going to say cooking." I lied with a grumble.

She laughed. "No, you weren't. Speaking of food, you want to order in Mexican? We can fool around afterward?"

"Do I love you?" I asked seriously. Of course, I wanted that. "You're a little minx, aren't you?"

She got horny at anything lately. Well, lately anyway, her moods came on at the most random of times: doing the washing, eating breakfast, and in the middle of the night. I had woken a couple times to her naked and straddling me. Not that I minded, I was just trying to keep up.

"What are you doing for your birthday?" Cassie asked, looking over at Sage.

If there was one thing I didn't know about her, it was her fucking birthday. How did I not know this? Oh, shit. I hoped it wasn't today.

She shook her head and tucked her feet under her bum as she wrapped an arm around my waist. "Nothing. Just staying here with my two favourite people."

"You do nothing every year." Cassie snorted back.

"No, I don't. Last year, I went out and met Oliver then got myself pregnant." She laughed back.

That took me for a shock. "That night was your birthday?" I asked, surprised.

"Yep. Spent it with you on a floor." Sage winked, her fingers stroking my side, and I knew what she wanted.

I shifted in my position and brought my leg up, since grabbing a pillow would be too obvious.

"So, in hindsight, I gave you a very memorable birthday present."

She grinned and nodded. "Mm, you sure did. You gave me the greatest present ever."

I raised a brow, leaning in and lowering my voice. "Maybe you'll get the same this year."

She looked at me, and I could see the heat in them. "I want you," she whispered. Lust was clear in her eyes, and I wanted her too, badly.

Tony looked at Meadow passed out in my brother's arms, and he smirked. "We all should go away for a week or two."

"Oh, yeah?" Cassie piped up. "But I can't fly. Remember?"

Even I groaned that time.

"Did I say a plane? And pregnant women fly all the time. Plenty of women have had babies before you. Your sister didn't complain this much when she was up to the duff."

Cassie shot him a glare and ignored him. "Camping again?" she asked.

"I'm not going camping again. Fuck that. With my kids? They were constantly bored out of their mind." Haddon added, now joining the conversation.

"No, you idiots. Let me finish talking. I meant that we should hire a riverboat and stay on it with just us. No kids. What do you all think?" Tony grinned, looking like an excited kid on Easter morning.

Sage sighed, and I felt the same way. "I don't know. I don't want to leave Meadow alone."

"Just think about it. You two need a break, and if you want to haul yourself away in a room for the entire trip and fuck each

416

other crazy, then go for it. But you both should take a break from all the shit that happened in the past few months. You deserve it. I think you need it," he said. He was dead serious and hadn't listened to any of the warnings we gave him as he reached over and took Meadow from Haddon's arms.

Never wake a sleeping baby.

# CHAPTER 34

"Of course, I'm worried. How can I not be?" I hissed and grabbed Cassie by the back of the arm, pinching her skin hard between my thumb and forefinger.

I was so over her mood swings. She might be pregnant, but I was ready to throw her off this goddamn boat that I agreed to go on. I didn't know why, but they wore me down, and I fell for all the excitement that was thrown at me.

The men winced as I let her arm go. Cassie's eyes filled with tears and she stormed off, mumbling something about everyone being mean to her and that she was pregnant and couldn't handle the stress.

Oliver patted Tony on the back and smirked. "I feel for you, bro. Good luck in there with that."

Tony scowled as he drained the last of his beer and tossed it in the bin, heading the way Cassie had taken off. Greyson was rubbing his own arm and shuddering as if he had been on the receiving end of the pain.

Julia giggled. "Oh, god. I remember being that hormonal. Although, I don't think I was that bad. Right, Haddon?"

Haddon froze mid-sip and nodded. "Sure, baby."

Somehow, I didn't think anyone believed him. Her giving him the daggers proved he was in for it later as well.

We had been out here for an hour, and all I wanted was my baby in my arms. I couldn't help but miss her terribly. She was staying with my parents. Oliver's Mum and Dad had Haddon and Julia's boys, and we thought it was best if my parents took care of

418

Meadow. Yes, we mostly wanted her to be watched constantly—something my parents were thrilled to do, their first sleepover with their granddaughter.

It wasn't an easy decision, and it took two weeks to finally give in and say that we both deserved to have this break. Eight days on a riverboat and no phone service and internet connection were going to kill us.

Oliver slung his arm around my shoulder and put his feet up on the table in front of us. "You drinking?" he asked.

I hadn't really thought about it. I was happy to sit back and let him enjoy his drinks. "I'm good."

"Baby, the last time I saw you drink was that shot of vodka. It's okay to have one, you know?" he said softly, kissing the spot behind my ear, which sent a shiver down my spine.

"Fine." I grinned, giving in and leaning over to take the can of Beam and cola from his hand. "I'll drink this then if it makes you happy."

"It does." He winked and grabbed my drink back before I could put the cool liquid in my mouth. "I brought you some vodka, lemon, and lime bitters. Thought that you might like something easy to start off with."

I pushed myself off the chair and gave him a grin, bringing my hand up and grabbing my boob with a lip bite. "Ollie, can you show me where they are? I seemed to have forgotten my way," I said in my most innocent voice.

Hell, as if I could lose my way on this boat. It was just two stories, and our room was up top.

Lust was clear in his eyes as he stood and grabbed my hand, leading me toward the stairs and up to the room we were sleeping in.

I giggled as he pushed me down on the bed and climbed on top of me with his own devilishly handsome grin. He pushed my hands above my head. "How much do you want it?" he asked, his eyes raking over my bare skin.

Bucking my hips up, I groaned. "Bad. I want you so bad."

"I don't believe you." He smirked. "Let's see if you're lying."

Before I could say anything else, his mouth was over my core and tongue deep inside me. Holy fuck. I couldn't even think right now as he pinched a nipple and assaulted me with his mouth. I wanted him desperately in my mouth. Hell, I wanted him in every part of me.

"Oh, shit! Oliver!" I cried, my hips thrashing up and down. I was ready to convulse until he stopped and kissed back up my stomach, teasing me. I hated him for it. I needed him and his cock inside me.

The moment he thrust, I couldn't stop the scream.

My chest rose and fell heavily as I lay down against his body. Oliver's hand brushed up and down my back. His cock was still pulsing deep inside me from his orgasm. I clenched around him and moaned softly as I raised my hips and slid off him. Sitting back up, he grabbed himself and ran his softening dick over my moist lips and rubbed cum that drizzled out, claiming me in a very sexy way.

"Bath or shower?" he asked, his lips brushing over my neck as we stood naked in the bathroom.

"Shower." I yawned. A bath would only put me to sleep. All the travelling we had done today was exhausting.

~

The guys cooked on the grill for dinner: fish and marinated prawn kebabs. We girls made a few different salads—well, Julia and I did. Cassie was still pouting, as she couldn't get in the hot tub due to being pregnant. I didn't think she realized that.

Ollie and I could barely keep our hands off each other, and Haddon and Julia looked more in love than I had ever seen. Poor Tony, he wasn't scoring too well. My sister was complaining yet again, and it was wearing him thin. Daniel was drinking and kept flashing me flirty grins, which pissed Oliver off. Greyson was his normal self and tanning.

"God, I really can't wait for this baby to be born. Maybe then you'll be less moody!" I teased my sister, finally having enough of her constant complaining.

This was meant to be my birthday trip—a fun and relaxing trip. So far, all Cassie had done was stress me out so much more. It was tiring. Everyone was on edge, and she didn't understand just how unbearable she had become.

Cassie just shook her head and scowled. "Look at you, miss goody two shoes. You get knocked up by a random man, and Mum and Dad didn't bat an eyelash. Yet here I am, twenty-six, married, and pregnant, and I'm being treated badly."

"Watch your mouth," Oliver said, his eyes staring right up into hers. He was pissed.

She rolled her eyes. "I was just stating a fact."

"You bring it on yourself." Tony sighed. "Cass, I love you, but even I'm ready to throw you over the fucking boat and let you swim back."

Her laugh was surprising. "Fine. Well, you can suck your own cock tonight and then fuck yourself for the rest of the trip. Don't expect any love from me!"

"My hand gives me more love lately than you have all year," he murmured and stood up, looking embarrassed and hurt as he headed away from us.

Haddon cleared his throat and rubbed his temples. Julia whispered something against his ear, and he nodded and kept his mouth shut. Cassie just sat and finished eating while Oliver was the one who stood and followed after her husband.

I knew what he was thinking.

She was starting to remind him of the woman who made his life hell.

"Cass, you need to stop it," I said quietly. "I'm sorry, but you're really mean. Tony's done nothing wrong, and you keep yelling at him. You just embarrassed him. Can't you see that?" I asked, hoping that if I spoke in a softer voice, then she'd not take offence to it.

421

Her eyes shot up and narrowed. "Mind your own business."

Sitting there, I pushed the food around on my plate and picked up my drink. It was just Haddon and I alone at the table. Cassie walked out, and Julia went to the use the bathroom. I took this opportunity to grill him about Oliver. Leaning forward, I tapped my chin and smiled a little.

"What was Oliver like growing up? Did he sleep around heaps?"

Haddon looked completely stunned. His eyes were wide as he shook his head from side to side. "Oh no. I know what you girls do. Not getting involved, Sage."

"I can stop you from getting laid." I tapped my fingers a little faster. "Julia may just listen to me."

"You wouldn't." He smirked.

"Wouldn't I?" I asked innocently. "Just give me some dirt on him. That's all I want."

He groaned, muttering something I couldn't make out. "Oliver wasn't like Tony if that's what you're getting out. Relax, Sage. He won't hurt you. I know you won't hurt him either." He stood up and grabbed his beer. Walking past me, he rubbed my shoulder. "What you two have is rare. Enjoy it."

That was what I ended up doing.

For five days, Oliver and I barely left the bedroom. We were completely into each other. The only time we did leave the room was when it was our turn to drive the boat. This getaway turned out to be what we really needed.

We were lying out on the deck with Cassie, who was still mad at me. She sighed and picked up another roll of sushi.

Being the annoying sister that I was, I said. "It's bad to eat sushi while pregnant."

It wasn't that I was pissing her off on purpose. I was just trying to be helpful and offer advice. She took it the wrong way.

"You have one baby. You're not a fucking genius when it comes to pregnancy."

"Raw fish isn't recommended, Cass, but whatever," Julia said beside me.

Cassie, being the drama queen, flung her plate of sushi over the side of the boat, and it fell into the ocean. "There. Happy now?"

Something was definitely off with her. Greyson just burst into laughter. "Oh my god. She just..." he said, clutching his stomach. "They all flew through the air like," he said and laughed harder. "Well, least we're feeding the fish then."

Julia and I giggled as Cassie stormed off. Daniel took her spot and just looked at us confused as we all kept laughing loudly.

~

OLIVER

"So things with you and Sage are pretty serious?" Daniel asked as I had my head stuck in the fridge.

I looked up at him. He couldn't still be serious. "Look, mate. I know you two have a past, but she's mine. Don't fucking try anything, and you can stop hitting on her."

"If you hurt her..." He stepped closer.

I scoffed. "You mean cheat like you did? Yeah, I have no intention of hurting her. We've been through enough as it is."

He crossed his arms and stepped backward, his back hitting against the counter. "I don't know what she sees in you. You cheated on your wife, got her kid poisoned, and then blew Amy's brains out."

Reacting on instinct, my fist flew into his mouth before he uttered another fucking word.

"Watch your mouth. You don't know fucking anything." I snarled and walked away as he grabbed a towel to wipe his mouth.

With all the shit that had gone down, no one really knew what happened to Amy or that she wasn't shot in the head. No, it was on the goddamn throat, and it was what she deserved.

~

It was the fifth time I had woken in cold sweat since her death. The nightmares only came when we slept apart. Sage wasn't handling hers too well. She was putting on a brave face, but I could see a deep trauma that still impacted our lives.

I'd do anything to take her pain away.

Tony came over, and I felt sorry for the guy. He was getting it bad lately. "Your missus is out on the deck, in the spa, alone."

"Alone?" I asked. My brows raised. I had yet to get her alone in there.

He smirked, swigging on his drink. "I'd say you've got ten minutes to get your ass up there before she comes to find you."

I laughed loudly. "I need a breather. My cock can't handle much more."

"Liar." He snorted. "You're having enough sex for all of us lately."

I left him to wallow in his own self-pity. This trip was actually quite depressing. I wanted to go home and hold my daughter. I hated that we had no signal. They probably picked this spot for that purpose.

Greyson passed me on the way. He was too quiet lately. It was always in my mind that one of the friends we had were working with Amy on whatever sick plan she had done.

I'd tried to get a copy of hospital security footage to see who the bastard in the room with Sage and Meadow was. I needed to know, and my lawyer was working on that.

Pulling my shirt off, I walked up the two steps and into the hot tub. Sage's eyes were on mine as I sat opposite her. She was making my cock hard in the string bikini she wore, and it didn't help that she looked like sex right now.

"Baby." I groaned as her foot slid over my lap and pressed against my groin. She sat back looking innocent as I held her foot in place and pushed myself into her. "I will fuck you in here if you're not careful."

I wasn't warning her. I was telling her.

Pulling her leg swiftly, she let out a shriek as I grabbed her by the hips and pulled her down on my lap. My mouth was hot with a hunger for her as my fingers slid in the bottom of her bikini. Her breathing was hard as I undid the lace tie and pulled my cock free.

"Ollie, we can't." She gasped as I thrust up. "The others."

I grinned as I looked over my shoulders. The others were lying on the couch and watching something on TV. My attention was back on her as she began to grind up and down, her slickness gripping me with each slide.

Her eyes rolled slightly as I slid my thumb over her hardened bud and rubbed slowly. Tightening, she silently came as we kept kissing. I blew seconds later with a guttural groan and laughed.

"Naughty girl. You like sex in public?"

"Only with you," she whispered through her own giggle.

"You want to go again?" I asked, sliding in and out of her slowly.

She nodded, but someone else answered for her. "If you do, I won't be responsible for getting my cock out and watching you two fuck." Tony winked as he turned around. "You're not as quiet as you think you are. I do have to give you props for the dirty talk. Never knew you had it in ya, bro!"

"Oh, god." Sage groaned, pulling her lips away from my skin. "Tony, stop being a pervert and go away."

He just laughed.

Our evening in the hot tub wasn't completely wrecked. We ended up getting drunk and fucking again when we were left alone. Then we headed up to our room where we screwed until neither of us could move. We did get a bang on our door from a pissed off pregnant woman, telling us to shut up. It only made me pound her harder and harder.

Growing frustrated with the amount of venom her sister spat out at everyone, I was ready to fucking lose it. I had no idea what her problem was. We were on a boat, and fishing and relaxing was the plan.

Today was my girlfriend's birthday, and I wanted her to just relax and enjoy herself. She'd constantly been worrying about Meadow and talking about just going back home. I hated that she was forcing herself to enjoy this trip even though it was meant to be for her.

~

As I put the last of the fruit in the bowl, I spun around and slammed my hand onto the cupboard. "Right. What's really going on? What is your problem?"

"Nothing." Cassie sighed.

I rolled my eyes and shook my head. "Stop lying. What is wrong?" I couldn't hide the snark in my voice at all. When she wouldn't answer, I kept talking. "Okay, fine. You're not going to speak, then you can listen. I don't know what your problem is or why you think yelling at everyone and pouting is making us enjoy our trip. It isn't. I will tell you this once and once only. Make her miserable today, and I will make your whole fucking year hell. I can have Tony out drinking every damn night and surrounded by women who will take his mind off a nagging wife.

"Don't look so surprised, Cassie. I fucked your sister when I was in a very unhappy marriage. You think Tony was a virgin when he met you? Hell, he'd fuck anything with legs before you came along. I know you're not the prissy virgin you claimed to be. You think we didn't know about you? How you were known as the town bike, everyone had a ride?"

"You're a pig." She spat.

I smirked. "No, sweetheart. I'm just done listening to women who think they can speak to men like they're a worthless punching bag and expect to get away with it. Stop being a sullen bitch and smile for once.

"I get you're jealous of Sage. Everyone can see that. What I don't understand is why. She's done nothing but help you and give you a job. She's the most generous girl I've ever known, and here

426

you are, bringing her down constantly. I should have knocked your teeth down your throat when you mentioned our daughter may be disabled. I wouldn't care if she was in a wheelchair and unable to walk, talk, or move for the rest of her life. You shouldn't either.

"Your true colours came out that day, and now I only tolerate you because I have to. Because you married my best mate and I'm with your sister." I leant in closer, making sure she understood just how furious I was with her right now. "I can't stand you and just because I'm talking to you, doesn't mean I like you."

I left her standing there in the kitchen crying and too shocked to form words. Hopefully, it got through her thick skull and she'd begin to treat others with more respect. Unless this was what pregnancy did to her, then we were all in for a hell of a ride. It was Tony I felt bad for. He had to go home to that.

Sure. I was a harsh prick to her. What I said was downright disgusting, but I was done trying. Nothing she said to me over these past few weeks could repair any of the damage. She brought this on herself.

"Morning, sleepy head," I said, softly kissing the bare shoulder of the birthday girl.

She moaned, mumbling something in her sleep, and then opened her eyes, rolling onto her back and covering her naked chest with a blanket. "Morning, handsome. You're dressed?" she asked, looking at my clothes and pouting. "Do I not get morning sex?"

I chuckled and kissed her again. "You can have all the sex you desire today."

"Really? Maybe we should see how many times you can blow before you're unable to get hard again." She winked and reached out to rub my groin. I moved away, and she groaned. She was always horny lately.

Letting out a loud laugh, I shook my head and stood back up. Undressing, I then slid in beside her and handed over her bowl of fruit salad and the Greek yoghurt that she loved. We fooled around while eating, kissing and feeding each other. I loved that we could just relax and have this playfulness without worry.

I slid my hand across her slim stomach, wiggling my brows. She blushed and wiggled hers back, looking down at my hand. She lifted her hand and rested it against mine. One look and we both spoke the silent conversation, agreeing to our future.

~

"This is perfect out here," she whispered, holding her mug of hot Milo.

It was just the two of us, not wanting to play poker with the others. I just wanted to spend the evening sober and sitting outside with the woman I loved, under the stars as the boat stayed still.

All that could be heard was soft water running and the frogs croaking. Today was a better day for us. She hadn't snuck off to cry or had a panic attack. It was beginning to look up, and even Cass had been pleasant for us all to enjoy.

I kissed the back of her hair and nodded, bringing my arms around her body tighter as she lay against me. "It is. It's perfect with you."

"If we ever get married, we should come here for our honeymoon, on our own," she said. Then I felt her body tense up. She noticed too. "Oh, I'm sorry. I didn't mean."

"Shh, baby. I know you didn't. But I agree with you. We should," I replied, not nearly as nervous as I thought I would be when I asked this question.

"We should?" she said again. Although, I could tell she didn't fully understand my question.

I opened my palm that had been holding tightly onto the diamond engagement ring in front of her. "We should," I said again and took the mug with my free hand, placing it to the table beside us and cupping her cheek. Her eyes glistened as she turned to face me while I slid the glittering ring onto her finger. "Marry me, Sage."

That wasn't a question. It was going to happen.

# CHAPTER 35

"Congratulations!"

My cheeks hurt so bad from all the grinning I had done since Ollie asked me to marry him. Hell, I had not expected that, and I was still in shock from it.

He had a freaking ring that he carried around for the entire boat trip because he was too scared that he would forget where he placed it or that I would find it in our room.

I slid my arms around his waist and looked up, completely happy and smitten as ever with him. "I love you."

"I love you, baby. You're glowing right now," he murmured against the skin of my cheek.

I blushed. He'd been making sly pregnancy comments to me. I just laughed and shook my head. "It's called a tan. I did sunbathe a lot while we were away."

"If you say so." He winked and tapped my bum with his hand as his other one held onto our daughter. "What do you think, princess? Do you reckon Mama has a baby in her belly?"

"Oliver." I laughed. "You can't say that to her."

He winked, and I reached over, taking Meadow when she held her hands out for me. She nuzzled against my skin, and I was completely happy right now.

His family, my family, and our friends were at our home celebrating our engagement. Just a small get-together with lots of food and plenty to drink. I wasn't drinking. More so that Ollie had put me on a ban.

Mum was gleaming as she held her champagne glass and walked over, giving me another lipstick kiss to the cheek. "My baby girl is getting married."

"Mum." I groaned. "Don't get emotional on me."

She laughed. "I gave birth to you, and I'll get as emotional as I wish. Oliver, look after her."

"Always do." Ollie shrugged, giving her a playful glare.

He fit so well with our family. There wasn't a doubt in my mind that things would change once we married. Although, Cass and Tony weren't doing so well.

She wasn't too pleased about hearing that Tony had screwed more women than he originally told her. The numbers were close to the hundreds. Sick man. I was thankful that Ollie's could be counted on one hand.

Open and honest, that was what we were, and secrets only came out eventually.

"Do you two have a date set?" Dad asked, nodding toward us.

We'd been engaged for four days. A date wasn't even on the calendar at the moment. Neither of us was in a huge rush. "We don't know. We're happy as is."

"Soon. We'll get married soon." Oliver cut in with a smile.

Soon. I liked the sound of that. There was no denying that I wanted to marry the man, but I also realised that he had his demons to battle still. There was going to be no pushing.

My sister sat on the couch as she rubbed her barely-there bump. We hadn't spoken much since the trip. She kept quiet after Oliver proposed. Everyone else was extremely excited for us.

Greyson took me by the hand and pulled me over to him, grinning like a hooligan as Oliver scowled behind us.

"What?" I asked, grinning as he placed his arms on my hips and began to slow dance.

I wasn't drunk enough for this. Or drunk at all.

"Are you happy?" he asked lowly.

"Oh my god. Not you too. I am happy. Why?" I asked.

He winked. "Just making sure. Now tell me why Daniel had a split lip?"

I giggled. "Ollie may or may not have hit him."

A moment later, I was being whisked into the arms of another man. The thick musky smell filled my nostrils as I leant against Oliver's body. Wrapping my arms around his waist, I held him closely. Here, it was just the two of us.

Lips lingering over mine, he pressed his body flush to mine, and I blushed as I felt his thick erection pressing against my belly. Turning me on at the most inappropriate times was his specialty. I grazed my nails down his back, and a throaty groan escaped his lips.

My eyes met his, and I swept my tongue over his mouth. The lights outside were low in the dark of the night like stars twinkling above us. There was splashing from the pool as people swam. His eyes were dark with lust as I pressed against him further. The music blocked everything else out.

"I need to use the bathroom," I said quietly. "Our bathroom."

He nodded, getting my hidden message as I walked backward and made my way inside. This man had driven all my senses wild. My hormones were uncontrollable. I couldn't think. I was hot, and each touch sent an electric spark through my veins.

I was pulling my panties off just as Oliver walked in. He closed the door and flicked the lock.

"Meadow?" I asked, reaching for his belt.

Our mouths were heavy over each other as he lifted me up, so I sat on the basin sink.

"Your mum." He groaned.

My hands stroked over his ready erection as his hands slid up my thighs, pushing them apart. We only had a few minutes before we'd be noticed. Hell, I was sure everyone possibly knew what we were both doing.

I couldn't think. I needed him.

431

His smooth, hard cock thrust hard inside. My insides clenched around him while adjusting to his throbbing length. Our mouths, tongues clashed against each other. His taste drove me wild and insane.

An animalistic noise came from his throat as my legs moved up his chest. I changed positions to feel him utterly deep inside me. His eyes were burning like the fire spreading down toward my core. "Oliver! Fuck!"

He groaned hard as he moved faster. "Not yet, baby. Wait for me!" He commanded.

Yes, because I could really hold my orgasm off. I was driven to the feeling, wanting it. He let out a throaty groan as his tongue lashed out and a firm hand gripped my ankle. I bit my lip, feeling my eyes roll as his mouth opened and his tongue swept out.

"Oh my." I groaned deeply in pleasure as he sucked on my toes. Tingles surged from my feet, etching straight up toward my groin. I didn't want to orgasm now. I wanted to keep feeling this newfound pleasure.

Oliver had never done such a sexy thing to me before. This was definitely happening again.

He sucked a little hard and kept his eyes to mine. Biting down, he then unclamped my toe and leant forward. "Cum with me, baby."

His husky voice sent me over the edge as I gripped his ass, grinding myself into him as I spread my thighs further apart. I needed to rub myself up and down all over him to prolong the pleasure. I didn't want it to stop.

"Oh yeah, baby." He throatily grunted, pumping himself deeper and faster as he reached climax. His hot cum spurted and filled me to the womb.

Gasping for breath, we both stopped. I could feel him pulsing inside me. I loved that I did this to him, loved that when he came, he grunted my name over and over as I did his. We were made for each other, as cliché as that sounded. We were.

432

He drew out, and I moaned as he left me empty. "Tonight, you're doing that again."

"You like?" he asked, pulling up his boxers that lay just under his ass. "Stop looking at me like that. I will fuck you again, baby."

In my post-orgasmic bliss, I smiled. "I loved it. I can't help but look at you like sex on legs. You're so fucking hot."

He smirked, reaching for the washcloth and running warm water over it before he wiped me clean. Bending down, his face was directly between my thighs. I was open and exposed. I was slightly embarrassed as he looked at my most private part.

"Don't blush, baby. You're beautiful," he said, leaning forward. His tongue darted out and ran up my still sensitive slit. I gasped, not expecting that.

My eyes rolled as I tilted my head back, hands reaching for anything to hold onto as he assaulted my core with his mouth. I groaned as he slipped a finger inside, then another while his tongue circled and flicked faster and faster.

The heat began to spread again. I was unable to hold it off. "Oliver, oh god." *Don't you dare* "—stop." I moaned loudly.

The bastard stopped and pulled away. "What's wrong?" he asked, his tongue licking his lips as he kept his fingers still inside me.

"No! Don't you dare stop!" I growled throatily. "Keep going!" I practically screamed.

He smirked and pushed his face back into my core, finishing what he started until climax reached my body and I convulsed over his mouth. Each stroke of his tongue sent a newfound pleasure to my system. The man knew what I loved, and he was good at it. He licked my clit longer and then faster as the orgasm intensified and reached the peak.

He then did the next thing I loved. He fucked me hard with his cock, grinding his pelvis into me with each thrust as my orgasm died and drove me right into another one.

~

Heading down the stairs, I left my fiancé in the bathroom to recover and fix her makeup.

Apparently, our two minutes turned into a good twenty minutes of lovemaking or fucking, as some of you would call it. It didn't matter if it were in a bed, slow and passionate, or on a sink, hard and raw. It was the same: making love.

My brother winked at me, slapping my back. He was pissed. "Tell me. Where did you and your missus sneak off to just now?"

I laughed. "Sage was sick. Just making sure she's okay."

"Sick my ass. You two are hopeless. Let me tell you something. Once you get married, the sex goes, as does the blow jobs," he said, sighing. "Julia used to be a wild horny girl. Now she's just." He stopped and grumbled. "Wild with anger."

"You do realize I was married before and had no sex life?" I reminded him sternly, not that I wanted to remember being married to her. "Now, I have a daughter, and I just fucked my wife twice in the bathroom. Nothing boring about that."

"Rub it in. Why don't you? You're still in the loved-up honeymoon phase. I doubt it'll last." He sighed and pulled a cigarette out, offering me one. I shook my head, declining. I'd given up for good. Hard but I was doing it.

Tony came over, deciding to join our guy talk. "I don't know what's going on, but Cassie is convinced if I blow in her, it's bad for the baby."

"Wait. Sage said when she swallows, it's actually healthy. Like eating a steak full of the good stuff." I winked.

Both men looked at me and rolled their eyes. For once, I loved that my sex life was better than theirs after all the times I had listened to them bragging and gloating about all the sex and head they received while I sat there, wishing I had that kind of sex life, but unfortunately, I didn't. Now I did, and I wasn't about to sit and be quiet.

Sage walked outside, looking flushed and gorgeous. She could deny it, but she was looking more beautiful than ever. Her cheeks were a slight rosy pink still. I loved the flushed look across her face when she came and how she turned into a minx that couldn't get enough.

"Our baby needs to go to sleep soon. She's looking exhausted and getting cranky." She laughed, covering Meadow in her arms with a blanket. "Ugh, Haddon. Seriously, go smoke that over by the fence."

My brother groaned. "Yes, boss." He winked and walked away.

We both laughed, and Cassie walked over, finally, after all these hours she spent sitting quiet and gloomy. "When do you want to leave?" she asked, avoiding eye contact.

"No idea. It's still early." Tony shrugged.

"Don't leave yet. We've not eaten dinner," Sage said, giving her a smile.

I didn't know how she could smile and act normal around her. I guessed faking it was the way to go. Cassie's eyes met mine, and she kept her expression blank, as did I. There was nothing more to say. It was one thing to speak to me and call me a fucking prick, but to attack the woman I love, I wouldn't allow that.

Daniel learned the hard way. It was about damn time he pissed off and left us alone.

Dinner. All of us sat outside and ate. The subject at the dinner table was our engagement and wedding. I didn't care where or how we got married. As long as she was happy, then I was happy.

"What about roses? They're always lovely." Julia smiled.

"Most people have roses." I pinched my temples and rubbed, sighing quietly. "Sage likes peonies."

Everyone looked up. I had even surprised myself for remembering the name.

Sage rubbed my thigh. "Yes, I do. Ollie brings me pink ones each week."

Julia let out a swooning noise. "Aw, at least one of the Bailey boys got the romance bone."

"If you want a bone, I can give you one." Haddon winked.

Everyone groaned, and my filthy-minded brother just laughed. Being the disgusting pervert he was, Haddon didn't have a filter. He'd say whatever was on his mind and then deal with the consequences later on. Judging by Julia's scowl and blush, he was tending to his own bone tonight.

"We aren't going to have a huge crazy wedding, just something simple, one that's very us," Sage said, spooning a mouthful of mashed potatoes to little miss hungry.

She let out a string of mm's as she ate and then opened up her mouth again for more. I could sit here and watch her forever. She was such a time waster.

"If you two planned a wedding, it'd be barefoot and casual. Please let us help?" Mum asked, giving us a hopeful smile.

I laughed. "There won't be any barefoot. You'll hear about our wedding when the invites are sent out. Until then, leave it up to us. Our wedding will be better than Tony's."

"If I remember, you two enjoyed yourselves that night." He winked.

The night of Tony's wedding. Yeah. I definitely enjoyed that. It was the time I saw her again, and she had been everything I remembered. Pregnant and that explained all the food she ate.

Dinner soon became desert, and I was eager for everyone to head off and leave.

Sage was lying down on the lounge chair, stroking Meadow's hair as she lay on her chest, just staring and not sleeping yet. She looked mesmerized by the stars and the big yellow moon shining out brightly. I didn't think she wanted to sleep and miss out on any excitement.

"She's had a big day. If she barely slept at your parents, then hopefully, she will sleep all night with us." I grinned. I was way too overprotective at the moment to let her out of our sight.

"You're not the only one, baby. I missed her so much. I can't wait to be with her tonight." Sage smiled, agreeing as she kissed her nose.

I took a seat on the edge of the chair near her foot and rubbed her leg. "I love you, Sage."

"I love you too. I can't wait to marry you. Tell me how you want your wedding to be?" she asked softly.

Thinking about it, I was surprised she'd ask such a thing. "With you, in a white dress and walking toward me."

She laughed softly. "Big or small?"

"Medium. Friends and family. Not in a church though," I said, smiling at her.

"No. I don't want a church wedding either. Garden or on a beach. I like twinkle lights. Maybe an evening wedding, something simple and pretty."

"You're pretty," I stated, leaning closer to her. "You're not simple though. You're amazing. I think we could have a wedding like that. It sounds good. Can I make another request?"

She nodded and laughed. "Yes, carnival food. Steak and all things that taste really good."

This was why I was crazy in love with her. She knew what I liked. She knew me. I was able to let her see all of me, and I got to see all of her—a side I knew she didn't share with others often. Leaning down closer, I brought my lips to hers and kissed her tenderly.

"Meet us upstairs, baby. I'll bring her up soon," I murmured over her mouth. The skin on her lips was so soft. She bit down on my lip and reluctantly pulled away.

I took Meadow from Sage and went to say goodnight to my folks. Mum was with Sage's mother, discussing wedding themes, cakes, and all the things we had talked about. They'd managed to pull Sage back into the conversation, and I could see her desperately trying to get away from them. Dad chuckled as he held onto his granddaughter and kissed her cheek.

"She's doing so much better now," Dad said as he rubbed Meadow on the head. She just looked at him and pouted then yawned and slumped her head against his chest.

Pouting was all she seemed to do. Although, she was gorgeous doing so, just like her mother.

"Yeah. She's doing fantastic. It's a relief. We haven't seen any signs of complications. All normal," I replied. She was a champion and recovered way beyond our expectations. We were still amazed and so damn blessed.

Dad chuckled, looking slightly hammered. "Who would have thought. Morphine and cough syrup? A damn lethal combination. She's extremely lucky to be here. I don't know how."

As he said that, I nodded until realization hit. Sage nor I hadn't mentioned morphine to anyone. A knot formed in my stomach, a sickening feeling as it hit me like a ton of fucking bricks. It was him. He had been in on it. My own fucking father betrayed me in the worst possible way. It made sense. He was there in the hospital. He was unnoticed. He was always around, and no one suspected a goddamn thing.

He looked taken aback as I instantly reached for Meadow and pulled her from his arms. I ignored the sob coming from her as I startled her.

"You," I said out loud, glaring at him as my anger boiled over like a thunderstorm.

# CHAPTER 36

Lying in bed, I waited and waited.

Oliver was meant to follow me up. Instead, he was still outside, and the noises were getting louder. My heart began to throb, and instantly, I knew something wasn't right. Getting up and throwing a jumper on, I took the stairs down and slowly made my way toward the back door.

Theo was drunk, and his face was red with anger. Oliver was glaring at him, his chest heaving up and down. Something had happened. Even Haddon was between them. I looked around, and I noticed Cassie holding onto Meadow protectively. She seemed relieved once she spotted me and began to make her way over.

"What's going on?" I asked in a soft whisper.

"Oliver's about to kill his father. I don't know what happened, but he's really angry," Cass said back. Julia shot us a glance and winced as Oliver's voice startled us all.

"Get out of my house now! I'm about to call the police. Don't think I won't!" He snarled.

Theo scoffed. "Now you grow a set."

"Dad." Haddon warned. "You should leave."

"No!" Oliver gritted. "You tell me why. I want to know why you did it."

Did what? I had no idea what was happening. Everyone looked just as confused as I felt, except for his father. He just looked at Oliver smugly.

Shaking his head, he pushed Haddon out of the way and stepped closer to Oliver. "What kind of man puts his dick in

439

another woman when he's married?" Oh, holy fuck. This couldn't be happening. "What kind of man did I raise? I raised a coward for a son. You had a wife who loved and doted on you, yet you fucked off with another woman."

"You're shitting me, right?" Haddon spat. "Do you have any idea what type of woman he fucking married?"

His dad nodded. "A beautiful and smart woman. He threw that away so whatever he was given he deserved it. Hell, I didn't think he'd be such a wimp. Can't handle a few punches. You're a pathetic disappointment. No son of mine takes a beating from a woman and instead of finding courage, he just dissolves into nothing. You're worthless."

"Theo, that's enough." Jean warned her husband.

He narrowed his eyes as he poked Oliver in the chest. "You couldn't even keep your wife satisfied. No wonder she came to me. I showed her how a real man looks after a woman."

I was going to be sick. His dad and Amy. This was going to mentally fuck Oliver up for good.

"You're repulsive." Oliver shoved him hard in the chest.

Loud gasps came from everyone, and Oliver just shook his head. His jaw was set, and his fists were balled up tightly. I knew what was coming. It wasn't going to end well for his father. I went to step forward, but Tony grabbed me by the waist, holding me back in place.

"He needs to do this himself. Let him take the bastard out," Tony grumbled angrily behind me.

"You were fucking her? What about Mum? Did you not think of her at all? Fuck!" Oliver ran both hands through his hair and fisted it. He closed his eyes and seemed to take a deep breath. "Tell me why Meadow? Why did you help her do it?"

If a pin had dropped, we'd have all heard it.

This had to be some mistake.

"I didn't know she'd go that far, but she wanted to teach you a lesson. Who knew you'd actually snap completely and go kill her?" He actually had the nerve to chuckle as if it was amusing.

"Your mother is just like you. She'll stick around and bury her head in the ground. You think she doesn't know about Amy and me?"

"I never!" Jean said, looking ready to pass out. My mother rushed to her and helped her take a seat.

"Bullshit. You coddle both these boys. They need to act like men. They let the women in their life take control and order them around. I didn't raise weak men!" Theo's face was almost purple as he yelled, looking between Oliver and Haddon.

Haddon shook his head and took a step back. He kept his eyes on his dad while speaking to Oliver. "Go for it. If you don't, then I fucking will."

Oliver's fist flung into his dad's face, and none of us had time to do anything. We all just stood as his dad stumbled back and fell down, knocked out with one punch. He didn't stop. Oliver bent down over his father's body and lifted him up by his collar.

"You're the weak one! You could have killed my daughter, you sick son of a bitch!"

One hand held Theo's collar, and the other pounded his father's face over and over. Blood covered his hand as he punched the man again and again. Haddon and my dad were trying to pull him off as Oliver kept lunging, yelling, and hitting him.

"You deserve to be dead with that fucking bitch!"

Meadow's scream seemed to have stopped him. He looked up, and guilt broke out all over his face as he realized he did this in front of her. Not knowing what to do, I grabbed her from Cassie and just took off inside.

She was sobbing loudly as I changed her and got her ready for bed. I was crying. What happened was too much. It was all coming out in the open. Oliver's own father hurt our daughter for some kind of punishment because he didn't fight back with Amy. This was sick and disgusting.

I lay in bed. My own cries were slowly wearing me out. The bedroom door was unlocked, and I waited, waiting for Oliver to come in and clean up or talk to me.

He never.

The next morning, I woke up to Meadow babbling on about something, and I rolled over. The bed was cold and empty on his side. I carried Meadow as I checked the spare bedroom and hoped Ollie was passed out in there.

He wasn't.

He was nowhere to be seen in our home.

Outside, I cleared up all the broken bottles and threw the food in the bin as Meadow crawled around the grass. The stench of leftovers made my stomach churn for the worst, and I was bent over the bin throwing up.

"Da. Da."

I wiped my mouth and looked over at Meadow. "Daddy is," I started but didn't know how to finish that. I had no idea where her daddy was.

~

Meadow and I were lying on the couch. I felt so hungover even though I hadn't drunk anything. She was getting sleepy as we watched *Tinkerbell*. The door opened and in stumbled Oliver, looking not as drunk as I had expected.

He was wearing a smile as he held a large box in his hand. I ignored him, trying to be mad with him, but I couldn't. He reacted the way anyone would have last night.

He sat down on the floor, blocking my view of the TV. "I shouldn't have left last night."

"Where were you?" I asked quietly.

"With Tony and Haddon. I've been around helping Mum pack," he said.

Meadow lifted her head and grinned. "Da. Da. Up!"

Ollie smiled and picked her from my chest, placing a kiss against her cheek. "Hey, baby. I missed you."

She pulled away and crawled over to her toys and began to play on the table with musical buttons. Oliver's attention was back on me. "Dad's been arrested. I couldn't let him get away with it."

"Oliver, what happened?" I asked quietly with a sigh. "I don't understand why he did it. He's your father."

"He's no father of mine. I don't know. Turns out, he and Amy had been fucking, and she got it in his mind that Meadow was a problem. The fucker believed her and agreed to help her. Some sick lovers plot for revenge." He spat out distastefully.

I sat up as bile rose in my throat. "I'm going to throw up."

My head felt heavy as I lay back in bed. Oliver was more worried about me right now. I tried telling him I was okay. He didn't believe that and carried me back to the couch. The news of Theo and Amy was sickening. Just thinking about them made me hurl. We could have lost our daughter. He knew the whole time. He held onto her and acted like the doting grandfather.

"Feel okay?" he asked, rubbing my forehead. "Want some soup? Or toast?"

"No. This is insane, Ollie. I can't even begin to imagine how you must feel," I said, taking his hand and kissing it. "I don't think I can eat anything. I feel sick to my stomach right now. What's going to happen to your father?"

"Don't worry about me, baby. I'm okay. It's Mum I'm worried about. Hopefully, he rots in hell. I'm sorry for losing it in front of her. I shouldn't have ever done that with Meadow or you around," he said, more regret filling his eyes.

He didn't need to apologize. "You know, what your father said? You're nothing like that. You're not weak. You're strong." I glanced to the box when I heard a noise, and I looked at it. "Ollie, what did you buy?"

A massive grin formed over his face. "Something for Meadow." He winked as his hands disappeared inside it, pulling out a black bunny rabbit and then a grey and white one on the other hand. "Meadow, look what Daddy got!"

Her hands and legs moved flat out as she squealed excitedly, charging toward him. I laughed, sitting up. "They're so cute and tiny."

I held one as we taught Meadow to gently pat them. She was sitting up happy as ever. "What are we calling them?" Ollie asked.

I shrugged while Meadow lay down on her tummy with her bum facing the air, giggling as she did a loud rumble in her nappy. Ollie chuckled. "Well, I say we call one of them Thumper."

~

OLIVER

*3 months later*

"This is pointless," Haddon muttered. "I don't want to be here."

"I know the feeling, but someone has to tell him." I sighed.

I held the orange envelope in my hands as we walked through the state prison and headed toward security. The last thing I wanted to do today was to be here, today of all days. Twenty minutes later, we were cleared to head through the doors and out into a room filled with chairs and tables.

Theo, as I now called him, wasn't hard to miss, sitting there with his greying beard and in an orange jumpsuit. He looked up with a small smile, but Haddon nor I didn't return it. We sat, and I slid the papers over to him.

"No hello?" he asked gruffly.

I scoffed. "You don't deserve fuck all. Mum signed. I suggest you do it as well."

"She really wants this?" he asked, looking at us both.

Haddon and I both nodded. Haddon spoke, "You fucked around on her and almost killed her granddaughter. I'd say you owe her this divorce. She wants nothing from you, and you'll be dead before you're eligible for parole."

"I never meant to hurt anyone," he said, rubbing his chin.

"Yet you did." I snorted with a growl. "Sign it. We need to go."

He looked up amused. "You can't share thirty minutes with your old man? Are you that angry with me, son?"

"I'm not your son anymore, and no, I don't want to be here with you." I wanted to take the pen and jam it in his neck, but I chose the pleasant option and just slid it over the table.

~

Haddon and I hadn't spoken much since getting back in the car. It was a two-hour drive back home, and we were on a deadline. The last thing I had wanted to do the day I got married was visit my father, but if it meant getting him out of our lives for good, then it needed to be done.

We decided to get married and not wait any longer. I was ready for it, and she was more than ready. We wanted to be a family who shared the same surname. After everything that we'd gone through, getting married was something we could look forward to and put all our demons behind us.

I wouldn't lie. We both struggled some nights. The nightmares seemed too real, or we would be a little bit more cautious when Meadow was with other people. We worried, and it couldn't be helped. We just needed to stick together. Talking to each other helped a great deal.

"Nervous?" Haddon asked. Tony handed over the flask with whiskey inside it.

I took it and had a shot, hissing as I handed it back. "Nope. Just anxious to marry her."

"She might back out." Tony smirked. "I would if I were you. Remember all that sex goes away."

I laughed.

"You know what your vows are going to be, right? Or is someone saying it and you will just repeat?" he asked.

"Nope. No idea. I'll just think of something up there. It'll come to me. I'm sure," I said confidently. I hoped it would come to me. Otherwise, I was going to be grinning like a fool and mumbling a bunch of words that hopefully made sense.

By 7:00 PM, we stood upon the grassy bank that overlooked a vineyard. Sage fell in love with this spot the moment we visited it. The sun was setting, giving this place a more intimate and romantic feeling. I just stood anxiously in my suit and waited for my bride to hurry up and get her down the aisle before I went and carried her myself.

When the music began to play, my nerves picked up.

"This is it. Still, want to stay?" Tony whispered.

"Absolutely." I nodded, keeping my eyes ahead.

Cassie and Julia were her bridesmaids, and they were wearing a pale pink dress. I didn't know what style it was called, but it was similar to what Sage wore in Cassie's wedding. Then came the little girl in a cream dress. Her dark hair was out and in loose curls with a lace band around her head. She was the only other girl here tonight that had my attention, our daughter.

She was walking and holding onto a bubble stick, dipping it in and trying to blow bubbles, but her breaths were too hard. She just followed down, looking more and more like her mother every day. Her big eyes lit up, and she grinned. "Daddy! Mama pree-tty!" she said, running toward me.

Everyone chuckled as I bent down and lifted her in my arms. "I bet she is. Where is Mummy?" I asked.

She lifted her hand, and she pointed toward where my almost wife had begun to walk. She held onto Mark's arm as he looked proud as a father. If I were to fall in love all over again, it would be in this moment, right now.

Her dress had been kept hidden from my view. Nothing over the top or too lavish, it was definitely her: simple and strapless with lace that showed off her curves. She was gorgeous. Her hair was all out and in loose curls. A small glittering headband kept it off her face. My thoughts, of course, drifted to what was underneath the dress, and my dick began to wake up.

When she reached me, she smiled. "I've missed you today."

"I missed you more, baby. Both of you," I said and kissed Meadow on the cheek. Badly, I wanted to lean forward and kiss Sage. "You're so beautiful. I can't take my eyes off you right now."

As the ceremony began, we took each other's hands. I tried to ignore my mother who was crying and at the same time smiling with pride in her eyes. Even though I had been married before, this felt like the only time for me. It was the real deal, and I couldn't wait until she had my last name.

I glanced over at Meadow. She was playing with the flowers by the table. Sage nervously squeezed my hands and took in a deep breath and began to talk with her soft voice.

"Oliver, I never knew what I wanted until I looked into your eyes. Then I knew I wanted it all with you. I take you to be my husband, my faithful partner, and one true love. I promise to encourage you and inspire you, to love you truly through the good times and the bad. I will forever be there to laugh with you and lift you up when you're down. When you're sick, I'll cook your favourite soup and get sick with you. To love you unconditionally through all the fun adventures in our life together. I love everything about you, from your smile to your blue eyes. I love the cute frown you have when you're concentrating hard, but I really love the way you let me in, that I get to see what everyone else doesn't. I get to experience just what an amazing and incredible man you really are, how much you love and care for those closest to you. For the way you look at me, you make me feel beautiful every day, and the first time you told me that you missed me, I fell harder. It's impossible for me to un-love you."

My heart was now pounding, and it wasn't my cock I had to worry about. It was my damn emotions. She was going to bring a man to tears right now. Her hands squeezed mine harder, and she blinked back her own tears.

"Nothing will come between us, except many more children, as many as you can handle. You're my everything, Oliver, and I'm so blessed to be able to call you my husband. Our children will be so blessed to call you their father. I can't promise to fix all of your problems, but I can promise that you won't have to face them alone. I'll be right by your side." She smiled and took the ring from Tony, sliding it on my finger. "I still fall for you every day, and I know that I want you today, tomorrow, next week, and for the rest of my life. You've got me, as I'm completely yours."

Holy fuck. "Can I kiss her now?" I asked the celebrant.

She laughed and shook her head. "Your turn. Then you can kiss her all you want."

447

I picked her hands up again and looked into her eyes, letting her know just how much she meant to me. "Sage. Before my life was joined with yours, I was incomplete. Before I loved you, everything was dark. Now that our lives are joined, I am full in love, in laughter, and in light. You are my everything, and I give all I have to you, that you may have all you want and need. The feeling hit me the moment we made eye contact. It was so immediate and powerful, far deeper and inexplicably beyond any calculation of time and place. You don't describe a feeling like that. You also can't replicate it or force it. You just let it flow in and around you. You go where it takes you, and it led me to fall more in love with you, Sage. You captivated me, and I knew once I had you, I could never let you go. I promise to love and care for you, and I will try in every way to be worthy of your love."

I was baring my soul to her, letting her know she had me completely. I was nothing without her.

"I will always be honest with you, kind, patient, and forgiving. I'll even admit it when I'm wrong." I took the ring and began to slide it on her finger, the ring I had designed just for her. "But most of all, I promise to be a true, faithful, and loyal friend to you. I'll take care of you, as your husband and father to our children. I will protect you always. I love you."

As soon as the woman announced us husband and wife, I kissed her hard as our families cheered us on and covered us with confetti.

After endless photos, we finally sat at the table filled with tea lights. The night sky was dark, and the lights were lit around us. Sage had done amazing organizing the whole thing herself. Dinner wasn't a set menu. They could get whatever they wanted.

My wife wanted dessert first, so that was what she got. Meadow was playing with her cousins, laughing as they waved glow sticks around.

Pulling my wife down onto my lap, I pressed my mouth against hers and smiled. "Mrs. Bailey, was today everything you imagined it to be?"

She wrapped her arms around my neck and smiled. "Indeed, it was. I'm so happy right now."

"You look beautiful. I love your dress, but I cannot wait to take it off you," I said huskily as I kissed her again.

In the middle of kissing, she pulled away and brushed her lips against my ear. "It was a little tight in the middle when I put it on today."

Pulling back slightly, I furrowed my brows as my heart began to speed up. Brows soon shot up as I stared at her blushing smile.

"Do you know what that means?"

"If you're saying what I think you're saying, then I think I'm going to cry," I said quietly. "Say it, Sage. Tell me the words, or I won't believe it."

She laughed softly, stroking my hair. "I'm pregnant. We're having another baby, Ollie."

"I knew it." I grinned and cupped the base of her neck as my other hand went to her stomach. I leant in, bringing her mouth back to mine. "I've never felt happier than right now."

# EPILOGUE

SAGE

"You're a dirty man, Mr. Bailey." I giggled as his fingers skimmed underneath my dress and tugged on the material of my panties.

He groaned as his mouth moved against mine. "I need you now."

"Ollie, we can't. Not here anyway." I gasped as his fingers entered me, clutching his back as he pushed me against the wall.

He let his lips run down my chest. He licked over my flesh and back up toward my neck. "Why not? We've fucked here before."

I shook my head, trying to ignore the loud yes that was almost escaping my throat. I ran my fingers through his hair and tugged. He let out a loud growl and ground his palm against me.

"You want me to stop, baby? I will if that's what you want."

I lifted my leg further up his body, wrapping it around his waist to keep myself steady. "Oh god, Oliver! Fuck me now."

Moments later, he sunk deep inside me, and I let out a pleasurable moan. We'd come back to the spot we first met, and Oliver thought it was perfect to visit the room our daughter, Meadow, was conceived in. I wasn't so sure, but with his hands feeling me up as we ground against one another on the dance floor and some extremely sexy dirty talk from my husband, I quickly agreed and let him lead me up those stairs again.

"You're so tight. Shit, baby." He grunted. "This won't last long. It's been too long." He groaned, sucking in a sharp breath as

450

he gripped my ass. Bringing me closer against him, he slid in and out, thrusting harder and deeper.

I didn't care how long it lasted. I just needed him in me.

Our breathing was heavy, and bodies were slick with sweat as we finished. I was hoping if someone walked in and saw us, they'd only assume we were making out, not making love. He slid out, and I moaned in delight.

"Thanks, babe. I needed that badly."

He chuckled, zipping himself up. "Bet you did. Now, we've got all night. I plan on taking you home soon and making you scream."

"Can't we sleep? The kids are gone for the night, and I miss sleeping." I pouted, standing up and pulling my dress down.

We now had two gorgeous children. Meadow was three, and Hudson would be two next week. He was so much like Ollie; it wasn't funny. He was also loud, full on, and bursting with energy. Meadow loved him to bits.

Pregnancy with him was completely different than when I was pregnant with Meadow. I ate constantly and not small amounts. I could sit up and eat everything in the pantry. Oliver thought it was hilarious, but he loved being a part of it all. My cravings were coconut water and candy. Oh god, I could eat all the candy in the world and still never be sick of it.

Sleeping wasn't as often as I'd like, but I wouldn't give up the nights curled on the couch with my family.

Oliver took me by the hand and winked. "Sleeping is for old people, and we're young, baby. You promised me a night of fun and all things dirty."

I laughed, following him out of the club room. "I did. I know. Okay then, let's go and have our night of all things dirty."

Tony and Cassie were slamming back the shots. Mum had their daughter, Ella. She was two, and she was a little demanding thing. Then again, Tony spoiled her to death, and anything she wanted, she got. It's amusing watching them as a family. Cassie's hormones returned after she gave birth. She was back to normal, being nice and even apologized to Oliver. They could now be in the same room and talk like they used to.

"Where did you two take off to?" Greyson asked, pulling away from his boyfriend, as they'd been sucking face most the night.

"Reliving memories." I grinned, glancing at Ollie who nodded.

His hand cupped my ass as he pulled me against his side. I loved how possessive he could sometimes be. "We were definitely reliving memories. Good memories."

"So you banged in a club again?" Tony snorted, slapping him on the back.

I laughed as I took a mouthful of my water, almost spitting it over myself. "Oh, we don't bang, Tony. We make love."

"Sweet love." Ollie corrected. "We're going to head off soon. Early night."

Cass pouted. "But why? It's not even midnight. We're out to drink and forget we have kids to take care of. Just relax and live a little."

"Cassie, Ollie and I have plans." I smirked. "Naked plans and we're taking full advantage."

We caught a taxi home, and I ran toward the front door as Oliver paid the driver. He wasn't far behind me as he came darting up the pathway. A grin spread over his face as I took the stairs two at a time. I barely had enough time to take my clothes off as Oliver attacked my body, pushing me down on the bed and straddling me.

His eyes burned with lust. "You ready, baby?" He wiggled his brows.

"For what? Another twenty seconds?" I teased and sighed. "Babe, we have to gets the kids from your mother tomorrow."

His eyes narrowed, and he smirked. "Who said you'll be walking out of this door? You're not going anywhere tomorrow."

I straddled him, and our naked bodies slapped together, and I rode him. My palms were against his chest as I sat up more, leaning back as I moved up and down. Moaning loudly, he filled me perfectly. It was pure bliss right now as his hips thrust up to meet me as I slammed down on him. His grunts and deep throaty groans were turning me on even more as he slapped my ass hard, pushing my core against him more.

"Oliver. Oh, holy fuck." One of my hands were on his thigh as I leant further back.

"Mm, baby. Cum for me. Cover my cock." He grunted. His thumb pressed over my clitoris as I grabbed my breast, pinching my nipple as I rode myself into an orgasm. His words, god, they drove me wild.

As soon as I came down from my high, I didn't hesitate to slide off and move down between his thighs. I took his swollen wet length in my mouth and began to suck deeply, moaning as I tasted us both.

"God. Sage."

His grunts picked up, and I pulled my mouth back with a loud pop. His stomach tensed as I stroked him hard and straddled his thighs. Grinding myself against him again, I jerked him off. Hot spurts of creamy white fluid shot up between us, covering us both as he came.

I knew how much he liked to rub himself into me after he came inside me. I couldn't help but slide myself around him, enjoying the view. We were both wildly sexual tonight, trying everything we hadn't done yet. His hand left pink marks on my skin. My hair was pulled. His back was scratched, and our sheets needed to be changed. We were a hot sticky mess, and after Ollie came a second time, his cock was ready to stay up all night.

The last thing I heard before I fell asleep was him talking about getting the kids in three hours.

~

Glancing at the clock, I yawned loudly. My eyes widened and my head pounded. It was almost 11:00 AM. Shit, we were still asleep and very late.

"Ollie." I flipped over to nudge him.

453

"Yeah?" he asked, walking into the bedroom wearing just a pair of boxers shorts. "Fuck, I haven't been this hungover in years."

"It's almost lunchtime. We have to go to your mum." I yawned again, sitting up in the bed and not bothering to cover my naked chest as the cover slipped down and revealed a breast.

He smirked. "Called her hours ago. She's taking them to the park and wanted to know if she could bring them back later this arvo. I told her it was okay."

"I love you." I smiled sleepily as I snuggled back under the blankets. "Get those boxers off, baby. I want some morning love from you."

His brows raised, and he grinned. "Oh, yeah? How much loving do you want?"

As he slipped between my thighs, I giggled when he began to tickle me. "Ollie, don't. I want you to make love to me."

"Oh, make love?" he asked, faking a shock. "But we're married with kids. We can't possibly have sex in the morning after last night. It's on a twice a week schedule."

"Oliver, we have it more than twice a week." I slapped his bare ass and ran my fingers closer to him.

He jerked away and shook his head. "Oh no, baby. No way it's happening again. Keep your fingers to yourself."

"You loved it." I reminded him.

"Yes, it felt fucking amazing, but so does every other time with you. I can go without it," he said, spreading my thighs apart. I groaned in soreness from the night before, and he easily slid inside me. Our bodies tangled into each other as we made love.

~

Sipping on the bottle of water as I lazily walked around the house, I stopped by Hudson's room and smiled. His room was full of trucks and cars. He was obsessed with Batman and cars. I felt Oliver's arm snake around my waist, and he slid something down the front of my bra. Looking down, I laughed and tilted my head back to give him a confused look.

"What is that for?" I asked, raising a brow.

454

"You know what it's for," he said with a shrug. "Want some company?"

I shook my head. "Nope. I don't know. What if it's not?"

He sighed and kissed my forehead. "If it's not, then last night should be a winner."

"Okay. Sit on the bed and wait for me," I said. I didn't get a chance to walk. He lifted me up bridal style, carrying me into our bedroom, then I walked into the bathroom.

This was nerve-racking. Exciting but it made me nervous. Oliver and I found that we loved being parents. We loved every moment of joy that our son and our daughter gave us. We definitely wanted more babies. It was a no-brainer that two was definitely the minimum we would have. The most, that was undecided.

I looked at the stick in my hand as I walked out of the bathroom. We were going to have an addition to our family. Oliver opened his eyes, and I could tell he was just as nervous as I was.

"Oliver," I said quietly. Then I grinned wide, jumping on the bed and straddling him. "Pregnant."

His grin matched mine while he sat up, leaning his back on our bed. He took the stick and read it. Shaking his head, he looked back at me. "You're giving me another baby. Fuck, I can't even begin to thank you for that, Sage."

"We made the baby together," I said in a breathy whisper as I leant down closer to him. "I can't believe it."

"Me either. I can't believe no one noticed that all you drank was water last night. You were sober, and no one said anything." He smirked.

That was definitely true. I pressed my lips against his while he wrapped his arms tightly around my waist. Pushing me back down into the bed, he slid down so his lips were on my stomach. Running his fingers on my flat stomach, he pressed a tender kiss to my belly.

My eyes filled with water as I looked down at him, watching him. "I can't wait to meet you. You're going to grow and cook in Mummy's tummy, then come out and meet us."

"Ollie," I said, holding back a sob.

"Mummy cries a lot. Your brother and your sister are going to adore you," he said softly, placing another kiss and then sliding back up to my side, pulling me closer. "Another baby. I am so happy. It feels like the first time I found out you were pregnant with Meadow."

I looked up and smiled. "It does?" I knew it did. I felt like this was our first child again.

He nodded. "It does. My life with you is happiness each day. I can't even explain how happy you've made me, Sage. You came into my life and saved me. Finding out you were pregnant with Meadow was the best feeling in the world. I love that we have our children. We made something incredible together. A daughter and a son, now another baby. I love you so much, Sage."

If I wasn't crying before, I was right now. "I love you too."

~

OLIVER

I looked over at my wife who lay exhausted in the bed. Her eyes were red from crying and hair tangled from sweat. Glancing back down at the small child in my arms, I couldn't be happier. After almost six hours, Sage had given birth to our healthy boy.

"I keep forgetting how small they first are." I smiled, placing a kiss against Archer's forehead.

"Remember this for a while," she said with a yawn. "It'll be the last one we have."

I shot her a look. "Okay," I said with a smirk. "If you say so." She would want another one when he was crawling around and not a baby anymore. Just like when Meadow started crawling, and then again when Hudson began to walk and then talk more. Her babymaking mood came on, and we were back into trying to get pregnant again. I gave her two years, and she would want to give Archer a little brother or sister.

Archie let out a soft cry, and I handed him back to his mother. He needed something I couldn't give him. Milk. She was a natural with him, with all our children. A perfect mother.

"Are you going to call them yet?" Sage asked as she stroked her finger down his little nose.

"I should, but I like this," I whispered softly.

"I know what you mean. I like it as well. Thank you for a perfect son." She smiled.

Leaning forward, I pressed my lips against her temple. "Don't thank me, baby. You did all the work. You're incredible."

She gave birth for the third time and still refused pain relief. I didn't know how she could do it. Although, her screaming and hand pinching was just as I remembered, brutal.

Life had thrown us a hell of a first year together. Who was I kidding? Life had fucked us over big time. Today, I was learning to put the past behind me. The times with Amy were my most miserable, and she rarely came across my mind anymore.

My father was still in prison, and I hadn't visited him since the morning of my wedding when my mother divorced him. He had called a few times and wrote, but those letters meant nothing to me. His words were meaningless. If he lay on his death bed, then I wouldn't be there to say goodbye.

He was dead to me after what he had done. He screwed the woman who tried to take our daughter away from us, all because he considered me a weak, worthless man.

Mum's better off without him. She sold their house and moved into a smaller one closer to Haddon and me. She adored the kids. She and Sage's mother were really great friends. Mum seemed happier. She had never gone to visit Dad, and I knew she wouldn't speak to him either.

Neither did Haddon. He and Julia were going stronger. A rough patch in the road and they both began to talk more. Although, neither wanted any more children. That was one thing they agreed on.

457

Sage and I weren't perfect. Sure, we had our small arguments now and then. If it got too heated, then one of us walked away until we were calm enough to talk it out. One thing we never did was go to bed angry. Life wasn't worth that.

We'd overcome so much. The strength that our love had was undeniably strong. We'd proven many times that when life fucked with us, we fucked with it right back. We're unbreakable.

Lies. It was the lies that brought me to a woman who saved my life.

Betrayal. I didn't regret cheating. It only opened my eyes to show me what had been wrong with my life.

Love. Sage showed me how to love. She showed me what it felt like to be loved.

Sage reached over and took hold of my hand. The love in her eyes was evident. "I love you, and I won't ever stop loving you."

Lifting her hand, I placed a tender kiss to her skin and looked into her eyes. She was all I needed, she and our children. "You're my everything, Sage. My rock, my life, and my future. Without you, I would never be the man I am today. I love you."

Six years ago, I had put myself in my own prison because I didn't want to have any interaction with society anymore. I didn't want to see anyone. Shutting them out felt like the only option. I felt too vile, too dirty.

Now, I knew it was wrong. What I went through wasn't my fault. I was a victim of domestic violence.

I could now say without a hint of embarrassment or shame that I had been abused by a woman. It had been an uphill struggle. I still saw a counselour, not as often, but I still went, just to talk if I needed to. Without the support of my wife, family, and friends, I never would have been able to leave that situation and grow from it. I got through the worst time of my life with help.

My sons, when they were old enough, I would tell them what happened to me. I wanted them to be aware that this did happen, more than people think. Every 14.6 seconds, a man is severely assaulted by his girlfriend or wife. People can joke about it. When old friends used to brag about their wife's cooking skills, I was silently thinking, *Yeah. You should see what my wife can do with a frying pan...definitely not cook with it.*

Today, I had my wife and my children to live for, to protect them with every being in my heart. I was the happiest man I had ever been.

I was a man who got out and moved on. I was a fucking survivor.

# BOOK YOU MIGHT ENJOY

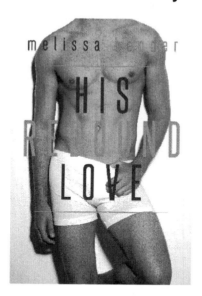

## HIS REBOUND LOVE
### Melissa Bender

*"You've been the first that I've kissed since her."*
*"So I'm the rebound…"*

I'm Jackson, Jack, or Jax. I don't really care what you call me as long as you scream it out in bed. Going back home to my parents at twenty-six is not my proudest decision, but after my shack-up girlfriend of two years went and f*cked someone else, I am left with no choice. She won't f*ck me but easily f*cked him. The cheating whore can go to hell for all I care, but she broke my heart for sure.

Six weeks into moping around in my room, my bitter, intoxicated arse has to get out and get moving. Getting over things isn't easy, but it has to be done.

Then I meet her, Sienna, a redhead with the brightest green eyes you'll ever see—those same eyes I imagined looking up at me as I jerked off in the shower months ago. She's perfect, almost too perfect, and she got me intrigued.

I have to man up and get my own place, so I'm getting a bachelor's pad…in Sienna's building. Not that I'm expecting anything. But one thing leads to another, and I find myself wanting her—falling for her. There's something more to her shy, nervous smile and the way she fumbles over her words whenever I push too hard…there's something more to that girl across the hall.

But am I even ready to be in another relationship? To try again? Will I ever get to quell her doubts about us? And when my past comes knocking on her door, will she let me in or send me walking out her life?

Sexy, steamy, and romantic, *His Rebound Love* is gonna make you believe in second chances, all while leaving your senses and inner desires tingling.

A standalone romance book. Guaranteed HEA. Grab your copy now!

# BOOK YOU MIGHT ENJOY

## BREAKING OLD HABITS
### Melissa Bender

*"I had one deal breaker between us—two, actually: you sticking your dick in another girl, and you going inside her house."*

I'm Ayla—Ayla Morgan, that chick with tats and long, black hair. Totally screams bad girl, right? Except I wasn't.

I'm just a regular twenty-two-year-old girl working at my mum's café. I'm honestly a good girl—unless we're talking about what goes under the sheets. And my tattoos? When you date an architect slash tattoo artist, I guess you just let him draw.

He's Griffin—Griffin James, my tattooed, extremely handsome, long-haired boyfriend with a glorious full beard. He's thirty-seven and has twin sons. I have moved in with them, and the kids love me as I adore them. Having them around is no big deal—but his ex-fiance from hell constantly turning up uninvited in our home is.

She lives just across the road and is having free-reign over our lives: stealing things and insulting me in front of the kids to boot. God knows what she has on her evil, conniving mind…but I bet it's about making my life a living hell and breaking us up. And Griffin's letting her, his idea of keeping the peace for the kids—or at least that's what he said.

For a long time, I believed him, willing to let things stay the same for the sake of my hot new love. But the ghosts of his past are haunting us…suffocating me, fucking me over, and breaking my heart. I am turning into a hormonal, paranoid mess—the kind of girl I swore I would never be.

Something has to give, or it's my mind that's gonna break.

Will I get him to change his ways? Will we ever escape Karen's nasty grasp? Griffin's old habits might just come back to bite him in the ass—bite him so hard that he realises just how much he wants it and just how close he is to losing it all.

A steamy, erotic romance book with just the right amount of kink and BDSM. Not for the faint-hearted. Grab your copy now!

# ACKNOWLEDGEMENTS

My loyal readers, thank you so much. Without you and all of your support, this wouldn't be possible still. I am so grateful for the love and support you constantly give me that pushes me to be the best writer and storyteller that I can be.

To Tinna, and the wonderful editing team I have, you are amazing, and I am so grateful that you gave me patience and understanding and let me tell my stories the way I dream them to be. From the cover, to the end of the book…I am extremely lucky to have you on my team.

My family and close friends, you know who you are. Thank you for always being there and cheering me on. Thank you for supporting me when I'm not sure of myself. Thanks for pushing me to be the best that I can be.

Dad, you mean the world to me. I love you.

Sweetly, Mel xx

# AUTHOR'S NOTE

Thank you so much for reading *Lies, Betrayal, Love*! I can't express how grateful I am for reading something that was once just a thought inside my head.

Please feel free to send me an email. Just know that my publisher filters these emails. Good news is always welcome.
melissa_bender@awesomeauthors.org

Sign up for my blog for updates and freebies!
http://melissa-bender.awesomeauthors.org/

One last thing: I'd love to hear your thoughts on the book. Please leave a review on Amazon or Goodreads because I just love reading your comments and getting to know you!

Can't wait to hear from you!

*Melissa Bender*

# ABOUT THE AUTHOR

I'm wife to a FIFO miner, mother of three, passionate foodie, and a vivid dreamer. Living in a small beach town in the lovely Tasmania, I spend my time between home and down at the beach, making memories and capturing the moments.

When I'm not glued to my laptop, I'm either in the kitchen creating recipes, cooking, or having a Netflix binge session. Often, I find myself drifting off into the world of make believe, getting lost inside the stories I write. I write because it's my passion. I want to create a world for my readers to get lost in. For them to swoon and fall in love the way I do with each character made. Oh, and I love starbursts!

Sweetly, Melissa xx

Like her on Facebook: http://bit.ly/MelissaBenderFB
Follow her on Goodreads: http://bit.ly/MelissaBenderGR
Sign up on her blog: http://bit.ly/MelissaBenderWEB

Made in the USA
Middletown, DE
03 November 2022

14039494R00281